CW00346938

THE LONELY LAKE KILLINGS

WES MARKIN

Boldwood

ALSO BY WES MARKIN

First published in Great Britain in 2023 by Boldwood Books Ltd.

Copyright © Wes Markin, 2023

Cover Design by Head Design

Cover Photography: Shutterstock

A CIP catalogue record for this book is available from the British Library.

Paperback ISBN 978-1-80483-758-0

Large Print ISBN 978-1-80483-759-7

Hardback ISBN 978-1-80483-760-3

Ebook ISBN 978-1-80483-756-6

Kindle ISBN 978-1-80483-757-3

Audio CD ISBN 978-1-80483-765-8

MP3 CD ISBN 978-1-80483-764-1

Digital audio download ISBN 978-1-80483-762-7

Boldwood Books Ltd
23 Bowerdean Street
London SW6 3TN
www.boldwoodbooks.com

For H and B

1

Bugger it!

On account of him now being an old man, it was a nightmare
for Frank Dowson to get over the fence on Breary Flat Lane with his
fishing gear. Still, he managed it, because nothing, absolutely nothing, was ever going to stand between him and a line in the water.

From habit, he cast cursory glances around him for any
observers before and after the climb. Not that anyone would've
stopped him. Yes, the lake and the lands around it beyond this
fence were private property but try telling that to the local youths
who smoked marijuana and had sex here, or the countless other
fishermen who plundered these waters.

Frank had always been _one of the many_. Who wants to stand out?
Life was much simpler when you blended in.

After scaling the fence, he took a deep breath and smiled. He
loved the smell of the lake. As if he was missing out on these local
opportunities just because someone owned this land! _No siree._ He'd
paid council tax to Knaresborough for most of his bloody life, and
no rich landowner was keeping this place from him!

Once he was over his fence, he glanced at his Rolex – a wedding present from his late wife – and saw that it was five-thirty. It was getting on to August, so the sun had already risen. In his younger days, he'd have been here much earlier. However, negotiating the undergrowth down towards the lake in waders, while clutching on to his tackle and bait, as well as his sandwiches and coffee, was no mean feat; to attempt it in darkness these days at his ridiculous age would've been a recipe for a visit to A&E, a long stay in hospital and a drawn-out recovery. Coming later wasn't a major issue for Frank these days anyway.

Retirement, eh? The promised land. No ticking clock!

Except when the sun came out in force that was!

If it started to frazzle him as it'd done last week, he'd be forced to pack up early. He took a quick glance up at the sky. It looked overcast, which gave him some hope. Although, humidity could end up an issue too.

He worked his way left through a patch of trees, purposefully moving away from the busiest area of the lake to the quieter side. Eventually, he stopped and considered. It was so tempting to head further into solitude. Away from the many other fishermen that would surely come over the fence in the next few hours.

He sighed. *No.* He needed to stay *one of the many.* Venturing on may risk his quiet life.

Because, up ahead, lost in the trees and undergrowth, was Harvey Henfrey's cottage.

And no one really went near that.

Harvey Henfrey had a right to be on this land, due to an agreement with the landowner – how he pulled that off was anybody's guess.

You see, Harvey was peculiar.

A man in his early fifties had no cause to be living out here like a recluse, without the comforts many took for granted, only venturing into town, sporadically, for supplies.

It was just plain odd. Harvey certainly wasn't *one of the many*!

However, although Frank had never met Harvey himself, he had it on good authority that the recluse was amiable enough. A man who didn't like to engage in conversation but wouldn't ignore the social pleasantries.

But straying too close to Harvey's property to fish wasn't the done thing. The man wanted to be alone. Let him be alone.

A few more steps wouldn't hurt though, would it?

A record number of metres later, he smirked at his adventurous nature, and then turned to face the body of water.

Due to the overcast day, it didn't sparkle as it usually did under the early morning sun, but God, did he feel that familiar rush of blood in his veins.

Some went skiing, some went scuba diving, some even jumped out of aeroplanes...

Frank Dowson fished.

And he knew of nothing else that could get his juices flowing in quite the same way.

Keen to get going, he increased his speed slightly – as much as his arthritic knees would allow anyway. He passed two trees and—

Stopped dead in his tracks, a coldness spreading over his chest.

Someone was sitting on the other side of the tree just ahead of him.

Not sitting with their back to a tree as was the convention, but rather, facing it, *leaning* into it. The tree was young, and the trunk relatively thin, so the individual, wearing a dress, had an outstretched leg either side of it.

The person's face was flat against the other side of the trunk and therefore, hidden.

'Hello?'

Nothing.

'Hello?'

The coldness in Frank's chest intensified, and he worried for his heart, which was probably still sore from last year's triple bypass. He glanced around, sucking in air, for a tree that he could lean against, but the closest to him was the one that potentially had a body behind it.

Fearing a panic attack, or worse still, heart failure, he focused hard on taking slow deep breaths, and when he was confident that he was no longer about to keel over, he said, 'Get yourself together, man.'

He took two large steps forward and looked at the person leaning into the tree.

'Mary mother of Jesus.'

The young woman had her right cheek pressed against the bark, so Frank could see into her wide and empty eyes.

Tia Meadows.

He groaned, picturing her face glowing behind the bar as she poured a pint for him in the White Bull three nights ago.

Her short, black bobbed hair failed to hide the dark wound on her forehead, which had bled down her face. Most of the blood was dry now, and the wound looked as though it was congealing.

Jesus wept! How old are you girl? Twenty?

Frank dropped his fishing tackle, bait, coffee and sandwiches, and put a hand to his mouth.

Without much thought, he said, 'Tia?' After her name had left his mouth, he had no idea why he'd bothered. She was dead. So clearly dead.

And then a thought walloped him hard: *This is Si Meadows' daughter! Si flaming Meadows!*

He reached for the mobile in his pocket, but when his hand felt the cold material of the waders, he remembered he hadn't brought it. 'Shit.' He deliberately didn't bring his mobile fishing with him. He wanted the solitude, after all. The peace. The quiet...

...like Harvey Henfrey...

Could the recluse have a phone?

He looked out at the lake, freezing in his mind the image of a leaning, old tree, hanging its branches on the surface of the lake. Knowing the part of the lake Tia's body was in line with would help Frank locate her again.

'Wait here,' he told Tia's body, knowing it was a useless request, but feeling strangely obligated to do so.

He attempted a jog.

He was quickly out of breath with pain radiating through his chest.

You foolish old man! Killing yourself ain't going to do anyone a bit of good.

After he'd caught his breath, he returned to a brisk walking speed.

Harvey Henfrey's stone cottage was surprisingly basic. Five metres by five metres at a push – it was smaller than Frank's double garage at home. Frank couldn't imagine holidaying in it for a weekend, never mind living in it.

He paused and thought: *Why would anyone subject themselves to this?*

He shook his head, admonishing himself again. This really wasn't the time to wonder what had happened in Harvey's life to lead to such drastic reclusiveness; there was a dead girl out there in the forest!

Tia Meadows.

The cottage door was level with the ground. He looked at the windows on the front to see if the occupant was looking out, but the curtains were drawn, and remained so.

Frank approached the door and knocked.

In such a tiny enclosure, you could be sure that the knocking wouldn't go unheard. Additionally, there should be no delay in getting to the door.

He knocked again, speaking this time. 'Harvey... I'm sorry... I need your help.'

Still nothing.

Shit. Now what?

He could head down to the lake and seek out an early bird with a mobile phone, or he could head back to Breary Flat Lane for a passer-by?

He looked down to his left to a small plastic table and chair and an empty mug. He noticed something beneath the table, something that must have fallen. He knelt, wincing when his arthritic knees complained. He reached under the table, took hold of a woman's black purse, and rose to his feet again.

He looked at the purse in his hand. If Harvey did have a partner, it was news to him.

A prostitute, perhaps? He rolled his eyes. *In Knaresborough?* Plus, if it was a prostitute, she probably would be streetwise enough to keep her purse safely by her side, not to advertise her possessions outside here.

Curious, he opened the purse and saw a multitude of cards crammed into the pockets.

He slid a blue card out at random.

A Barclays Visa Debit card.

It couldn't be.

The coldness in his chest flared again.

No... No...

He traced the raised letters that spelt out *Tia Anne Meadows*.

Then, sighting the driving licence, he slid it out with a thumb, and looked at Tia's portrait.

Glowing. Healthy. Young.

Alive.

He heard the clunk of a lock in the cottage door.

The purse, the driving licence and the bank card slipped from his hands. He backed away.

How have I, one of the many – a simple man, ended up here?

He clutched his chest. The door swung open. It was dark inside. All the other curtains must have been drawn too.

Frank couldn't hear anything over the sound of his own heart, and his own breathing, but he could see Harvey in the shadows.

A gravelly voice. 'You shouldn't be here.'

'I... I...' *What do I say? What do I do?*

'Tell me what's wrong.' Harvey said, stepping out. He was pale, unshaven, and his greasy white hair was a mess.

'I... there's a...' Frank noticed a knife in Harvey's right hand, pressed against his thigh.

Frank tracked Harvey's eyes as they fell to the purse and the cards on the ground. Harvey's eyes then moved slowly back up to Frank.

Harvey stepped towards him.

2

Detective Chief Inspector Emma Gardner found her brother downstairs eating breakfast at an ungodly hour.

Looking down into his bowl, Jack Moss stirred his porridge with a spoon. 'Sorry Sis, did I wake you?'

Gardner stood at the open kitchen door. 'Would I be standing here at four in the morning otherwise?'

Jack continued to stir his porridge. He was yet to look up. 'I thought I was being quiet.'

'I've cop sense, remember? It's better than Spidey-sense. Someone breathes two floors down, and I wake up, heart beating like a drum.'

Jack rested the handle of his spoon on the lip of his bowl, and finally looked up. 'Doesn't sound too pleasant.'

'It's got me out of a few scrapes.' She touched the scar on her chest where the knife had punctured her lung all those years ago. *But maybe not all of them*, she thought.

He pushed his long hair behind his ears and regarded her for a moment. 'Do you think I'm one of those *scrapes*?'

A borderline sociopath who fractured my skull as a child, and served time for mowing someone down in a car? 'No, of course not.'

He scratched his goatee. 'So, you've seen enough by now to know that I'm different... that I've changed.'

Sociopaths are very good at masking who they really are. 'I'm getting there.'

She pulled the chair out opposite him and sat down. 'I don't want to keep having this conversation. Right now, my concern, *our* concern, is that seven-year-old girl.'

Jack nodded. 'Rose loves you. Her auntie Emma.'

'Don't, Jack.' Gardner shook her head. 'Just don't. You may be my brother, but I didn't get where I am in my career by being a pushover. Save the manipulation.'

'It's true, Rose told me—'

'*Stop*,' Gardner said, raising a finger. *Because I don't want to get attached.*

She stared into her brother's eyes. And saw it again. That same look she'd seen when she was ten, and he was eight, and they were alone together in Malcolm's Maze of Mirrors, just before he'd swung that rock and fractured her skull. Simply because she'd called him a 'weirdo' only moments before.

This familiar look caused a cold sweat to break out on her back, but she didn't want to show weakness. 'Rose is my niece.' This was true. Gardner had made the necessary checks. Jack Moss was named as her father on her birth certificate. 'And you've made it clear that you're going to be involved in her life. I'm helping. That's all. It's what Mum and Dad would've wanted.'

'Do you think I'm bad for my daughter, Sis?'

You've a personality disorder, Jack. You're not safe. 'I don't know... I hope not.'

'Her mother is a drug addict. Am I not the better option?'

She stared at Jack, trying to read him. But, as was always the case, she failed. He never gave anything away.

She sighed and looked down at the table. Her involvement in her brother's situation was complete madness. If the social workers had opted to take Rose into care, then Jack would not be in her house and she'd be solely focused on getting her own life back together – which was, incidentally, also a complete mess. But the social workers were working hard to keep Rose with her mother, Freya, who was now in recovery. *Apparently.* The authorities had been annoyed several months back because Freya had allowed Rose to journey up to Knaresborough for the weekend with Jack, but the authorities had moved past that, and had now intensified their support in educating Freya into making the right decisions. They were in the process of trying to integrate Jack into Rose's life in a more measured manner.

Gardner knew that the social workers were only trying to do the right thing here, but how was she able to fight off the nagging feeling that this was all destined to fail?

And if it did fail, what then? Could fostering Rose herself be an option? Was she really in the position to do that with a crumbling marriage, and a daughter of her own to worry about?

'Being a father has changed me,' Jack said. He placed his palms together as if he was praying. 'I just want to do what is right by Rose. That's all.'

'You get your life back on track, Jack. You get a job. You show you can be part of society. Then, everyone will believe you, not just me.'

Jack nodded. 'And then I'll be able to eat porridge in the middle of the night without waking you?'

She managed a smile. 'One step at a time. Now, I'm going back to bed.'

Jack pushed an envelope over the table.

She raised an eyebrow. Really? Jack had remembered her birthday?

'I think my Spidey-sense is stronger than yours,' Jack said. 'I woke up because someone posted this about thirty minutes ago.'

Gardner picked up the envelope. She turned it over and read her name and address. They'd been written neatly with a fountain pen. There was no stamp.

She opened it.

It was a card with a piece of toast on it. Across the top was written:

A birthday toast for you.

Despite the humour, Gardner was not amused. Who in their right mind posted a card at three-thirty in the morning?

She opened it.

It seemed they weren't going to say.

The card read:

Happy Birthday Emma.

She looked at the back of the card, and there was nothing there either.

What the...?

'It's your birthday?' Jack asked.

Gardner nodded.

'Happy birthday.'

'Please,' Gardner said, glaring at him. 'It's really not important.'

'Whatever you say, Sis.'

After she returned to bed, she tossed and turned for several hours, wondering who the bloody hell had sent her a birthday card at three-thirty. Who does that? It'd certainly never happened to her before. The only people she knew around here were on her team, and the thought of receiving one from them was, frankly, just odd. Especially considering she'd told no one about her birthday.

In the early morning, after sunrise, her mobile phone interrupted her racing thoughts.

She read the caller's name and with a burst of adrenaline, answered, 'Ma'am?'

'Emma,' Chief Constable Rebecca Marsh said. 'It's not good news, I'm afraid.'

Well, I didn't think you were phoning to wish me happy birthday…

3

Detective Inspector Paul Riddick had been awake for over an hour but had not moved a muscle for two reasons.

The first was entirely selfless. He didn't want to disturb Paula Bolton. The nurse he was currently dating had endured the mother of all shifts at Harrogate District Hospital yesterday, and that paled into insignificance compared to what they had lined up for her today.

The public sector, eh?

The second reason for not moving, however, was entirely selfish. It'd been a humid night, and the bedsheets had long been abandoned. Consequently, he'd had the best part of an hour to gaze on her naked form.

And wasn't that a gift from above?

But, alas, it was time to move. He slipped carefully from the bed, crept to the door and took down his dressing gown from the hook. He couldn't resist a peek back; she was now awake.

'Sorry.'

She shook her head, closed her eyes and stretched out. He

looked over her body again, and then at the bedside clock. Maybe he could be a little late for work?

'Nothing says sorry like breakfast in bed,' Paula said, playfully.

'Toast?'

'Ambitious! Is that all there is?'

'Yes... if it's not out of date.'

Paula raised an eyebrow. 'What happened to: *I'm going food shopping this weekend*?'

'When I said that, I was going to go... but then I didn't. I haven't got any butter either. Sorry.'

Paula laughed. 'How the hell do you survive?'

'Badly,' Riddick said. 'That's why we always stay at yours.'

'Dry toast and coffee will be fine.'

'Cool,' he said, tying up his dressing gown. 'I can't promise milk in the coffee though.'

'A glass of water?'

'A glass?' Riddick said, smirking.

As he descended the stairs, he heard her call out, 'That promise to go shopping has been made three weeks running.'

Riddick turned into the kitchen. He looked at the table. For a moment, he thought about his wife, Rachel, sitting there. She'd passed away over two years ago, but he'd only stopped communicating with her at that table three months back.

Figure that one out. Grief worked in mysterious ways.

He filled the kettle, turned it on, and then examined the bread. It was a couple of days out of date, but a quick check of four separate slices under a light bulb showed no mould, so he slipped them in the toaster.

He opened the instant coffee tub and pounded at the solidified block of granules with a teaspoon until he'd broken off enough to at least colour a mug of hot water. Then, he filled a glass under the tap for Paula.

He smiled.

Despite the breakfast shit show, he realised that he was feeling something he'd not felt for a long time. Contentment. Dare he say it, a small measure of happiness?

He checked over his shoulder again at the table behind him. For the first time in three months, his heart didn't completely drop over the absence of Rachel and the twins. There was still guilt, yes, but he really did feel like he was getting some semblance of control back.

He took the breakfast upstairs on a tray. Paula had rescued the bedsheets from the floor and had covered herself.

'Now, that's disappointing,' Riddick said, nodding down at her.

She reached up and took the tray from him and positioned it in the centre of the bed. 'As is breakfast,' she said with a wink. 'This might convince you to finally knock the takeaways on the head and get to the—'

Riddick's mobile phone rang from his bedside table. He went around to see who it was.

'Bloody hell,' Riddick said.

'What is it?' Paula asked, raising her eyebrows.

'Someone trying to ruin breakfast.'

'Is that even possible?'

'Oh, it's possible,' Riddick said, answering the call. 'Good morning, ma'am.'

4

Gardner stood beside the blue and white police cordon which was plastered to the fence. Breary Flat Lane wasn't the widest, but the black major incident van and some panda cars had negotiated their way in to form a long line and block off the dog walkers and joggers.

Gardner looked left and right. There was still no sign of the press. Thank the heavens! There were many reasons for disliking them, but none more so than the fact that they'd released information to the public in the last case without her say so. Worse still, the information had been leaked from someone in her own team. How she wished she knew who'd it been, but so far, all attempts to identify them had failed.

Ray Barnett had logged her in. The tall, black DS had also provided her a white over suit.

As she was getting into the suit, Paul Riddick marched towards her alongside the vehicles. He didn't look in the best shape. She tried to keep the suspicion from her eyes.

'What?' he hissed, indicating that she'd failed in her discretion.

'Nothing.'

Riddick glanced around, checking no one was listening in. 'Just because I haven't shaved and put a dollop of wax in my hair, doesn't mean I've been getting pissed all night.'

'I can smell perfume.'

'Rumbled,' Riddick said. 'I fell off the wagon and drank a French fragrance that was 70 per cent. It had real bite.'

'I never said you were drinking.'

'You didn't have to. It's written all over your face, boss.'

'Well, shoot me for keeping an eye on you. Who's this mysterious woman anyhow?'

Riddick waved her closer. 'She's...'

She leaned in to listen.

'Ms *mind your own business.*'

She pulled back and shook her head. 'You've been dating a month. Why can't you just tell me? You're a child, Paul.'

'You wouldn't even know her.'

'Not the point. Anyway, I could get to know her?'

'I don't think so.' Riddick laughed. 'I've told her I don't come with baggage. A surrogate older sister checking my cupboards for vodka bottles every time she comes round would be considered baggage by many.'

'Older! Only by a bloody year—'

Chief Constable Rebecca 'Harsh' Marsh coughed. She was standing on the other side of the fence in her white suit. She must have overheard some of the conversation.

'Ma'am,' Gardner said, the blood flying to her cheeks.

'Nice perfume, DI Riddick,' Marsh said, smirking.

Riddick looked away and shook his head.

'However, as interesting as your love life is, Paul, can you continue to bicker later? We do have some rather pressing matters to attend to on the other side of this fence.' She was looking directly at Gardner as she said this.

Until that moment, Gardner had considered Marsh's nickname, 'Dr Frank-N-Furter' as rather unfair. Yes, she wore dark make-up, and had a rather masculine appearance, but that was as far as the similarities with the mad scientist in *The Rocky Horror Picture Show* seemed to go. However, right now, Gardner saw the likeness in all its glory. In her irritation, Marsh looked unhinged.

'Of course, ma'am,' Gardner said.

'The body...' Marsh looked at Riddick. 'It's Tia Meadows.'

'Really?' Riddick said, his eyes widening. 'Bloody hell.'

Gardner, who was recently seconded from Wiltshire, had no idea who that was.

'That's awful,' Riddick said.

'An understatement,' Marsh said. 'She's twenty years old.' She looked at Gardner again. 'You know, since you walked into Knaresborough several months back, Major Crimes has never been busier.'

Gardner almost apologised but realised in time that she shouldn't rise to it.

'Tia Meadows,' Riddick said, shaking his head.

Marsh sighed. 'Yes. Our crimes seem to be getting more major by the bloody day.'

'Does anyone want to bring me up to date on who this girl is?' Gardner said, feeling a surge of irritation. 'I am the SIO after all.'

* * *

After Gardner had been updated on who Tia Meadows was, they scaled the fence and began trudging towards the crime scene. Marsh took the opportunity to explain in more detail the sequence of events, beginning with Frank Dowson's discovery of the body. En route, the trees, and the number of white-suited forensic officers, thickened around them.

Over to the right, Gardner could see a large body of water.

'Private land,' Riddick said to her as they walked. 'Always strange to think someone could actually own a lake that big.'

'It seems easily accessible for private land?' Gardner said. 'All you have to do is hop over a rotten fence.'

'Yes,' Marsh said. 'And it *is* regularly hopped over. Nothing will keep the fishermen away, come hell or high water. I think the owner gave up long ago.'

A tall, white-suited woman stepped out in front of them. Gardner recognised her as Chief Forensic Officer, Fiona Lane. She looked at Gardner and then Riddick. 'As you get closer, please do your best to stay on the protective plates.'

Gardner nodded. It felt condescending, but she guessed the chief forensic officer being overly pedantic was better than incompetence – Gardner had witnessed that more than once in her career.

A few steps later, Gardner saw the SOCOs congregating off to the right, near where the body would be. Gardner was about to turn when Marsh pointed off ahead, instead.

Gardner paused to find out why.

'That's the direction in which Frank Dowson ran after finding the body. Straight to Harvey Henfrey's hut,' Marsh said.

'I can't see the hut,' Gardner said.

'It's still a little distance from here, and behind the trees,' Marsh said. 'Harvey Henfrey likes to keep himself as far from civilisation as he can.'

'A recluse... Interesting... What's he like?' Gardner asked.

'Not a bad bloke, actually,' Riddick answered.

Marsh turned and stared at Riddick. She pointed in the direction of the body. 'If he did *that*, he's a bad bloke.'

'Of course,' Riddick said. 'I'm just saying! You know, after the press hung me out to dry, I bumped into him in a store. He was the only person that didn't sneer at me and turn the other way back then.'

'You share common ground,' Marsh said. 'Neither of you are good with people.'

Riddick looked away.

Gardner also felt uncomfortable. Marsh was not in the best of moods. She interjected before this exchange became any more heated. 'Well, Harvey is in custody. If he's responsible, we'll know soon enough.'

Both Marsh and Riddick nodded in agreement, but she could see the anger on Riddick's face over the unduly harsh comments.

Marsh sighed. 'It's getting crowded over there and Dr Hugo Sands is in the middle of it all. By my reckoning, he'll lose the plot in the next five minutes, so I'll hang back. I've seen Tia already. It's not pretty, I'm afraid. Not pretty at all.'

'Okay, ma'am,' Gardner said. 'We'll take a look.'

'After you've finished there, come back here. Both of you. I'll take you to Frank Dowson... That's not pretty either, I'm afraid. That poor man.'

* * *

Gardner didn't expect to see Detective Sergeant Phil Rice there. Being short and completely bald, Rice may not have looked the part, but he did fancy himself as a northern barbarian. He had an uncanny knack of offending everyone, and even those laughing at his controversial attitudes and jokes were only doing so to avoid being his next target. Despite this, he'd proven himself very efficient in Gardner's last investigation, and demonstrated that, on the whole, he was driven for the truth and justice.

Rice looked between Gardner and Riddick, nodded down at

Tia, and said, 'Gives new meaning to the term *tree-hugger*, doesn't it?'

Gardner shook her head, inwardly sighing. 'I didn't expect to see you, Phil.'

Rice pointed over to where Marsh was still standing. 'The chief constable wanted me close on this one, boss. She described my performance on Operation Eden as impeccable.'

Riddick snorted. 'You helped, sure. Impeccable? Really? I mean no fights broke out in your presence this time, which is an improvement, but impeccable? Come on!'

Rice glared at him. 'Go and ask the chief constable. Anyway, what's bothering you? Are you still pissed off that I called you out on investigating the Winters' suicide?'

'No, I wasn't pissed off,' Riddick said. 'I just don't like you. Two completely unrelated topics.'

'Do you mind?' Dr Hugo Sands said, looking up at Rice, and then over at Riddick. 'Have some decorum!'

Gardner glared at Riddick. 'He's right.' She looked at Rice. 'And Phil... you may have the chief constable's backing, but I'm the SIO. I accept you pulled a blinder in Operation Eden, but I'm not having conflict on my watch. Do you understand?'

Phil nodded. 'Yes, boss.'

'Let's crack on then,' Gardner said, kneeling and looking into Tia's vacant, open eyes. Her head looked misshapen and there was a mess of blood on her forehead and cheeks.

'Did she die from this head wound?' Gardner asked.

Dr Hugo Sands never fared well with questions. He'd often stare at the questioner for a long period of time before answering, even if the response was monosyllabic, making them wonder if they'd just asked the most ridiculous thing in the world.

Gardner knew she should appreciate his careful consideration of answers, as it gave her valid information to work with, but sometimes she craved something, even if it was just conjecture; however, he was never prepared to give that up.

'I can't confirm that until she's been on my table...' Sands finally said. 'However, she was positioned like this post-mortem.'

'I could have told you that,' Rice said. 'Who dies hugging a tree?'

Gardner glared at him.

'Sorry,' Rice said and looked down.

'So, when did she die?' Gardner asked.

Sands took a while. 'I lifted the front of her shirt. Blood has settled in her stomach, where she'd been lying face down. That must have been at least six hours ago now, as the blood has become bluish. The flesh is still turning white when pressed though so it's not hit my twelve-hour cut off point. I'd say she died between eight last night and two in the morning.'

'Thanks,' Gardner said.

'Hopefully, I'll be able to refine that down a little more for you after I get her back on the table, but there're always so many variables.'

Sands smiled at Gardner. It was creepy for him to smile at her in the same breath as he'd said he was going to cut the victim up and pore over the pieces. But that was Sands all over. He was different. And, in fairness, probably rather effective for being so.

She looked at Riddick. 'You told me before that Tia is well-known on account of her father, Si Meadows. Can you give me more detail on that?'

'Of course,' Riddick said. 'He has the monopoly on most of the building work that goes on in Knaresborough. All of it, some reckon. Doesn't matter which local company you use, money finds its way back to Meadows.'

'After years of being heavy handed with the opposition,' Rice said, 'Meadows doesn't really have any opposition any more.' He looked down at Tia. 'Which makes this all the more unexpected.'

'All murders are unexpected,' Gardner said.

'Not like this boss,' Rice said. 'Whoever did this has put themselves at the mercy of Si Meadows – and believe me, that isn't where you want to be.'

'So, Si Meadows is the Godfather?' Gardner asked, rolling her eyes.

'If you work in trade' – Riddick shrugged – 'I guess he pretty much is.'

Gardner sighed. 'And Tia is the apple of his eye?'

'Aye,' Riddick said.

'So, another shit storm over Knaresborough?' Gardner asked.

'A big one, yeah,' Rice said.

'Great.'

Another case weaved into the fabric of a close-knit community. Gardner inwardly sighed. Emotions always ran high in investigations like this. She suspected trying times ahead. 'Well, at least we have another starting point other than the old recluse, Harvey.'

'Tia courted her own controversy too,' Rice said. 'She was a barmaid at the White Bull – the rowdiest pub in Knaresborough. In fact, she was working there last night apparently.' He looked at Sands. 'So, we can narrow down your window when we find out what time her shift finished. Somehow, between the end of her shift and now, she ended up here. By all accounts, she was a bit of a slapper.'

'Jesus,' Riddick groaned. 'I hope that what you just said never gets back to her father.'

'I'm police, he's not stupid enough—'

'His daughter's dead, Phil. You think he's going to be arsed about your tea-stained badge?'

Rice shrugged.

'And also, I never want to hear that expression again from you, Phil,' Gardner said. 'Devaluing victims has got you in trouble before

– let's nip it in the bud this time. Who did you hear that from anyway?'

'Just some mates of mine that drink in the Bull. Always flirting with lads apparently. Not wearing enough clothing. You know that kind of thing?'

'You mean perfectly acceptable behaviour in the twenty-first century?' Riddick asked.

'Not if she were my daughter! Anyway, why is everything so politically correct these days?'

'Because, Phil,' Gardner said, looking down at the girl's lifeless eyes, 'daughter of the Godfather, barmaid, promiscuous; none of that truly defines anybody. The only thing that matters is how and why this short life has been cut.' She looked up at Rice with a furrowed brow. 'Rowdiest pub in Knaresborough? Knaresborough gets rowdy?'

'Yes,' Rice said. 'On account of the gypsies. We're inundated with them this time of year.'

'Travellers, you mean?' Gardner said with a raised eyebrow.

'In fact,' Rice said, pointing off over the lake, 'they're on the rugby field over there. A stone's throw from here. So, we may want to mark them up as suspects.'

'Or as potential witnesses?' Gardner sighed, standing. 'Nothing like some late summer discrimination to put us firmly under the media spotlight, Phil. Can we have more of the impeccable detective, please, and less of the northern knuckle-dragger?'

Rice glowered.

Riddick whispered in her ear. 'Boss, knuckle-draggers aren't just from the north.'

She grinned in his direction. 'Noted. Let's go and look at Harvey's hut.' She looked back at Rice. 'And *you* look up the word impeccable on your phone, and I'll consider keeping you as part of the team.'

As they walked back in Marsh's direction, Riddick said, 'Impeccable, my arse. I reckon he's shagging Dr Frank-N-Furter. Why else would she elevate the prick?'

Gardner considered Marsh, and she considered Rice. Now, that really was a peculiar combination that turned her stomach.

* * *

'Harvey Henfrey lives in there?' Gardner asked, pointing at the hut.

'Yes,' Marsh replied. 'They do say minimalism is popular these days. People rejecting materialism and living with next to nothing.'

'Sounds like any Yorkshire man to me,' Riddick said.

Gardner noticed Marsh smile. Was the tension from earlier thawing between them?

'This is beyond minimalism,' Gardner said. 'A tiny stone hut. What's the next step called?'

'Having sod all?' Riddick ventured.

'Makes sense,' Marsh said.

'He must love nature.' Gardner looked around at the unkempt grasses and undergrowth, and the trees looming over the dishevelled hut. 'Think of the bloody insects. Also, does he not get cold in the winter?'

'Has a small generator for electricity, and a gas tank around the back,' Marsh said. 'Don't be fooled. He still has some comforts.'

'Fifty seems a little young to completely withdraw from society,' Gardner said.

'Is it?' Riddick said. 'I know I've felt like doing it a few times.'

A white-suited SOCO emerged from the door of the hut, holding a bag. He stopped to talk to Tony Reid, the exhibits officer, who made a note of the evidence in the book.

'Who is with Harvey Henfrey at the moment?' Gardner asked.

'Lucy.'

Gardner nodded. *Good.* She'd been impressed with DC O'Brien on her last case.

'After he was arrested,' Marsh said, 'he was taken down to the station in Knaresborough. You can both stop in there on the way back to Head Office.'

'How was Harvey's arrest?' Gardner asked.

'Calm for the most part. He did ask Lucy whether she'd kill someone and leave the body in her own back garden.'

Riddick snorted. 'A fair question.'

'Tia Meadows' purse was outside his hut.' Marsh pointed out a small table. 'Underneath that.'

'Suggesting she could have been killed here,' Riddick said, 'prior to being dragged and displayed on that tree. Dr Sands reckoned the lass was lying face down initially.'

'We might be sitting on an open and shut case here.'

'Maybe,' Gardner said. 'All feels a little convenient though, don't you think? Harvey taking the trouble to move the body, but leaving the purse at his front door. Might as well have put a bow around it. It's not rational.'

'Look where he lives.' Marsh shook her head. 'Is this rational? If his DNA is on that purse, you'll have enough for the CPS. I'll fast track it.'

'If it's a stitch up,' Riddick said, 'wouldn't the murder weapon be easy to find?'

'Well, no sign of it yet. They've searched the hut top to bottom.'

Gardner stepped away from Riddick and Marsh and surveyed the lonely hut for a moment. *Why are you out here, Harvey, all on your own? What happened to you?*

She turned back to her colleagues. 'So, you said before that it wasn't pretty with Frank Dowson, ma'am?'

'Oh yes. Follow me.'

* * *

Frank Dowson was sitting on a fallen tree behind the hut, staring out over the lake, looking all of his seventy years and then some.

A young, uniformed officer had been comforting him and stood when she saw Gardner and Riddick approach.

She gave a shake of her head to indicate that he wasn't in a good place, and then left them.

'Mr Dowson?' Gardner said, sitting on the fallen tree beside him.

'Would've been a great day to fish.' Frank nodded at the lake. 'It was cracking the flags all last week, and earlier this week, it was still savage hot. Today is just right for it.'

'I'm sorry for what you went through, Mr Dowson. I'm DCI Gardner, and this is DI Riddick. Is it okay if we ask you a few questions?'

'Frank, please. Do you think you could recover my equipment from where I dropped it by that poor girl? Won't be able to replace it on my pension in a hurry, I can tell you!'

'We'll see what we can do,' Gardner said, despite knowing that recovering his rod from an active crime scene would be problematic. 'Frank, can you briefly talk me through what happened?'

'*Again?* Don't you guys communicate?'

Gardner smiled. 'We do... but second-hand information is never quite as good. And I'm the senior investigator on this case. You, Frank, are the most important person right now.'

'How so? You got the bastard already!' He sighed. 'Okay then, if we must.'

'Thanks Frank.' Gardner pulled out a notepad and readied her pen.

Frank described his jaunt down to the lake at sunrise, and his discovery of Tia Meadows. He shook his head. 'I honestly thought my ticker was going to pack in – I only had it rewired recently!'

'Have the paramedics checked you over?' Gardner asked.

'Yes... they want a more thorough look at the hospital, just to be sure, but they don't think I'm in any immediate danger.'

'I'm glad to hear that, Frank,' Gardner said.

'What a monster!' Frank shook his head. 'That girl always had a smile for everyone... A real good lass. Someone who'd give up her seat on the bus for you. Yeah, she were one of them. They don't make them much like that any more, I can tell you.' He lowered his head.

Gardner allowed him a moment to reflect, before saying, 'Frank... I wasn't aware you knew her. I'm sorry for your loss.'

He waved the comment away. 'It's okay, love.'

Gardner hated being called *love*, but when it came to witnesses, especially those raised in a completely different time period, she forced back any reaction and remained patient.

'She served me in the White Bull many a time, but truth be told, I know her father more than I did her. Si is a strong man, but he won't come back from this. I mean, who *can* come back from this? She was such a gentle, sweet girl.'

'How do you know Si Meadows?' Riddick asked.

'He drinks in the White Bull. We weren't tight or anything, but he could shoot some pool. And I like pool.'

'What happened after you found her?' Gardner asked.

Frank explained that he didn't have a mobile, so he thought Harvey Henfrey would be his best option at summoning help. 'And then I found the purse.'

'So, you handled the purse, and the driver's licence?' Gardner asked.

Frank nodded. 'I've already explained this.'

'Just confirming,' Gardner said, making notes. 'We'll probably find your DNA on it.'

'I'm an old dog. I don't know much about all that,' Frank said. 'But, after I saw that purse, and Harvey, that monster, came to the door, I...' He paused and looked down as if ashamed.

'Ran?' Riddick asked.

'Of course!' Frank hissed. He turned narrow eyes onto Riddick. 'He had a knife in his hand and I'd just seen what he'd done to that poor girl!'

'Where did you run to, Frank?' Gardner asked.

'Over that fence and all the way back down Breary Flat Lane until I got to Quinn's house.'

'Quinn?'

'Greg Quinn. An old buddy. He let me use his mobile to call you lot in.'

'I see.'

'And then, you know the rest. I led you lot to that poor lass.'

Gardner nodded, still making notes.

'I also watched you arrest that bastard.' He wagged a finger at Gardner. 'Don't you go believing any of his bullshit, love. I saw it in his eyes when he opened that door to me. He did it all right. That man ain't right in his head.'

'How much contact have you had with Harvey before today, Frank?' Riddick asked.

'Same as the next man, son. He comes into town every now and again. He seems polite enough, but he's not interested in conversation.' He narrowed his eyes. 'We now know exactly what he's interested in, don't we? Bloody psychopath.'

Gardner took some more details down regarding Frank's personal life, but this was rather brief. He was childless and widowed. He lived on a modest pension, whiling away his twilight years hunched over lakes. He seemed to have a good word for nearly everyone he spoke about, apart from Harvey, of course.

'A wrong 'un. Always known it, always said it. A blatant wrong 'un.'

* * *

They left Frank to dwell on a fishing expedition that never was, and a life that was no more, and returned to Marsh at the front of the hut.

'I'm going to take a look in,' Gardner said.

She nodded a greeting at Tony Reid, who was down on his knees, pulling at fibres on the doorframe with tweezers, and then peered into the hut.

There was a small kitchen at the back with equipment so archaic that it may actually be worth something to an eccentric collector. She recalled the gas tank around the back. She wondered if Harvey Henfrey possessed a carbon monoxide detector – she'd seen lethal setups in her time, but never anything this extreme.

In front of the kitchen lay a small pile of old cushions alongside a folded-up bedsheet, which, she assumed, served as a makeshift bed in the evening.

No television. No radio. And no sofa.

Gardner had seen drug dens and squats which were more liveable.

There was only one thing of note. A large bookshelf that covered half a wall and must have been about two and a half metres long. It reached the ceiling and was stocked full of books.

'Harvey likes to read then.'

Tony Reid, who was kneeling beside her, looked up. 'All crime books, too. Fancy that?'

'Yes, fancy that,' Gardner said.

You'd think with such wide reading into crime, she thought, *you'd have been more creative when disposing of the body.*

* * *

Marsh took a phone call, leaving Riddick and Gardner to wander back alone through the woodland to the crime scene.

Up ahead, the SOCOs were still gathering evidence under the watchful eye of Fiona Lane; Sands was still hunched over the body; and Rice was still hovering around like a fly on shit – loving his recently acquired bump in importance.

'Mr Impeccable... Impeccable at being a complete tool,' Riddick said.

Gardner couldn't hold back a chuckle, but then she took a deep breath and said, 'All right, Paul, but enough's enough; let's rein this in now. I know you dislike him, and I know he doesn't cover himself in glory with his views from the dark ages, but he's shown capability.'

'Behind a desk, maybe. Away from other human beings.'

'Yes, true—'

'And look, he's not behind a desk.'

'Also, true. Yes... I see that... but be patient. It won't be long before he is again.'

'Patient! Let's hope he doesn't screw up the investigation before that happens. You know, regardless of what Harsh Marsh says, at least I know how to handle people.'

'I know. The chief constable was just letting off steam. You know how she gets.'

'I have to admit to a time when I worked at being unapproachable and obnoxious.' Riddick nodded in Rice's direction. 'But for him, it is a natural talent.'

'Let it go.'

They heard shouting. 'Where is she? Where the bloody hell is she?'

Gardner looked in the direction of a squat, burly man with a shaved head.

'Shit,' Riddick said. 'That's Si Meadows.'

The victim's father. 'How? I mean, the press aren't even here yet – how does he know?'

'Take your bloody hands off me!' Si said, brushing Barnett aside, which was no mean feat considering the DS's impressive size.

Gardner stepped forward and sandwiched herself between Si and the route to his daughter. He was still some distance away from Tia. Gardner hoped he'd not seen her yet. She glanced behind her. Sands was now on his feet, standing alongside Rice, blocking the view as best they could. Even if Si could have seen through this wall of people, he'd only catch sight of her legs; her face was on the other side of the trunk.

Gardner was about the same size as Si. It gave her no confidence. The man was wide, his face weathered, and his expression hard.

'Is it her? Is it Tia?' Si had a deep, loud voice. The words vibrated through the air around Gardner and hurt her eardrums.

'Mr Meadows, I need—'

'Answer the goddamn question, woman!' He clenched a fist. 'Is it my daughter?'

'Why're you here, Mr Meadows? Who told you—'

'Quinn phoned me. He told me old Frank had found my daughter. They're wrong. Tell me they're bloody wrong.'

Gardner thought back to Frank's mention of Greg Quinn – the man who lived at the bottom of Breary Flat Lane, who'd let Frank ring in the body.

Gardner could see Barnett drawing closer, behind Si. If Si lurched for her now, Barnett would be able to restrain him. It gave her some relief and some confidence to address the bereaved father. 'I'm sorry, Mr Meadows. I really am—'

'Don't you dare.' Si pointed at her, tears in his eyes. 'Don't you *dare!*'

Gardner looked him in the eyes. 'I'm sorry. There's a body. Several people have recognised her as Tia.'

He flinched. It was as if Gardner had struck him across the face and silenced him.

'I'm so sorry. We really are, Mr Meadows. There may be a time for a formal identification, but not now. In my experience, it just never works out well without some time—'

'My little girl?' Si furrowed his brow.

'Mr Meadows, let us help you. It is better that you let us take care of it for now.'

Si turned his head from side to side. He looked confused, as if Gardner was speaking a language he couldn't understand. 'My little girl?'

Gardner put a hand on his shoulder. He looked down at her hand. Tears filled his eyes.

Barnett, who was still looming behind Si, made eye contact with her. His expression seemed to suggest that he felt the same as her now. The panic was over. Si had become more malleable—

Suddenly, Gardner was flung to one side and her legs were gone from beneath her. She landed on her backside and banged the back of her head against a tree.

'Tia... God, no... Tia!'

Rubbing the back of her head, Gardner looked up at Si. He had moved forward towards his daughter's body. Sands had scarpered, and Rice had taken several steps back. Barnett was following Si. She noticed also, Riddick waiting in the wings.

'My little girl...' Si's words were quiet and broken now, almost like the sounds of a dying animal. 'What have they done to you?' He placed one hand on the tree and leaned over his daughter. 'What have they done?'

'Mr Meadows,' Gardner said from the ground. 'You mustn't make contact with her.'

Si reached out to touch Tia's face. Gardner nodded at Barnett.

Barnett grabbed him by the arms and yanked him backwards. Rice came in to assist.

'Get off me!' Meadows' voice was full of anger again. He shouted profanities.

Barnett and Rice had moved onto an arm each, and they fought to edge Si away from the body. Their faces were taut.

'I'll kill you all. Get off me!'

Rice, the weakest of the two officers by a country mile, was struggling to stay upright. His feet were starting to drag through the undergrowth.

Shit!

When it was clear that the emotion flowing through the distraught man was giving him inexplicable strength, Riddick came to support Rice.

'*Get off me!* My little girl...'

Together, all three officers managed to drag him to the ground.

'Tia! Tia!'

He banged his head on the ground, and froth broke out from the corners of his mouth.

'My Tia!'

Gardner rose to her feet and stood over her officers as they fought to keep Si pinned down. All three of them were red and flustered and gritting their teeth. She wondered how much they had left in their tank.

'Let me go or I'll kill you all!'

It continued like this for quite some time before Si Meadows finally broke, sagging under the weight of three exhausted police officers, and wept.

Gardner took a deep breath. She'd seen countless reactions to the death of a loved one. All of them so different. All of them heart-breaking.

She never really got used to it.

5

'It felt like he'd the strength of ten men!' Riddick said from Gardner's passenger seat.

Gardner glanced at him before returning her attention to the road. 'Are you okay?'

'Yes... I've had my fair share of grief, but I don't remember turning into the Hulk.'

'Really? *You* never lose control? That's what you're telling me?' Referring, of course, to his swing first, ask questions later approach that she'd had to rein in when she'd first met him.

'He practically assaulted you, boss.'

'His daughter has just been murdered.'

'Still... knocking you over? You probably should report it.'

'We do enough by the letter of the law. Today is a day for empathy.'

They parked in the Castle Gate car park and headed into the Knaresborough police station. There was an elderly couple talking to the desk sergeant about a lost phone.

Riddick interrupted them. 'Sorry.' He sounded anything but.

After giving his request, the desk sergeant made a call, while the elderly couple looked at Riddick with disgust. A young officer came flying out. He was still carrying adolescence around with him in the form of acne and patchy facial hair. His enthusiasm couldn't be faulted though. 'Constable Jackson, ma'am.'

'Good morning,' Gardner said.

Riddick simply nodded.

'I took the liberty of finding out all I could about your man,' Jackson said, sounding eager as he then filled them in.

Harvey Henfrey was fifty years old and had lived in this area his whole life. Prior to uprooting to a basic hut by a lake ten years ago, he'd lived in his late parents' home in Scotton. He had no priors, and no employment history, and wasn't currently registered with the council to vote.

'Never worked?' Riddick asked. 'Bollocks, surely?'

Jackson pointed out how much Harvey had sold his parents' home for.

'Well, that should keep his head above water,' Gardner said. 'Especially if you're going to reduce your cost of living as excessively as he's done.'

As they walked towards the interview room, Riddick shook his head. 'My dad always said never trust a man who's never worked a day in his life.'

'Did you agree?' Gardner asked

'Agree? You think I ever agreed with my father about anything? He was a prick.'

Gardner tried not to smile. 'Well, sponging off Mummy and Daddy your whole existence doesn't make you a murderer.'

'It's a good job,' Riddick said. 'There'd be an epidemic of them around these parts. Thoughts on Harvey then?'

'The man wants to be a ghost. So, why kill someone, leave them by your hut, and sacrifice all that beautiful anonymity? Does he really want to be one of Britain's most infamous men? I shouldn't think so.'

They entered the interview room. Harvey Henfrey was a gaunt man, who despite years of not working, and living deep in nature, had not aged particularly well. He looked like he could do with a good meal and, Gardner thought, a good night's rest on a proper bed rather than that heap of old cushions she'd cast her eyes over in his hut.

Harvey's hands were clamped together on the table, and after seeing Gardner and Riddick enter the room, he closed his eyes.

They sat opposite him. 'Mr Henfrey, I'm DCI Gardner, and this is DI Riddick.'

His eyes remained closed.

A man who regularly closes himself off from the real world, Gardner thought. *I guess closing his eyes is all he has left in his armoury now.*

She looked down at his knuckles which glowed on his clamped hands. *Signs of struggle? Is there something you want to say?*

Gardner looked up at the camera in the corner of the room and kicked off the interview with the date and time.

'Obviously, it's your right not to talk to us, Harvey,' Gardner said. 'But ask yourself – will it help you? From where we're sitting, it just doesn't look good.'

With his eyes closed, he started to bob his head up and down as if he was listening to music. *Or some voices in his head, perhaps?*

Riddick and Gardner exchanged a look.

Harvey had already waived his right to a solicitor before they arrived. Usually, you'd rip the suspect's arm off for this act, but right now, Gardner was wondering if he'd be better off with a solicitor. Counsel might breathe some sense into a man that had seemingly drifted off someplace else.

'Harvey,' Riddick said, 'Tia Meadow's body was found close to where you live. Her purse was found under the table outside your hut. Add to that, you threatened Frank Dowson with a knife...'

Gardner looked at Riddick. Her deputy SIO was very good at getting to the point and baiting a person of interest. She left him to it. *Maybe, he'll succeed in waking the stubborn recluse up?*

'Everything seems rather cut and dried, Harvey,' Riddick continued. 'This interview is a formality. Your chance to set the record straight on why you did what you did.'

Nothing.

'Why did you kill Tia Meadows?' Riddick asked.

Harvey stopped bobbing his head and opened his clenched hands. Gardner felt a rush of adrenaline...*do we have lift off?*

The recluse started humming to himself.

Gardner slumped back in her chair.

'What kind of monster are you?' Riddick said, the volume in his voice rising. 'She was twenty years old. Practically still a kid, and you knocked the life out of her! Isn't it worth a simple comment? How about her father, Harvey? Have you nothing to say about the mess you've created for him?'

Harvey turned his head from side to side.

So, you are listening?

She looked at Riddick. This was horrible to watch, but they were breaking through. She nodded for him to continue.

'And you left her there in the dirt... threw her away. Couldn't you have at least returned her to those who gave a toss?'

Harvey wasn't simply turning his head – he was shaking it now.

Riddick was on the verge of shouting. 'Wouldn't she have sex with you, was that it?'

Gardner put a hand on his arm, attempting to rein in her feisty colleague.

'God forbid, are we going to discover that you had sex with her without consent?'

Harvey's eyes snapped open. 'Wash your filthy mouth out, young man.'

Gardner tightened her grip on Riddick's arm, indicating that he stopped now. That was enough!

Gardner then stared at Harvey without talking, letting the pressure build up on him.

Harvey's eyes darted between the two officers. 'I wouldn't do that... I *didn't* do that.'

Gardner nodded to show she was listening.

Harvey's eyes filled with tears now as they continued to dart between his interrogators. 'I didn't hurt her.' He reached out across the table.

Gardner resisted the urge to snap her arm back, so Harvey's hand could settle on hers. It felt right to offer him some reassurance and gain some trust after snapping him out of his trance.

His watery eyes fixed on hers. 'I've never hurt anyone.'

And then something unexpected happened.

Gardner believed him.

* * *

As their interview with their prime suspect wound on, it became very apparent that Harvey Henfrey was a gentle and nervous man. The nerves could be an act, yet Gardner became more and more convinced that this was the real Harvey. Even the most convincing sociopaths struggled to feign this sustained level of tenderness.

Gardner had let his hand rest on hers for a short time to keep him calm and reassure him. It seemed the best way to get him to talk now that the trance was broken.

'So, you knew who Tia Meadows was?' Gardner asked.

Harvey nodded. 'She was nice.' He smiled and looked down at his hands which were now flat on the table rather than clenched.

'I used to see her at Tesco's when she was working there. I remember her helping me with those annoying self-service machines.' His smile broadened for a second. 'She had a good sense of humour. Told me to kick the machine if it gave me any more trouble, and she wouldn't tell anyone. Happy girl... always so happy.'

Gardner recalled Rice telling them that Tia Meadows had been working the bar at the White Bull last night. 'Did you ever drink in the White Bull?'

'No.' Harvey shook his head. 'I don't drink. I also don't do well in social situations.' He looked up. 'I like to read. That's what I like. Pretty much all I like. Nature too, I guess.'

'I saw your books,' Gardner said. 'An impressive collection. Crime fiction?'

'That's my poison. Ever since *The Big Sleep*.'

'Chandler?' Gardner asked.

'Yes... do you read him?'

Gardner shook her head. 'I used to read; not any more.' *I also can't stomach crime writing. Not with what I've got to go through daily.*

'That's a shame. Reading is a great distraction from what's going on in here.' Harvey pointed at his head and looked at Riddick. The recluse appeared engaged in this conversation, and far less nervous than he had done seconds ago. 'You?'

Riddick didn't reply straight away. Gardner suspected he was weighing up whether to keep this part of the interview cordial to provoke a slip up or go in guns blazing again. 'My head is too cluttered to read.' Cordial, then.

'Because you're a detective.' Harvey's eyes widened.

Gardner detected excitement in the suspect's tone of voice.

'One of the reasons,' Riddick said.

Gardner's heart sank. Riddick's other reason was the great loss he'd experienced. The death of his wife and two children.

'I also have books on mindfulness,' Harvey said. 'Do you know about mindfulness?'

'I know of it,' Gardner said. 'I don't practise it. I rarely get time to live in the moment.'

'You should try it,' Harvey said, giving her a gentle nod. 'Sometimes, I sit and stare at that lake for hours. Nothing else. Just staring and appreciating. I call it Lonely Lake, you know?'

'Why?' Gardner asked.

'Sometimes I sit and watch the fishermen, or even the people that come alone to sit and think. I rarely see people together. There's something about this lake. It draws in those who are lonely.'

'Like you?'

'I guess.'

'I assume you know the lake and the area around it very well then?' Riddick asked.

'Been there a while.'

'Ten years I believe,' Riddick continued. He leaned forward and creased his brow. 'So wouldn't you have heard something out of the ordinary? Someone disturbing the area?'

'Maybe in winter, but in summer, the insects can make a racket! Not a bad racket, mind. It helps me sleep.' His face fell and he looked down at the table. When he looked up, Gardner detected genuine sadness again. 'Did she suffer?'

Gardner said, 'Let's continue with what you know, first, Harvey.'

'I didn't wish her any harm! I don't know how many times I have to say it.'

'Once we've all the facts, you can have a short break,' Gardner said. 'Now, you said earlier in this interview that you've no idea how Tia Meadows' purse ended up beneath your outside table?'

'I don't. I really don't.'

'But Lonely Lake and the trees around it are your world, Harvey? You must be tuned in to the sounds. Wouldn't you have heard someone outside the hut... someone putting it there? Earlier you told me that you heard Frank Dowson outside your home before he knocked, so how did you not hear someone putting the purse there?'

'I don't know... I guess they must have made an effort not to disturb me? Also, like I said, the insects can be so loud. I mean I could've been asleep? I'm a heavy sleeper.'

'Whoever did this to put you on the radar must have taken quite a risk in planting that purse,' Riddick said. 'Any ideas who, or why?'

Harvey shook his head.

'You read a lot of crime books,' Riddick said. 'So, you know that we'll test the purse thoroughly. We'll know if you handled it.'

'I know. But I did handle it.'

'Why?' Gardner asked.

'Well, Frank dropped it when he ran. I was curious. After I picked it up, and realised it was Tia's, I just put it back on the ground. I don't know why. It just seemed the sensible thing to do.'

'Okay,' Gardner said. 'Say we give you the benefit of the doubt: you didn't leave the purse on or under that table earlier for Frank to discover, and you didn't kill Tia Meadows... Why pull a knife on Frank Dowson?'

Harvey flushed and shook his head. 'It's hard to explain.'

'But you can see how it looks, can't you, Harvey?' Riddick said.

'I can...'

'The CPS will value it as more evidence against you.'

'I live alone. Completely alone. Since my mother died ten years ago, I've had no company.'

'Your choice,' Riddick said.

'Yes, you're right.' Harvey looked at Gardner as he spoke. He was clearly sensing her as a sympathetic ear. Gardner couldn't claim it was an act; she was genuinely feeling it. She was really doubting Harvey's guilt. 'I never wanted it any other way. Still don't want it any other way. But when you live alone for so long, and not just alone, but *away* from everyone else, you become a lot more... I don't know... cautious? I guess you lose that complacency everybody has around each other.'

'So, what're you saying?' Riddick asked.

Still looking at Gardner, Harvey said, 'I'm saying I was nervous. No one has knocked on that door in years. And this man, Frank, he didn't just knock, he *pounded*. It's hard to describe how I felt in that situation. It wasn't panic, but there was vulnerability. Yes, I felt vulnerable.'

'So, you went for a kitchen knife?' Riddick said with an incredulous tone.

'Not exactly, no. I was cutting mushrooms for my breakfast. I already had the knife in my hand. It was an intense situation and... and... well, I never raised the knife. I never went for him. He just ran.'

Gardner made a note to get confirmation of the chopped mushrooms in the hut. Then, she looked up to see Harvey's eyes firmly on hers. She could see the desperation in them. She could also see the trust he was developing for her.

Riddick said, 'You told Frank that he shouldn't have come.'

Harvey nodded. 'I'd have said that to anyone. No one should be coming. That's not what I want.'

'He'd just found a murdered girl!' Riddick said.

'I didn't know that. If I'd known, and he hadn't run, I'd have helped.'

'But the lack of alibi is a major problem here, Harvey,' Gardner said. 'You were in the hut, alone, for the entire window of time. That does you no good.'

'The truth does me no good?'

'Sometimes the truth isn't enough,' Riddick said. 'You know that from your books. We need evidence. This is all on you without it.

Surely, you see that?'

Harvey's face twitched. His eyes darted between the officers again, before settling again on Gardner. His eyes were practically screaming at her for help now. 'You know, I don't need to read crime books to know that leaving a body near where you live isn't the best way to avoid suspicion! Does that count for anything?'

'Not if you did it on purpose as a canny way to talk us out of your guilt,' Riddick said.

'Did you go out at all last night between 8 p.m. and 2 a.m.?' Gardner asked, clutching at straws for him. 'See someone? Did someone see you? What did you do exactly?'

'I read *The Girl with the Dragon Tattoo*.'

'I'm afraid Stieg Larsson can't give you an alibi,' Riddick said.

'I only have what I have,' Harvey said, frowning. 'I will tell you the truth about everything. The first I heard of what happened to Tia Meadows was when I was arrested.'

'What's your relationship with Tia Meadows' father, Si?' Gardner asked.

'Relationship?'

'Well, do you know him?'

'Barely.'

'You're both fifty. Both born and bred in this area,' Gardner said.

'We went to the same school, even shared a couple of classes, but we were never friends. Not really.'

Gardner made a note.

The interview continued for some time, turning circles on itself. Eventually, Gardner made the call to put it on hold, and run a briefing to launch an investigation.

'How long do I have to stay here?' Harvey asked.

How long is a piece of string?

'Initially, it's twenty-four hours, Harvey,' Gardner said.

'But the chances are we'll be applying for an extension,' Riddick said.

'Can I have something to read?' Harvey asked.

'I'll see if there's anything I can do,' Gardner said. 'You should also get a solicitor.'

'I don't think there's any point. You'll get to the truth before any of that's necessary. I trust you.'

'Real life isn't always like the books,' Gardner said. 'We're far from all the answers.'

'And you're far from proving your innocence,' Riddick said.

Harvey looked down at the table again, clenching and unclenching his fists. 'When I was a child, Mum always used to tell me it never pays to be different. I've spent the last forty years proving the truth of that statement. I'm here because I'm different.'

'No, you're here because evidence was found on your property, and you've no alibi,' Riddick said.

'But that's my point. Someone is doing this to me. It's the same as being bullied at school. People target those unlike themselves.'

'You're fifty years old, Harvey. You live completely alone. You only socialise with shop assistants. Who's going to have targeted you?' Riddick asked.

'You'll see soon enough,' Harvey said, still looking Gardner in the eyes, rather than Riddick. 'You'll see how mean people can be.'

And Gardner knew he was right.

6

Gardner was lost in her thoughts on the way to HQ.

'Go on then, what's wrong?' Riddick asked from the passenger seat. 'Spit it out.'

'A dead girl, and an innocent man bang to rights? What do you think is wrong?'

'Bit early to start throwing around the word *innocent*.'

'Intuition, Paul.'

Riddick snorted. 'How many good people have come a cropper from intuition over the years?'

'Anyway, let's save it for the briefing and the team,' Gardner said. 'Meanwhile, I appreciate that you're on cloud nine after your hot date, but have a shower at HQ before the briefing, you reek of perfume.'

'Yes, boss, if I must, but I've started to like it.'

'And it does kind of suit you, Paul. Smooths out your rough edges, but I need everyone focused in the briefing, not dabbing at their eyes with a tissue.'

Riddick laughed. 'Now I've a personal question for you, boss...'

'Nothing like some good old-fashioned deflection.'

'Any news from Barry?'

'No, my marriage remains in the toilet. Although when someone hits flush is anyone's guess.'

The turmoil over how Anabelle was going to feel about her parents' broken marriage was difficult to navigate. Gardner was glad her eyes were on the road. It meant that Riddick wouldn't see the sadness in them. A brave face was the best course of action. Especially alongside a man who had more than his fair share of demons to bear.

'However, there may be a silver lining.'

'Go on.'

'Tell you what, you spill your beans, and I'll spill mine.'

Riddick laughed again. 'Nice try. Nah. Not interested enough.'

Gardner sighed. 'Okay, I'll give you a sweetener. Someone hand-delivered a birthday card to me in the middle of the night.'

She sensed Riddick's eyes on her.

'I don't know where to start with that one, boss.'

'Say what's on your mind.'

'Firstly, it's your birthday! Thanks for leaving your good friend here in the dark over this.'

'My birthday lacks importance. Go on, secondly?'

'Secondly... who's posting you a card in the middle of the night?'

'Anonymous.'

'You said this was a silver lining?'

'It's nice to have some attention.'

'From a stalker?'

Gardner rolled her eyes. 'Let's not assume it's a stalker.'

'When someone hand-delivers an anonymous card to you in the middle of the night, then you can be absolutely 100 per cent sure that it's a stalker.'

She thought back to her sleepless night. She'd be lying if she said it hadn't unnerved her; however, it seemed more appropriate to pass it off with humour. At least for now, anyway. 'So, it wasn't from you then?' Gardner asked, smiling.

'Might have been if you'd bothered to tell me. Anyway, I've crossed lines, but stalking someone is one step too far, even for me.'

'Why sound so horrified? There's worse things to be in life than *my* stalker, surely?'

'This conversation is developing into something way beyond ridiculous, boss,' Riddick said. 'To conclude though, let's just agree that the birthday card is weird.'

'Can't I just hold onto the hope that it's romantic?'

'Why?'

Gardner shrugged. 'Because my own husband and daughter still haven't phoned to wish me happy birthday.'

'I'm sorry.'

'Shit, eh?'

Again, she was glad her eyes were on the road, so Riddick couldn't gauge the true sadness in them.

'There may be a good reason?'

'There's a reason, all right. My husband – soon to be ex-husband at this rate – is a prick?'

'No comment.'

'So, can you see why a girl might hold out some hope that there's an admirer out there?'

'And if it turns out to be Jeffrey Dahmer?'

'We'll cross that bridge when we come to it.'

'Or *escape* over it more like.'

* * *

Unlike the first briefing in the last operation, Gardner felt she now had the measure of her eleven-strong, predominantly male, middle-aged Major Investigation Team; however, in the same way she had last time, she headed to the bathroom beforehand to ready herself.

Tucking her shirt in and adjusting her suit top was a pre-requisite; as was ensuring her bobbed brown hair was neat. She threw back some tic tacs, crunched them, and then winked at herself in the mirror.

Her march into IR2 couldn't feel more different this time. All the officers in the room fell silent. It made her feel like DCI Michael Yorke, her mentor and hero when she'd been back in Wiltshire.

It also made her feel on top of the world.

She did, however, hold back the proud smirk itching for release.

Checking Marsh wasn't in the room, she said, 'It was suggested earlier that until recently, the MIT never really saw major incidences... So, it's a good job the southerner turned up to put you all to work.'

Most of her audience laughed.

A hand shot up. It was DS Ross.

'John?'

'I agree! It was *way* quieter before you got here, boss! Peaceful, even.'

Gardner smiled. 'If you want peace and quiet, John, it can be arranged. There're requests for someone to supervise the toilets by Knaresborough Town Hall. Apparently, the complaints are flooding in about a defecating miscreant.'

'That's above his paygrade, boss,' O'Brien shouted.

Gardner laughed. Lucy always handled herself well in this swamp of bigoted testosterone.

'John probably is the defecating miscreant!' Rice called out.

Gardner turned back to the board while her team bantered for a moment longer. Any second now, they'd appreciate it was time to get serious. They did and silence ensued. She smiled again. In a lot of ways, she was growing fond of her team. Getting to know them was really starting to yield benefits. She knew their strengths and weaknesses, and the tasks she'd assigned – pinned to the board in the plastic wallet – were as bespoke as they could get.

She read out the randomly generated operation name from the top of the board.

'Operation Bright Day.'

Her eyes fell to the picture of Tia Meadows extracted from her Facebook page. Heavily made up, but it was no disguise to the natural beauty shining through.

Operation Bright Day – what a name!

Nothing delightful about this day... nothing delightful at all.

She turned and looked at Riddick. He was sitting nearer than he'd done on the last investigation. On Operation Eden, he'd skulked near the back. An outcast and loner. The Harvey Henfrey of the incident room. Bringing down Neil Taylor, and his previous DCI, Anders Smith, had elevated Riddick's status, and his colleagues had become more willing to accept him back into the fold. When she informed them all that he'd be deputy SIO on the case, there were no grumbles this time. She nodded at him with pride. He'd made huge steps.

He better stick to his promise to keep my birthday quiet though, she thought, *or I'll string him up by his gonads!*

'Matthew, are you ready?' Gardner asked a lanky man in an old, creased suit.

The HOLMES 2 operative, Matthew Blanks, nodded, his long black hair flapping back and forth.

'Tia Meadows,' she said, pointing at the picture on the board. 'Twenty years old.' She let the words hang there for a time.

'A bonny lass,' someone remarked.

'Yes,' Gardner agreed, turning back. 'Heart-breaking. I think we can all appreciate what an impact it will have on our community.'

Our? Did she just say our? Did she say that because she was starting to feel at home?

'Hopefully, boss, it won't be dragged out,' Rice said. 'Not when we have the bastard in custody.'

Gardner took a deep breath. She'd hold off on her reservations around Harvey's guilt just a little while longer.

She turned back and pointed below Tia's picture to where she'd written the location of the body and the time it was phoned in by Frank Dowson: 5.55 a.m. She read it out.

Gardner then pointed at a photograph of Frank Dowson standing proudly in his fisherman's waders, holding a massive fish in one hand. His details were also carefully written beside him.

'Tia was recognised by Frank Dowson, several of our officers, and then, regrettably, by the father, Si Meadows, who arrived at the scene after being contacted by Greg Quinn, who resides on Breary Flat Lane. He was the man who Frank ran to after Harvey approached him with a knife. Si Meadows made quite an impression at the crime scene.'

She pointed to a picture of the wide, squat man who'd upended her and left her with a nasty lump on the back of her head.

'What a prick,' Rice said. 'He needs to be hung out for that.'

Gardner turned. 'No,' she said, sternly.

'He hurt you, boss!' Rice protested.

'I said no Phil. Are you a father?' She didn't wait for an answer. 'We move on from what happened. Are we clear?'

Rice nodded.

Gardner surveyed her team. 'What do we know about Tia Meadows? Popular and well-known around Knaresborough. A socialite by all accounts.' She looked at Rice to warn him off any disparaging remarks. Hearing her referred to as a slapper because of her dress sense and conversations with boys had been more than enough for her to bear in one day. Her look didn't dissuade him.

'And sexually active,' Rice said.

'She's twenty, Phil,' O'Brien said. 'How many twenty-year-olds aren't sexually active?'

'I just thought it was important to cover every base,' Rice said.

'Do you know of anyone she was having sex with, Phil?'

Rice's face reddened. 'Well, no, but you could just tell, you know? I've drunk in the Bull on occasion. She was, you know, very—'

'Confident?' O'Brien asked. There was irritation in her tone.

'Yes,' Rice said.

'So? You're from another time period, Phil,' O'Brien said.

'Maybe, but I'm also your superior!'

'And I'm yours,' Gardner said with a raised eyebrow. 'So, unless you have anything concrete, Phil, regarding partners, can you keep your narrow-minded assumptions to yourself?'

Rice looked down, reddening further.

'She'd a number of jobs,' Gardner continued. 'She did shifts at Tesco in town, and worked behind the bar at the White Bull. Two pockets of information ready for us to rustle through. We also, of course, have the previously mentioned father, Si Meadows, infamous around here for dominating the building trade. It's an important area and needs unpicking.'

Riddick had his hand in the air.

'Paul?'

'Tia's mother left a long time ago,' Riddick said, reading from notes. 'When she was seven. She ran off to Greece with a lover, apparently. She never returned to the UK. Her whereabouts are now unknown, but we'll try our best. Tia lived with her father.'

Matthew Blanks tapped away incessantly on his laptop, recording details. Gardner wondered how he could see through all that hair. She prayed he tied it back when he was at the wheel of a car.

'Si Meadows rejected our offer of a FLO,' Gardner said. 'Paul and I will talk to him first. No one else is to go near him until I am certain he's calmed down. Tia's shift at the White Bull finished at eleven last night I'm led to believe. Dr Sands believes she died before 2 a.m. so it will be interesting to see if she returned home prior to her death.'

DS Ross put his hand up.

'John?'

'That lake. It's a fair walk from the White Bull in town. Twenty-five minutes or so? It seems an odd place for Tia to be walking to at that time, and it's nowhere near where she lives.'

Gardner decided it was now time to broach her doubts. 'Sands believes that the body was moved from somewhere. She died face down, from a suspected head wound, and was transported to that tree, and positioned. As far as we know, Harvey doesn't possess a vehicle. Which means, if he did do it, he potentially could have done it at his hut and dragged her through the woods.'

'What would Tia Meadows be doing with someone like Harvey Henfrey?' Barnett asked.

'Good question, Ray,' Gardner said. She paused and looked between their faces. 'Thing is, I don't think she was ever with him...'

There was a stunned silence. Faces creased. Some shook their heads.

Gardner continued, 'Both Paul and I have spoken to Harvey. We haven't taken him at face value, we can assure you, but he's convincing. He's not an individual experienced with socialising, and so you'd imagine inept at deceit and betrayal. If he's lying, he's doing it extremely effectively – better than I've ever seen it.' *Even better than my own brother, which would be impressive.* 'I know this doesn't confirm his innocence. But ask yourself: why would he keep the body a stone's throw from his home, and then hold onto a purse –

not a small purse by the way – but a rather large one that couldn't possibly be overlooked?'

The silence remained. Faces stayed creased. Heads were still shaking.

Well, it was worth a shot, Gardner thought. 'I'm just highlighting that we're keeping our options open. I want this case investigated thoroughly. *He'll* be investigated thoroughly too.'

She could sense their relief.

'We need a good look at Tia last night. What happened at the White Bull? Where did she go afterwards? There's CCTV around the town; we should be able to piece that together sooner rather than later. Meanwhile, we can be going door to door on Breary Flat Lane and adjacent streets. Someone could have transported her body there, or, at the very least, seen her walking there.'

It felt like the right moment to bring the briefing to a close.

'Until we know otherwise, I don't want any of you considering this an open and shut case. We need to throw everything at it. Let's think about motive for a start. If you're really convinced that Harvey killed Tia, bring me the reason why. It's not enough to just tell me he's odd, or different. In your eyes, he's been odd and different for fifty years, and he's never killed anyone – at least that we know of. Despite being popular and well-liked, Tia was targeted. This might make it easier to locate the person bearing a grudge. They're obviously few and far between. Let's build up a picture of Tia's life. Best friends? Boyfriends? Girlfriends? We have her mobile and we're acquiring call logs. We also need to crack open the dungeon that is social media. Medical problems? Unlikely at her age, but worth squinting at.' She paused. 'We've been here before, not that long ago, and I'm asking you to go again, as well as you did last time, and we'll clear this up, I've no doubt. As I mentioned, DI Riddick and I will be speaking to Si Meadows. He's a large character in this small area, so it seems an important point. Could he have been targeted?

Was his daughter a way to get at him? I've assigned tasks and pinned them to the wall. We will reconvene at 6 p.m. Thank you.'

Feeling as if she hadn't paused for breath, she turned her back to her team and took one. Then she stared at a photograph of Si Meadows.

She rubbed the lump on the back of her head.

Let's hope he's calmed down, Gardner thought, *or at least realised that we're on the same side.*

7

Large glass of whisky in hand, Si Meadows opened the front door of his massive home and regarded Gardner. His eyes were puffy and red. He took a big gulp, sighed and said, 'I hope I didn't hurt you.'

'I'm fine,' Gardner said.

She was surprised at how quickly he'd calmed down. Was it the alcohol? Well, whatever the reason, she welcomed it.

Si gave a swift nod. 'It's all rather hazy, you know? I wasn't thinking straight.' He took another mouthful and then rubbed at his eyes.

'It's understandable. We're so sorry for your loss. Can we come in please?' Gardner asked.

Si looked at Riddick and then back at Gardner. 'It depends.' He finished the whisky.

'On?' Riddick asked.

'On whether or not you tell me where that freak is.'

'Who're you referring to?' Gardner asked, knowing well enough the answer.

Si snorted. 'Give me a bastard break.'

'It's yet to be established who's responsible,' Riddick said.

Si sneered. 'Yet to be established? Is that how it works these days? Is that how *weak* you folks have become? Everyone else knows it's that freak; why're you two so confused?'

'I understand how you must feel, Mr Meadows—'

'*No,*' Si said, pointing his empty glass at her. 'You've no sodding idea how I feel.'

Gardner felt the back of her head throb as her heart rate started to increase.

Si's eyes swept over Riddick. He paused for a moment. 'I guess you might do.'

'Sorry?' Riddick said.

'I guess you might know how I feel.'

Riddick was stunned into silence, so Gardner moved the conversation on quickly. 'Mr Meadows, if the person you're referring to is guilty, you can be sure we'll know sooner rather than later. Right now, we need to gather the evidence to ensure whoever is responsible faces justice.'

'Justice?' Si said. 'Did you get justice, DI Riddick?'

Gardner looked at Riddick. His eyes were wide. She needed to put a knife in this interaction immediately. 'Mr Meadows—'

'Boss, it's okay,' Riddick said, holding the palm of his hand in her direction. 'Mr Meadows, I believe in our system.'

'You do, do you?' Si raised his eyebrows.

Enough! 'Mr Meadows,' Gardner said. 'This isn't serving any purpose. Can we please just come in?'

Si narrowed his red puffy eyes, thought about it, and then nodded. 'Whatever.'

He turned and Gardner followed him into his home. As she did so, she glanced back to Riddick and whispered, 'Maybe it's best if you wait in the car.'

Riddick ignored her and went in anyway.

* * *

If the size of the house hadn't given away the fact that Si was loaded, the décor certainly did.

Gardner didn't read *Hello* magazine, but had, on occasion, picked it up in a doctor's waiting room. This was the kind of house a rich celebrity would live in. Si had buried himself in a wealth that evaded the vast majority of the world's inhabitants.

She recalled Harvey's hut earlier.

The two men may appear to have polar opposite lifestyles, but weren't they, in fact, very similar? Hadn't both of them isolated themselves from the world they inhabited?

The lounge they currently occupied was massive, and Gardner couldn't handle the space between the sofa she and Riddick sat on, and the one that Si occupied. Rather than speak loudly and impersonally across the room, Gardner left Riddick and went to sit on the same sofa as their host. Si simply stared into space, blankly. He'd got himself another drink but hadn't offered them one.

She followed Riddick's line of sight to a fully stocked bar beneath a chandelier.

A penny for his thoughts?

She hoped he wasn't being plagued with temptation.

She looked back at Si. She was yet to meet a builder on a premiership footballer's wage. The suggestion that Si was overseeing and controlling all building trade in Knaresborough suddenly carried a lot of weight. She recalled her quip that he was like the Godfather.

His high profile might just give them answers.

After all, there never was a king without enemies and traitors, was there?

She pulled out her pad. 'Has Tia always lived here with you, Mr Meadows?'

'Yes... Where else would she live?'

'Tia was twenty. She may have spent time elsewhere before now. With her mother for example. Do you know where your ex-wife is?'

'No. Tia has always been with me. That bitch left for Greece when Tia was seven. Good riddance. We haven't heard from her since.'

With all your money? Gardner thought. *Wouldn't she be tempted back? Is she paid to stay away... or worse?* Gardner made some notes. 'How had your relationship with your daughter been?'

'She's my daughter! Ask a better bloody question.'

'All relationships are different, Mr Meadows. Unique.'

Si looked at Gardner and narrowed his eyes. 'It was perfect. Our relationship was perfect. We were best friends. She talked to me about everything.'

'Everything? Even her personal life?' Gardner asked.

Si creased his brow.

'Boyfriends?' Gardner prompted.

'Of course. She hasn't had many though.'

Contrary to what DS Rice believes, Gardner thought, making notes. Although why would she give credence to a man who wore bigoted attitudes like badges of honour?

'I believe she had a couple of jobs,' Gardner said. 'She worked at the White Bull most evenings, and also did some shifts at Tesco.'

'So?' Si shrugged.

Gardner opened her mouth to answer, but Riddick got in there first. 'Why?'

'Why what?' Si asked.

'Why was she working for minimum wage when you have all this?' Riddick asked.

Her deputy SIO was direct, but not wrong.

Si took another mouthful of whisky. 'She wanted to work. I told her she didn't have to. She knew I'd pay for her to do whatever she wanted – education or otherwise. Even offered to set her up a business. Fiercely independent, you see. Like me. I fought for everything I have. She seemed set on doing the same.'

Fought, Gardner thought. *In what way have you fought, Si, I wonder?*

Gardner continued to probe Si and Tia's relationship. Si made it seem idyllic. *Too idyllic?* It sounded as though they spent every free moment together, eating, watching television and chatting with never a bad word passing between them. The fact that Tia 'wasn't very interested in boys' cropped up again, and so too, did Gardner's memory of Rice's dismissive comment.

'Where were you last night, Mr Meadows?' Gardner asked.

'Why?'

'It's the same question we ask everyone. We do it to eliminate—'

'Have you not been listening to a word I've been saying?' He shook his glass. 'She was my *everything*.'

'No one is denying that,' Riddick said.

Si stared at Riddick. 'Were you asked the same questions?'

Gardner interjected. 'The circumstances were very different. We're here about Tia, and you. Let us help you, Mr Meadows.'

Si and Riddick regarded each other for a moment.

'Okay, fair enough,' Si said. He nodded at Riddick.

Riddick's nod in return was quick and barely perceptible, but Gardner clocked it.

Is this a connection between two people who've lost everything?

'I was drinking at the White Bull,' Si said.

'While your daughter was there?' Gardner asked.

'It's my local. Always has been. Tia knew the risks when she took the job – she knew full well that I wouldn't stop drinking there. I wasn't keeping an eye on her...' Gardner watched one of the saddest expressions she'd ever seen close over his face. 'Although of course I was.'

Gardner allowed him a moment. She looked over at Riddick, who wasn't making notes. That always irritated her. She held up her pad to gesture he do the same. He rolled his eyes and reached into his pocket.

'Mr Meadows, who were you with in the White Bull?' Gardner asked.

'Terry Montgomery and Frankie Lane. There's plenty of other people who can tell you I was there too.'

'When did you leave?'

'After last orders. Must have been around eleven.'

'Where did you go?'

'Here... home.'

'How?'

'I walked. Fifteen minutes. No point in waiting on a taxi.'

'Did you come home alone?'

'I wasn't with Tia if that's what you're asking.'

'Who were you with then?'

'For pity's sake. Does it matter?'

'Yes,' Gardner said.

'Why? I wasn't with Tia, nor did I see her after that. Sometimes, she stays back late at the White Bull for a couple of drinks. I went to sleep, and it was only in the morning, around seven, that I noticed she'd not come home. Then, I got *that* call off Greg Quinn first thing... and...' He finished his whisky.

'Who did you go home with?' Riddick asked.

Si tapped his foot and scowled.

Riddick persisted, 'Who?'

Si stood up. 'It's nothing to do with Tia. It's nothing to do with anything.'

'You need someone to confirm your whereabouts between eleven and two in the morning, Mr Meadows,' Gardner said.

'Or what?' Si said, glaring at her. 'You'll arrest me?'

Gardner took a deep breath. She thought of another way of approaching it. 'Mr Meadows. No doubt we'll get the CCTV footage from town and, hopefully, from other points on your route home. We'll find out anyway. By saving us this time now, you empower us to get on with finding the truth.'

'Shit,' Si said, turning and marching over to the bar. 'Shit, shit, *shit*!' He refilled his glass, slammed the bottle down and stared thoughtfully at it for a time.

Gardner looked over to Riddick, saw that he was about to speak, and then steadied him with the palm of her hand. Riddick paused.

'I was with Luke Donnelly,' Si said. 'He works behind the bar with Tia. In fact, they're the same age. They were good friends.'

Gardner made a note. 'Thank you. What were you doing with Luke Donnelly?'

He drank a mouthful of whisky. 'I bumped into him outside the takeaway. We were walking in the same direction... Not much else to it...'

Really? Gardner thought. *Seems like you're carrying something heavy here.*

'Did you come back here with Luke?' Gardner asked.

Si swirled the whisky in his glass.

Gardner and Riddick exchanged a look.

'Did you go back to Luke's?' Riddick said.

Si looked up at Riddick. 'Yes.'

Riddick looked at Gardner then back at Si. 'Why?'

Si opened his mouth, but no words came out.

'Mr Meadows?' Gardner prompted.

'For a drink,' Si said. 'Okay? Just a bloody drink.'

'Did Tia know about this?' Riddick asked.

Si slammed the glass down. 'I promise you that this is irrelevant.'

'Can we decide that, Mr Meadows? Did Tia know you were having a drink at Luke's?'

'No, of course not,' Si said. 'She wouldn't have liked it.' He drank more whisky. 'Shit.' Empty glass in hand, he pointed at Riddick, and then turned his finger on Gardner. 'No one can know. Do you hear me? No one can know.' He was slurring his words now.

'What time were you with Luke until?' Gardner said.

He narrowed his eyes. 'About five. Then I came back here and grabbed an hour or so before... before... Quinn phoned... to tell me... ah Christ, you know already.' He ran a hand over his forehead. 'You can't tell anyone.' He pointed again. 'You listening? You *can't* tell anyone.'

'If it doesn't become necessary to share this information,' Gardner said. 'We won't. But we *will* have to confirm it with Luke.'

Si sighed and poured himself another drink.

When he returned to the sofa beside her, Gardner tried to prompt more information about Luke Donnelly, but met nothing but steely stares and monosyllabic brush offs. Riddick asked him questions about work, but he seemed content to tell them he'd retired. In fact, he kept emphasising that he'd retired two years ago at the grand old age of forty-eight.

Si didn't look like he had much left in him. A couple more whiskies and he'd be unconscious on the sofa. So, Gardner prioritised her question. There'd been one she was teetering around, but had been apprehensive about launching into too early. 'What's your relationship with Harvey Henfrey?'

'*Relationship*?'

'Yes, that's correct.'

'These questions just get better and better!' He drank some more whisky.

Great, Gardner thought. At this rate, her interviewing technique may put him in a hospital bed to have his stomach pumped.

'Try this for a relationship: the man has ruined my goddamn life!'

'So, before today, did you know who he was?'

'Of course I did. Everyone knows who he is. He's a freak that lives out by a lake where all the wreck-heads and fishermen loiter.'

'You and he are both the same age,' Gardner said.

'And?'

'And you've never socialised?'

'Socialised?' He guffawed and gestured around his house. 'Have you looked around, DCI. What can me and him possibly have in common?'

Quite a lot if you ask me. Both of you seem like prisoners in some way. 'So, just to confirm, you've never spoken?'

'We went to school together, okay? We were sat next to each other in maths one year and we chatted, but we never got close...' His mouth remained open as if he was tempted to say something else. A second or so later, he must have thought better of it, as he closed it.

Gardner made some notes. 'Can we see Tia's room please?'

Si went to the bar and poured the last of the whisky into his glass. 'If you must.'

* * *

Considering the grandeur of the rest of the home, Tia's bedroom was modest. It was relatively small with limited furnishing. The room was comprised of a queen-sized futon, a dressing table scattered with cosmetics, and some lilac-coloured furniture. She had various posters of boy bands on the wall, and a wooden box overflowing with stuffed toys, neither of which seemed appropriate for a twenty-year-old.

'I'm sorry for the mess,' Si said from the doorway. 'I did always try and tell her.' He broke off and walked away. Gardner could hear him sobbing on his landing.

Gardner glanced at Riddick who looked pale. Had Si's constant references to his tragedy got on top of him? 'I've got this if you need some air,' she said.

'It's okay,' he said, continuing to look around the room.

The mess Si had been referring to was an exaggeration. A few scattered cosmetics, an unmade bed and a wooden box that couldn't shut from all the toys wasn't exactly what you'd call a disaster zone.

Gardner ran her eyes over some framed photographs on the wall. Most of them were of Tia and her father in different locations throughout the world: the Eiffel Tower, the Great Wall of China, the pyramids of Giza. *Impressive.* Tia had been to more places in her teens than Gardner would get to in her lifetime. There were a few photographs of her with friends. The same friend never seemed to appear more than once though.

She glanced up at Riddick, who was running his eyes over a bookshelf, which, at first glance, contained a lot of teenage fiction. They'd already agreed not to touch anything. It could be prudent to call in forensics at some point. Outside, she could still hear drunken sobbing.

Gardner was about to suggest that they call it a day here, when she heard the melodic twinkling of a wooden music box.

She moved over to where Riddick was watching a pink ballerina twirl to the plucking of a steel comb.

She glared at him, annoyed that he'd opened the box up.

Si's sobbing grew louder, and she realised he'd moved up close behind them. Recalling her experience earlier, she stepped out of his way.

Riddick did the same.

Then, the distraught bereaved father clutched the wooden

musical box in both hands and lifted it so the ballerina was level with his eyes.

Gardner felt guilty for darting away in fear and considered placing a hand on the broken man's shoulder.

She thought better of it.

She was in a pressure cooker of emotion right now, and she didn't want to do anything that might cause it to boil over.

She looked over at Riddick and gestured they leave with a nod of her head.

At the door, she turned to Si and said, 'Thank you, Mr Meadows. I will arrange someone to call and make the offer of a family liaison officer again. I think you should give it serious thought. There really is no shame in having some support.'

He didn't respond. He just stared at his daughter's twirling ballerina.

'We'll see ourselves out, Mr Meadows. Please contact us if you need anything.'

On the stairs, Riddick turned to her. 'There's no way into him right now.'

Well, if anyone knew how Si Meadows was feeling at this moment in time, then you could be sure Riddick did.

8

Gardner contacted Barnett and asked him to visit Luke Donnelly to confirm Si's alibi.

'He's gay?'

'Seems that way.'

'That's crazy.'

'Really? I know we're in deepest, darkest Yorkshire, Ray...'

'No... I don't mean the fact he's gay, boss, just that... Si Meadows! The man has controlled the building trade in these parts for as long as anyone can remember.'

'Can't you rule with an iron fist *and* be homosexual?'

'Yes, I guess. I'm sorry. It just seems strange to me that one of the most intimidating men in North Yorkshire is gay. I must be old-fashioned. I'm—'

'Don't worry, Ray, I'm winding you up. I think, like you, that homophobia probably still exists in the underworld – and I don't expect the testosterone-heavy summit to be forward-thinking. You can be certain that Si doesn't want anyone to know about his interest in young men. And Luke is young. He's only twenty. Same as his daughter. Oh, and Ray?'

'Yes, boss?'

'Take Lucy to the interview for the experience.'

Gardner was keen to nurture O'Brien.

After ringing off, Gardner phoned ahead to the White Bull. The landlord, Bertie Thomas, agreed to meet her and Riddick at the door.

* * *

They couldn't park in the town square because it was the middle of the annual FEVA arts and crafts festival, and the place was rammed. They managed to find a spot behind the square next to the Methodist church.

As they walked through the heaving town centre, Gardner heard the squawking tones of Punch as he argued with Judy. She paused outside Caffè Nero behind a crowd of giggling children. For a moment, she was seized with nostalgia and was back, as a child, watching the shows on the beaches in Dorset.

She recalled Punch hitting Judy. A few years ago, she'd read about how inappropriate that was, and the clamour for change. This was one performer who'd listened.

Judy was now the one hitting Punch.

She failed to see how that made it okay, but thought it was at least nice that Judy was getting her own back as she caught up with Riddick outside the White Bull.

'Impressive building,' she said.

'Yes. Many of our buildings were constructed from the stones of the Knaresborough castle wall in 1648, following the order from parliament to dismantle royalist castles.'

'It gives the place a quaint character.'

'You may change your mind when you see inside,' Riddick said, holding the door open for her.

Bertie Thomas was a short, plump man with very few remaining strands of white hair that he still went to the trouble of dyeing and combing over. He wore a pressed white shirt and a black bow tie. To Gardner, he looked more like a washed-up door-to-door salesman than a pub landlord.

'Come in,' he said. 'I've not opened yet. The place is empty.'

The White Bull was the type of pub that looked passionately old-fashioned on the outside but fiercely modern on the inside. Gardner couldn't stand the whizz bang of fruit machines and was glad they were unplugged. She also didn't care much for the sound of pool, so was glad to see the lights above the tables were switched off. The White Bull was the type of place you came to watch live sports; Blind Jack's, over the square, was the pub you ventured into for a more rustic experience.

'Drink?' Bertie asked.

'Just water, please,' Gardner said.

'Coke, thanks,' Riddick said.

'I guess the days of *The Sweeney* are long gone?' Bertie asked. 'You know the first pub I worked in did a thriving trade from the local constabulary. Actually, I think, looking back, it was most of the trade. Times change, I guess. The police are the ones dealing with the drinkers, rather than doing the actual drinking these days.'

He was looking at Riddick as he said this, which Gardner thought ironic, considering all the DI's recent troubles were with alcohol.

Once Gardner had her water, and Riddick his Coke, Bertie stood over them while they sat.

'Please sit, Mr Thomas,' Gardner said.

'I can't. Not at the moment.'

Riddick looked around the pub, confused. 'It's empty.'

Gardner kicked Riddick under the table.

'I just can't,' Bertie said. 'Medical reasons.'

'Ahh,' Riddick said, his cheeks reddening.

'Age and dignity. They're not good bedfellows,' Bertie said. 'And please call me Bertie.'

'Well, Bertie, thanks for seeing us. As I explained on the phone, it's about Tia Meadows.'

A look of sadness passed over Bertie's face in much the same way it'd passed over Frank's, Harvey's and Si's at the mere mention of her name. This didn't surprise Gardner too much. Tia had been twenty years old with her whole life ahead of her. What was heartening was the fact that she'd clearly held a lot more respect than Rice had suggested earlier at the crime scene.

'Beautiful smile,' Bertie said. 'One of them, you know?' He touched his ears. 'Ear to ear. Lit up her whole face.'

Gardner nodded. 'How long has she worked for you?'

'She didn't just work here.' He blinked a few times, clearly forcing back tears. 'She was my friend.' A tear broke away and he caught it with the back of his hand. 'But I was also her boss... yes. In my fifteen years of running this public house, I can absolutely guarantee that Tia Meadows was one of the best things that ever happened to this place.' Bertie put his palms in the air. 'She always brightened up the room. She had this way.'

'How long has she worked for you?' Riddick asked, demanding the answer to Gardner's earlier question.

Gardner was grateful for the impatience in Riddick's voice. Better to just get to the point.

'About two years, give or take.' Bertie paced from side to side. 'More comfortable if I just keep moving.'

'And did you notice anything out of the ordinary last night?' Riddick asked.

'What do you mean?'

'Well, did she *seem* different in any way?'

'I didn't notice anything. Her father was here last night, so she was on her best behaviour.'

'Best behaviour?' Gardner quizzed.

Bertie smirked. 'No flirting.'

'Flirting?' Riddick asked. 'Who does she usually flirt with?'

Bertie's face dropped, and he looked concerned that he'd maybe said the wrong thing. 'Well, not so much flirting.... More chatting, I guess. She was a chatty girl, Tia. Could talk a storm up with any customer when there were others to serve.'

'So, she was less chatty because her father was here?' Riddick asked.

Bertie shook his head and sighed. 'I guess what I mean is... sorry if this comes out all wrong... but, it just always seemed to be *men* that she got caught up with in conversation. So, I guess it was flirting, and yes, she did less of it when her old man was in.'

Gardner smiled. 'Could it be because men were going out of their way to engage her in conversation? And thought better of it in the presence of Si Meadows?'

Bertie thought about it and nodded. 'I guess that makes sense.'

'Nothing stands out from last night?' Riddick asked.

'This is the White Bull,' Bertie said, smiling. 'Everything stands out. Ordinary here is different from ordinary in most pubs.'

'Elaborate.' Riddick was now sounding extremely irritated.

'I can't recall anything involving Tia, I'm afraid. There was a scrap – again, a usual occurrence. This one involved Si, coincidentally. Old rogue...'

'Come again,' Riddick said. 'Si Meadows was involved in a *fight*?'

Bertie nodded. 'I can see how that may look. But fighting isn't uncommon. Some punters would even admit to liking a scrap in here.'

'What happened, Bertie?' Gardner asked, unable now to keep irritation from her voice also.

He gestured at the pool tables with his thumb. 'It's amazing what a game of pool can do to the most level-headed of men.'

'So, Si had a fight with someone over a game of pool?' Gardner asked.

'Not exactly...' He shook his head from side to side and was looking remarkably paler than he had done five minutes ago. 'Look, I don't want to get him into trouble here; he's one of my best customers.'

'Really, Bertie?' Riddick asked. 'Or are you just scared of him? Like most people are in this area? And that's fine... it's probably quite *normal*... but listen, *I* know that he will want you to help us find whoever did this.'

'I guess. Okay. Si has it in for travellers. To be fair, most people have it in for travellers. Have you seen the mess they make? But no one quite dislikes travellers like Si. It's business, you see. They go door to door offering odd jobs and poaching work. All building work goes through Si in this area. That's the way it is, you know?'

Gardner nodded and the look she gave Riddick probably spoke volumes. How was this situation going on unchecked in the twenty-first century? Her priority was the murder right now, but she'd be back to cast an eye over this dodgy monopoly built up by Si Meadows.

'When the travellers are in town, we become their pub of choice. We do get quite busy but, as a result, we become more volatile. I employ from a bouncer agency in Leeds when they're in town. The money I make from them dwarfs the cost of the bouncers, so it's worth it. Scraps break out, and then the perpetrator is evicted. What can I say? The rougher the night, the better the takings! It's a dog-eat-dog world. So, anyway, the travellers, by and large, know to keep their distance from Si. And, to his credit, he usually keeps his distance from them due to his unpredictable

temperament. But, last night, a young upstart marched over there' –
he thumbed at the pool table – 'and provoked him.'

'Provoked him?' Gardner asked. 'How?'

'He challenged him to a game of pool.'

Gardner creased her brow. 'How's that provocation?'

'Trust me, when it comes to Si and travellers, that's provocation.
He runs a strict "do not chuffing talk to me" policy.' Bertie laughed.

'Who is this lad?' Riddick asked.

'I don't know. Never seen him before. He obviously didn't know
who Si was either, unless he was suicidal. Lad couldn't have been
older than twenty.'

'I assume you checked his ID at the door then?' Riddick said.

Bertie avoided eye contact. 'Of course. Anyway, Si beat the living
shit out of the kid. At least, until Reggie and Dez, my two bouncers,
separated them.'

'I take it you evicted both from the premises?' Gardner said.

'I evicted the lad,' Bertie said.

'But not Si?'

Bertie again avoided eye contact. 'He didn't start it.'

Gardner shook her head. 'That's not what you just said.'

'That's exactly what I said. They shouldn't communicate with
him.'

Riddick snorted.

Bertie looked at him angrily and fiddled with his bow tie.

'You didn't evict Si, Bertie,' Riddick said, 'because Si isn't the
kind of man you evict. Not without consequences.'

Bertie was sweating as he paced now, and not on account of his
piles. 'This is his local. He's a valued customer.'

'Whatever,' Gardner said, holding her hands up. 'Put local poli-
tics aside for a second. Tell me what happened next.'

'Not a great deal,' Bertie said. 'The travellers that came in with
that lad – about ten I reckon – just carried on drinking. I thought

there would be more camaraderie between them to be honest, but
they seemed happy to cut this lad loose. Maybe they'd warned him
about Si and the idiot ignored them? I don't know. Everything went
smoothly from that point on until chucking out time anyhow.'

'Nothing else involving Si and Tia?' Gardner said.

'Nothing. To be fair, considering the clientele, it was a relatively
quiet night. Everyone filtered out after eleven.'

'And Si Meadows too?' Riddick asked.

'Yes... of course. Tia obviously stayed to help clean up, but her
father left on the dot. With Terry and Frankie if I recall.'

Gardner nodded. That did tally up with what Si had said about
leaving with his drinking buddies prior to meeting up with Luke
some time later in a takeaway. 'Do you know where Tia went after
she left?'

Bertie shrugged. 'Why would I know that? Home, I'd assume?'

'Was Luke Donnelly working here last night?' Riddick asked.

'Yes, why do you ask?'

Gardner glared at Riddick. *Don't be starting a hare running!*

'Just getting a complete picture,' Riddick said. 'What is your
relationship with Luke like?'

'Fine, I guess,' Bertie said. 'Never really got on with him like I
got on with Tia. Very camp...' He raised an eyebrow. 'Wouldn't be
surprised if, you know...' He didn't finish.

'Wouldn't be surprised if what?' Riddick asked.

'Well... if he had alternative tastes.'

'Alternative tastes?' Riddick rolled his eyes and smiled at Gardner. 'What you on about?'

'Gay,' Bertie whispered.

Riddick looked around. 'There's no one here but us, Bertie. No
need to whisper.'

Amusing as it was, Gardner kicked Riddick under the table to
stop him playing.

'Were Luke and Si friends?'

Bertie pulled his head back, wearing an incredulous expression. 'Odd question. Luke and Tia were thick as thieves, yes. But Luke and Si? Never seen them talking. Doubt I ever would. Chalk and cheese them two. One is fifteen stone of pure testosterone, and the other, well... you know...'

Riddick said, 'Has alternative tastes?'

He winced when Gardner cut him off with another kick.

Gardner and Riddick continued to probe Bertie a while longer, but it seemed the information had peaked with the revelation surrounding Si's fight. Because it was the first she'd heard of it, she assumed that the CCTV footage supplied from the White Bull had yet to be scrutinised. She'd contact Rice on the way to see the travellers to ask him to view the entire evening's recording between now and the briefing, so he could capture the most relevant parts for the team to view – the fight, no doubt, being the highlight.

After thanking Bertie, Riddick grabbed two coffees from Nero. Punch and Judy had finished, but the stage was still set up for the afternoon show. Gardner cast her mind back to those Dorset beaches with her family. Watching that show, sitting alongside...

Jack.

Her brother never laughed. Not once. The other children did, but not him.

She remembered being in her bed one night, listening to her father's lament as he argued with her mother. 'It's like a dead man has crawled up inside my son.'

9

Si Meadows danced.

Holding his daughter's wooden music box, he focused on the pirouetting ballerina who had one leg cocked against the other and one arm outstretched in the air, and kept pace with her.

Tears streamed down his face.

'Tia...'

He increased his speed and was suddenly turning faster than the dancer. Yes, he was uncoordinated, clumsy and occasionally stumbled, but he didn't care.

His eyes never strayed from the wooden figure.

They were always on her.

His Tia. His daughter. His baby. His *everything*...

'How you danced! When you were on stage, everyone only had eyes for you.'

I only had eyes for you.

He moved faster. Dizzy now, but still he turned. Still he cried.

'Come back to me, baby.'

The music stopped. The ballerina stopped.

Si stopped.

The world around him continued to move, so he fell to his knees, and screamed.

* * *

Later, his voice sore from the screaming, he crawled over to Tia's bed and hoisted himself onto it. Without looking, he grabbed one of his beautiful little dancer's framed photographs from the wall.

He lay back and held the photograph at arm's length above his face.

Him and Tia with their backs to Stonehenge.

The smiles on their faces. A glorious time. Look at that sky!

Red sky at night. Shepherd's delight.

The red sky at night made him think of his old scout hut on the River Nidd.

And that night.

The *one* that'd changed everything. He went downstairs and grabbed another bottle of whisky from his bar.

The old scout hut was still firmly on his mind.

He thought of going there.

Why not?

He had nothing else to do...

Taking his bottle, he headed out to his car to revisit old wounds.

* * *

His wounds were deep, but so were the wounds on the scout hut itself.

The doors were missing. It didn't matter. The roof had fallen in long ago and attempting to go inside would be suicide.

The council had pinned up warning signs everywhere, and

notices of its demolition. Si snorted. The hut was long overdue its levelling.

He circled to the back of the hut, stood on the bank of the River Nidd and stared out over the slow running river.

He drank from his bottle and moved his eyes up to the cloudy sky.

Far too early for a red sky at night.

But the thought was another reminder, nonetheless.

1982

Always on the lookout for some mischief, ten-year-old Si Meadows regularly set off for cub scouts half an hour before it started.

Tonight, Si had decided that the mischief was down on the bank of the River Nidd behind the scout hut, in which his father, and before him, his grandfather, had learned to tie knots, while promising to do their duty to God and royalty.

The sky was a brilliant red from the descending sun, giving enough visibility to manoeuvre the bank. He heard his father's voice in his head. 'Red sky at night, shepherd's delight. Be good weather tomorrow, Si.'

Si walked the muddy banks strewn with the remnants of a party the previous evening. Fag packets and beer bottles. From those either too skint to drink in the pub, or those who were far too young to get in one.

Si sneered over the thought of his uncles and cousins, who would've been among the revellers. His people, the Meadows, certainly got about. He hated most of them. Always ruffling his hair and calling him 'Baby Si-by' because of his puffy cheeks and small build. Bastards.

'You need to stop smoking, Si-by – it stunts your growth.'

Raucous laughter.

Sod off, Uncle Bryan. If you ruffle my hair when I've grown, I'll break your bloody finger off!

A cold breeze rushed in over the Nidd. His cub scout jumper, with its smattering of badges – although not as many as some of the others – fought off some of the cold, but he was wearing his school shorts out of season, and he shivered.

What choice did he have? His father spent most of their money on booze, and so his mother hadn't bothered replacing his trousers following his last growth spurt. No way was he wearing trousers so that every Tom, Dick and Harry could point at his exposed ankles and cry, 'Has your cat died, Si?'

He reached into his pocket and pulled out the red Swiss Army Knife his father had given him. He stroked the engraved letters. SM. Stuart Meadows. His father was a bastard, but giving him this had been one of his better moments. He slipped the knife back in his pocket and patted it to check it was securely in there. It was his most prized possession.

Si mindlessly lined up three bottles on a tree that had toppled long ago.

Then, he selected a few rocks from the banks. Rocks big enough to smash, but not too big that he couldn't throw them a decent distance.

The sun was almost down and the red sky was darkening. He watched pools of light spring up on the Nidd and followed them up to the source. From the houses on the opposite side of the Nidd, glowing windows stared at him like the eyes of a predator.

'Piss off!'

He turned and threw the first stone.

It struck the central bottle, but the glass didn't smash; it simply toppled back onto the bank behind.

However, it still classed as a score. And with his first shot too! 'One,' he hissed at the predator's eyes.

He drew back his hand to launch the second stone.

'Queer!' The loud voice in his head made him jump.

The stone whistled harmlessly over the remaining two bottles and landed with a thud in the undergrowth.

He shook his head. He thought he was over this.

Ignoring the shaking in his throwing hand, he pulled the next stone back for another go.

'Puff!' the voice in his head shrieked.

Another miss.

Jesus, it was days back. Let it go, just let it go.

This time he expected the voice, and so kept focus. The bottle on the left toppled. 'Two! Take that!'

The success didn't seem to help his confidence though. The shaking intensified and he broke out in a sweat. He needed to pull himself together. He yanked back his trembling hand and waited for a cool breeze to steady him before launching.

'Si-by is gay-by!' his inner voice cried.

No strike.

Shit! Two stones left.

Si noticed his face was damp. He looked up at the sky, hoping it was raining but already knowing it wasn't. He wiped at the tears with the back of his jumper sleeve.

He thought back to that moment again, three days previous, sitting on the swing at the park alongside his best friend for as long as he could remember. The source of his greatest laughs.

He pushed the memory aside to throw another stone. This time without lining it up. It sailed clear of the bottle.

The voice in his head came louder. 'Bender!'

He wiped his eyes again.

Back in that memory, his best friend reached up and put his hand on Si's face. Si let it stay there for a time and found himself lost in his friend's blue eyes. Then, he felt his friend's lips on his... warm... soft... He pulled away and stood, pointed down at his friend and shouted, 'You're disgusting.'

Again, he pushed the traumatic memory aside. He drew back his hand to throw the stone. He wouldn't be pressured by the voice in his head this time. This had to be his moment to take control. He launched, shouting, 'You ruined everything!'

The bottle shattered.

'Three!'

The back door of the scout hut started to rattle – someone was unlocking it from the inside. Had he been heard?

Si sprinted up the muddy bank, kicking aside fag packets and bottles.

He made it to the side of the hut before he heard the back door open.

'Who's there?' It was the voice of Baloo, one of the cub scout leaders. A grumpy bastard who was well into his fifties.

'Who's there?' It sounded like a growl this time.

It was typical. Baloo had no patience. Why did he want to work with kids in the first place?

Si heard the back door slam.

He looked at his Casio digital watch. Cubs started in fifteen minutes.

He circled back around to the front of the hut. The door, which had been recently repainted, badly, had blistered. Under the red sky, the hut looked as if it was covered in boils.

After checking his face was dry with his fingertips, Si reached for the handle. He was no longer in the mood for mischief, and he'd be happy to just get into the warmth. It was possible some of the other cub scouts may have turned up early; although, that could include his best friend. Ex-best friend. Awkward.

He tried the handle. The door was locked.

Strange.

He placed his ear to the door and listened.

And then everything changed.

* * *

Si's mobile phone rang.

Luke Donnelly.

He answered and allowed Luke to speak first. 'Si, thank God, I'm so worried. The police want to talk to me.'

'Tell them the truth.'

'Okay.'

'And then you can tell them it's over.'

Silence.

'Did you get that?' Si asked.

'Yes... Si, are you okay? I'm worried—'

'Listen carefully to what I'm about to say, Luke. Listen very carefully.'

'I'm listening.'

'I'm expecting a red sky tonight. A red sky.'

'I see... Where are you now, Si? Can I come to you?'

Si looked at the baby blue sky. 'A *blood* red sky.'

'Si?'

'Listen carefully. If you ever call me again, I'll cut your throat.' He hung up and dropped his phone into his trouser pocket.

He then held his bottle of whisky up to blue sky and squinted, looking through the bottle. Amber.

Tonight would be red.

Red sky at night.

Shepherd's delight.

10

After Barnett had contacted them to report that he'd spoken to Luke Donnelly, and confirmed Si's alibi, Gardner and Riddick headed to the Knaresborough rugby field.

'I could take you for a birthday drink, later?' Riddick said.

'I don't do pity drinks.' She laughed. 'Besides, you've already been in one pub today; that's enough of a risk. I'm not letting you go into another.'

'If I was going to fall, I'd have done so by now.'

'Thanks for the offer, anyhow. I'll be sure to do the same on your birthday. If you don't have a hot date with... sorry... what's her name again?'

'Ha. Nice try. Turn left here. So, you going to spend your birthday with Jack?'

'Jack certainly doesn't do pity. In fact, he doesn't do sympathy, compassion and many other emotions either.'

'Is he that bad?'

'You know what he did to me as a kid?'

'Yes. But I felt like doing that to my own sister on a daily basis.'

'Did you?'

'Of course not.'

'I rest my case.'

'Only because if I'd have fractured her skull, she'd have fractured mine back.'

'You're suggesting I should've got him back somehow?'

'Well, it's never too late. I'll do it if you like.' He cracked his knuckles. 'I owe you after all.'

'If I have to listen to him say he's changed one more time, I might take you up on that promise.'

'Could he be telling the truth?' Riddick said.

'Absolutely not. But he has a daughter, which means I've a niece, which means he's better off where I can keep an eye on him until I can figure out what the hell to do.'

'Is there actually anything you can do?'

'I don't know, Paul.' She sighed. 'But while he's got a roof over his head and he's out of trouble, I'm doing all I can for Rose. If she needs me, I can ensure a safe place. And with her mother being a spiralling drug addict, it can happen anytime.'

'Noble of you. But it's a risk if Jack's still dangerous.'

'I know. And if Anabelle and Barry were with me, there's no way this would be happening. But as it's just little old me, I've taken the gamble.'

Gardner took her eyes off the road to look at Riddick briefly. His eyes were on her. He was listening intently. She suddenly realised how good it felt to open up to someone. She'd spent nearly every evening in Knaresborough lost in her own pained thoughts, thinking she was alone, when the very best person to hear her cries may have been on her doorstep all along.

Riddick said, 'Over here, boss.'

Gardner didn't need it pointing out.

The travellers had taken over an entire rugby pitch. There were countless caravans, some in much better condition than others. There were also a few quad bikes and motorbikes dotted around.

'Park by these boulders,' Riddick said, pointing. 'They're usually piled up here to block vehicles from entering, but as you can see, they've been dragged aside by the guests.'

'Where does the rugby team relocate to?' Gardner asked.

'Well, actually, they don't really use this pitch any more. They use the pitch outside the club.' He pointed off to the other side. 'This one is mainly left to the dog walkers.'

Gardner could hear barking dogs and could see quite a few of the larger variety loitering around the caravans.

'I guess the dog walkers go elsewhere when they're here?'

'Well, it's either that, or Fido gets eaten,' Riddick said.

Gardner sighed and opened her door. 'Come on. I doubt anyone is coming out to welcome us in. And tread lightly, Paul.'

'I'm getting warnings now?'

Gardner stepped out of the car. 'I'd give you a warning even if we were going to a kid's birthday party. I've seen you in action, remember?'

'Look, if they've done nothing wrong, they've nothing to worry about…'

'They've illegally commandeered the local area!'

'Good point.'

As they walked towards the caravans, Gardner said, 'Now we've dealt with the drinking, we need to work on the tolerance.'

'Tolerance lowers your guard,' Riddick said.

When they reached the first caravan, a large Alsatian came flying in their direction, but was yanked back by the rope that tethered it to a wooden post.

Froth spewed from the corners of its mouth and as it barked, it displayed a set of teeth that could bite through metal.

'You think it wants to play ball?' Riddick asked.

The dog remained some distance from them, but Gardner still took some steps backwards. She'd always been a fan of dogs but had seen enough in her career to know that some were capable of severe damage.

She heard laughter from two teenage boys outside a caravan to her right, who were clearly amused by Gardner's unease. She glared at them, and they resumed what they were doing before Gardner and Riddick had infiltrated the camp: kicking a football to one another.

An old man in a grey jogging suit opened the door. He was sucking hard on a cigarette and, judging by the depth of the many wrinkles on his face, this was something he'd been doing his whole life.

'DCI Gardner and DI Riddick,' Gardner said, holding up her badge.

The old man squinted, shaking his head as if he was experiencing a close encounter of the third kind.

The dog continued to bark aggressively.

'Your dog, sir?' Riddick said.

The man furrowed his brow as though he was struggling to hear.

'Is this your dog, sir?' Riddick repeated, louder.

The old man pointed at the Alsatian and raised an eyebrow.

'Yes,' Riddick said.

'Tyson? Do I look crazy?' The man grinned. He didn't have a great deal of teeth left, and those he did, were twisted and discoloured.

'He's got attachment issues,' a middle-aged man said, coming up alongside Riddick and Gardner. The man's entire head was shaved apart from a short mohawk that ran down the middle. He had a vest on and clearly kept himself well conditioned with weights. 'Can I help you?'

Gardner showed her badge and made the introductions. 'And your name, sir?'

'Tommy Byrne.'

'Is Tyson chipped, Mr Byrne?' Riddick asked.

Tommy walked over to Tyson and petted him on the head. He stopped barking and started to whimper instead as he kept his beady eyes on the invaders.

'Only Tyson's owner would know,' Tommy said.

'And where can I find this owner?' Riddick asked.

'In an urn, I'm afraid. We share responsibility for Tyson now.'

Gardner inwardly sighed. 'Look, we're not here to discuss dogs.' She looked around the site, noticing there were a lot of different breeds and many of them were barking. 'I'm sure if any of them were dangerous, you'd have taken the necessary precautions.'

Tommy nodded.

'Tyson's the least of your worries,' the old man at the caravan door said. He pointed in the distance. 'Deidra over there. Now that's who you want to talk to. She got a right mean cat. Lottie, she called.' The old man held his fingers up like claws and bared his teeth. Unfortunately, baring his teeth did not have the desired effect as he didn't really have many.

'We insist all dogs are registered,' Tommy said.

Gardner wondered how you registered a dog with no fixed address but decided that there were more pressing issues.

'Are you in charge here?' Riddick asked.

'In a fashion. So I'll also tell you that we're complying with the council,' Tommy said. 'They claim to be in the process of proving that they own this land, and this encampment is unauthorised. We're awaiting the outcome of their investigation.'

Gardner was familiar with this process. It could take some time. She imagined the residents around here, especially those on Hay-A-Park estate, would be feeling rather frustrated.

'The council have also been making enquiries about health, welfare and our kids' education. They've been more than happy with what they've heard.' Tommy sounded fully up on his rights. A useful skillset when living outside society.

'Mr Byrne—'

'Tommy, please.' He gave a wide smile. Unlike his elderly companion, he had a full set of gnashers which looked well maintained.

'We're here about an incident that occurred in the White Bull public house last night,' Gardner said.

'Are you referring to the incident regarding Rod?'

'That depends what happened to Rod,' Riddick said.

Tommy shouted over to the boys playing football. 'Oi, gobshites, get Rod now, will ya?'

Gardner and Riddick exchanged a look as the boys scurried away.

'We're good people here,' Tommy said.

'We never suggested otherwise,' Riddick said.

Tommy smiled and eyed Riddick up and down. Then he nodded. 'Glad to hear it. I can't abide ignorance.'

A crowd of three skinny young men, barely out of their teens, approached.

'Sorry,' Tommy said, turning to the three boys. 'I asked for Rod. I didn't realise we'd three Rods on site?'

The central boy stepped forward. He was limping and his face was a mess of bruises and cuts. 'No, I'm Rod... not these.'

Tommy guffawed and looked at Riddick as he spoke. 'Yes, Rod, you idiot. I know who you are. Not one of our brightest.' He whispered the last part, but Rod would most certainly have heard.

'Everyone knows who you are, Rod,' one of the other lads said. 'Everyone here has banged your sister—'

'Piss off, boys,' Tommy said.

The two other lads turned and sloped away.

'What's your surname, Rod?' Riddick asked.

'Child,' Tommy said.

'We can take it from here, Tommy,' Gardner said.

'Isn't there a rule about minors or something?'

'How old are you?' Gardner asked Rod.

'Twenty,' Rod said.

'But in here,' Tommy said, touching his head. 'He's a minor.'

'Can we just talk to him alone, please, Tommy?' Gardner said.

Tommy nodded and turned away.

Gardner and Riddick took Rod to one side and briefed him as to why they were here. Several times during the conversation, Gardner wondered if Rod had suffered a brain injury during last night's confrontation with Si Meadows. He spoke slowly, without much detail, and seemed fairly accepting of what'd befallen him; most people would've been seething.

'I just wanted to play,' Rod said. He winced and groaned. 'I meant no harm.'

'Did you know who he was?' Gardner asked.

'An old man.'

'Hey,' the old man said from the doorway of the trailer. 'He was pretty handy for an old man, eh? Look at the state of ye!'

Gardner rolled her eyes. That man clearly had sharper hearing than he'd made out earlier if he could hear from there. She turned and called over to him. 'Can you go back into your caravan, please?'

He grumbled and went back inside. Gardner waited until he'd closed the caravan door.

'So, you approached Si Meadows and asked him for a game of pool?' Gardner said.

'Is that his name?'

Gardner nodded.

'Yes. I did.' Rod nodded, and then realised his mistake. 'Ow...' He grabbed the back of his neck.

'Did no one warn you?' Riddick asked.

Rod looked confused by the question. 'I just wanted to play pool... He'd been on there all night.'

'Well, I think you'll be giving pool a miss for a while now,' Riddick said.

Gardner looked at Riddick.

'After he started beating me, they threw me out!'

'Did that feel fair?' Riddick asked.

Rod shrugged.

'Did any of your friends help or come back with you?'

'No,' Rod said. 'I found my way back easy enough.'

Afterwards, Gardner got her phone out and found the picture of Tia Meadows that she had on the board in the incident room. She showed it to Rod.

He grinned inanely.

'Ever seen her before?'

'No, I'd remember. She's fit—'

'All right, fella, enough,' Riddick said. 'She was in the pub last night, serving.'

Rod had another look. It took him a moment, but eventually he nodded. 'Yes. I remember now.'

'Did you talk to her?'

Rod shook his head. 'No.'

'You sure?'

'I'd remember. She's fit and I like her hair.'

'Two very important qualities in a lifelong partner,' Riddick said, rolling his eyes at Gardner.

Gardner and Riddick continued, somewhat desperately, to probe him but got nothing.

On the way off the rugby pitch, Riddick sighed. 'What a waste of bloody time.'

'Was it?' Gardner said.

They stopped by the car and looked at each other.

'Go on, then, enlighten me, boss,' Riddick said.

'Not saying it's anything yet, but...' She held up her phone and showed a photograph of the two young men that had approached with Rod. 'They were watching us chat. I snapped them on the sly when I was showing Rod the picture of Tia. Notice the boy on the left with the poor excuse for a moustache.' She used her thumb and forefinger to zoom in.

The boy looked as if he was about to throw up.

'Hung over?' Riddick asked.

'Possibly... but if not, I've a feeling that we're going to be back here to ruffle some more feathers sometime soon.'

11
———

Harvey Henfrey's request had gone unanswered. No crime book, but at least some kind soul had thrown him a pack of cards.

Being a dab hand at solitaire, he dealt the cards out quickly on the bed and hunkered down.

One hour turned to two, before quickly becoming three, and then tumbling down onto four.

Every now and again, he stopped to think about his parents. Life had never been the same since they'd passed. They'd understood him. They'd been the only people he could spend time with in his adult life.

He thought about his mother's red dress, which she always wore to dinner on special occasions in the house – on birthdays, Christmases etc. And he thought of his father's pipe, which he'd smoke by the window because his mother hated the smell.

He also thought about how his mother and father would both hold him tight, when he had *those* nightmares. Even at the age of thirty-nine, the year before they went, they'd hold him.

And now he missed that – them holding him – more than ever.

Eventually, exhausted from the events of the day, he drifted off
to sleep.

* * *

'Harvey... Harvey...' the creep said, moving in closer. 'We talked about
this. We'd an understanding.'

Harvey kept his arms folded and forced back tears.

He'd cried before this day, in this same situation, many times, but
today felt different somehow.

Harvey kept his eyes down, because he knew that looking into those
bloodshot eyes would shrink him. And today he wanted to fight back.

Today, he wanted to show strength.

Harvey tightened his arms across his chest. 'Leave me alone.' Too
quiet. *'Just... you know... piss off.'* Better. Louder.

'Where does a ten-year-old learn to speak like that?' he asked, leaning
in closer. 'You know, when I was your age, my mother would wash my
mouth out with soap and water.' His breath stank. 'Why did you come
then, Harvey? Why did you come to me only to refuse?'

'Because...' Harvey felt his strength evaporate. 'Because...'

Someone filmed my mother with a man.

'Because...'

They gave you the recording.

'Because...'

You're threatening to show everyone.

'Because...'

You're a disgusting, old bastard.

The creep said, 'Because a cat got your tongue?'

Harvey felt the hand on his thigh.

And then it was gone. All that strength he'd talked into himself on the
way over, that he'd felt building within him on this plastic chair,
disappeared.

Like air from a balloon.

'Please... please...' Harvey said.

'Please... please...' the bastard mimicked, rubbing his thigh. 'You sound just like your mother.'

Now the tears were back.

'Do you want to watch the video of your mother again?'

'No.' Please. Anything but that again.

'I have it, you know. In the back?'

Harvey shook his head. He felt the tears streaming down his face. The disgusting man squeezed his thigh.

'I could show it to your friends. We could all watch it tonight?'

Harvey hung his head in shame.

He felt the creep's hand in his hair.

He didn't resist.

He'd shrunk again. He'd been reduced. He felt hollow, boneless even, like a sheet of skin draped over a chair.

'Why must we fight, Harvey?' he said. 'Why must we argue, every time? I can be nice, you know.'

He squeezed Harvey's thigh again, tighter this time.

'You know how nice I can be,' the bastard said.

Harvey felt the creep pulling at his belt...

Eyes open, sitting upright, Harvey opened his mouth and released a guttural wail from deep inside. He covered his face with his hands, twisted and moaned, until he'd confined the past to the past, and the terror had subsided.

He sat up and brushed the playing cards onto the floor.

It'd been over a year since he'd last had that dream. He thought he'd buried it well. Today's stress had drawn it back to the surface.

A police officer opened the cell door. 'Is everything okay?'

Harvey looked at him. 'I made a mistake. I never should have let it all back into my life.'

'Let what back in?'

Harvey thought about telling the officer everything but stopped himself just in time. He lay back on his mattress. 'I'm tired... I'm confused.' He rolled onto his side and stared at the brick wall. 'And I need to rest.'

12

'Okay, then, you win,' Riddick said. 'Her name's Paula.'

Gardner pulled over to the side of the road and turned her incredulous expression towards Riddick.

Riddick laughed. 'Don't be daft.'

'Daft? I thought this day would never come. You've been dating this woman for a month now, and this is the first time you've told me anything about her!'

'Well, I wanted to make sure it was going well.'

'And?'

'I like her.'

'How much?' Gardner said with a raised eyebrow.

'It's been a month. I'm not about to move her in. Besides, not sure she deserves that.'

'Yes, poor lass, I've seen your music collection.'

'Eh?'

'Spandau Ballet?'

'I like music from my childhood. Nothing wrong with that. Anyway, start the car, boss. You got what you want.'

'Occupation?'

Riddick sighed. 'Nurse. Now' – he pointed at her feet – 'foot to the floor, or I'm getting out, and you're going to see Dr Hugo Sands all on your own.'

She started the car. 'He's not that bad, you know?'

Riddick smirked and winked. 'Really?'

'I said "not that bad". A pathologist that refers to their "table" with such fondness is certainly not my type.'

After turning left, Gardner threw another smile at her passenger. She was glad he was opening up to her. Was it because she'd opened up to him earlier about Jack and Rose?

He returned her smile and then she focused back on the road.

Were they growing even closer?

It seemed that way.

And Gardner would have to admit, it felt good.

* * *

It didn't shock Gardner watching Sands pace enthusiastically around Tia's corpse on 'his table' – she'd seen this many a time from pathologists – but it did make Riddick's insinuation that she was attracted to him really jar with her.

She preferred her men to view a dead twenty-year-old as a tragic loss rather than an intriguing piece of artwork.

'There's no doubt.' He was currently pointing out the wound on the front of her head. 'The blow caused a great deal of trauma. Her death would've been quick.'

Riddick sighed. 'Any idea what she's been hit with?'

'There's residue from a brick in the wound. But, word of warning, she could have fallen and died by banging her head on said brick.'

'Well, if that was the case, why move her all the way to the tree by the lake?' Riddick asked.

'That's your job,' Sands said with a shrug.

To frame Harvey, Gardner thought but kept her opinions to herself.

'I've also narrowed the time of death down to between 12 and 2 a.m. My rationale is in the reports. Along with my findings regarding the movement and positioning of the body. So, are you ready for what's next?' Sands didn't smile, but his raised eyebrows spoke volumes about how much he enjoyed his work. He looked over at his young, white-suited assistant. 'Phyllis?'

She came over and helped Sands roll the stitched-up victim onto her front.

Her back was a mess of broken lines and discolouration.

'Good lord,' Gardner said.

'Lacerations and bruising are all consistent with a sustained period of whipping. A belt was most certainly used and' – he pointed to some darker bruising – 'buckle side first.'

'Post-mortem?' Gardner asked, hopefully.

Sands shook his head. 'Afraid not. It would've been very painful.'

Gardner flinched. *Thanks, Hugo, I get that.*

She shook her head. It'd been a while since she'd seen anything this bad. This was torture. Plain and simple.

'Bloody hell,' Riddick said.

'Someone wasn't happy with this girl,' Sands said, looking down at her ruined back.

You think? Gardner thought.

'Oh... and she was two months pregnant,' Sands continued.

'Shit,' Gardner said, thinking, *is there anything else you want to throw at me?*

Shaken up by these two pieces of information, Gardner struggled to take in Sands' blow-by-blow description of all the science behind his findings but knew it would be in his report that had been emailed over to HQ.

If there was one thing that Sands was good at, it was crossing the t's and dotting the i's.

Outside the mortuary, Gardner peeled off her white suit.

Twenty years old, pregnant and whipped.

She felt sick; it was fortunate that it'd been a while since she'd eaten.

Riddick tried to speak, but she held her hand up. 'Just let me process this, please, Paul. Wait until we're back in the car.'

He nodded. 'Of course, boss.' He looked concerned.

For all his bravado, Riddick could also be sensitive and understanding.

'DCI? There's something else.' It was Sands. He'd emerged from the mortuary behind her.

'Yes, Dr Sands,' Gardner said, turning, taking on a professional pose again. She didn't know how much more she could take, but she didn't want Sands seeing any vulnerability.

'It's personal.'

'I'm sorry?'

Sands looked up at Riddick.

'Of course,' Riddick said. 'Don't mind me.' He turned and walked away.

Gardner remained confused. 'I don't—'

'I've tickets for Ed Sheeran.'

You have to be kidding me.

'And I was wondering—'

'I'm married!' *And I've just, seconds ago, learned that a pregnant, twenty-year-old woman had experienced great suffering before her death.*

'Ah... I'd noticed that it'd gone,' Sands said.

'What?'

'Your wedding ring.' He pointed at her hand. 'Sorry if I called this wrong.'

She couldn't believe she was having this conversation. She shook her head. 'I've got to go,' she said, turning to walk away.

'Happy birthday,' he called after her.

* * *

After Gardner filled him in, Riddick was speechless. They drove in silence for a few minutes.

Eventually, when Gardner pulled over to empty tic tacs into her mouth, he opted to break the silence. 'That's not Valium, you know.'

'Next best thing,' she said and bit down with a crunch.

'I knew he was odd,' Riddick said. 'But to just come right out and say that... in there... in *that* context. Well, it's bonkers.'

Gardner swallowed the mints and then eyed Riddick suspiciously. 'Did you tell him it was my birthday?'

'Yes, I mentioned it over beers at the pub last night with him! Have you forgotten I didn't even know myself?'

Gardner sighed. 'Well how did he find out?'

Riddick shrugged. 'No idea. Marsh? Maybe he researched you?'

Gardner shuddered.

'Wait,' Riddick said. 'You don't think... that card... it's from Sands?'

Of course, Gardner had already considered this. She shrugged and sighed. 'I don't know.'

'Wow,' Riddick said. 'Sands is your stalker.'

'Shut up, Paul,' Gardner said, indicating to move the car back out.

Riddick clicked his tongue. 'Well, look on the bright side, he's creepy, but I doubt he's dangerous.'

'Shit, Paul! Look, I can't think about this now.' She pulled out and accelerated. 'We're about to run a briefing.'

'Okay boss. But one more thing... please.'

'It'd better be relevant.'

'Ed Sheeran.'

'What about him?'

'He's good.'

'I don't agree.'

'Still, if he has tickets, you should—'

'Sod off, Paul.'

'Yes, boss, fair enough.'

13

After the double whammy of the post-mortem and being hit on by the person conducting it, Gardner's head was understandably cluttered. Fortunately, she'd some time before the briefing, which she used to ready the whiteboard as well as clear her head.

Before addressing them all, she looked up at the large whiteboard she'd been working on. Operation Bright Day was swelling.

To the right of the board was a large aerial image of the lake, the surrounding woodland, Harvey Henfrey's hut, the spot where Tia was found, the surrounding country paths, the field currently occupied by travellers and the rugby club.

Tia, heavily made up, remained at the centre of the board. Smiling. Unaware of the fate that awaited her. *The belt and its buckle.*

Red lines sprang from the victim linking to: Si Meadows, the cash-rich, broken father, who oversaw all building trade in the area; Knaresborian recluse and prime suspect, Harvey Henfrey; and Tia's close young friend, Luke Donnelly, who also had a line connecting him to Si, due to their sexual relationship. Gardner had also written the name of the traveller: Rod Child. She didn't have a photograph for him yet, but he'd found himself in the wrong place at the wrong time in the White Bull, and so had earned himself a solid line to Si Meadows.

Gardner narrowed her eyes. *Three lines already for you, Si.*

Additionally on the board were places of interest such as the Tesco on the high street where Tia conducted her day shifts and the White Bull in the town centre in which she conducted her evening shifts. One of her officers had also pinned a map of Knaresborough to the bottom corner of the board and meticulously, with a red pen, drawn out the route she'd have usually taken home from the White Bull.

Gardner looked over her team of eleven and saw from their flustered, tired faces, that they'd put in a shift today. She caught a smile from Lucy O'Brien in the room and returned it, glad for any female heartbeat in this male-dominated room.

She began by feeding back on the day's findings before handing over to Riddick who worked his way through the pathologist's report. After announcing Tia's pregnancy, he handed every officer a photograph of the whip marks.

'Someone punished this lass,' Rice said. He sounded sad, and Gardner welcomed this sign of emotion from someone who'd been far too dismissive of their victim earlier.

'Is this religious in some way?' Rice asked.

'What makes you say that?' Riddick replied.

Rice shrugged. 'Always thought of whipping as either a punishment or a religious ritual for some reason.'

'You're thinking of self-flagellation,' Barnett said. 'Flogging oneself to cause mortification of the flesh. It's seen as a spiritual discipline.'

'Yes... that... maybe...' Rice squinted. 'How do you know so much about it?'

'Part of my philosophy degree at university was religious studies,' Barnett said.

Gardner nodded. 'Anyway, the whip marks weren't self-inflicted. Sands would've picked up on that. So, I think we run with the idea that someone just wanted to punish Tia Meadows.'

'Sick bastard,' Rice said.

Lots of his colleagues nodded.

Matthew Blanks paused from banging away on his keyboard to push his long hair behind his ears, and Gardner caught a wide glimpse of his wide, focused eyes.

'Forensic results are hopefully going to start coming in tomorrow,' Riddick said. 'The chief constable has signed a small fortune over to it. The nature of the case.'

'Thank you, Paul,' Gardner said.

'Our resident religious philosopher, Ray, next,' Gardner said, smiling at Barnett. 'The CCTV from the area?'

'As I told you before, it's not great news... Knaresborough feels like it's in the dark ages sometimes. We picked up Tia leaving the White Bull at 11.15 p.m., which tallies up with what the landlord told you, boss. Tia makes her way down the high street. As you can imagine, there's a lot of CCTV on the high street, but when she takes her right turn onto King James Road, we lose track of her. We've checked with neighbours, but no one saw her arrive home. And Si Meadows didn't return home from Luke Donnelly's until this morning, so he cannot verify she was there.'

'But we *know* that she didn't head to Breary Flat Lane straight from the White Bull?' Gardner asked.

'That's correct, boss.' He looked at his notes. 'Also, door to door has been slow near the lake and crime scene on Breary Flat Lane itself. Due to the current high number of travellers in that area, locals have been subjected to a lot of vehicles and individuals coming and going, so nothing is standing out to them.'

'According to Sands, she didn't die by that lake, but was taken there,' Gardner said. 'Supposing that Harvey Henfrey isn't our man, then is it plausible that she could have been killed elsewhere, and then driven up Breary Flat Lane and carried over that fence?'

A few members of her team shook their heads. They didn't like this hypothesis. It was much easier to think that this was down to Harvey.

'Heavy work,' Rice said. 'You'd have to be strong and have the poor lass in a fireman's lift. My money would be on her just walking there after returning home. She'd have had time in Sands' window.'

'But why would she walk there?' Gardner asked. 'Midnight by that lake? Why?'

'Meeting a boyfriend?' Rice suggested.

'She's twenty,' Riddick said. 'Does she need to sneak around?'

'With Si Meadows as your dad,' Rice replied, 'it's probably best to.'

'I don't buy that,' Gardner said. 'She was old enough to have boyfriends. Si may have taken a keen interest, but I doubt there was an outright ban on them.'

'Unless one of those boys was a traveller?' Barnett said.

All eyes flew to Barnett.

Bloody good, Ray.

She wrote 'traveller?' with the list of people connected to Tia.

'So, I'm going to narrow down to three options,' Gardner said. 'One: she was murdered away from the crime scene sometime after turning off onto King James Road, and then driven to Breary Flat Lane and dumped by the lake. Two: after returning home, Tia went back out to visit a traveller boyfriend by the lake and was murdered there. For both these options, framing Harvey Henfrey could have been premeditated, or could have just been an afterthought. Three: Tia went back out to see Harvey for some, as yet, unknown reason, and he murdered her...'

A number of hands went up.

'I wasn't taking a vote,' Gardner said.

The hands came down.

'Okay, Phil, please share what you discovered earlier.'

Rice stood and came to the front. He went over to the board and pointed at somewhere on the map.

'The Co-op service station on Boroughbridge Road. For three consecutive mornings, *including* yesterday, Tia Meadows withdrew two hundred pounds at this cashpoint. That was her maximum daily allowance from Barclays. We do have a camera on the cashpoint which films her withdrawing the money, but she's always alone.'

'So, we need to find out what she's spending money on,' Gardner said. 'Toxicology should be back tomorrow, so we may be able to rule out drugs then.'

Rice stood there, nodding, clearly proud of his discoveries, dragging out his stay at the front of the room. She noticed a few of his colleagues rolling their eyes.

'And, Phil, what else?'

'Well,' Rice said, 'phone records show regular calls to three numbers over the past month. The first number is her father's. The second and third are unregistered numbers. She's speaking to two individuals on burner phones.'

'Well done, Phil.'

'No problems, boss.' He grinned, all teeth.

'Tomorrow, you can find out what she's been spending her money on, and who she's been calling.'

'Consider it done.' Still all teeth.

She inwardly sighed when he finally went to sit back down.

'If you turn your chairs around, you'll see that Lucy has set up the screen at the back of the room.'

Everyone complied.

'The boss asked me to scour through the White Bull's camera footage from yesterday evening,' O'Brien said. 'I've tried my best to select moments that I consider relevant. There're four cameras positioned around the pub, which gives us over twenty hours of footage, and it is available on our system now if you want to view any of it this evening, folks.' She grinned. 'I warn you that some of the footage isn't for those of a nervous disposition... Phil.'

Rice gave her the finger. 'See a single shake? Still as ice.'

'Should've seen Phil when he got back from that crime scene,' DS Ross said. 'Disappeared into the shitter and we didn't see him for best part of an hour.'

Laughter.

Rice turned the finger on Ross.

'John, Phil, enough,' Gardner said. 'Lucy?'

O'Brien hit play on her laptop and the grainy projected image took up a large chunk of the back wall.

One of the cameras was positioned in the corner of the pub, above the front door, and covered the travellers gathered in front of the bar. O'Brien moved through several interactions between Tia and different travellers who bought drinks. It was unclear what they were saying, but Tia was quick with the service, offering them large smiles, but little conversation. It seemed Bertie had been right about her not being chatty that evening – potentially because her father was there.

Then, Gardner saw who she was looking out for. 'Pause please, Lucy.'

Gardner hoisted her phone from her pocket. She went to the picture she'd taken earlier on the campsite of the young man with the moustache who'd looked ready to vomit, nodded, and then passed her phone out to the team. 'Pass it along, look at the picture, please.' Everyone did. When she got the phone back, she said. 'Okay, play, Lucy.'

O'Brien obliged.

'Now look who Tia is serving,' Gardner said.

Sure enough, the boy about to spew his guts out at the travellers' site was at the bar. This time there was a lot of conversation.

Did you miss this, Bertie? Gardner thought.

A few times, Tia reached over the bar to playfully tap the young man with the moustache on his arm.

'Shagging, I reckon,' Rice said.

Gardner and Riddick exchanged a glance. She suspected Rice would make that assumption if he'd simply come in to ask for directions to the local store. However, they certainly appeared to know each other well. They'd be back at the travellers' camp tomorrow to ruffle those feathers.

As the footage wound on, the travellers became drunker and rowdier, annoying other punters in the bar and many around the pool tables, who kept glancing over.

One of those punters was Si Meadows.

Eventually, a familiar traveller, who could barely walk straight at this point, approached the pool tables, bouncing off several of his friends and some tables en route. 'Pause it, please, Lucy,' Gardner said. 'That's Rod Child. We spoke to him today.'

'Not the sharpest tool in the shed,' Riddick said.

'Aye,' Rice said. 'Anyone swaggering over to where Si Meadows is drinking is clearly not functioning properly.'

'Hardly swaggering,' O'Brien said, playing the footage again. 'He can barely walk.'

The other travellers gathered behind Rod cheered wildly.

Clearly egging him on, Gardner thought. *Who needs enemies with friends like those?*

There was an audible gasp from her team as Si laid Rod Child out. Laid out being an understatement. Si pummelled him. If not for the large bouncers trucked in from Leeds, it would've ended in hospitalisation.

'For asking for a game of pool?' Rice said. 'You sure you don't want to put him through the wringer for what he did to you, boss? This bastard's a danger to society, no?'

Looking at that, Gardner couldn't disagree. But right now, she felt there were bigger fish to fry.

'Unbelievable he's still in there,' Barnett said as they watched Si continue to play pool.

'Now, let's watch this sequence of events closely,' Gardner said. 'Last orders come and go, the travellers leave... Look, there's Bertie twiddling his bow tie – good takings, I imagine – pleased, despite the extreme violence. Si and his friends leave, fifteen minutes of tidying, Luke Donnelly leaves to meet Si, according to their story...'

'Disgusting; he's practically a child!' Rice said.

'Now, Tia is laughing with Bertie...'

'Notice how he puts his hand on her shoulder and leaves it there,' O'Brien said. 'She makes no attempt to move it...'

Rice looked horrified. 'That's a step too far. He shouldn't be leaving his hand there.'

'As if you wouldn't, Phil,' O'Brien said.

'I prefer a woman my own age, thank you,' Rice said.

'Why not find one then?' O'Brien said.

Laughter.

Finally, Tia exited the pub and O'Brien stopped the recording. 'And there she goes.'

Surprising everyone, Riddick stood up. His eyes flicked between O'Brien and Rice angrily. The bantering had got to him.

'Yes, there she goes,' Riddick hissed. 'To be whipped and snuffed out.'

O'Brien looked down. Rice glanced around for a friendly face but didn't find one.

The room fell silent.

* * *

Marsh had been in attendance for the latter part of the briefing and, after the team had left, she asked Riddick and Gardner to stay back.

She leaned on the back of a plastic chair and it bent slightly under her impressive upper body strength. She eyed Riddick. 'Are you okay, Paul?'

'Yes, ma'am.'

'Are you sure?'

Riddick smirked. 'You don't seem to think so.'

Marsh returned his smirk. 'I appreciate that we don't want a circus atmosphere in here, Paul, but let's not suck all the life from the room.'

'It's a murder investigation, ma'am.'

'You're also surrounded by living, breathing human beings. This isn't a morgue. What's up?'

'Nothing.'

'*Bollocks.* What's up?'

'Just something playing on my mind.'

'Share, please.'

Riddick went to the board and pointed. His finger settled on the photograph of Si Meadows. 'Three lines. One to his daughter, one to Luke Donnelly and one to the traveller, Rod Child.'

'Connections are good,' Marsh said.

'Yes. Except when the man is also connected to the man who killed my family... ma'am.'

For the first time ever, Gardner saw the colour drain from Marsh's face. She stood up straight and stopped crushing the plastic chair. 'Ronnie Haller?'

Riddick nodded.

Gardner chewed her bottom lip. Drug-dealing Ronnie Haller had been taken down by Riddick and was serving time for two murders. Ronnie had ordered the car bomb that killed Riddick's wife and two daughters out of retaliation.

'The bastard's in jail.' Marsh looked at Gardner. 'Thoughts?'

Gardner shrugged. 'News to me, ma'am.'

'Before Si made himself millions by getting his claws into every business in these parts,' Riddick said, 'he ran with Ronnie Haller. Way back, ma'am. When they were both starting out.'

'Way before my time,' Marsh said.

'And mine. It was back in Anders' day.'

Ex-DCI Anders Smith had been Gardner's predecessor. For most of his career, he'd taken a rather old-school approach to justice, but had been Riddick's mentor and close friend until recently. He was currently in jail for murder and corruption. It'd been Riddick who'd uncovered the truth and exposed his former best friend. So, for obvious reasons, the topic rarely came up in conversations.

Riddick continued, 'Si Meadows got away from Haller and out of drugs a long time ago after discovering his own talent for manipulating and intimidating people into handing over shares in their businesses.'

'So, why your concern now?'

'Just the obvious, ma'am. One dealt drugs and the other shakes down businesses. They're both gangsters and form a living, breathing Venn diagram. Which means they overlap.'

'I know what a Venn diagram is, Paul,' Marsh said and sighed. She looked at Gardner. 'What do you think?'

Gardner shrugged again. 'I need some time to process this.'

And she would take that time, but still, she didn't see a great deal in this. It almost felt like Riddick was clutching at straws. Had Si Meadows' loss of a child triggered Riddick again? Relit the trauma over losing his own children?

Marsh sighed again and looked at Riddick. 'Okay, I appreciate it's worth looking into, Paul. It might turn out to be nothing... perhaps. Hopefully.'

Riddick nodded. 'I agree.'

'So, look into it, Paul, and then bloody rule this connection out. You need to be focused on the here and now. The past is best where it is for you, if you catch my drift.'

'I completely catch your drift, ma'am. I don't want to go back to that place either. Not at all.'

'Like I said, hopefully, you won't have to,' Marsh said. She looked at Gardner. 'But if there're signs he is, Emma, you come and see me.'

Gardner nodded.

Riddick grunted. 'I'm not a bloody child, ma'am.'

Marsh grinned and held her hands aloft. 'You're all my children.'

14

Si glanced into the mirror above the chest of drawers. Bloodshot eyes and flaky, dry skin. Fatigue and despair.

He chased down the vision with whisky.

His mobile rang. He put down his glass, saw it was Larry, and answered, 'What?'

'Si, I'm sorry. I know it's not a good time, but it's Reggie; he's just not playing ball—'

'*Reggie?*'

'Yes. Reggie.'

Seeing his glass was empty, Si drank straight from the bottle. His throat and stomach burned.

'Si? You there?'

'You phone me about Reggie, *now?*'

'Sorry, Si, I understand, I'll—'

'What about him?' Si put his hand on the handle of the top drawer.

'Not playing ball, like I said.'

'Ah, I see,' Si said. 'So, kill him.'

Silence.

Si stroked the front of the drawer.

Larry said, 'Okay, I see I was wrong to phone, I'm sorry—'

'Kill. Him.'

Silence.

Si opened the drawer.

Larry said, 'Okay, you're not making sense... I'm going now.'

'Bang, bang, you're dead,' Si said. He hung up the phone and threw it onto the chest of drawers beside the bottle of whisky.

He reached into the drawer and lifted out a cardboard folder. He brought it to his nose and sniffed it.

Really? Issey Miyake? Tia's favourite perfume.

Had she gone through his drawers? Looked in this folder? Discovered... found... read... *investigated*?

Or was the scent his drunken imagination?

He picked up the bottle, left the mobile and took the folder over to his office desk.

After putting the bottle down on his desk, he sat in the large leather chair, and laid the unmarked folder out in front of him. Clutching the edge of the table, he regarded the folder as if it was contaminated.

He looked at his Swiss Army Knife beside the article. Hesitantly, he picked it up and regarded the printed initials: SM. Not for Si Meadows. For Stuart Meadows. His long dead, alcoholic father. He freed the largest blade.

Two more gulps of whisky later, he returned his eyes to the folder.

Keeping his pen knife in his hand, he shook out the one item in his folder. The newspaper article.

He didn't look down at the photograph.

Didn't need to.

The bloody thing was ingrained in his mind.

That monster.

Smiling.

Si slammed the point of the knife down into the smiling monster's head, pinning the newspaper article to the table.

Then, he turned his head to one side and threw up.

15

Gardner was driving into her estate when her phone started ringing. She answered on the hands-free.

'Happy birthday!' Anabelle shouted.

Gardner smiled. 'Thanks, pudding.'

'Did you get my card, Mummy?'

'Yes,' Gardner lied. Barry probably posted it late. 'I loved it.'

'I drew both of us together on the beach. Can we go, Mummy? Please?'

'Yes. Soon. It sounds like paradise, pudding.'

She pulled into her driveway, killed the engine and continued to talk with her daughter. She felt tears in the corners of her eyes as she considered how nice it would be to put her arms around her little girl right now. Later in the conversation, Anabelle mentioned that she had been to Alton Towers on Sunday.

Nice of you to mention it, Barry!

'Wow,' Gardner said. 'Did you have a good time?'

'Amazing. We went on the log flume. It was freezing! Sandra got drenched.'

Sandra? Gardner's blood ran cold. *Sandra?*

'Who's Sandra?'

'Daddy's friend. She's nice.'

'Okay, Ana,' Barry said in the background. 'Can I talk to Mummy now, please?'

Been rumbled, Barry?

'Bye Mummy. Happy birthday, I love you.'

'You too, pudding. As soon as I can, I'll get us to that beach.'

'Emma, happy birthday,' Barry said.

'It's almost over now.'

'Yeah, sorry. I meant to call earlier, but it's been a nightmare day at the office.'

'Nothing to do with *Sandra* then?'

'Sorry?'

'Who's Sandra?'

'She's just a *friend*. From work. Look, I don't want to argue. There's nothing to get wound up about here.'

'I see. A friend.'

'Yes! She separated from her husband recently and I said she could tag along with me and Ana to Alton Towers.'

'You could have asked me instead?'

'It was a last-minute thing! I told you about Ana's grading at gymnastics. This was the treat for her.' Barry sighed. 'Also, it's just a theme park. I know you hate them. I didn't think you'd be fussed.'

'Not fussed about my daughter?'

'I don't think that.'

'Well... why not at least phone?'

Barry guffawed. 'You're *always* busy.'

'An excuse. You haven't tried for ages.'

'Because when I do, you brush me off... *every time*. What's the point?'

'Nonsense. If I'm in the middle of a murder investigation, it's not a brush off.'

'You're always in the middle of something, Emma. And... never mind. I don't—'

'No, say it. And?'

'You took in that psycho brother of yours.'

Frustration surged through Gardner. 'There it is. The real reason. You know he has a daughter. Our niece?'

Someone vulnerable.

'*You* have a daughter.'

'I *see*. So, I shouldn't help her?' She shook her head in despair. He just didn't get it. *Refused* to get it. 'Should I just let her suffer?'

'No, of course not. Look, Emma, I don't know. Point is, you're not with us any more. It's hard to have conversations like this!'

It's hard to have any conversation with you these days. 'You were supposed to come up here!'

'It wouldn't have worked. You've no time to help us settle. And you're desperate to get back here within a year. You know it's not a good idea to subject Ana to an upheaval.'

Gardner nodded. She did agree. However: 'Your solution to the problems we're having is to replace me with another woman for family days out, and then forget my birthday?'

'You're always so over the top.'

'Is "piss off" over the top?'

'Yes.'

'Good. Piss off.' She hung up.

She punched the steering wheel. *Was that conversation the death knell of my marriage? Replacing me that quick! Kind of impressive, Barry. I really didn't think you had it in you.*

Her heart was beating flat out and she felt compelled to head inside, drink a bottle of wine and cry herself to sleep. She pocketed her phone, exited the car and headed up the path.

The front door flew open. Rose charged down the path with her pigtails flapping in the air behind her. 'Happy birthday, Auntie Emma!'

Gardner swept her seven-year-old niece up in her arms and kissed her on her cheek. She turned once, holding tightly to her, before setting her back down. She knelt and gripped her thin cheeks between both her hands and then patted the front of her flowery dress. She looked like Anabelle.

'It's great to see you Rose.' *I really didn't expect that.*

'It's your birthday, Auntie Emma, and there's cake.'

'Rose, I told you not to spoil the surprise,' Jack said from the doorway.

'Sorry, Daddy,' Rose said.

'Seeing you is the surprise,' Gardner said, kissing Rose on the head. 'Anything else is just icing on the cake.'

'Oh there's icing all right,' Jack said.

'Lots of it!' Rose said.

Gardner stood. 'You best take me in and show me.'

Jack was staring right at her, a false smile plastered on his face.

She returned his smile but couldn't bear to hold his eye contact. *Grand gestures.* He was trying, but she was still convinced he was full of shit.

* * *

It was only after demolishing Cedric the Caterpillar that Gardner was able to get Jack alone.

Rose was on the sofa watching a famous male celebrity send millions of British hearts into a flutter by delivering a bedtime story on Cbeebies.

In the kitchen, she said, 'Explain.'

'Her mother had another overdose.'

'Shit,' Gardner said. 'How is she?'

'Recovering.'

'Thank God. What's going to happen now?'

'I don't know. All I know is that I got a call this morning to come and collect her. It seems that signing those forms, Emma, and placing me in your residence has earned their trust.'

'I'm a DCI, Jack. Are you surprised?'

Jack said, 'I'm sorry that I'm throwing your life into chaos, Sis.'

Gardner grunted. 'Don't flatter yourself, Jack. My life was in chaos long before you showed up.'

'Still, if it's ever too much?'

'Stop going through the motions, Jack. I've already agreed to help keep her out of care. I'll make up her bed and get her down to sleep.'

'Thanks. What about your birthday?'

'What about it?' She paused at the door and turned back. 'The best birthday present you can give me this evening is to leave me in peace to drink wine.'

'Whatever you want.'

16

For Riddick, fighting his way out of a foul mood was like fighting his way out of a steel cage. Knowing that tequila was no longer his go-to answer for this, he texted Paula several times on the way back from HQ, desperate for her company when her shift finished.

It was only when he was in The Wharfe, waiting for his fish and chips, did he receive his reply.

I'm sorry.

Sorry for what? He thought.
He texted back.

Why?

'Salt and vinegar?' the young man behind the counter asked.
'Please.'
'Say when.'
Riddick watched the young man raise an eyebrow when it was clear that the 'when' wasn't coming anytime soon.

Lay it on thick, son. Who cares? My blood pressure is already through the roof today...

Eventually, the young man stopped of his own accord, probably fearful of breaking some law for selling unsafe food.

On the walk back, Riddick texted Paula again.

For what???

This time, she replied.

For everything.

Bloody hell, Paula. I can't be bothered with these cryptic messages right now!

Realising that his mood was achieving the impossible and souring further, Riddick kept his head down as he walked past Dawn till Dusk, unsuccessfully fighting back the thought of the alcohol which inhabited the shelves in there.

He tried calling Paula, but her phone was off.

What the bloody hell have I done?

He thought back over the morning. Apart from her disappointment that he hadn't done a decent shop since the last time she'd stayed, he could think of nothing.

Was there someone else? An old boyfriend?

His imagination on overdrive, he turned onto his road.

Up ahead, the Bentley in his driveway made his stomach turn.

Surely not...

Any lingering doubts were dismissed when he was close enough to read the personalised number plate: M41 NNE

His stomach turned again.

Marianne Perse. The toxic freelance journalist relentless in her drive to destroy Paul Riddick.

Years back, after Riddick had investigated a mother following the suicide of her teenage daughter, the press had smelled blood.

In some ways, Riddick could understand that. He'd been forced to investigate the mother after something the father had revealed, and he'd not gone about it as subtly as he could have done. For many, him being hung out to dry had been his just desserts.

However, Marianne Perse hadn't been content with just that. Instead, she'd gone for total and utter annihilation, happily selling her stories to the highest bidder, desperate for him to lose his job.

To this day, he never quite understood why she'd struck up such a vendetta. Had she experienced suicide in her own life? Is this why it'd become so personal to her?

He recalled the moment Marianne had approached him following the death of his wife and children to ask him how it felt now he was at the heart of a tragic story rather than looking in at one from the outside.

He gritted his teeth, marched over to the Bentley on his driveway and slammed his fish and chips down on the roof. He yanked open the door.

He wanted to tell her he was inches away from setting fire to her car with her sitting inside it. And that would only be the start. He'd also like to throw in the idea of defiling her blackened corpse after. However, he knew that she'd be recording this, so going gentle was his best option.

'What the bloody hell are you doing on my property?'

That really was as gentle as he could go.

Marianne smiled at him. As was usual, she wore dark red lipstick and her hair was expensively coiffed. She turned down the dance music blaring from the speaker. 'DI Riddick, thank you for seeing me. We need to have a—'

'I never agreed to see you. Get the hell off my driveway.'

Marianne clicked the radio off and then smiled at Riddick again. 'We need to have a conversation.'

'I want you to go. *Now.*'

'Maybe I should come in?'

'Aren't you listening?' He squeezed the bag of fish and chips on the roof, wondering whether it was more trouble than it was worth to empty it all over her upholstery.

'It's in your best interests to hear what I have to say, DI—'

'You've five seconds to leave before I lose it.'

She sighed. 'I wanted to do this with more decency.'

'You've never done anything decent in your life! Four seconds.'

She reached over to the back seat for a brown envelope.

'Three seconds.' He drummed his fingers on the roof of the car.

She held out the envelope. 'Take it.'

He shook his head. 'Two seconds.'

She proffered it again. 'Trust me, you want to see this. At least give yourself a fighting chance.'

That didn't sound good. He snatched it from her hands. 'One.'

She reached over the passenger seat for the door handle. 'You'll want to speak to me shortly.' She closed the door.

'Like a hole in the head.' Riddick stared at the brown envelope in his hand.

It was only when Marianne was reversing that Riddick realised the fish and chips were still on the roof. He darted forward and grabbed the bag. Then, he gave her the finger, and muttered to himself, 'Ruining my life is one thing, but spoiling my fish and chips is one step too far.' He stood in his driveway as she drove away.

* * *

After reading Marianne Perse's article: 'Corruption: Back from the Dead', Riddick paced the room, keeping his hands clasped behind his back, fighting the urge to smash things.

'Shit, shit...'

Is this really happening?

He leaned over the article on the coffee table again.

Paula Bolton, a nurse at Harrogate District Hospital, entered a month-long relationship with DI Riddick despite protestations from her friends and family. A relationship that started off with great passion and excitement soon became a test of endurance.

Paula, how could you? Surely this is a bloody nightmare?

If not, he'd been sold down the river.

He reread the entire article, hoping it wasn't as bad as he'd feared on the first read.

It was false hope.

The article would be more appropriately named: 'Bad Boy Paul Riddick'.

Because Paula had exposed everything.

Everything.

His guilt over the Winters case and the way he treated the bereaved mother. The pain and turmoil he felt over the loss of his family, and the suggestion that he was in part responsible for what happened to them with his reckless approach to police work. His close relationship with ex-DCI Anders Smith, who was now serving time for murder, alongside countless inferences that Riddick had slipped outside the law with Anders on many occasions. Then came the icing on the cake.

His struggles with alcohol.

Even though his reputation with the public still languished

somewhere in the toilet bowl, this article would most certainly hit the flush.

His phone rang. The number was unknown.

'I'm going to sue you, Marianne.'

'A waste of money, I assure you,' Marianne said. 'The article is well sourced.'

'By someone who lied their way into my life?'

'I don't know what you're talking about, DI Riddick.'

'You put Paula up to this.'

'My source came to me.'

'And you paid her well I expect?'

'I've found a newspaper that will run the story. They believe it ticks the appropriate boxes.'

'Is one of those boxes defamation of character?'

'The article makes it clear that this is one person's view. The readers can make up their own mind if they believe it.'

'She's an NHS nurse and I'm a disgraced police officer. You've not given me much of a fighting chance, have you? This is character assassination.'

'You chose your path a long time ago, DI Riddick. However, it isn't over for you... not just yet. I'd like to offer you an opportunity.'

'From you?'

'How about an interview with your side of the story?'

'Do you think I'm completely insane?'

'You said I've not given you much of a fighting chance, but I'm presenting one to you on a platter.'

'Marianne, I've seen your skills with editing; the last thing I'm going to do is let you put me on tape. I'll save it for a courtroom. For my lawyer who will tear you and your source to pieces.'

'I thought you'd say that. It's a shame. I genuinely think—'

'Shut up, Marianne. There's nothing genuine here. You always wanted to destroy me, didn't you? The fact is though, you won't win.

I've experienced far worse than you could ever imagine. Your attempts are pitiful and are too little, too late. This is nothing. I'll shrug it off.'

'Bent coppers always come unstuck eventually, DI Riddick. I'm surprised you've lasted as long as you have.'

'You know nothing about me.'

'Have you read the article? I know you well enough. Last chance. You want to schedule an interview?'

Riddick hurled his profanities and hung up.

He immediately tried to phone Paula, but again, she didn't answer.

But she wasn't going to, was she?

She'd taken him for a complete fool, made herself some easy money, and wouldn't have any appetite for a debrief.

He texted her.

How could you?

Then:

If they print that story my career is over.
Do you not feel anything? After knowing what I went through?

His phone indicated that the messages were read.

He waited for a reply.

When one didn't come, he threw his phone on the sofa, bent down, gripped his glass coffee table and overturned it. It crashed into the TV cabinet, smashing everywhere.

He saw the picture of himself on the article staring back at him through shattered glass.

No longer hungry, he abandoned his fish supper and stared at the kitchen cupboard for some time.

His *empty* kitchen cupboard.

He held up his hand in front of his face and watched it shake.

Not now... Not again.

He stood and paced the kitchen. His stomach was doing somer-saults. Unless he calmed soon, his heart would surely blow.

You're a weak, weak man, Paul Riddick.

He left the house for Dawn till Dusk.

One beer... that's all...

Just one beer.

* * *

He fulfilled his promise to himself to only have one beer. Then, he chased it down with tequila. It didn't take much tequila to make him unsteady. It'd been several months, so his tolerance was down.

Not wanting to return home just yet to face the article again, he wandered around Knaresborough until he found himself in the area of Aspin, outside the impressive home he'd visited earlier. He slipped the open bottle of tequila next to one of the trees that lined the long, impressive driveway and staggered to the front door.

He pounded.

No answer.

He pounded again. 'Open up!'

The door opened.

Si Meadows stood there in loungewear. His T-shirt read: *Best Dad in the World.* He had a crystal glass filled with whisky in one hand.

'You look pissed,' Riddick said.

'Pot calling the kettle black?' Si said. 'What do you want? Is it about Tia? What have you found out?'

'No,' Riddick said, eyeing the glass in Si's hand. 'It's not about that.'

Si scowled. 'What do you want then?'

Riddick pointed at him. 'Ronnie Haller.' He inched his finger closer. 'What do you know about Ronnie Haller?'

Si pushed his finger away. 'That he's in jail. That's all I know.'

'That's not enough.' Riddick shook his head. 'What's your relationship with him?'

'You can't handle your drink,' Si said. 'And you're wasting my bloody time.' He started to close the door.

Riddick thrust his foot out, stopping the door closing. 'You slam the door in coppers' faces regularly?'

'Only washed-up coppers.'

'*I'm* a detective inspector.'

Si nodded. 'Christ knows how. Now get your sodding foot out of my door.'

'Answer the question: what's your relationship with Ronnie Haller?'

'We don't have a relationship,' Si said. 'Now, get your bloody foot out of my door. Because, if you don't, I'm going to break it off. My day has been bad enough already. I don't fancy a night in the cells.'

'You used to be mates with him when you were younger.'

'Eons ago! Back when you were wet behind the ears and dreaming of being an honest copper. Now get your foot out of my door.' His eyes narrowed. He clenched a fist.

'He killed my family.' Riddick thumbed his chest. '*My family.*'

Si maintained his scowl for a moment longer, but then his expression suddenly softened. His eyes widened, he unclenched his fist and took his other hand off the door.

'My family,' Riddick said, tearing up.

Si nodded and sighed. 'Yeah, I know.'

Riddick wiped a tear away with the back of his hand. Then, he steeled himself. 'Do you know anything—'

'I don't,' Si said. 'Honest. Listen, I'd nothing to do with that. I wouldn't be part of *anything* like that. A man's family is off limits.'

Riddick looked down.

'I'm sorry for what happened to you,' Si said.

Riddick lifted his eyes back up. 'You think that monster, Haller, had anything to do with Tia?'

Si flinched. '*What?* No! If he did, he'd be dead already.'

Riddick thought about those words. *Dead already.*

He took his foot from the door and turned to face the driveway. *Dead already.*

He staggered away.

'Now you tell me, something, DI Riddick,' Si called after him. 'Tell me who you think killed Tia.'

'I don't know.' Riddick held his hand up to bid Si farewell.

Riddick drew closer to the tree; he could almost taste the tequila. He felt his mouth water, and a warm sense of anticipation in his stomach.

A hand landed on his shoulder, and he turned to face him.

'Did Harvey kill Tia?' Si said. 'Answer me.'

Riddick looked down at the hand on his shoulder. 'Take your hand off me.'

'It was him, wasn't it?'

'I don't know.'

'Bullshit. You must have an idea.'

'An idea isn't the truth, Si.'

'It's a bloody start!'

'Or a one-way ticket to paranoia. I know, I've been there.'

'Tell me. Was it him?'

'You really want to know what I think?' Riddick asked. 'You may not like the answer.'

Si squeezed Riddick's shoulder. 'Yes.'

'I don't think it was him.'

Si narrowed his eyes and shook his head slowly. '*Bollocks.*'

'I told you you wouldn't like my answer.'

'No... Harvey did it. I know he did. He killed my baby.'

'What makes you so sure?' Riddick said, frowning. 'What do you know?'

Si opened his mouth to reply, but then closed it again and looked away.

'What do you know?' Riddick repeated.

Si took his hand from Riddick's shoulder. 'Nothing.'

Riddick shrugged. 'In that case...' He turned and resumed his journey to the bottle.

'Who else could it possibly be?' Si raised his voice behind him.

'You can be sure we're looking into everything,' Riddick said.

'You're too busy drinking. Look at the state of you!'

'Pot calling the kettle black,' Riddick said, reaching down for the bottle. He unscrewed it and took a large gulp and then staggered away.

'It was Harvey. I *know* it was him,' Si called behind him.

Riddick raised his hand in farewell.

17

Following that birthday bottle of wine, drunk alone, Gardner's head didn't want to come off her pillow next morning.

She took her hangover to task, in the same way she always took her hangover to task, by rolling out of her bed and into her running gear.

Opting for greenery, she ploughed into the fields and farms of Knaresborough, where she soon regretted forgetting to take her antihistamine tablet. Her hangover was soon replaced by excessive sneezing and watery eyes.

With no small amount of coincidence, Gardner found herself jogging past the travellers' camp on the rugby pitch. The sun had only just crested the sky, but the travellers were already up in force – how could you not be with so many loud, unsettled dogs? Some of the younger men were already chipping the football about on the outskirts, while several younger women were going about tasks such as hanging out washing, cooking food or tending to the pets.

It was plain to see which gender had it best in their world!

She heard a wolf whistle. She looked at a lad that couldn't be much older than fourteen. He gave her a toothy grin. She ignored him, not wanting to cause a scene, especially as she'd be back here later to speak to the moustached traveller she'd snapped on her camera. The one that had been flirting with Tia Meadows in the White Bull camera footage.

She passed the rugby field and turned right down a country lane that framed the lake.

Lonely Lake.

Or so Harvey had named it.

As she ran, she looked down at the ground in disgust. There was loose tissue paper blowing in the wind. Evidence that the travellers had opted to use this path as a toilet.

She picked up the pace.

Several nettles stung her legs as she moved too quickly to avoid them, but it was a small price to pay to escape the unsanitary conditions.

She took a right onto Breary Flat Lane.

It was early, but there were still some dog walkers about. She nodded a greeting to them as she passed and smiled when a cock-apoo yapped in her direction and then pulled on its lead.

'Rosie!' a middle-aged man hissed at his dog.

'It's fine,' Gardner said, pausing to stroke Rosie.

Rosie then started to lick Gardner's legs.

'Sorry about that,' the owner said. 'If it's any consolation, it means you've worked up quite a sweat.'

'I put that down to the humidity, not my effort levels,' Gardner said, looking down at the cockapoo. 'Thanks Rosie, you soothed my nettle stings.'

Gardner left the owner laughing and continued. She paused by the fence that she'd scaled yesterday to reach the crime scene. Police tape was stuck on it still, however, it hadn't deterred the regular trespassers. She could hear talking.

Was there any point in dressing them down?

Deciding against it, she prepared to jog away when she recognised one of the voices.

She scaled the fence and wound her way through the patch of trees to the crime scene.

'Have you got the lake clearly in the shot?' Marianne asked her photographer. 'Readers like a lake. Lots of mystery... potential.'

'Yes, Ms Perse,' Gardner said, approaching. 'You've your very own Loch Ness here.'

'Except' – Marianne smiled and winked – 'this monster is on land.'

The crime scene was still set up with a blue and white cordon, evidence markers, and protective plates. It'd already been harvested, but it may need to be revisited. 'Did you not see the cordon on the fence?'

'Sorry, no. Must have missed it,' Marianne said, looking smug and proud in her tight, summery dress, which was totally unfitting for a ramble through the undergrowth by a lake.

The photographer, on the other hand, kept his head lowered. He knew that this was crossing lines. At least he had the decency to feel ashamed of himself.

'Fortunately,' Marianne said, pointing at Gardner. 'The monster is in custody. Thanks to you, DCI Gardner. You're really turning out to be a commodity around here.'

Commodity! 'Could you leave the crime scene, Ms Perse?'

'Okay.' Marianne crossed over the cordon with her photographer. 'Is it okay to stand here?'

'Not really; this is private land.'

Marianne put her hand to her chest and chortled. 'Every fisherman in North Yorkshire has plundered this lake.'

'I don't know anything about that,' Gardner said, 'but I do know that if you don't leave this land now, I'll be forced to file a report. The owner may also opt to press charges.'

'I think our owner is otherwise preoccupied by the fact that he granted a murderer the right to live on his land, don't you?'

'You seemed to have tried and convicted someone already, Ms Perse. Doesn't that sound familiar? This is my final warning.'

Gardner stood there while they walked past her. When they were a metre or so behind her, Marianne said, 'I guess I'll have to wait for the press conference?'

'Yes,' Gardner said over her shoulder, 'like all of your colleagues.'

'There's something else I've been meaning to catch up with you about, DCI Gardner.'

Gardner sighed and turned. 'Make it quick, please.'

'DI Riddick. I was wondering if you'd give us some comments on his conduct and his general approach to policing.'

Gardner flinched. What a change in topic. And massively incendiary too. 'Keep walking, Ms Perse.'

'Some personal titbits about your working relationship would be welcome. I say working, however, if there's anything else between you, that wouldn't go amiss either.' She smirked.

'Why in God's name would I do that?'

She raised an eyebrow. 'Extra money? Those pay freezes must have hurt these last years—'

'Money doesn't float my boat.'

'Then, maybe just talk to me out of decency.'

Gardner shook her head. 'You've no idea about decency.'

'Speak to DI Riddick today,' Marianne said. 'Things are about to get very warm around him. Actually, warm is putting it mildly. Hot, more like. He could do with friends in his corner. Why not give me his side of the story? I'll print it word for word.'

'Are you recording me?' Gardner asked.

'No, of course not. I don't have your permission, do I?'

'No, you don't. So, listen very carefully to what I say.'

'I am.'

'Sod off, Marianne.'

Marianne nodded. 'That came through loud and clear.'

'And if you don't, I'll find time following this investigation to turn your life upside down. I'll investigate everything you've ever done, and if I get so much as a sniff of anything foul, I'll come after you so damn hard.'

Marianne nodded. 'I thought we could have reached some sort of agreement. Seems not.'

Gardner watched them both walk away, fighting the sudden urge to pick up a stick and throw it hard in Marianne's direction.

Marianne turned back and called out, 'Oh, I almost forgot DCI. You may want to check out Harvey's hut. It seems he's had some visitors.'

Jesus, Gardner thought. *What happened in your life to make you such a bitch?*

* * *

There'd been visitors all right.

Angry ones by the looks of it.

Red graffiti across the side of the hut indicated their motivation.

Drown in your lake, murderer.

Shaking her head, Gardner approached the front door which had been kicked clean off its hinges.

The smell made her gag, so she covered her mouth as she looked around.

The shelf of books was on its side. The pillows he slept on had been split and emptied. And someone had smeared excrement up the walls.

18

DC Steven Hastings had been given strict instructions to keep an eye on Harvey overnight.

His orders from his superior couldn't have been clearer. 'The man is a wrong 'un. If the victim's purse isn't enough to convince you of that, consider that he lives by a chuffin' lake in a hut like Huckleberry Finn's drunk father! Keep your eyes on him all night. If he tops himself, it's on you.'

Initially, Hastings did a good job. He looked in on numerous occasions and watched Harvey sweat and ramble to himself in an anxious sleep, but in the early hours, Hastings drifted off. He was only human, after all.

Fortunately, the first time he'd done this, he was woken by another of Harvey's night terrors in which the old recluse had screamed, 'Don't touch me!'

Relieved that he'd not slept through a suicide attempt, Hastings had popped his head in, told the freak to get back to bed and then paced around the station to try and keep himself awake.

All may have been fine if he hadn't have taken a break for some YouTube videos and drifted off for a second time.

Hastings woke. He noticed the daylight immediately and realised he must have slept the rest of the night away.

Luckily, his superior hadn't stumbled in on him.

He stood, yawned and stretched and thought of Harvey. He wandered towards his cell. 'Harvey?'

There was no answer. Probably still asleep.

He pounded on the door. 'Harvey, you awake?'

If you weren't before, you will be now!

Still no answer.

He opened the hatch in the cell door.

No Harvey. Blood on the sheets.

Panic exploded in his stomach.

No... no... no...

With a shaking hand, he worked through the keys until he found number five. He thrust it in the keyhole, unlocked it and opened the door. He stumbled in.

His eyes fell to his left where Harvey lay.

Covered in his own blood.

19

Riddick looked a shambles and Gardner couldn't take her eyes off him.

There's no way he could accuse her of being paranoid this time; his eyes were like two piss holes in the snow!

It had to be something to do with Marianne Perse.

Things are going to get very warm around him...

He could do with friends...

Riddick had also retreated to the back of the incident room, where he used to loiter prior to his new-found confidence. She tried to make eye contact with him, but he was having none of it.

She focused herself and continued the briefing.

Matthew Blanks had phoned in ill with a bad stomach. Apparently, he had been sickeningly explicit in his description of the ailment, which stood to reason. He spent every day, reporting everything in minute detail – it'd be a hard habit to break, so there'd be nothing subtle in his description of explosive diarrhoea.

Consequently, she'd tasked Rice with making notes. After his brief comment that he felt picked on by having to do this, he huffed and puffed his way through operating the laptop, making Gardner regret asking him.

Gardner had already described the state of Harvey's vandalised hut to the team, and they were in the process of discussing who could be responsible. It soon became clear that no one had the foggiest, so they'd place that on the back burner while forensics gathered some evidence.

Lucy O'Brien then took the floor. She'd pulled an all-nighter but still didn't look half as bad as Riddick. She showed everyone camera footage. 'This was from outside the first house on Breary Flat Lane. They have a security camera on loop. This was four days ago.'

Tia Meadows walked straight past the house, wearing shorts and a T-shirt. She had a backpack over one shoulder.

O'Brien changed the footage. The location was the same. 'Three days ago.'

Tia strolled past again. This time in a flowery frock. Same backpack.

'Two days ago.'

Another shot of Tia – this time wearing jeans. Same backpack.

'Only from the daytime,' O'Brien concluded. 'Nothing of her at night.'

'Because she wouldn't have been caught on camera, if she was already dead and in the boot of someone's car,' Gardner said.

'Yes,' O'Brien said. 'We've run all the vehicles, and we're following up on all of them. But bear in mind that the murderer could have driven in from the other side of Breary Flat Lane via Hay-A-Park. No camera footage on that side I'm afraid.'

Gardner nodded. 'Yes, but this gives us a fighting chance. Please make sure that we've communicated with all drivers by the end of the day. Back to Tia in the daytime though; what was she doing on Breary Flat Lane three days running?' She turned to the whiteboard. She prodded the picture of the moustached lad she'd snapped yesterday. 'Ray's traveller.'

'*My* traveller?' Barnett asked.

'You suggested it, remember? The love affair?'

Ray nodded, looking proud.

'DI Riddick and I will be heading to the rugby club later to speak to this lad. Lucy, please tell everyone else what you've found out.'

'I correlated the times of those three two-hundred-pound cash withdrawals from the cashpoint at the Co-op service station on Boroughbridge Road with these times Tia was caught on camera on Breary Flat Lane. They're roughly ten minutes apart each time. She went here directly from the cashpoint.'

Gardner looked between the faces of her team as they processed this.

'Shit,' Rice said, tapping away. He looked flustered. 'Slow down.'

Gardner ignored him. 'So, each time she withdrew money, she headed to either Harvey Henfrey, or to the travellers.'

'Maybe she *was* buying drugs from the travellers?' Barnett said.

'Toxicology came through this morning,' Gardner said. 'Tia did not have drugs in her system.'

'Well, I'm certain she wasn't trying to buy one of those caravans.' Rice shook his head and carried on typing. 'She took the money to Harvey. The more I think about it, the more it just feels... obvious?'

Gardner looked at him. 'Harvey had thirty pounds in his possession. If he'd ever had this money she'd withdrawn, what did he spend it on? Ray has done some good work tracking Harvey's recent movements, but it seems there aren't many. There was a trip to Sainsbury's three days earlier, but we have CCTV footage of him emerging with *only* two bags of groceries – so, unless he's gone for champers, we can assume he didn't spend six hundred quid in there. He does have a bank account, but he hasn't used it within the last week, and he's never deposited that amount of money.'

'Harvey lives out in the wilderness, boss,' Rice said. 'He could've hidden that money under a stone somewhere.'

Fair point.

'Still,' Gardner continued. 'I'm suspecting one of two things has happened here. Either, Tia has given that money to that traveller she appears cosy with on the footage, or she was building up her money to buy something by taking out her daily maximum amount. But this isn't logical – who does that? Wouldn't you just use your card for the full amount in the shop? However, if she had that money on her person, Tia's murderer could've taken it from her purse before planting it outside Harvey's hut.'

'Or it could still be in her room?' O'Brien ventured.

'True. It's due to be searched. Phil, you have an update?'

'Nothing regarding those two mysterious phone numbers yet,' Rice said. 'Maybe one of them belongs to our suspicious traveller.'

'Harvey definitely doesn't have a phone?' Barnett asked.

Gardner shook her head.

'Remember that stone in the wilderness I just flagged up?' Rice said. 'The one he may be able to hide things under?'

Gardner inwardly sighed. 'If it makes you feel any better, Phil, I'll get forensics to go and pull up some rocks while they're looking at the vandalised hut.'

Rice nodded, looking proud of himself.

Marsh called Gardner over from the door of the briefing room. As she exited, she glanced up at Riddick, realising he'd yet to say a single word. 'DI Riddick?'

'Yes, boss.' He stood and shuffled to the front of the room to take over.

* * *

After hearing what Marsh had to say, Gardner resumed her position at the front of the incident room. She took in the worried expressions on several of her team members' faces. They'd obviously clocked how pale she now looked. Rice, however, had yet to notice and was still banging at the keyboard, cursing as he did so.

Gardner began. 'As well as Frank's, Harvey's DNA was on the purse. He picked it up after Frank dropped it. Tia's DNA is also there. No one else's.' She steeled herself for the next bit. 'However... DNA from Tia has been recovered inside Harvey's hut.'

There were a couple of grunts. Rice clapped his hands together. 'Gotcha!'

'We have some of Tia's hair follicles on his chair,' Gardner continued. 'She was definitely in his hut at some point.'

'The CPS will like this, I expect,' Rice said, smiling.

'There's something else...' Gardner said. 'Harvey was found this morning in his cell, blood everywhere.'

Several members of her team gasped.

'What happened?' Barnett asked.

'He'd been dragging a pack of playing cards over the skin on his arms for the best part of the night.'

She saw several of her officers wince.

'Shame he didn't nick an artery,' Rice grunted.

'Watch it, Phil,' Gardner said, fixing him with a stare.

'Is he going to be all right?' O'Brien asked.

Gardner nodded. 'I think so... He's sore and weak, but it's not critical. One more thing,' Gardner added. 'While he was delirious, he told the paramedic that attended to him that he loved Tia Meadows.'

Rice looked around the room, nodding his head, a 'told-you-so' expression on his face. Gardner realised that if he issued the words, 'case closed', or anything of the like, she'd probably end up flooring him.

20

Si hadn't slept a wink.

Deliberately.

If he'd slept, he'd have had to wake up and confront reality again.

Not appealing.

Instead, he'd drunk himself sober. At least, that's how it felt to him. He was under no illusions that others would beg to differ.

He wandered back to the decrepit old scout hut. He stood and looked at the yawning hole where the front door used to be. He considered crawling in. You wouldn't get far, and you would most certainly be risking your life, because the collapse of the remainder of that roof was long overdue.

Even if, by some miracle, you survived the raining debris, there wasn't anybody in the immediate vicinity to hear the catastrophe and arrange your excavation.

It certainly wouldn't be a nice way to die.

Si crawled through the yawning hole.

Not far in, his path was closed off by a fallen beam and a pile of plasterboard. Unable to stand, he rolled onto his back and stared up at another beam, which, although badly damaged, was still managing to hold up part of the roof.

Easy. A swift kick. Peace and quiet.

Tempting. To end his existence in the place that had so significantly impacted his life back in 1982.

On the night an angry ten-year-old boy had come to the scout hut thirty minutes early to smash bottles on the bank of the Nidd and think about his best friend kissing him.

The night of the red sky.

* * *

After hearing that sound, Si gently tried the handle, but the front door of the scout hut was locked.

He placed his ear to the door again, waited, heard the familiar voice again and then sprang back from the door, his heart suddenly thrashing in his chest.

His best friend. Scared for his life.

Si darted back around the hut, checking the windows en route, but all the curtains were drawn.

When he reached the back door, which Baloo had slammed shut only moments ago, he placed an ear to it. The hammering of his own heart made it difficult to hear anything, but when he really focused, he was sure he could hear a whimpering sound, like a small animal in fear.

He turned away from the door and looked up at the darkening red sky, thinking: Shout? Run home? Kick the door down?

The door.

Si had heard the rattle of the back door being unlocked by Baloo, but he couldn't recall the rattle of it being relocked...

He reached into his pocket for his Swiss Army Knife and popped the largest blade.

Then, despite burning fear in his gut, he tried the handle.

The back door glided open.

The scout hut was a large room with a storage cupboard by the front door. At the rear of the room, where Si had just entered, there was a tiny open plan kitchen. To go through into the main space, you had to lift a hatch.

Si was not about to lift that hatch because Baloo was currently standing on the other side of it, leering at him.

Si was smaller than most boys his age, so Baloo's stoop didn't bring him completely level with the boy, but it did bring him close.

Close enough for Si to see the flecks of red in his yellowing eyes, and the bluish tinge in his thin lips.

'I heard you out the back. Not surprising, is it?' Baloo tapped the hatch with his crooked finger. 'Always a Meadows. Causing problems. Your father was a pain in the arse too.'

Si held the army knife behind his back. Should he bring it around and announce the threat?

He heard the whimpering sound again. He took a step to the side and peered into the large room and gasped.

He'd been right. It was him.

The boy who'd kissed him was hunched over on a white plastic chair. He was wearing his cub scout jumper, but his trousers were in a crumpled pile at his feet. He still had his socks and underwear on. He was sobbing into his hands.

'Harvey?'

He didn't look up.

'Let him go,' Si said to Baloo, revealing the knife.

Baloo's eyes widened.

'Now!' Si's voice shook, betraying his fear.

Baloo's eyes returned to normal, a ghost of a smile flickered across his face, and he shook his head. 'Why? He's okay. He's where he belongs... And, you know, we start in ten minutes or so. He was just about to go and get ready.'

Harvey turned his blotchy face in Si's direction.

Si felt his heart sink. 'Are you okay, Harvey?'

Harvey stared at Si, opened his mouth as if preparing to reply, but then closed it as if deciding against it. Was that shame on his face, or distress? Harvey put his face back in his hands.

'He's fine,' growled Baloo.

'No, he isn't.'

'Yes, he is. And this isn't for anyone else to hear about.'

Si narrowed his eyes and inched forward, knife in front of him now. 'Who said anything about talking?'

Baloo creased his brow. 'Really?'

'Let him go,' Si continued.

Baloo thought for a moment and then smiled. His lips stretched, growing bluer and thinner as a result. 'He's not a prisoner. He can go whenever he wants.' He called over his shoulder, 'Do you want to leave Harvey?'

Harvey didn't remove his face from his palms.

'Harvey... go if you want.' Baloo continued to smile.

'I'm okay.' Harvey's words were muffled by the palms of his hands.

Baloo cocked his head. 'See? Maybe it's you who should go instead?'

Si shook his head. 'No... this is wrong.'

'Wrong? Harvey and I have a special understanding.' He sucked in his bottom lip for a moment and then released it. 'But I suppose we could have a special understanding too?'

'I'd kill you first.'

Baloo rolled his eyes and grunted. 'The fight never lasts, boy. I know all about you Si. In fact, it was Harvey who told me everything that happened between you and him on that swing.'

Si looked over at his friend. Harvey dropped his palms from his face and looked at him guiltily.

Queer. Puff. Si-by is gay-by. Bender.

'We're alike, Si,' Baloo said, sucking at his bottom lip again. 'All three of us, tonight, in this room. So alike.'

Si shook his head.

'Fighting it...' Baloo continued, nodding down at the army knife. 'Violence?' He shook his head. 'What does it solve?'

'It's not true!' Si said. 'Whatever Harvey told you is a lie! I—'

'True enough to cause a stir in the community though, boy. The Meadows clan have a reputation to uphold after all.'

'Piss off!' *Si felt himself welling up.*

Baloo held his hands in the air. 'Let's make a deal. You keep my secret, and I'll keep yours and Harvey's.'

Queer. Puff. Si-by is gay-by. Bender.

'There's no secret!' Si said.

'Come now, really?' Baloo said. 'Did you not share that special moment?'

'Nothing happened.'

'Are you sure? Think about it.'

Si was locked in the moment again. Harvey's lips on his. Did he pull away instantly? Or had the kiss lingered?

No one could know. Ever. He looked at the knife in his hand. But did he really have it in him to kill an old man? Would he even succeed?

'Think clearly about this,' Baloo said. 'If you try to hurt me, you're done. If you talk, you're done. Just walk away, Si.'

Si looked over at his best friend. Harvey looked lost, desperate and in need of help.

But... Queer. Puff. Si-by is gay-by. Bender.

It would ruin his family.

Shit.

'I'm sorry, Harvey.'

Harvey nodded. Did his friend understand? Really? Was that possible? Si turned and sprinted from the hut.

Under a blood red sky, he ran home and never said a word to anyone about what he'd just seen.

* * *

Sweat was dripping from Si's face. It was boiling inside the collapsing scout hut, and there was very little air.

His phone vibrated.

Despite being in an enclosed space, he was able to slip it from his pocket. He looked at the screen. It was Larry again. He'd been ignoring his calls for a while now. 'What's up?'

'Thank God, I've been phoning you all morning, Si. Where are you?'

He took a deep, hot breath. 'Reminiscing. What do you want?'

'Harvey Henfrey was taken to Harrogate District Hospital this morning.'

Si started to sit up, stopping himself before clocking his head, disrupting the beam, and potentially ending his existence. 'Why?'

'I don't know. But he's alive. He was sitting up in a wheelchair.'

'Thank God,' Si said. And he meant it. When Harvey died, he wanted to be looking him in the eyes. 'Was Iain discreet? Where is he now?'

'Iain followed them to the hospital car park. He's still there. He's certain he's yet to be seen.'

'Okay, keep him there, but don't let him go in. We certainly don't want them tightening security around Harvey.'

'There's something else.'

'Go on.'

'Some of the lads did something for you.'

Si blinked sweat out of his eyes. 'What?'

'They visited the prick's hut. Did some damage.'

'On whose request?'

'No one's. They wanted to do something for you.'

'And who do you think the police will look at for that? Did you know about this?'

'No. I... sorry.'

'What the hell are you doing? You're supposed to be keeping them in line.'

'They're angry, Si. They think they're showing their solidarity with you.'

'Fools. They'd better have been careful.'

'The police will only find broken furniture and dog shit.'

'If they come calling for me today, Larry, then you're taking the fall for this.'

A pause. 'I understand, but I'm confident. And Si? I can get more details on Harvey's admission. One of our boys is hooked up with a lass that works there. A nurse.'

'Good. Phone me when you know anything. And one more thing, Larry.'

'Yes?'

'No more surprises.' Si hung up and slipped the phone back into his pocket. He looked up at the loose beam and its promise of a quiet eternity.

Not yet.

After debts have been paid.

He turned and crawled back out.

21

Gardner was pissed off with Riddick for abandoning her outside HQ due to personal reasons.

'I just need to do something; it won't take long.'

Despite Gardner pleading for the reason why, Riddick hadn't been forthcoming. More than likely it would be something to do with the death of his family and that snake, Marianne Perse, so she was going to have to let her deputy SIO get it out of his system. Barking orders at him would be a non-starter. She prayed to God that he wasn't heading down a path that would force her to contact Marsh with concerns.

After driving to the hospital alone, she asked Harvey's police guard to wait outside the room while she spoke to him. The police guard wasn't over the moon about this, but Gardner was insistent.

Once the police guard had relented, she sat beside Harvey's hospital bed, looked down at his bandaged arms, and then up at the drip.

'For hydration,' Harvey said.

'You gave them a scare at the station.'

'I'll be fine. No major arteries nicked.'

'Why'd you do it?' Gardner asked.

Tears were forming in the corners of his eyes. He opened his mouth to speak, but then evidently changed his mind over what he was going to say and closed it.

When it was clear that Harvey wasn't going to say anything, she readied her notebook and got to business. 'How close were you with Tia Meadows?'

He looked away. 'I told you: I don't have any relationships.'

'Really? So, why'd you tell the paramedic you loved her?'

He shook his head. 'I don't recall...'

'I see. So, she was *never* inside your hut then?'

He looked back at her and thought for a moment. He sighed. 'You've found something, haven't you?'

'Her DNA, Harvey.'

He licked his dry lips. 'It isn't what you think.'

'It's going beyond what I think now. The CPS will have enough to prosecute.'

The tears in the corners of his eyes slipped free. They ran down his cheeks. 'You'll just be wasting your time while this monster walks free.'

'I guess that's your choice?'

He sighed. 'Okay, I do remember saying that to the paramedic. It's true.'

'Why did you love her?'

'Not because she was beautiful, although she was. No... it was more because of how kind she was. And, you know, she was such a good listener.' He stared off into space.

'A man with no relationships, eh?'

'If things had been different, and I'd have had a daughter, I think she'd have been exactly like Tia. Warm, non-judgemental. Everything the world doesn't seem to be any more.' He paused, still staring into space as a smile spread across his face.

Gardner put her hand on his upper arm just above where a bandage ended. 'It's time, Harvey. Tell me about Tia. There's no shame in finding someone. Finding a friend. If that's what happened.'

'After my parents... you know' – he looked away – 'passed. There's no one I'd have allowed into my life. No one. But she was different. She broke through the peace I'd given myself.' His smile remained, but there were more tears. 'And I'd never felt happier.'

Gardner kept her hand on his upper arm.

'She came to visit me.' He wiped at a wet cheek with the back of his bandaged hand. 'Fourteen times, in fact. I counted. Over two wonderful months. *Fourteen times.*' He looked down. 'There won't be a fifteenth.'

Gardner took a deep breath, steeling herself emotionally. 'Tell me about it.'

* * *

Thud. Thud.

Harvey flinched. It was rare for anyone to knock on his hut door. The occasional tyke on the end of a dare. If so, it wouldn't happen again, the kid would be running by now.

Thud. Thud.

The knock was insistent and determined.

He peeled back the curtain and looked through the window.

She had short, black bobbed hair and unblemished white skin. She didn't look dangerous.

He didn't arm himself before opening the door. 'Can I help you?'

'My name is Tia Meadows.'

Meadows.

The word came like a wave, crashing hard into the shore.

'Meadows,' he repeated back to her.

'Yes... Tia Meadows. Are you okay?'

No.

'Yes.' His hands shook. 'Are you related to Si Meadows?'

'He's my father.'

Harvey felt Si's lips against his and saw the sorrow in his eyes just before he turned from him at the back of that scout hut.

He opened his mouth to reply to Tia, but nothing came out.

'You know my father, don't you?'

'I'm sorry,' Harvey said. 'It's better if you—'

'He has a picture of you and him together in his drawer. When you were children. I know it's you because he wrote your names on the back. He also has other photographs. Ones taken over the years.'

'Over the years?' Harvey had watched Si run away from him in the scout hut. There hadn't been any years after that. At least, not years of them together.

'Well, pictures of you. Alone. None with you and my father together.'

'Oh.'

'I thought you'd be able to tell me why.'

Harvey put his fist to his mouth. 'Sorry... I... I haven't spoken to your father in forty years. I'm not too sure.'

'Please,' Tia said. 'Anything you can tell me will help.'

'Help with what exactly?'

'To understand him.'

'That might be difficult.'

'I agree. My father is a man who refuses to be understood.'

Harvey sighed. 'You know, maybe that's for a reason? Maybe it's just better that way.'

She pulled off a backpack, unzipped it, reached in and pulled out a photograph. She thrust it into Harvey's hand.

'That's you standing alongside my father at cub scouts, and...' She reached into her bag again.

Harvey stared, mouth open, at his ten-year-old self. Beside him in the *group of other cub scouts was Si, and at the back, hunching slightly, was...*

She held a newspaper article in the air.

There he was again...

Baloo...

Sneering outside the courthouse.

Harvey's eyes panned over the headline: 'Fifty-eight-year-old scout leader, Miles Cook, found not guilty of child abuse.'

Harvey gulped. 'What a thing to find.'

Tia nodded. 'Now, you can see why I'm here.'

'Yes, I think you'd better come in.'

* * *

'So inquisitive,' Harvey said and smiled. 'She'd have made a great police officer.' He pointed at Gardner, wincing because he had to move his damaged arm. 'You'd have liked her. She'd have badgered anything out of anyone, like that detective I used to watch on television. Columbo.'

Gardner smiled. Her hand was still on his upper arm.

'Mum and Dad used to watch that with me when I was young, and just before they passed, we watched them all over again...'

Gardner was still stuck on the words, 'Not guilty of child abuse.' She had a sickening feeling gnawing at her stomach that this investigation was heading down an even darker path.

'She found all of this in her father's drawer?' Gardner asked.

Harvey nodded.

'Who is Miles Cook?' Gardner asked.

'One of the *true* monsters. Back then, he was our cub scout leader, Baloo.'

'And where is he now?'

Harvey shrugged. 'Good question. He left Knaresborough and I never saw him again.'

'Who was he accused of abusing?' Gardner asked.

'His name was Bernard Fielding. But it was his word against Miles, and the monster lived to terrorise another day.'

Gardner made a note of Bernard Fielding and Miles Cook.

'You won't be able to talk to Bernard,' Harvey said.

'Why not?'

'He hanged himself in his parents' garage before he turned twenty.'

'Good lord.'

'Yes, I told you Miles was a monster.' He stared off into the distance, clearly reflecting. 'He ruined lives. *Destroyed* them. The truest of monsters.'

Gardner sighed, looked at her hand on Harvey's arm again, and then up into his sad eyes. 'He abused you too, didn't he?'

Harvey took a long, deep breath in through his nose. 'My mother and father had issues at the time, I won't deny that, but I was a happy boy, you know? I reckon my life had some promise... may have come good if the monster hadn't derailed it. Yes, he abused me all right.'

'Did you not say anything? Back Bernard up?'

Harvey shook his head, and more tears ran down his cheeks. 'No. I should've done. Maybe it would have put him in jail. There isn't a day goes past that I don't regret it. Could I have saved other boys my fate? But, you know, Miles was clever. He made sure he had power over us before he ever touched us. He knew how to keep us silent. It's easy to fall into his trap when you're ten.'

'Apart from Bernard?'

'Yes, apart from Bernard. The monster's one mistake: underestimating Bernard.'

'What did he have on you, Harvey?'

'My mother. Way back then, my mother and father were struggling to make ends meet. Many years later they told me they were practically destitute.'

Harvey looked away and remained silent for a time. 'My mother... Jesus... she was desperate, *so* desperate. The warmest person, but so desperate...'

Gardner squeezed Harvey's arm. 'What happened?'

'She prostituted herself. I don't know how many times. I only knew this because of Miles. Miles had a friend, another monster like him, who paid my mother and then recorded it on film. Threatened to expose her.'

Gardner's heart was heavy. 'I'm so sorry.'

Harvey shrugged. 'I loved my mother. God, how I loved her. And he knew that. I'm not sure what he ever had on Bernard. I never found out. Not enough, I guess. Although, let's not take away from Bernard's bravery, which went unrewarded. That poor boy.'

'You've suffered too, Harvey. As have all his victims.'

'Yes, but I'm alive.'

She looked at his bandaged arms and thought of his shit-smeared hut. *But are you, Harvey? Are you truly alive?*

'How did Tia find you?'

'Everybody knows who the town freak is, don't they?' Harvey rolled his eyes. 'The more you try to hide yourself away, the more the bastards take notice. Do people welcome non-conformists where you come from?'

Gardner nodded, conceding his point. 'So when Tia came to you, did you tell her everything?'

Harvey nodded. 'Didn't really have a choice. Like I said, she was insistent. She was my Columbo. Besides, she'd found this mountain of evidence from Si's drawer. She just wanted to fill in the gaps. To know what her father had to do with this whole sorry business.'

'And?'

'After I told her, I defended him. Remember, he was a ten-year-old boy too, scared of the consequences.'

* * *

'But my father just ran away!' Tia said. 'Left you. That's awful.'

'Is it?' Harvey said with a raised eyebrow. 'He was ten. He was scared for himself and his family's reputation in the same way I was.'

'Because he was gay?' Tia said, nursing her tea.

'Different times, Tia. It would've been a mess. You can't expect a child to be able to deal with those feelings.'

Harvey had allowed Tia use of his one chair, but it didn't feel right for him to behave like a slob and sit on the cushions lying on the floor, so he leaned against his bookcase instead.

'I always suspected he might be gay,' Tia said. 'He never seemed to have any girlfriends and I've caught his eye wandering over at young men a few times. Do you think you and my father would've ended up together, if not for, you know...'

'We were ten, Tia. And confused.'

'Have you ever been married?'

He shook his head.

'A girlfriend? A boyfriend?'

'No.'

'But that's so sad.'

'I had Mum and Dad. That was enough.'

'But now? You're alone?'

'I'm fine, Tia.'

'Is it because of what this man, Miles Cook, did to you?'

'Honestly, Tia, thank you for your compassion, but don't worry. I'm content... in a way... and I guess that's more than some. I just prefer to be left alone these days. Just the way it is.'

'Sorry, Harvey,' Tia said, putting her cup down on the floor. 'I should leave...'

'God, no,' Harvey held the palms of his hands out. 'I'm happy for you to be here.'

'Are you sure?'

His eyes widened and he smiled. 'Yes... I am. Absolutely. I just find it hard to trust people, but I trust you. Because of your kindness. Besides, I've also got a lot of tea so there's no rush. Nothing but tea, in fact, so it may get boring, but still, please stay as long as you want, and I'll keep boiling that kettle.'

She smiled.

'And tell me about yourself, Tia. Tell me what you've got going on in your life? Shouldn't you be off at a university somewhere?'

'Don't you start!' She guffawed. 'My father is livid about that.'

'Sorry—'

'No, don't be. It's just... I don't feel quite ready yet. That's all.'

Harvey nodded. 'It's an expensive do, anyway.'

She waved a hand. 'It's not so much that. My dad will pay. Actually, he's offered to send me off there in a Porsche in an effort to bribe me. That's how he solves everything... with money.' She suddenly looked embarrassed. 'I'm not showing off.'

'I didn't think that at all. I'm very glad he's done so well for himself.'

Tia looked down at the floor, thinking a while, before saying, 'Actually, there's another reason I don't want to go. Not just yet, anyway.'

'I see,' Harvey said, smiling. He finally succumbed to the temptation of comfort and lowered himself down onto the cushions.

'But it's kind of a secret...'

'I understand,' Harvey said.

'Yet I know some of your secrets. Maybe it would be fair to share one of mine with you? But my father would be horrified if he knew. Actually, everyone I know would be horrified!'

'You can rely on me not to be horrified. I also promise not to tell your father. So, what's the scandal?'

'It would be a scandal.' She sighed. 'Maybe I'm like you, Harvey, maybe I'm just different.'

'Unique, Tia. That's the deal, here, okay? You're unique. One-of-a-kind. Inimitable. Okay?'

'My father will never accept what's happening. Never.' She wiped a tear away and then looked at Harvey. 'You're so nice... I suddenly feel like I can tell you anything. The reason I haven't left Knaresborough is because someone is coming back in a couple of weeks. Someone I got very close to last summer.'

'Who?'

She looked off to the right, at the wall of his hut. 'Over the lake. On the rugby field.'

'A rugby player?'

Tia laughed. 'No, silly. A traveller.'

'Ah,' Harvey said.

'Yes.' Tia nodded. 'It's a tale as old as time. I've fallen for someone I shouldn't have. My family's greatest enemy.'

'Greatest enemy? Why?'

'Something to do with trade,' Tia said. 'They bring competition to my father's business. They offer services out and undercut prices.'

'I wouldn't know anything about it.'

'Neither do I really. But I do know this: if my father finds out, I'm dead!'

Harvey smiled. 'I don't believe that for a second.'

'Okay... but my boyfriend would most definitely be dead. And I can't be having that.'

'So, what're you going to do?'

'To begin with, I'm going to keep it within these four walls... with you.'

'I see.'

'It'll be the world's best kept secret.'
'It will be. I'll never expose it. Come what may.'

* * *

'Do you know the name of this boy she fell for?' Gardner asked, her thoughts circling around the moustached boy she'd snapped the previous day.

'Aiden.'

'Aiden what?'

'Just Aiden, I'm afraid.'

'Did you find out anything else about this Aiden?'

'She was in love. He was gifted every positive adjective under the sun. Gentle, affectionate, kind. She claimed he was very different to those he lived with. Who was I to suggest that it might be a façade, and people aren't always who they appear to be? I didn't want to scare her off because... well, you know...'

'Because what?'

'Because she was my friend.' Harvey sighed. 'Stupid, I know.'

'And why is that stupid, Harvey?'

'Well, look at me!' His eyes were now red from the crying. 'I'm the freak who lives in a hut. I don't *do* friends.'

'How many times did she visit you?'

'I told you. Fourteen times.'

'Why would anyone do that unless they liked you?'

'Sympathy?'

Harvey's eyes filled with tears again. If he was Tia's killer, he was quite the actor. That wasn't to say that she hadn't met her fair share of actors in her time.

'Did her father ever find out she was visiting?' Gardner asked.

'No, and as far as I'm aware he never found out about Aiden either.'

'And you didn't meet Aiden?'

He shook his head. 'No. But I think he was stringing Tia along. She'd waited all this time for him to return to Knaresborough while he was galivanting off around the country doing God knows what. And he was about to do it again... His people never stayed longer than six weeks or so. Such a beautiful girl; such a heart in her. She could've, *should've*, done so much better for herself.'

'Did you ever find out if she confronted her father about what she'd discovered in his drawer?'

'She never mentioned it again.'

'What did you do when she visited?'

'All sorts. We talked, mainly. She liked to read, so we shared some books. I'd an old backgammon set so I taught her how to play. She enjoyed that immensely.' He looked off into the distance. 'Started to beat me more often than not.'

'Did she ever give you money?'

'No, of course not. What kind of question is that?'

Gardner made a few notes while Harvey fiddled with the bandages on his arm. He chuckled and Gardner look back up at him. 'What is it, Harvey?'

'Just thinking about how crazy this all is. After my parents died, I never wanted human company ever again.' He looked at Gardner. 'Tia changed all that. Gave me hope... and now...' He looked away, narrowed his red eyes and glared ahead. 'You must find whoever did this, because it wasn't me. Someone out there hurt that lovely, innocent young woman, and placed that purse at my door. They knew exactly what they were doing. Blame the freak. It's an easy sell.'

Gardner nodded. *Yes, it was. Too easy.*

They talked for a while longer. Before Gardner left, she put her hand on Harvey's upper hand again and met his eyes. 'If this is the truth, Harvey, then I'm sorry. So very sorry for everything that has happened to you.'

Harvey nodded and smiled.

'But until I know exactly what happened to Tia, then you've to stay in custody; I hope you understand that?'

He nodded again. 'You could take that guard away, and I'd stay right where I was. Like you, I only care about one thing: finding the person who did this to Tia.'

* * *

Gardner hit one of the toilets in the hospital. She sat in a cubicle for a moment, feeling tearful. Harvey's pain was significant, and now she could understand his eccentricities and his chosen lifestyle. Of course, she couldn't rule him out. There was a mountain of evidence against him and, some would argue, there was clear motive: revenge against Si for abandoning him in his hour of need, the hour that would go on to define the rest of his tortured existence.

But his connection with Tia had seemed so tender, or, at the very least, had been presented by him as such.

She thought of her brother, Jack, and his claims he'd changed.

Her husband, Barry, and his claims that he wasn't having an affair and was interested in saving their marriage.

Her deputy SIO, Riddick, and his claims that he was fully in control.

All these people making their promises.

Were they all about to let her down?

Unlike that broken man in the hospital bed who had kept his promises to Tia, despite the whole world being against him.

Standing up, Gardner straightened out her suit and opened the cubicle door. Alone, she stood staring at her reflection, checking there were no tears visible on her face.

God forgive any of her people if they were lying to her.

Because, if there was one thing Emma Gardner wasn't, it was a pushover.

She narrowed her eyes.

And if any of them believed this, they were going to get a nasty surprise.

Outside, she phoned one man who didn't seem to ever hide behind a façade, to the disappointment of many of his offended colleagues.

She filled Phil Rice in on the abuse angle and then said, 'Miles Cook. We need to know where he went.'

'To his grave, I imagine. I hope. Bastard paedo.'

'Don't use that word around me, Phil. I don't like it.'

'What? Bastard?'

She rolled her eyes.

'I'll find the paedophile.' He emphasised the word.

'He was found not guilty, you know, *just* remember that.'

'I'm looking at a photograph of him now. How any jury could spare that man...'

'This isn't Victorian England, Phil, we don't condemn people on physical appearance.'

'Shame—'

'Phil. I've a headache. I phoned you because you get things done. Miles Cook. Get something done.' She hung up.

Then, she journeyed off to the rugby pitch to visit the travelling community's answer to Romeo.

Aiden.

Second name still unknown.

22

After parking up, Gardner phoned Riddick.

When he didn't pick up, her anxiety intensified.

What're you up to, man? I'm blowing this investigation wide open and my wingman is AWOL.

In no mood for the yapping dogs at the travellers' site, she took a few on in a staring contest as she passed them by, buoyed on by the fact that the most aggressive looking ones were tethered to posts.

Tommy Byrne, the traveller with the mohawk, emerged from behind a caravan. 'You again?'

She recognised the Alsatian he had on his lead. Tyson. Or, rather, she recognised his froth-covered canine teeth, and his loud bark.

'Yes, Tommy, me again,' Gardner said. She nodded down at Tyson. 'You adopted him?'

'Trying to. He still has attachment issues.'

'He certainly looks as if he wants to attach himself to something.'

'He'll be fine as long as I hold this lead.' The muscles flexed in Tommy's exposed, tattoo-covered chest and Gardner was glad he'd the upper body strength to keep the beast in check. 'Anyway, don't get the wrong impression. This is him in a welcoming mood. He must like you. He wasn't so tender-hearted when the chap from the council turned up earlier.' Tommy squinted. 'Are you here for Rod again? Surely not? He's a barmpot... He couldn't even string a sentence together before that prick brayed him at the Bull, so now you've got no chance.'

'I'm here to talk to one of the young men who was standing alongside him yesterday.' She pointed to the spot where she'd spoken to Rod the previous day.

Tommy shrugged. 'A lot has happened since then. We've been busy.'

Gardner looked left and right at the multitude of people lying about drinking coffee. 'Looks that way. It's the one with the moustache.'

'Male or female?' Tommy asked and then laughed.

'His name's Aiden.'

Gardner was sure she detected a flash of concern on Tommy's face. She was equally certain his response was delayed.

'A moustache, male and Aiden equals Aiden Poole.'

'Okay, Tommy, where is Aiden?'

Tommy chewed his bottom lip. He was measuring his responses. He was frustrating her.

'Tommy?'

Eventually, the irritant stopped chewing and sighed. He looked resigned to Gardner's discovery. 'I guess you know that he was shagging that girl that died. She was a right warm un.'

'Warm un?'

'Bit of a slapper.'

Gardner felt a surge of anger. She looked away and managed to rein in her temper. She looked back at him. 'You didn't think that was important information to share yesterday?'

Tommy shrugged. 'How'd I know it's important? I'm not a copper.'

'Aiden's girlfriend is killed a fraction of a mile from where you're camping, and you don't think that's important? Maybe Rod isn't the only barmpot around here!'

Tommy ran a hand over his mohawk. He grinned, but his narrowed eyes betrayed the fact that he wasn't really amused.

Riddick would've appreciated her caustic tone.

'Take me to see Aiden Poole please, Tommy.'

'You know,' Tommy said, holding his finger up. 'I think he went out earlier.'

She took her phone out.

'What yer doing?' Aiden said.

'This is a murder investigation. If I'm forced to go door to door around your caravans, I'm going to need a bigger team.' She looked around with wide eyes. 'A much bigger team.'

'Hang on,' Tommy said, not even pretending to be amused now. 'I think I might know where he is. Follow me. But he didn't kill her, you know? The lad was loved up.'

Tommy turned. Tyson didn't turn with him, content to continue sizing Gardner up.

'Tyson!' Tommy said, yanking on the lead. The dog yelped and reluctantly turned. Gardner followed man and beast into the heart of the travellers' camp.

* * *

When Aiden Poole opened the door, he wore the same look of nausea she'd seen in that photograph yesterday. Almost immediately, without any introductions, Aiden set out his stall. 'I loved Tia. I loved her *so* much.'

Gardner nodded to show that she'd heard his cry. 'Mr Poole. My name is DCI Gardner. I'm genuinely sorry for your loss, but I do wonder why you didn't come over to speak with me yesterday when I was here? Or better still, headed to the station to tell us that you were in a relationship with Tia?'

'I... I...' He didn't finish. He hung his head.

'Told you,' Tommy said from behind her. 'That boy ain't no killer. Just a loved-up puppy.'

She turned her head. 'Thanks Tommy. I can handle it from here.'

'I'll linger around outside here—'

'Doesn't Tyson need his morning walk?'

'He's had it. And the last thing he needs is another shit. Two today already. The beast is a walking tank of fertiliser.'

Gardner ignored him, followed Aiden into the caravan and closed the door behind her.

The caravan itself was clean and orderly. Aiden sat down on the edge of his bed at the end of the caravan and put his head in his hands.

He didn't offer her a seat. Gardner didn't care and was content to lean against the kitchen unit. 'So, why haven't you reached out, Aiden?'

He shrugged but didn't lift his head. 'For what? For you to suspect me? I didn't see Tia that night after I left the pub.'

'Who were you with?'

'There was a crowd of us. I'll give you a list if you want? Lots of people can vouch for me.'

I'm sure they can, Gardner thought, pulling out her notebook. *Massive question marks over it being the truth though.* 'Go on then.'

After she wrote down the list of names, she asked, 'Can you tell me your phone number, please?'

He looked up and told her.

The number matched one of the three numbers recovered from Tia's phone log. 'This is an unregistered number?'

'Unregistered?' Aiden stroked his long moustache – a clear, but failed, attempt to add maturity to his baby face. 'Yes. I guess. We don't register anything. We just pay as we go.'

'Aiden, phone logs show that you've been in touch with Tia Meadows very consistently over the previous year.'

He nodded. 'We loved each other. Haven't I explained that?'

'Could you explain how you met Tia?'

'I was drinking in the White Bull. She was behind the bar. We got talking, you know, how people do, and we... well, we hit it off.'

'And you entered into a relationship?'

Aiden nodded.

Gardner gestured around the caravan. 'Did you spend time together in here?'

Aiden creased his brow. 'Of course. Sometimes. What're you getting at? Are you asking if we slept together? Tia's a proper lady if you know what I mean. So, no, we didn't sleep together right from the get-go if that's what you're implying.'

It wasn't, Gardner thought, but nodded and made a note anyway. She also thought back to Tommy's suggestion that she was a bit of a slapper. *What had he meant by that? Maybe, he was just doing it to be antagonistic?*

'She made me wait a time,' Aiden said.

'How many times do you think she was here with you?'

'Not many, to be honest.' He sighed. 'Not enough. Bloody baggage, you see.'

'Baggage?'

'Her father.'

Gardner took a deep breath. Si Meadows was everywhere. Never mind the connecting lines on the incident board, he cropped up in nearly every interview too. The beating of Rod Child. The horrifying childhood experience with Harvey Henfrey. And now here, too? *In what way was Si Meadows baggage, Aiden?* She exhaled slowly, measuring where to take this line of questioning. 'Do you know her father?'

'Not personally, no.'

'Yet, you say he was a problem in some way?'

'He was controlling. The reason she rarely stayed here was because he'd have hit the roof if he ever found out. She had to be so bloody cautious.'

'Did Tia mention why he was like this?'

'He hated travellers. He was a tradesman in the area, and some of the boys on the site offer trade jobs. He didn't like being undercut.'

Tradesman! More than that; he bloody ran the area.

'So, what did Tia tell her father when she actually stayed here?'

'Sometimes, he was away on business. Other times, she told him she was staying at a friend's.'

'Did he ever suspect? Did you ever have any problems?'

'As far as I know, he never found out. I saw him a few times in the White Bull, but he seemed none the wiser. Fortunately. I saw what he did to Rod! Although, I doubt the lad felt it.' He pointed at his forehead. 'Like a plank of wood up here that boy.'

'Still, it must have been difficult,' Gardner said.

'Aye. That man got in the way all right. I wanted her to come with me last year when we left for the next place, but she never had the courage to. How could anyone have any courage with that prick as a father?'

Gardner made notes. 'If you were so in love, wouldn't it have been hard for you to be apart for most of the year?'

'It was hard, yeah. She did slip away for the occasional day to meet me wherever we were camped, making up God-knows-what excuses to keep that old bastard sweet, but those days were few and far between. You've seen yourself how many phone calls there were. Life was tough.' He stroked his moustache again and looked down. 'And it just got tougher.'

'Must have been expensive for you on a pay-as-you-go?'

'She was worth it. Besides, she did most of the calling. Pays to get a contract and get those free minutes, although her dad was minted anyway.'

You can say that again.

'It sounds like you were in a very frustrating relationship, Aiden.'

'Didn't stop me loving the bones of her though.' Rather than fiddling with his moustache, he was now playing with a pendant on the end of a gold chain. It looked like a bird in flight.

'I don't suppose you ever suggested meeting her father?' Gardner asked. 'An attempt to plead your case as it were?'

'Once or twice. But she always shut that conversation down quickly.'

'What did she say?'

'That it was suicide.'

'Did you buy it?'

'She was fairly convincing. Tia never minced her words. She said, clearly, that if her father ever found out about me, I'd be dead. But love would've seen us right, you know what I mean? It felt like destiny.'

She imagined Riddick taking an opportunity to quip, 'A regular Romeo and Juliet. So, tell me, what next for the star-crossed lovers?'

'Did you ever consider trying to approach him without her permission?' Gardner asked.

'She'd have hated me for it. So, I left it. Also, I...' He paused. He let the bird pendant fall back against his neck and returned his fingers to his moustache.

'What?' Gardner said. 'What were you going to say?'

Aiden sighed. 'You see where I live? I've a responsibility to my people too.'

'What do you mean?'

'Well, bringing the local bulldog, Si Meadows, to our doorstep wouldn't be my most selfless move.'

'But your people knew about Tia?'

'Yes, well.' He nodded to his right as if to gesture outside the caravan. 'It did become a problem. Tommy told me to knock the relationship on the head. Said he'd looked into the father and discovered he was bad news.'

'I take it Tommy is in charge around here then?'

'He's in charge, but he's a good man... and he's good for us. People listen to him. I wanted to listen to him, but, well...'

'When did Tommy tell you to knock the relationship on the head?'

'A couple of weeks back.'

'I'm assuming you didn't then.'

'No, I couldn't. Told him I'd rather leave the camp than give up on her. Anything else, I told him. Anything else I'd do in a heart-beat. But giving up on Tia was not an option.'

'You're still here. I guess you won Tommy round?'

'Tommy does have a reasonable side. I made him understand.' He paused. 'He gave me a chance, but warned me to be discrete. And he made me promise to end it if Si ever found out.'

'Surely you knew that one day he would?'

'Yes, but I was desperate. Anything to buy me more time with Tia.'

'Tommy doesn't seem like a pushover to me.'

Aiden looked away. 'He isn't. I think he just realised what she meant to me.'

You're lying. Something else happened here. To do with the money perhaps? Six hundred pounds in three days was a lot of money for Tia to withdraw. Did she give it you? Tommy, perhaps? Was this what changed Tommy's mind? Three cash withdrawals of two hundred pounds? More to follow if she hadn't died?

Gardner parked this line of inquiry for a while. She didn't want to risk getting him too riled so early in their discussion. Instead, she continued to question him over the nature of the relationship.

Aiden enjoyed talking about Tia. He talked of dreamy looks punctuated by smiles. He was quite the poet. Their relationship had begun tentatively but quickly became passionate and intense, or, at the very least, that's how he remembered it. Love could be blind. Gardner reminded herself that this was only one side of the coin. He shied away from discussing sex directly, but it was evident that this area had not been lacking in their relationship. After almost half an hour, he'd given a convincing case that his feelings had been genuine. He was tender whenever he spoke of her, and his feelings of loss seemed to be breaking him.

'Where did you go when you left the White Bull the evening before last?'

'Straight back here with the boys. Didn't I tell you that already?'

You did. But I wanted to double check.

She took a list of all of Aiden's alibis for the journey home.

'After you arrived back, what happened?'

'What always happens. We gathered in the centre around the fire and drank some more.'

The list of alibis grew.

Not that they're reliable alibis, anyway, Gardner thought. She doubted Tommy or anyone else on this site for that matter, would think twice about protecting one of their own. She probably would've considered this quite noble if not for the fact there was a brutal murder involved.

Still, it needed checking. She'd ask two of her team members to come down and take statements after she'd left.

'Did Tia ever give you any money?' Gardner asked.

'What? Why do you ask that?'

'Well, she had access to a lot, and well...' She looked around, thinking how best to word this. 'I guess your lifestyle operates on a smaller budget.'

'What do you think this is? I loved her. I wasn't using her!'

'I'm not suggesting that, Aiden. Not at all. We just know that she was in possession of money in those last couple of days. A reasonable amount. Could you have any idea why?'

He shrugged and looked down. 'Like you said, she had access to a lot. Her father was loaded. Maybe she got it from him?'

She got it from a cashpoint. The question is – did you know about it? 'Six hundred pounds? Does that mean anything to you, Aiden?'

'No.' He glanced at the side of the caravan as he said this, and Gardner wondered if he was considering Tommy standing outside.

The peculiarity surrounding Tia's large withdrawals felt relevant. She made further notes.

Gardner knew the next part of the interview was going to be very difficult, but there was an important question that needed asking and answering.

'Tia was pregnant, Aiden.'

The colour drained from Aiden's face. He opened his mouth to respond, but nothing came out, and he simply closed it again.

He didn't know. She asked anyway, 'Did you know?'

He didn't open his mouth this time. He simply turned his head from side to side.

'It was early. She may not have known herself.'

Aiden looked like he was going to vomit.

'Do you think the baby was yours?'

He lowered his face and pinched his eyes.

'Aiden? If you could please answer?'

His body trembled a few times. He looked back up at her with red eyes. 'We were careful.'

'How so?'

'Condoms.'

'Every time?'

Aiden nodded. 'Does this mean the baby wasn't mine?'

'No,' Gardner said. 'It can still happen.'

But it opens up the very real possibility that Tia was with someone else.

Gardner gave Aiden a couple of moments to collect himself. He looked broken. 'Aiden, can you come to the station and give us a DNA sample? It will help us to rule you out, and we can also look into the other issue?'

'At whether the baby is mine or not?'

Gardner nodded.

Aiden sighed. 'Of course.'

Gardner steeled herself to direct a big question at this wavering man. 'Who do you think killed Tia, Aiden?'

Aiden looked more confused than shocked now. 'You've got him, haven't you? The freak who lives out by the lake? Harvey Henfrey.'

Gardner couldn't help but see the irony in a traveller calling someone who chose to live outside of society a freak but kept her thoughts to herself.

'We're still investigating that possibility,' Gardner said. 'Did Tia ever mention Harvey to you?'

Aiden shook his head. 'No.' He paused. 'But if he didn't do it, who did? I'd look at her father. Si Meadows. Vicious prick. You should have seen the way he dismantled Rod. The man has a serious screw loose.'

I saw it, Gardner thought. *And you're right, it wasn't pretty.*

'He scared her,' Aiden continued. 'I know that.'

'How so?' Gardner asked.

'He was quick to anger. She also felt intimidated by some of the people he knocked around with.'

Gardner made notes but didn't seem to feel she was making further headway.

She moved the focus on to Aiden's lifestyle. She had to admit that the nomadic lifestyle sounded intriguing. In fact, with her sudden move from Wiltshire to North Yorkshire, she was kind of living it. There were many times in her life when she'd found herself ground down by the monotony of life; maybe constantly upping sticks was not a bad life choice after all.

Finally, she bid him farewell. 'Please go to the station for that DNA test, Aiden. Once again, I'm sorry for your loss. I'll be in touch.'

When she left the caravan, Tommy and Tyson were no longer there. This was a shame as she wanted to ask him questions regarding his warning to Aiden about staying away from Tia. She was also curious to know if he'd had anything to do with the large cash withdrawals she'd made.

As she reached the outskirts of the campsite looking for Tommy and Tyson among the multitude of travellers and dogs, she glimpsed two people ahead on the country road parallel to the site. An adult and a child. Both were standing still and staring in this direction.

It was difficult to see who it was due to the sun in her eyes, but there was something about the way the figures held themselves which made them familiar.

She squinted and shielded her eyes.

Jack and Rose.

Brother and niece.

An innocent stroll?

Have they seen my car?

Are they looking for me?

She held up her hand and waved, wondering if they could see her, standing among the caravans.

Either they couldn't see her or had chosen to ignore her.

As she watched them walk away, a thought hit her. One that sent a shiver running through her whole body.

Has Jack been following me?

She shook her head. *Get a grip, Emma.* It was a popular walking route. Who wouldn't stop to glance at this eyesore that had descended onto the rugby field?

Trying to shake off her uneasy thoughts, she continued to look for Tommy. Eventually, she bumped into the old man from the day before. He was still smoking like a chimney.

He took great pleasure in telling her that Tommy had now gone out for the day and that he had no contact details for him.

Despite knowing it was a lie, Gardner felt too shaken up by her brother's sudden appearance to put up a challenge and headed out of the site. It was time to touch base again with Knaresborough's most controversial figure – Si Meadows.

23

Ronnie Haller may have been no spring chicken when the door to freedom had been closed off to him, but he hadn't looked like he did right now – haggard and broken.

Haller had always been a well-built man. However, rather than holding him upright in an imposing manner, his muscles now seemed to drag him downwards, making him hunch over.

Admittedly, his teeth had never been a dentist's dream, but at least they'd been useable. Now, they were hanging loosely in diseased gums and Riddick suspected anything apart from soup would be a challenge.

It may not have been possible to take much pleasure from Haller's continued existence, but Riddick couldn't deny himself a brief smile over his decay.

Following the briefing, it'd taken Riddick a reasonable amount of vodka back home to get him into this prison without having a panic attack. He'd done the right thing and used a taxi service to carry him here; getting pulled over with his current blood alcohol level would lead to an immediate suspension. Despite being way over the limit to drive though, it seemed he was masking his inebriation well. None of the prison guards had yet to bat an eyelid.

He'd seen Haller several times since that fateful day, but on each of those occasions, he'd been in a courtroom. This was the first time he'd been opposite Haller since the interview room on the worst day of his life.

The day Haller had killed his family.

Haller was chained to the table. A guard stood a metre behind Riddick.

He pondered his options. *Could I get my hands round Haller's throat before the guard seizes me? Maybe. Would I have the chance to squeeze? Unlikely.*

On the way in, he'd been searched thoroughly. He possessed nothing to split open one of the bastard's arteries, and he doubted he'd be able to garrot him with a shoelace.

'Glad to see you looking like shit, Ronnie,' Riddick said, sitting and gripping the underside of the table.

Haller prodded at wobbling teeth with his tongue for about ten seconds, before he said, 'You're no oil painting either, son.'

'Don't call me son.' Riddick exhaled a long deep breath through his nose. 'I'm here to ask you a few questions.'

Haller laughed. 'Questions? About what, son? Sorry, *Paul*. Don't you already know everything about me? Do you remember telling me you read me like a book?'

'I remember.'

'Just before you put me in here.' Haller rattled his chains.

'Listen, Ronnie. Someone has died.'

'Two people die every second.'

Riddick tried to ignore him. 'Her name was Tia Meadows.'

'What makes her more important than all the others?'

Keep going. Ignore his attempts to antagonise. 'Tia was very young, and she didn't—'

'I. Don't. Care.' Haller smirked.

Riddick slammed his fist on the table. 'I'm not here to play games.'

Haller shrugged.

Riddick sensed the guard closing in behind him, nervous about his erratic behaviour no doubt. Riddick held up his hand. 'I'm okay. Sorry.' He sized the smug prick up again. 'She didn't deserve what happened to her.'

'Does anyone?'

Riddick shook his head. 'This is useless... I knew it would be. I need to get out of here.'

Haller chuckled. 'Hasty. Okay. Say I answer your questions. Then what? You leave me to rot?'

Riddick glared at him. 'You already have done. No... this time, I'll be leaving you to die.'

'Not much of an incentive.'

'No, but it's all you get. Tia. Meadows. If there's any humanity in you, talk to me.'

Haller tilted his head one way and then the other, cracking the bones in his neck. 'I read about it.'

'You know her father, don't you?'

'I do.' Haller snorted, coughed up phlegm and spat it on the floor.

'Ronnie!' the guard said.

'Sorry sir. Wouldn't want to lose my privileges now, would I? Leeds United this weekend, after all.' He winked at Riddick. 'In UHD. Sixty inches.'

Riddick was sure he could feel every bead of sweat crawl out of every pore in his body and run down his skin. 'I need you to tell me about Si Meadows.'

'Everyone knows him,' Haller said. 'Why trouble yourself to talk to me?'

'You ran with him.'

'Eons ago. And, again, many others have run with him, not just little ol' me.'

Riddick felt disappointment flooding his body. The bastard opposite him was right. Why had he troubled himself? Subjected himself to such turmoil on a whim?

'I'm going to break it to you now, Paul. There's nothing for you here. Si's daughter is dead. So what? Between you and me, the screw behind you and these four walls, it couldn't have happened to a nicer bloke.'

Riddick stood and leaned over the table. 'Who said I cared about *his* feelings? She was innocent.'

Riddick took his hand from the table and turned. He looked down at his shaking hands and up at the guard, who regarded him with a raised eyebrow. He was better off out of this room.

'Always the good man, eh, Paul? Looking for justice. Defender of the innocents?'

Riddick took a step forward towards the guard and the exit.

'Okay... okay... don't get your knickers in a twist, son. You're here now,' Haller said. 'I may not be able to bring that poor little lass down by the lake back to life but let's see what we can do.'

Without turning, Riddick said, 'Unless you've something that can help, Ronnie, I'm not staying.'

'How about a bargain, then?'

Riddick turned, clenching his shaking hands into fists. 'I've told you. No bargain. You could offer up the name of the murderer and I wouldn't even consider it. You're never getting out of here. Suggest it again and I'll break you.' He glanced back at the guard as he said this, wondering if any decent human being would oppose this idea.

'Why does it always have to be so dramatic with you, Paul?' Haller said. 'What do you think I was going to ask for – a reduced sentence? Even if it was reduced, I'd still die in here. I also get my privileges already – UHD, remember?' He smirked. 'No, Paul, I want something else.'

Riddick walked back to the table, put his hands on it and leaned over. Every inch of his skin felt as if it'd set alight. 'Just give me an excuse, Ronnie. Just one excuse...'

'No excuse, but how about a question? One question,' Haller said. 'How about it? Answer me one question. A single, *solitary* question and I'll sing like a canary.'

You're being baited, Paul. Haller knows nothing.

As far as Riddick's ideas went, this had to be his worst to date. 'I'm done here.'

'Even by your standards, Paul, this is a new level of hot-headedness. For the sake of one question, I might be able to tell you something about Si Meadows that could turn your pathetic little investigation into a bloody meteorite.' He raised a hand in the air and mimicked a soaring meteorite. He even made the sound effect.

'Do it then, *dammit*! Ask your bloody question!' Riddick's face suddenly felt hot.

Haller cleared his throat.

'Ask it!' Riddick felt as if his eyes were going to burst.

'Okay...' Haller smiled. 'Why am I still alive?'

Riddick creased his brow and stared at Haller. He opened his mouth to respond but nothing came out. *Walk, Paul. Walk now. He's playing you.*

'Why am I still alive?' Haller repeated.

Riddick shook his head. 'What?'

'It's simple really. Why am I still sitting? Breathing? Talking?'

Riddick, who continued to shake his head, stood up straight. *This was wrong. This conversation was all wrong.*

'Okay, I can see you need help; let me elaborate,' Haller said. 'You see, the thing is, if that had been my family in the car that went boom... well...' His chains rattled as he pointed at Riddick. 'If you'd done that?' He pointed back at himself. 'To my family? Then you'd be long dead, son. Long dead. So, the question is a good one. Why am I still alive?'

Riddick lost control of his breathing. He felt his eyelids tremble so hard that the room took on an almost strobe-like effect.

He felt the guard's hand on his shoulder. 'Let's leave it there, Detective Inspector.'

He cracked his knuckles and closed his eyes. In the darkness, he saw:

Rachel.

Lucy.

Molly.

Riddick's eyes snapped open. He shook off the guard's hand, pounced and closed his hands around Haller's neck. 'How dare you... I'm going to—'

There was a tight grip around his chest, and a yank that almost took his footing away.

'—kill you!' Riddick managed to finish.

Riddick saw the distance from Haller rapidly grow as the guard pulled him back. He heard the door to the visiting room swing open.

Riddick surged again, closing some distance to the murderer.

'Harry, help me!' said the guard who was gripping him.

Riddick continued to fight in the guard's grip for a moment, but once Harry had brought his restraining hands into the equation, it was clear his brief stand was over. He wasn't getting free of two men.

Haller continued, 'It's not because you're weak, Paul... and it's not because you're a coward, anything but. Shall I tell you why I'm still here?'

'Shut up,' Riddick shouted. 'Shut your disgusting mouth.'

'They were a burden. Your family. They saddled you. You're like me, son. You can't handle baggage. That's why you let me live...' He smiled, showing his rotting teeth. '*Gratitude.*'

Riddick kicked up his fight against the guards again, tears of rage in his eyes. '*Shut your mouth!*'

'I gave you freedom, son. I lifted the pressure off you. Having to worry if you lived or died, leaving them alone to fend for themselves. It was my mistake. If I'd have known that I was doing you a fav—'

'I'm going to break your neck!' Riddick thrust again and made it closer, his fingers almost reaching the killer's face.

Stretching... stretching...

'Kill... you.'

But then his strength faded, and his control was gone. The guards dragged him back and wrestled him through the door.

* * *

Outside, he called a taxi and waited, wishing he had some more vodka to steady his nerves. Of course, he'd not brought any with him. He'd never have gained entrance to a prison with a hipflask.

The anger burned fiercely inside him as he paced the car park. He looked up at the imposing gates of the prison.

Why am I still alive?

He hadn't expected such a question.

Why am I still alive?

The problem was – it was a *bloody* good question. 'Why are you still alive?'

He stopped pacing and slipped a photograph of his wife, Rachel, and his twins, Lucy and Molly, from his wallet.

He stared at their immortalised faces.

For years, he'd imagined their presence. The way they looked had never changed.

Because it never would change.

He looked up at the prison gates again and saw again that monster smiling at him.

'Why are you still alive, Ronnie Haller?'

The phone rang. The number was unknown. 'Hello, DI Riddick? It's Harry. One of the guards from before.'

'I know who you are. Again, I'm sorry. If you've changed your mind, I understand. You probably should report it,' Riddick said.

'Look, Detective Inspector, we discussed this already, and we meant what we said. This *isn't* going any further,' Harry said. 'That man in there is evil, pure and simple, and what he did... well, I can't imagine. I'm so sorry.'

'Thanks,' Riddick said, wondering if Harry would still have the same view after reading Marianne Perse's impending article. How would he react to discovering that he'd just allowed a corrupt, alcoholic officer access to a dangerous prisoner?

'But that's not why I'm phoning, Detective Inspector,' Harry said. 'After you left, Haller spoke to me. He asked me to tell you three things. All relevant to your investigation.'

Curious. Riddick's heart started to beat faster. 'Go on.'

'Firstly, Si Meadows is gay.'

Riddick inwardly groaned. *Yes... we know that already.*

'Secondly, Haller wants you to know that he thinks Si Meadows has it in him to kill his own daughter rather than let the truth get out.'

'Sounds to me like he's got it in for Meadows and is just trying to score points,' Riddick said, not bothering to reach into his pocket for his notepad just yet. 'You said there was something else?' His heart settled back down as his hopes quickly faded.

'He said one more thing. I wrote it down as quickly as I could because it sounded so accusatory. Do you have a pen?'

He kept his phone pinned to his ear with his shoulder to free his hands, and plucked out his notepad and pen. 'Yes. Ready.'

'He said, "Paul Riddick took me off the street, then he took Neil Taylor off the street. But he left two foxes behind. Si Meadows and Rhys Hunt. Two tight foxes."'

Rhys Hunt. Another local businessman with lots of money and few morals. Based in Harrogate.

So, Rhys Hunt was tight with Si Meadows. Nothing special there. All crooks in North Yorkshire were tight with Meadows. Unless... Was Haller pointing out something relevant out here? But why would he steer the investigation this way? A wild goose chase to frustrate, or was there something in it for him?

'Sounds like most of our bitter old convicts,' Harry said. 'Jealous that his fellow gangsters are still enjoying their freedom, but I thought you should know immediately.'

'Yes, thanks... And sorry... again.'

He circled Rhys Hunt with his pen.

He looked up at the prison. *Why am I still alive?*

He looked back at the circled name.

God, Riddick thought, *I hope this snippet of information was worth it.*

He pocketed the notepad and pen, and contacted Si Meadows. 'I need to talk to you.'

'About? You've something new?'

'Where are you?'

'I'm in the White Bull.'

He watched the taxi drive into the car park. 'I'll be right there.'

Two burned-out alcoholics meeting in a pub in the afternoon to discuss a murder investigation – what could possibly go wrong?

24

Si's vehicle was in his driveway, but Gardner got no response when she hammered on his door.

She eased herself around the house, looking through windows, but struggled to see any signs of life.

'Shit,' she said, returning to the front door and knocking, unsuccessfully, a second time. She tried his mobile phone number and was sent through to voicemail. She tried again and put her ear to his door to see if she could hear it ringing inside. She couldn't. It didn't really confirm anything. The phone could be on silent, or he could be at the back of the house somewhere she wouldn't hear it anyway.

She tried his mobile a third time and left a message that it was extremely important he contacted her.

Then, she contacted Barnett.

'Shit, Ray. Si's car's here, but there's no sign of him. We need to talk to him.'

'Do we get a warrant to go in?'

Gardner thought about it and shook her head. 'No... too soon. We don't have enough. I'm not kicking down the door to go in based on the fact he knew Harvey when he was ten. I'll keep trying his phone. Post a message to keep an eye out for him, Ray. He's not in his vehicle, so number plate recognition won't help.'

After she rang off, she called Riddick again.

He was the second bastard in as many minutes to ignore her call.

She shook her head. Riddick off the radar was just as bad, if not worse.

A single glance at history would tell you that.

25

After paying the taxi driver, Riddick entered the White Bull and looked around. He sighted a couple of old drunks in the corner, who, despite sitting together, weren't communicating. They simply stared blankly at their half-empty pint glasses as if something awful had frozen them in this sorry position a long time ago, any hope of recovery slipping away with the sands of time.

Is this me, too?

The thought stabbed at Riddick. He'd climbed out of hell already this year, and in less than twenty-four hours he'd fallen back into it. Would he get another chance to climb out? Or had he completely blown it?

He looked towards Si hitting balls on the pool table. It was the same pool table he'd been using when he'd assaulted Rod Child. The bereaved father paused to chalk up his cue. He looked in Riddick's direction, gave him a swift nod, took his shot, potted a red ball, and then reached over for his drink.

Riddick looked up at the rows of bottles behind the bar and glanced over at the old drunks again. He felt his insides melting.

Bertie, wearing a multicoloured bow tie today, stepped out of a door behind the bar. 'DI Riddick.'

There was a loud clack and successive thudding sounds as several pool balls found pockets. 'I'm here to speak to Si.'

Bertie nodded. 'Coke again?'

Riddick gritted his teeth and didn't reply.

'Something stronger?'

'Put a double vodka in,' Riddick said, looking away in shame.

Bertie winked. 'Won't tell a soul.'

Won't matter if you do. Marianne's article's about to tell the world. 'Don't sweat it, Bertie,' he said, looking back at the landlord.

'A copper with balls,' Bertie said and smirked again. 'Thought those days had passed. You remind me of Anders—'

'*Finish* talking now, Bertie, and pour the drink.' He put a ten-pound note on the table.

'Behave,' Bertie said, filling the glass. 'It's on the house.' He pushed the drink over.

Riddick took it, left his money on the bar anyway, and approached Si.

Si was lining up a shot on a yellow. He looked at Riddick from the top of his eyes. 'Do you have anything for me?'

'Like what?'

Si struck the yellow with aggression. Riddick was surprised when it hit the lip of the pocket and went in rather than over. 'The truth of what happened to my Tia.'

'If I had the truth, Si, I wouldn't be standing here now.'

'That's disappointing. I just ignored three calls from your superior. I thought it best to hear what you had to say first. Thought you'd be more forthcoming.'

Gardner? Why has she called you?

Riddick had also ignored a bucket load of calls from her too.

'Did she leave a voicemail?' Riddick asked.

'Yes. Just told me to get in touch.'

'You should... after I leave.'

'Maybe. But if you don't know anything, will she?'

'It's possible.' Riddick took a large mouthful of vodka and coke.

Si smirked and nodded at the glass in Riddick's hand. 'Thirsty?' He propped up his cue and reached for his own glass. 'Doesn't help that much though, does it?'

Riddick grunted.

Si continued, 'It still feels as if there're a thousand razor blades running over every part of my body... simultaneously. But I guess if anyone would know that, then you would.' He raised an eyebrow at Riddick. 'So, what's the secret?'

'The secret?'

'The secret to how to stop the razor blades?'

'There isn't one – at least not one I know of.'

'Jesus, Paul. Can't you give me the usual line about time being the great healer?'

He shook his head. 'It's all bollocks. I warn you now, Si, the razorblades never go away. Every day, they still cut. Still hurt. You won't ever be allowed to heal. You'll just live alongside it.'

Si snorted. 'Well, you're just what I need.' He looked down at his remaining pool balls. 'You're a barrel of bloody laughs, Paul.' He lined up a shot, but then changed his mind. He straightened up and squeezed his eyes with his thumb and forefinger, and sucked in a deep breath. Eventually, he dropped his hand back down and returned to his shot.

And missed.

Still leaning over the table, he looked up at Riddick angrily. 'I'll kill whoever did this.'

Ronnie Haller's question suddenly went through his mind: *Why am I still alive?*

Riddick steadied himself against the table as he took another mouthful.

'Slow down man,' Si said, nodding at Riddick's drink. 'You'll be good for nothing.'

'I went to see Ronnie Haller.'

Si raised an eyebrow and finally straightened up from his duff shot. He held the cue in both hands. Riddick wondered if he might lash out with it if he didn't like the direction of the conversation. 'Why?'

'Because I haven't forgotten *who* he is. *What* he is. I thought he might know something.'

'Pointless. Haller had nothing to do with Tia.'

Riddick nodded. 'I agree. He's incarcerated and vulnerable to retaliation. Why would he take that risk?'

Si said, 'Precisely. He knows well enough what would happen.'

Because you're both cut from the same cloth, aren't you? You both use violence to communicate... to live your foolish lives.

And yet...

Haller's question burned through his brain again. *Why am I still alive?*

Haller had taken everything from Riddick. Everything. Yet, here Riddick was, still clinging to morality. Doing the right thing.

Who was the real fool in this room?

'Does it surprise you that he's still alive after what he did to me?' Riddick asked.

Si cocked his head and looked at Riddick. 'Not really, no.'

'Really?'

'Yes. Your world is different. I don't think it's comparable. Apples and pears.'

'Explain what you mean.'

He shrugged. 'You're strong, I guess. To believe in your justice takes strength. But, in my world, it's different, Paul. In my world, that isn't justice. To let the bastard live is weakness. But it's apples and pears.'

'Ha,' Riddick said, 'I feel anything but strong. You know the prick asked me why he was still alive?'

Si smirked. 'Bastard always did have a knack at getting in people's heads. My advice to you is to push him right back out.'

Riddick finished his drink.

'So, now we've established that Haller didn't hurt my baby,' Si said, lining up a shot on another red. 'Then we're back with Harvey...' He potted the red. He lined up another. 'Incarcerated, not incarcerated, it won't matter.' He potted. 'Different world, remember?'

'Apples and pears,' Riddick said. 'But as I said to you yesterday, Si, I'm not inclined to think Harvey killed Tia.'

'Then, why's he *still* in custody? Seems not everyone is in agreement with you.'

'These things are complicated.'

Si lined up his final ball. The black. 'Seems straightforward to me.'

'You do realise what you're saying to me, here, Si? Do you think I won't report a potential crime?'

'You think I care at this point?'

Si potted the black. He stood up straight, cracked his neck and lay the pool cue on the table. He reached over and finished his own drink.

'Okay, I've been transparent with you. Your turn. Tell me about Rhys Hunt,' Riddick said.

Si froze and looked down into his empty glass. He didn't speak for a time.

'Talk to me,' Riddick said.

Si slammed his empty glass down. 'Where're you going with this?'

'Haller told me that you and Rhys were close.'

'Haller always likes to stir shit. I know Rhys, yes. He owns a chain of new cafés in Harrogate. My company did the building work for him. Hardly best friends with him though.'

'He referred to both you and Rhys as two tight foxes.'

Si snorted. 'He always thought he'd a way with words. The only thing he was ever good at was doing a number on people. And he's really done a number on you! You need to get yourself together. Why would Haller help you? You're the reason he's rotting in a cell.'

'When was the last time you saw Rhys?'

'You know, if I wasn't otherwise preoccupied, I'd be in mind to visit Haller... put a sock in his mouth myself. But I assure you Paul – you're barking up the wrong tree. I helped Rhys a couple of years back with these cafés, but that's as far as it goes.'

'Did Tia know Rhys?'

'Wrong. Tree. And a massive waste of time. You've got the man, Paul. Harvey. Nothing in what you're saying is convincing me otherwise.'

Riddick sighed. Was Haller playing him?

Si sat on his stool. 'You having another? My shout?'

'I should go and you should phone DCI Gardner back.'

'Why? She won't have any surprises.' Si looked around the pub and sighed. 'You know Tia loved dancing... she was good at it too. She went to dance school when she was three. I just keep thinking of her dancing. Don't get me wrong, seeing her dance, it's one of my fondest memories, but I can't seem to shake it from my mind. It's on a constant loop. God, she seems so alive when I... never mind.'

Riddick nodded. 'That's why you've chosen that memory. Your mind is trying desperately to keep her alive. For me, it's when I pushed my daughters on a roundabout. They went nuts for it. Kept screaming at me to go faster. On and on they went. I ended up hunched over a bench in the park, trying not to be sick. But I love that memory.'

'But my memory is... so... doesn't matter.'

'Painful?'

'Yes. I'm worried I'll end up resenting it.'

'You won't. The pain reminds you that you're alive *and* that they're still alive as long as you are. Eventually, you'll be able to control when and how you experience these memories... to a certain extent.'

'I don't think I ever want to forget.'

'You won't. I promise you, you won't.'

Several minutes elapsed in which both men remained silent, lost in their thoughts.

Riddick saw Haller's mouth moving. *Why am I still alive?* He saw the bastard sneering again.

'Si, I need to ask you for something.'

'Go on?'

As Riddick made his request, he felt his stomach and heart turn upside down. This was a road he'd never imagined being on. And now he was walking it.

Si listened to his request and then looked him in the eyes for a short time, before saying, 'The answer is yes. And don't punish yourself for this, Paul. Sometimes those apples and pears have more in common than they realise.'

26

Riddick contacted his third taxi of the day to take him to HQ. Once he was out of the vehicle and in the car park, he called Gardner. Despite her sweary insistences to the contrary, he held firm to his demand that she filled him in on her discoveries before he shared his own experiences.

Her findings rocked him.

The Aiden Poole angle was interesting, but it was the connection between Si Meadows and Harvey Henfrey which really hit home.

'Do you think Si was abused by this Miles Cook too?' Riddick asked.

'I don't know. I'd ask Si if I could find him.'

'Shit boss, if I'd known, I'd have asked him,' Riddick said, knowing he was about to feel the force of Gardner's wrath.

'You what?'

'Sorry. I've just been with him at the White Bull.'

Riddick let her vent over his maverick behaviour before he explained, in detail, his experience with Ronnie Haller at the prison. And Ronnie's claim that the Harrogate-based businessman

Rhys Hunt was close with Si, followed by Si's counterclaim over a pool table that Riddick had been sent on a wild goose chase by the convict.

Gardner was silent.

'You still there?' Riddick asked.

'Yes... I haven't dropped the phone just yet, but I'm close. Jesus, Paul! Ronnie Haller? Si Meadows? You really have been off gallivanting. You could have phoned me, or in the least, answered my calls.'

Riddick said he was sorry, but she could probably tell he wasn't really, and they ended their conversation with a promise that Riddick would contact her after he'd researched Rhys Hunt at HQ. Gardner, meanwhile, was going to head to the White Bull to catch Si before he left and confront him over that fateful day at the scout hut when he was only ten years old.

After ending his call with Gardner, Riddick's phone rang. He looked down to see that it was Paula Bolton.

Instinctively, his finger went for the answer button, almost forgetting her responsibility for his sudden fall from the wagon, but he managed to hold off at the last second.

'Screw you,' he said. *You don't get to explain why you sold me down the river.*

For good measure, he texted these exact words to her once the phone had stopped ringing.

* * *

It'd been a trying twenty-four hours, but the sight of those two old drunks in the White Bull had inspired him to fight his way back onto the wagon.

Two cups of coffee, black no sugar, seemed a good place to start.

As he drank his second cup, he thought:

Ronnie Haller.

Marianne Perse.

Both of these people turned Riddick's stomach. Both had already damaged his life irreparably but neither seemed to have lost the hunger to continue doing so.

'Over my dead body, I'll let either of you damage it any more,' he said out loud before wiring himself on a third cup of coffee to try and fend off the inebriation and cravings.

Then he spent over an hour on the computer.

Researching Rhys Hunt.

Rhys' similarities to Si were striking: working class boy, savvier than his peers, relied upon and trusted by top dogs such as Ronnie Haller. Both of their familiarities with the nuances of the street had accelerated their careers until they were the top dogs themselves. Si had assimilated the building trade in the local area by any means necessary, while Rhys had built his monopoly in wine bars and cafés, predominantly in Harrogate.

Rhys was younger than Si at forty-five and had no children. On the internet, Riddick viewed many photographs of Rhys and his wife, Lorraine, together. And, while Lorraine was pretty enough, she certainly wasn't the glamorous wife he'd expect a man of his criminal stature to have, especially one who went out of his way to have the sharpest suits and priciest haircuts.

He researched the building contracts that had been given to Si from Rhys' registered company. Riddick was no lawyer, but on the surface, it appeared legitimate. But it was always going to, wasn't it? These people weren't amateurs. Away from the official looking papers, heads will have been cracked and bribes would've been made.

So, what next?

Dragging Rhys Hunt in for questioning based on a loose comment from Haller would look desperate. And although he wasn't concerned about his own reputation, which would soon be in tatters again anyway, he didn't want to upset Gardner's investigation.

He didn't give up though and spent some time looking over the evidence they'd accrued so far on HOLMES 2, trying to find any possible links to Rhys Hunt. It was only when he decided to take another look at the footage from Tia Meadows' last night in the White Bull that the key Haller had slipped into this lock, finally turned.

Rhys Hunt had been there.

Heart rate accelerating, Riddick forwarded through the footage.

He shook his head in disbelief when he witnessed Rhys and Si playing pool together, a total of three times. They laughed, joked and bought each other drinks. On several occasions, they had arms around each other's backs like old friends.

Si, you're taking the complete piss! First, you neglect to mention your connection with our prime suspect Harvey Henfrey, and now you're blatantly lying about your relationship with this man.

Riddick shook his head in disgust. This footage had given Haller credibility. What were Rhys and Si up to together?

This wasn't the only element of the footage that caught Riddick's attention.

On three occasions, Tia Meadows walked over to Rhys' table to collect glasses. On each occasion, Rhys stopped whatever he was doing – whether that be talking, drinking or playing pool – to greet her warmly and talk *at* her. She never really entered into a conversation, she'd reserved that commitment solely for Aiden Poole, but she was clearly very familiar with Rhys. If anything though, she looked *very* uncomfortable and struggled to meet the older man's eyes.

Again, Riddick thought back to his conversation with Si. He'd said that he didn't think his daughter even knew Rhys.

It beggared belief!

Si Meadows was hampering the investigation into his own daughter's murder.

And for what? To protect Rhys? Protect some dodgy dealings? Wouldn't he be over this by now?

He phoned Gardner. 'Did you find Si?'

'No, he'd left the White Bull,' Gardner said. 'I'm on my way back to HQ. What did you find out about Rhys Hunt?'

He told her. 'So, we must go and see Rhys.'

'Yes.'

'I had trouble starting my car, so I got a taxi in.' He flinched as he lied. 'Can you pick me up in the car park? His place isn't far from here.'

27

Gardner waited in the car park at HQ for Riddick to climb in beside her. She was suspicious and couldn't help but eye him up and down, but to be fair, he didn't look pissed.

'I take it you booked your car in to be looked at?' Gardner asked.

Riddick nodded but avoided eye contact with her. 'Be a couple of days yet though. Forge Garage are snowed under. They'll come and tow it over as soon as they can.'

Why're you lying to me? She opened her mouth to voice her annoyance but then held back. If he was drinking, at least he wasn't drink-driving. It wouldn't be enough to save his career, but it might spare some lives and keep him out of jail. She inwardly sighed. 'Hunt's address?'

Riddick told her and she punched it into the satnav.

'You think we're onto something here then?' Gardner asked, driving out of the car park.

'Well, don't take my word for it; watch the video footage for yourself.'

'You're my deputy SIO, why wouldn't I take your word for it?'

'Because this has started from Ronnie Haller and you're dubious – it's written all over your face.'

Never mind Ronnie Haller; I'm dubious about your mental health, Paul. 'Rightly so, perhaps?'

He sighed. 'I guess. Yes. Because if anyone wants me walking into the eye of a shit storm, it'll be Haller.'

'Let me do all the walking with you from now on then,' Gardner said. 'So, I've got your back. I assume you know Si better than most after your tête-à-tête at the White Bull? As I can't ask him yet, want to hazard a guess as to why he'd keep his history with Harvey from us?'

'Where to start?' Riddick said. 'He's a successful and wealthy racketeer – he'll want to keep that moment of cowardice from public knowledge.'

'But he was *only* ten years old. Does it class as cowardice when you're that young?'

'Will he see it like that? No. He'll see it as weakness. Add in the fact that he had feelings, even at an early age, for someone of the same sex – not something he'll want to shout about.'

'So, this all comes down to testosterone and image?' Gardner asked.

'Wouldn't be the first time, would it?'

'To be honest, I'm surprised he hasn't just let it all out though. Si seemed deflated the other day when we saw him. He certainly looked as if he'd had enough. He confessed his sexuality to us, so why bother holding back on Harvey? I really don't think it serves any purpose for him. Si left Harvey to be abused by Miles. The CPS will love this. Harvey's motive is there. Plain as day. Revenge.'

'Unless,' Riddick said, his eyes widening, 'Si's biding his time? Keeping it secret in the hope that Harvey doesn't stay under lock and key and becomes vulnerable...'

'I don't follow...'

'I think Si is maybe eyeing up a different kind of justice.'

Gardner shook her head. 'Hasn't he got too much left to lose?'

'No,' Riddick said. 'He's already lost everything. Trust me, I know.'

'I guess you could be right.' Gardner sighed. 'Well, at least Harvey's safe still under lock and key, and is likely to stay there for the foreseeable anyway.'

Gardner indicated right and stopped at some traffic lights.

'You haven't said that much about Aiden Poole,' Riddick said.

'In the same way I don't fancy Harvey for her death, I also don't fancy Aiden. It's the way they both talk about her. They were completely in awe of her. It seems Tia had a knack of capturing people's hearts and souls.'

'Did you pick up on any possible motive there?'

'Aiden disliked Si, bitterly. He was an obstacle to their relationship, even if Si never actually found out about the two of them. But you'd go for the obstacle itself, surely, not the woman you adored.'

'Unless Si *did* find out?' Riddick said. 'Maybe Si threatened to end their relationship and, you know, he's untouchable? Maybe, Aiden thought, if I can't have her, no one can...'

Wouldn't be the first time I've come across that, Gardner thought. *But no.* Try as she might, she just couldn't reconcile herself with the idea of Harvey or Aiden being guilty. The dreamy looks on their faces while they spoke of Tia, the tone of adoration in every word they used about her, the despair they now felt... No, the guilt had to be elsewhere.

Or was she just hoping it was?

Was it just too tragic to consider someone with such love for another, using a belt on them before knocking the life out of them with a brick?

'But there's something going on with those travellers,' Gardner continued. 'And I don't just mean with Aiden. The one in charge,

Tommy Byrne, seems to have an agenda. I mean, I'm not surprised that they want to keep us out of the way – they would do at the best of times – but I do feel he's hiding something. Aiden was warned off Tia by Tommy because they knew Si Meadows would be a problem. However, he continued to see her. How did that slide? I reckon this six hundred pounds Tia withdrew from the cashpoint came into play. Did Tommy start to see Tia as a cash cow rather than a liability?'

'It's possible,' Riddick said and shrugged.

Gardner indicated to turn right. 'Almost there. You let me lead on this, remember?'

'Don't you always?'

'You told me you were worried about Haller setting you up, somehow. This interview needs to be as measured as we can get it.'

'I agree.'

* * *

Riddick regarded the intricately carved door handle depicting four barely clad women pushing a canoe down the stream and demonstrated his usual level of tolerance. 'What the bloody hell is wrong with the world?' He stepped to one side and gestured for Gardner to knock.

'It's art,' Gardner said, knocking.

'To me, it just looks pornographic.'

Gardner smiled, wondering what strange pornography Riddick was subjecting himself to, when a middle-aged woman with long, curly brown hair opened the door. She wore no make-up and her tie-dye dress had seen better days. She was a larger woman, but it clearly wasn't fat on her. She looked very well built and muscular.

After confirming she was Lorraine Hunt, and showing her identification, Gardner asked if Rhys was home.

'Yes. Please come in.'

She led them into an impressive lounge which had its own bar and looked out on a garden so impressive you could hire it out for small weddings. While Lorraine left the lounge to get her husband, Gardner looked at Riddick, and said, 'Si and Rhys have similar tastes in interior design.'

'Good news,' Riddick said. 'In the future when they share a cell, they won't have to argue over décor.'

She watched Riddick walk over to the mantlepiece. 'Would you look at that!'

Gardner came alongside him. There was a picture of a much younger Lorraine holding a trophy. She was in a bikini – her body was even larger than it was now. The definition in her muscles was accentuated by the oil on her skin.

'A bodybuilder,' Riddick said.

'Long time ago now that,' Lorraine said from behind them.

'Impressive.' Gardner turned. 'Have you won many competitions?'

'A couple when I was younger.' She flexed a bicep. 'But age and responsibilities catch up with us all.'

Gardner regarded her impressive bicep. 'Looks like you still have it to me.'

'I try my best... when I can.'

Riddick turned from the picture. He suddenly looked impatient. 'Is Rhys coming down?'

'I called up to him. He's on a business call. He won't be long.' She moved quickly, gracefully, and she seemed to have a permanent grin on her face as if she was on recreational drugs. She sat on the same sofa as Gardner and Riddick, alongside them. Gardner looked down; she was bare-footed and had a large tattoo of an eagle on her ankle.

'He's always working, you know. There was a time – long ago, before the business, we had a lot of fun...' She patted Gardner's leg. She also continued to smile despite the sad tone in her voice.

Suddenly feeling uneasy over Lorraine's odd behaviour, Gardner returned the smile. 'Do you think he'll be long? We're short on time.'

'No, no. He won't be a moment, I promise,' Lorraine said, reaching under the coffee table.

Lorraine pulled out a photo album and opened it on the table. 'Festivals,' she said. 'We lived for them. Mags, next door, she lived for Caribbean holidays. Not us. Mud and music, that's what juiced us... once upon a time.'

She pointed out photographs of herself and Rhys when they were barely out of their teens. In some photographs, they were covered in mud. In others, they lounged in the sun with plastic beer glasses in hand, smoking dubious looking roll-ups.

'Glastonbury, Reading, Donnington... We went to them all.'

'Looks nice,' Gardner said, glancing to her right at Riddick, who couldn't look any less interested.

Lorraine pointed at a photograph of a flattened tent. Three young adults were lying around it. Lorraine wasn't one of them and Gardner assumed she must have been the photographer.

'The wind,' Lorraine said. 'That night we had to sleep under the stars.'

'Sounds romantic,' Riddick said.

His threshold has been breached already. Gardner glared at him.

He nodded to show he'd reined himself back in.

Gardner turned back. She considered probing the dreamy wife over Rhys' connection to Si but decided that it was best to leave her to her nostalgia rather than create any tension before her husband's arrival.

'Wait. Can I see that please?' Riddick asked.

'Of course,' Lorraine said, passing the photo album over Gardner's lap.

Gardner turned and watched her colleague's eyes widen as he looked at the spliff-smoking teens. He prodded one of them. 'That's Si Meadows, isn't it?'

Gardner looked. Riddick was right. Younger, waif-like, but most certainly Si.

Lorraine nodded. 'Yes, and Priscilla.'

Priscilla. His ex-wife. The one who'd eloped to Greece when Tia was seven. She was still to be located.

Gardner and Riddick exchanged a glance, before Riddick asked, 'How close were you four?'

'Best friends.'

'Really?' Riddick said. 'Best friends?'

Gardner heard the anger in her deputy SIO's tone of voice. He clearly wasn't best pleased with Si's continual deception.

'Were,' Lorraine said. 'This was a long time ago. Since their marriage broke down, I don't have time for Si any more. An arrogant man!'

'And Rhys – does he have time for him any more?' Gardner asked.

Lorraine shrugged. 'You'll have to ask him.'

'Do you know where Priscilla is?' Gardner asked.

'Sorry, I don't. She went such a long time ago. She met someone in Greece last I heard. She couldn't live with Si any longer. That man was so controlling. Such a sad story. That poor girl, Tia. We still send her gifts.'

'Gifts?' Riddick said. Now he sounded surprised rather than angry.

'You know that we're her godparents, don't you?' Lorraine asked.

Gardner widened her eyes. 'No, we didn't.' Gardner looked at

Riddick and then back at Lorraine. 'You are aware... aren't you, Mrs Hunt?'

'Aware of what?'

'Of what happened to Tia?'

At first, she looked confused as if she didn't, but then her face darkened as if she suddenly remembered. 'Yes. God. How horrible. Such a loss.' A tear formed in her eye.

This woman isn't well.

Gardner looked at Riddick. His expression confirmed that he was having similar thoughts. She was glad he hadn't verbalised these thoughts though because she could guarantee that he'd have delivered them without much, if any, tact.

'I can only imagine the pain her parents feel,' Lorraine said. She put her hand to her mouth. 'Does Priscilla know?'

Not unless she reads the British press in Greece, Gardner thought.

'Imagine whose pain?' a man asked from the doorway.

'Tia's parents,' Lorraine said. 'Losing a daughter.'

Rhys was a good-looking man and was content to wear his money and wear it well. Styled, coifed hair; a sharp suit; glowing cufflinks, and the centrepiece – the polished Rolex. 'Why would I want to imagine it? It's horrible.' He eyed up Gardner and then Riddick. He kept his eyes on Riddick. 'You need to lock that recluse up for the rest of his life.'

'I'm DI Paul Riddick. Sorry, but could you tell me who you're referring to?'

Rhys guffawed. 'Don't play silly beggars, DI. You know full well who I'm referring to. Harvey Henfrey. It's all over the bloody papers.'

'Mr Hunt... I'm DCI Emma Gardner.' She waited until he managed to force his eyes back on to her. *Yes. I'm in charge. A woman. Get over yourself.* 'Just because he's in custody, doesn't mean he's guilty.'

'She was found on his bloody doorstep!'

Gardner inwardly cursed the press. Journalists such as Marianne Perse really did make their jobs more difficult.

'And according to the papers, it's open and closed,' Rhys said. 'So why are you here?'

'Forget the papers, Mr Hunt,' Riddick said. 'Just because something claims to be non-fiction, doesn't always make it so. So, let's get back to reality.'

Not now, tiger, Gardner thought. *Let's start smoothly.*

Rhys approached his bar, talking over his shoulder at them. 'Well, if what I'm saying is wrong, then what *everyone* is saying is wrong. Listen, she was our goddaughter, we're devastated. How can we help? If we can help, we will do.'

'Could you please come and sit then?' Gardner said.

'Yes... in a moment.' He continued his journey to the bar.

Her status meant nothing to a man of his wealth.

'We haven't the time for this, Mr Hunt,' Riddick said.

He stopped and turned at Riddick's command.

Not her status then. He was just another misogynistic prick in a long line of many.

'Because,' Gardner said, losing patience and cutting in before Riddick, 'as is the case in many investigations of this nature, there're *other* persons of interest.'

His flinch suggested he detected her accusatory tone. 'Okay. Can I at least pour myself a drink? Please?'

Gardner took a deep breath and nodded. At least it might settle the arrogant fool down a bit.

He poured himself a large glass of Scotch at his bar. 'Well, ask away.'

'When did you last see Tia Meadows?' Gardner asked.

'I can't remember. I may have bumped into her in town several months—'

'Listen, let's speed this up,' Riddick said. The impatience and frustration in his voice was evident. 'You saw her the night she died, in the White Bull. We've got the footage. I'm not going to play any more of these games, Mr Hunt. It seems to me that there's a growing number of people involved in this investigation who are vastly underestimating our abilities—'

Gardner reached behind herself and tapped Riddick's leg.

'So, let's try again, Mr Hunt,' Riddick continued, softening his voice. 'What did you talk about at the White Bull?'

Rhys put his glass down and sighed. 'Something and nothing. She was my goddaughter. I was pleased to see her, and I told her so. Honestly, before then, it'd been a while. I couldn't even tell you how long. Half a year? More maybe? I sent her gifts on her birthday several months back.'

'But you're tight with her father, Si Meadows?' Riddick asked.

'Once upon a time, yes.'

'No... I think you're still tight,' Riddick said.

Rhys took a large mouthful of his Scotch. 'You do, do you? Who told you that?'

'I've seen the footage remember.'

'Of two old friends having a drink and reminiscing? It's not a regular occurrence. We're as far from tight as can be.'

'Come on, Rhys,' Lorraine said. 'You know that's not true. We should try and help here.'

Rhys' eyes widened. He stared at her. His mouth hung open slightly.

'Mrs Hunt,' Gardner said, turning to Lorraine, 'could you explain what you mean—'

'No,' Rhys said. 'She can't. In fact, I'd prefer it if she left the room. Unless you suspect her of something. Do you?' He paused. 'No... didn't think so. Listen, I'll tell you this. Whatever my wife said before I came in the room, and whatever she says now, means very little. I'd disregard it.'

Gardner looked at Lorraine. She was staring ahead, grinning.

Rhys said, 'She's under the doctor's care... has been for a while now.'

Lorraine narrowed her eyes but was still smiling.

'It's been a hard couple of months,' Rhys said, nodding. 'With medication changes and the like—'

'I hate you,' Lorraine said, shaking her head.

'Lots of side effects too,' Rhys finished.

Lorraine touched the table and looked between Gardner and Riddick. She'd finally stopped smiling. 'There was a time, like I said, long ago. We were happy.' She stood. 'Long, long ago.'

She reached down and squeezed Gardner's shoulder. 'I hope you find whoever did this. For Tia.' She then left the room.

Gardner looked at Rhys, horrified that he had spoken so callously about his wife. All was not well in this marriage, and here was a bastard if she'd ever met one.

Rhys shrugged. 'She'll get over it. One of the side effects. She forgets our conversations.'

'I'd say that was a very fortunate side effect,' Riddick said.

'You're quite smug, you know that,' Rhys said, replying to Riddick with a caustic tone. 'You know she's a sick woman? Do you have any idea what I've had to suffer?'

You? Gardner thought. *What about her?*

Riddick said, 'You may want to paint this picture of you and Si as distant acquaintances and convince us that your wife is suffering delusions of some kind, but I've just seen photographic evidence in her photo album that you four made the happiest double daters since Abba. So, before I give up doing this the gentle way, Mr Hunt, and escort you down to the station for a formal interview, making sure I make enough of a fuss while doing so to get Mags' tongue wagging next door, can you please tell us what is going on between you and Si Meadows?'

Direct, Gardner thought. *As he always is. This could go one of two ways... Thrown out, door slammed in face and solicitor called... Or...*

'Okay.' He sighed. 'We're buddies. Always have been, always will be. So what?'

The second way then, Gardner thought. *Thank Christ.*

'Doesn't mean much in this situation anyway,' Rhys continued, approaching the sofa without the swagger in which he'd approached the bar. He sighed before he sat, swirling his drink around his glass.

'Why such a song and dance then?' Riddick asked.

'Because I sometimes employ his services. It's in our best interest to present a purely professional relationship. Appearances matter in my line of work.'

'It didn't look like you were keeping your relationship too quiet the night Tia died,' Gardner said.

Rhys shrugged. 'A few drinks and you throw caution to the wind – you know how it is. Besides, it's the White Bull. No one of any relevance drinks in there. Mainly travellers and old drunks.'

'So, you're admitting that your relationship with Si Meadows would get tongues wagging? What have you two been up to exactly?' Gardner said.

'Jesus.' Rhys shrugged. 'Honestly, it's not like that. It's as I said. We just want to keep up the pretence that our relationship is purely professional. Do I need a solicitor?'

'I think you might do,' Riddick said.

Rhys swore under his breath. 'Listen, you're here about something completely unrelated. Tia's death has nothing to do with our friendship. Nothing at all.'

'Okay,' Riddick said. 'Be *completely* transparent about your relationship with Si, beyond this idea of it being purely professional. Then, we can put a line through it.'

Rhys sighed and began. He discussed their youth together. At Riddick's prompting, he also mentioned their brief time 'working' for Ronnie Haller on 'odd jobs' which were 'all above board'. Gardner noticed Riddick gritting his teeth and tapping his foot impatiently during this part.

Eventually, Rhys reached Si and Priscilla's messy divorce about thirteen years back, and the fact that Lorraine and Si's friendship had crumbled as a result. 'But, yes, I stayed in touch with Si. We sent gifts to Tia, as I've explained, but apart from the odd drink at the White Bull when I saw her – there was minimal contact. And the appearance of a professional relationship with Si is crucial. You must understand how people think in our world. It's easier for Hunts Ltd if other businesses don't believe I give any preferential treatment to Si's companies. I've to present myself as unbiased when offering contracts, or you can soon start to find yourself very alone. As good as me and Si have been for each other, you don't want to close all your other avenues, so I share the wealth out a little, and dispel any notion of favouritism. One day we might not have each other any more – what then? We present vulnerability and then... well, that could be dangerous.'

'You said minimal contact with Tia,' Riddick probed. 'Yet you looked very happy on that footage when you saw her... and she looked rather uncomfortable. What should I read into that?'

Rhys screwed up his face. 'I don't know what you mean. I was pleased to see her. As for her, well, young people can be like that, sometimes. Shy around their elders. I really don't know where you're heading with all this.'

Gardner made notes. She glanced over at Riddick. He didn't look convinced by Rhys' claim – mind you, Riddick never looked convinced by anything.

'What did you give her for her birthday?' Riddick asked.

Rhys shook his head. 'Are you serious, DI?'

'Of course. Why wouldn't I be?'

'Money... hundred quid or so I think. To treat herself.'

'I'd be much happier to see someone if they gave me a hundred quid!' Riddick said.

Rhys rolled his eyes. 'You do know her father is worth a packet? I doubt a hundred pound would've impressed her all that much.'

'Let's return to the night in question,' Gardner said. 'Where did you go after the White Bull?'

'Home, of course. I had Lorraine pick me up. She'll confirm it for you.'

'Lorraine? Isn't she under the care of a doctor and experiencing a change in medication?' Riddick asked.

Rhys sneered. 'She can still drive; probably shouldn't like, but hey, I'm not the doctor.'

'Still, probably safer to get a taxi?' Riddick said.

'I tried to phone one, but they were all tied up in Harrogate,' Rhys said.

Bollocks, Gardner thought. *I'm sure the best tipper in town wouldn't struggle with a taxi.*

Gardner noticed that Riddick had taken his phone out of his pocket and was looking at the screen. When she tried to see what he was doing, he held it away from her. 'If you'll excuse me for one moment,' Riddick said. 'I just have to make a call.'

'Now?' Gardner asked.

'Yes, I'll explain in a moment. It may be relevant.'

He exited the room.

'He's got a real chip on his shoulder that one,' Rhys said.

To be fair, the best officers usually do. 'He doesn't like obstruction of justice, Mr Hunt. He doesn't feel that some of our witnesses, present company included, have been as transparent as they could have been considering the traumatic nature of this case.'

'I've nothing for you regarding what happened to Tia.' He put his hand on his chest. 'I assure you. Yes, she meant the world to me, I won't deny it, but I rarely actually saw her. Myself and her father thought it was better that way.' There was the muffled ring of a mobile phone. 'I'm sorry.' He reached into his inside suit pocket and pulled out his phone. Gardner noticed that the ringing remained muffled, despite the phone being removed from the pocket.

Rhys face paled as he acknowledged the inactive phone in his hand.

'You've another phone, Mr Hunt?'

He looked up at her. 'Yes.'

He reached into the other jacket pocket and hoisted a second mobile phone out – this time the ringing became clearer.

'If you need to take that, we can wait,' Gardner said.

'No need, I'll get to it later.' He killed the call.

'How many phones do you have, Mr Hunt?' Gardner asked.

He glared up at her. 'How many do you have? Isn't it common to have a personal one, and a work one?'

Gardner nodded. 'So, two then?'

'Yes,' Rhys said. The phone started to ring again. 'Shit.' He killed the call again.

'Maybe it's important?' Gardner said. 'Please feel free to answer.'

'No, it's okay...' The phone rang a third time. 'Bloody hell.'

'Answer the phone, please,' Riddick said from the doorway.

'No, I, it really isn't necessary,' Rhys said, ending the call.

Riddick walked into the room, pressing something on his own phone.

Gardner watched Rhys' finger trace the side of the phone,

hunting the power button. His phone rang again just before he cut the power.

Silence.

Rhys was looking down, shaking his head.

'It's strange,' Riddick said. 'Every time I call this unregistered number we found on Tia's phone log, your phone seems to ring.'

Paler than ever, Rhys slipped the phone back in his pocket.

'I think it may be your number?' Riddick asked.

'I want a solicitor.'

'Considering you rarely saw Tia,' Gardner said. 'You certainly spoke to her a lot. Over ten times this month alone according to that log.'

'I'm not saying anything else until I have a solicitor!'

'Could you ask him to meet you at the station?' Gardner said. 'I think it's best we get you on record.'

28

After interviewing Rhys Hunt in the presence of his solicitor, Gardner and Riddick returned to run the briefing and feedback to their team.

Gardner felt frayed and, try as she might, she just couldn't stop her mind flitting back to the moment she saw Jack and Rose at the rugby club, staring into the travellers' campsite.

An innocent walk, perhaps? An innocent child asking her father why there were so many caravans in one area? Or was something more sinister at play here? Had Jack been following her, and if so, why?

Realising that she had the eyes of many an eager officer on her, and she was more distracted than a child in an amusement arcade, she handed the reins over to Riddick. He did a stellar job of recapping through the growing list of suspects, which had, after the previous couple of hours, grown to five.

'Our main boy, Harvey,' Riddick said, tapping the picture of the recluse that lived by the lake. He ran through everything they had on him, before concluding with motive. 'He could have an axe to grind against Si Meadows after he abandoned him to the paedophile, Miles Cook, when they were children.'

O'Brien said, 'A long time ago; why wait until now?'

'Still solid motive though,' Rice said. 'And we've the evidence. Tia's presence in his rotten rat hole? The purse? But hey, who am I to complain.' He folded his arms. 'I need the overtime.'

'No location on Miles Cook either,' Riddick said. 'He left Knaresborough following the trial and was reported missing in Blackburn, Lancashire, over twenty years ago. He's now presumed dead.'

'No great loss,' Rice said.

Riddick nodded and then summarised Tia's father before O'Brien added, 'He's a repressed homosexual. And image is everything to a man like Si. He's no stranger to violence and could do anything to protect his reputation.'

'In the Knaresborian underworld?' Rice asked, his words laced with sarcasm.

Riddick hit back, 'Have you forgotten Anders? Neil Taylor? Come on, Phil. You know the place is worse than many realise.'

Rice shrugged. 'Chancers! Hardly a dark underbelly.'

The dismissive sarcasm that was signature Phil Rice snapped Gardner from a distractable mind. Rather than admonish the irritating DS, she pointed at the next suspect along. 'Tommy Byrne, leader of the traveller camp.' She talked through what she knew about him, which she realised was very little. He'd be getting a more thorough grilling first thing tomorrow. 'He's obnoxious. He didn't want Tia Meadows going there because he was concerned about Si making problems for their camp.' She looked at Rice as she said the next part. 'Quite a fearsome reputation for a *chancer*? This has made me wonder about the six hundred pounds Tia withdrew over those three days. Was Tommy paid off? Or, worse still, maybe Tommy just took Tia out of the picture completely before her father could find out?'

Finding her focus and confidence again, Gardner continued with her recap of Aiden Poole. 'Infatuated is an understatement, but love is a rollercoaster, as we all know, and so we need to probe further.'

'Maybe Tia called it off with him?' Barnett suggested. 'Rejection is a powerful trigger.'

'I agree, which is why I need a bag load of sensitivity... so I've tasked you with taking another run at him in the morning, Ray.'

'Send in the gentle giant,' O'Brien said and grinned.

'I'm not that gentle.' Barnett scowled.

O'Brien reached up and stroked his shaved head. 'There, there, putty cat.'

Barnett shook his head to knock off O'Brien's hand and then stared ahead with a confused look on his face, as if trying to determine if this was complimentary or not.

The team were yet to hear about the final person of interest, Tia's godfather, Rhys Hunt. Gardner handed the floor back to Riddick for this one. He left out the part involving his visit to Haller.

'Another immoral businessman,' Barnett said.

'Capitalism baby,' Rice said. 'It's an aphrodisiac for rats. Makes them breed.'

Gardner regarded him. *Do you have a controversial view on absolutely everything, Phil?*

'We brought him in and took a statement,' Riddick continued, shrugging off Rice. 'But we didn't hold him – regular phone calls with your goddaughter aren't an offence.'

O'Brien said, 'How about a secret phone and the constant lies about how much contact he had with her?'

'It's infuriating and suspicious, but it isn't getting him jail time. However, he just became a major person of interest in my eyes.'

Rice said, 'You reckon? Ten phone calls in the last week? I mean, what was his excuse?'

'They got on like a house on fire,' Riddick grunted. 'Although it certainly didn't look that way on the footage from the White Bull.'

'How frequent were the phone calls before that?' O'Brien asked.

'They were there. But far more sporadic. They go back about a year, one or two a week, and then disappear completely prior to last summer. They peaked over the last seven days.'

'He was shagging her,' Rice said. 'She broke it off and then he hounded her, hence her awkward response in the White Bull.'

'His goddaughter?' Barnett said. 'That's disgusting.'

'Is it? They're not related,' Rice said.

'I'm sure the church would disagree,' Barnett said. 'To them, it would be an abomination.'

'Do you go to church?' Rice asked.

'No,' Barnett said. 'But it's still disgusting. He's in a position of responsibility.'

'He's not a teacher,' Rice said.

'Let's run it past Si and see if he shares your views,' Barnett said.

'Let's not,' Gardner said. 'However, there may be something in what Phil just said. Rightly, or wrongly, this relationship may have happened. And let's not forget Tia's pregnancy. The obvious father is Aiden, but now potentially we have Rhys. And if it's Rhys, then we have motive right there. Keeping the truth from Si. I've requested DNA tests on the baby so we can find out who the father is. Hopefully, the results will be with us tomorrow.'

Inevitably, anchoring their discussion with the five suspects brought a raft of hypotheses and suggestions. The conversation continued, unabated, for a significant length of time. Gardner welcomed the distraction from the concern over her brother's presence at the rugby field, but there was a pulsing in her temple which quickly became more painful under the fast, loud voices.

When she did call time on it, she indicated tomorrow's assignments pinned to the board with a word of warning. While they were all sleeping, she'd likely be dwelling on Operation Bright Day into the early hours of the morning, and the tasks were subject to change. However, a potential head start was there if anyone wanted it.

After the room had cleared out, she approached Riddick. She really wanted someone to talk to about everything weighing on her mind but knew that Riddick himself was saddled with something at the moment. 'Good job,' she said.

'Might be my last one,' Riddick said.

'I don't follow.'

He told her about Paula's betrayal and Marianne's impending article.

So, Gardner thought, *that's what Marianne had meant that morning by the lake.*

Things are going to get very warm around him.

He could do with friends.

This wasn't good. Not at all. Especially in the middle of a murder investigation. However, she needed to steady Riddick. 'Nothing we can't handle.'

'I'm going to stop by Marsh's office on the way back to give her the good news,' Riddick said.

'You want me to come with you?'

'A bodyguard? Nice, but no. This is my music. I'll face it alone.'

'Marsh will be supportive.'

'Like last time?'

'This is different. You've done nothing wrong.'

'Drinking on the job?'

'It's Paula's word against yours.'

'Everyone knows it's true... you know it's true.'

Gardner sighed. She thought they were past this. She didn't

want to lose Riddick. Not only was he a good officer with razor-sharp instincts, but she was... well... fond of him. But there were skeletons in this boy's closet, and if she'd discovered anything in her career, it was that skeletons always had a habit of becoming quite animated at the worst possible times.

29

Si parked Larry's Lexus in the covered car park.

His number two had hated handing over the keys to his new pride and joy. But needs must. Si wanted to be off the radar for a time.

He turned the radio on, but then turned it immediately off. Music, since Tia's death, had become irritating.

His eyes panned over the whisky bottle in the passenger footwell.

Empty. Whatever. Good.

He needed some control back for the next step.

But, as the alcohol wore off, the burning in his chest made a sudden return.

He focused on it, tried to understand it. Scalding anger? Aching loss? Crushing despair? A combination of all three?

Si looked at the palm of his hand, the Devil's hand, and then closed his eyes...

Tia clutched her cheek and hissed at him. 'Animal! Is this why Mum left?'

He raised his hand again. 'How long have you been seeing the old bastard by the lake?'

'Long enough to know what happened.'

He slapped her with the back of his hand this time, across the other cheek. 'How could you?'

She shielded her face. 'Stop, Dad. Please, I'm pregnant...'

He came back to the car park. This had been the moment. When the burning sensation in his chest had begun. Not *after* her death. But in that moment. The scalding anger. The aching loss. The crushing despair. *Then.* Before her death.

Again, he went back into the memory...

He stumbled backwards and slumped down onto the sofa. 'Is it his? Harvey's? Was this his twisted idea of revenge? Did he rape you? God... did you let him?'

Tia stormed out of the house.

Back in the car park now, Si realised how deranged he must have seemed to his precious daughter.

And the worst of it all: he still hadn't got the answer to his questions.

He reached over to the passenger seat for his wheel brace and then exited the Lexus.

He left the covered car park and looked up at his destination. The Harrogate District Hospital beneath a crimson sky.

Red sky at night.

He started forward.

30

As Gardner drove into her housing estate, she recalled the words of Mrs Halliwell, one of her more interesting teachers. 'When the sun is low in a sky loaded with dust and moisture particles, only the longer wavelengths make it through, while the shorter ones, blue, for example, are scattered. What's the longest wavelength in the colour spectrum? Emma?'

'Red.'

The sunset was staggering.

Gardner thought of a split blood orange.

This in turn made her think of the Merlot in her kitchen as she turned onto her street.

Her breath caught in her throat. There was a small crowd of neighbours around her home.

Her front door was open; two people were scrapping in her garden.

She slammed the brakes and, without bothering to kill the engine, pounced from her vehicle. She slipped past several neighbours who had phones pinned to their ears.

The scrap was now an assault.

Her brother was straddling someone and raining blows down on their face. She squinted, trying to see who it—

Tommy Byrne!

She couldn't see his face clearly, due to the pummelling, but she could see his mohawk.

The blow from Jack's right fist came at a steady tempo and consistent speed, and looked more like someone using a bicycle pump than delivering a beating.

'What the hell is going on?' she shouted, looking around the crowd. 'He's going to kill him.' She charged onto the grass. 'For God's sake, help!'

She put her arm around her brother's neck and pulled him backwards. Unfortunately, it was like pulling on a pile of cemented bricks. 'Jack... Stop...'

Her earlier plea had hooked a neighbour, so when she yanked again, someone pulled with her. Jack came off his victim and hit the ground.

'Shit,' Gardner said.

Tommy's face looked broken; blood bubbled from his mouth.

But he's breathing... Thank Christ, he's breathing...

She glared at Jack, who was now sitting up and staring off into space. His expression was blank. She felt the cold sting of the stone as it bit into her head at Malcolm's Maze of Mirrors when she was a child—

Rose?

She looked up at her open doorway. 'Where's Rose?' she shouted at her brother.

No reply. His eyes didn't move. He remained ice cold.

She gave the neighbour who'd helped her a swift, grateful nod, and then swung around to the crowd. Not all of them would know her. 'I'm DCI Emma Gardner. We need an ambulance.'

'No,' Tommy said.

Gardner turned back.

He was sitting up now. His mohawk was slanted one way, his nose the other. 'No, just help me up.'

The neighbour who'd helped with Jack proffered a hand. Tommy took it and, groaning and wincing, managed to get himself to his feet.

Tommy swayed. 'I need to go.'

'No, you don't, Tommy,' Gardner said. 'What're you doing at my home?'

'Ask him.' Tommy nodded at Jack and spat blood on the floor. He swayed some more before turning.

'You're not going anywhere,' Gardner said.

Tommy put his middle finger up.

She moved to stop him, but a sudden scream froze her.

Rose!

She spun in the direction of her open front door.

To the soundtrack of the sirens from the nearby emergency services, she sprinted into her home. 'Rose?'

There was no sign of her downstairs, and Gardner's anxiety levels intensified when she was unable to find her upstairs either.

She stood on the landing. 'Rose? Where are you?' She listened, hearing little over her thumping heart.

Make a noise, Rose! Show me where you are...

She went back into the guest bedroom, where Rose slept. The sheets were cast aside. Apart from that, nothing. 'Rose?'

She dropped down to her knees.

The young girl was under the bed, on her back, with her hands pinned over her ears. *Thank God.*

'It's Auntie Emma. Come to me.' She offered a hand to Rose.

At first, Rose looked hesitant. *She's terrified.*

'Please,' Gardner said. 'Let me help you.'

Rose took her outstretched hand and Gardner helped her

wriggle out. Then, in the corner of the guest room, Gardner clutched her crying niece to her chest.

Outside, she could hear more commotion. The emergency services were here.

Rose said, 'I had a bad dream. I'm sorry.'

The scream?

'Then, when I woke up, there was so much noise.'

'It's fine,' Gardner said, holding her niece close. 'Everything's fine.'

When Rose had settled, Gardner lay her on the bed. 'Don't worry, Rose.' She kissed her on her forehead. 'I'll make everything right.'

If it's the last thing I do.

Gardner placed Rose's favourite teddy bear, a squashed-up dog aptly named Pug, in her arms and told her to hang tight while she ended the commotion outside.

She sprinted down the stairs. Her brother needed to be taken into custody. Tommy, to the hospital.

When she got outside, two responding officers stood talking to the neighbours.

She ran over to them. 'Do you have him?'

A young, uniformed male turned. 'Who?'

Shit. 'Jack. My brother. He was assaulting someone on the lawn.'

'I'm afraid not. He ran, apparently,' the officer said.

She looked at the group of neighbours that must have informed him of this. She almost said: *no one thought to stop him?* but held back. She shouldn't expect a civilian to wrestle down a dangerous man like her brother.

A paramedic was standing by an empty ambulance, looking confused.

'Bloody hell,' Gardner said. 'Tommy left too? He was a mess!'

She looked at several of her neighbours, who either avoided eye contact or shrugged.

She introduced herself to the uniforms. 'You need to find Jack Moss and take him into custody. He's a dangerous man. And get the paramedics to the travellers' site up at the rugby field to treat a man called Tommy Byrne. He was barely walking. Then, let me know, so I can talk to him.'

Shaking her head, she stared up into the red sky, thinking about those shorter wavelengths of the colour spectrum being scattered.

It was just like life in general really. At any second, everything we thought was in place could just be scattered.

Everywhere.

31

To Riddick, the sky looked like it was on fire.

Just like his renewed war against alcohol.

He lowered the kitchen blind and went back to sit at the kitchen table where the tequila awaited him.

Riddick looked at the phone number Si had scribbled on the back of a beer mat in the White Bull.

He heard Haller's voice. *Why am I still alive?*

'I don't know,' Riddick said.

They were a burden. They saddled you. You're like me, son. You can't handle baggage. That's why you let me live. Gratitude.

'Not true.'

I gave you freedom. I lifted the pressure off you. Having to worry if you lived or died, leaving them alone to fend for themselves.

'I loved them. You ripped out my soul.'

It was my mistake. If I'd have known that I was doing you a fav—

Riddick slammed his hands down on the table, cutting off the voice. He looked at the bottle of tequila and sighed. *What's the point?* It didn't stop the torment.

Nothing stopped the torment.

He stood up and walked over to the kitchen unit where he'd left the impending article: 'Corruption: Back from the Dead'. Then he looked at the pay-as-you-go phone that he'd purchased earlier. He'd already unwrapped and charged it.

From behind him, he heard the clicking of knitting needles. He turned to look at Rachel sitting at the head of the kitchen table.

'No,' he said. 'No, I didn't mean for this. For you—'

'To come back again?' Rachel said with a raised eyebrow. She nodded at the bunny rabbit she was knitting. 'Who's going to finish this for Louise?'

'You already made one for our niece; she'll be fine.' He shook his head. 'This isn't right. I'm sorry. I put this behind us. I let you rest. I moved on.'

She nodded at the beer mat with the phone number on it. 'Is this moving on?'

Riddick rubbed his stubble. 'I tried, Rachel, I really did.'

She fixed him with a stare.

With the new pay-as-you-go phone, he sat back at the table. 'I guess I still need you.'

'You *think* you still need me, Paul. But do you? You stopped Anders, remember? And now you've got Emma to help you. And that psychiatrist, Doctor—'

'I thought all of that was enough, but maybe I was wrong...'

'Why? Because someone wants to drag your name through the mud again? You've beaten that before; you can beat it again.'

'Not just because of the article.'

Haller's rotting teeth. His decaying face. *Why am I still alive?*

'He's a dead man behind bars. His life is over. Don't let him make you believe otherwise. Let him rot. Let him decay. You have justice.'

'Do I? I just don't feel it, you know. At least, I don't *think* I feel it.'

He rubbed his eyes. 'God, it's so confusing. I don't know what I want.'

'Closure?'

He looked up at Rachel. 'Yes, that's it. Closure.'

'But will you ever get it? Does it matter what you do?'

Riddick's hand settled on the new phone. 'But I must try. I must keep trying.'

'I never told you to stop trying, Paul, but searching for something that isn't there *isn't* trying. It's futile.'

Riddick looked up at his dead wife with tears in his eyes. 'I know what you're doing. I know why you're here. My doctor explained it.'

'That I'm a coping mechanism? That I'm not really here? That you're talking to yourself?' Rachel asked, continuing to knit.

'Kind of,' Riddick said. 'You're also my voice of reason.'

'Am I now?' Rachel said, smiling. 'I like that. Well, if that's the case, Paul Riddick, listen to reason and do not use that phone.'

Riddick picked up the phone and turned it on.

'What're you doing, Paul?'

He dialled the number Si had given to him.

He placed the phone to his ear and listened to the ring. He wiped tears away with the back of his hand. 'I've had enough of reason. It doesn't work.'

After he'd made the call, he smashed the phone and its SIM to pieces. He then drank from the tequila bottle, in silence, next to empty chairs.

Rachel and his daughters were gone and never coming back.

Like himself.

Gone and never coming back.

32

The only thing keeping Si from the door of the Harrogate District Hospital was sheer willpower. Marching inside with a wheel brace concealed beneath his jacket was doomed to failure. Harvey would be under the watchful eye of the police.

It was clear that adrenaline combined with a high-blood alcohol level had brought Si on a futile journey. He stood there while the red sky quickly blackened and the only light source became the windows of the hospital, the headlights of the readied ambulances parked near A&E, and the glowing cigarettes of patients who occupied the benches out front.

Fighting the urge to embark on a suicide mission with every ounce of his being was tiring. He took a seat on a bench beside a smoking patient, keeping his wheel brace concealed, and sighed.

'Bad news?' the smoking man asked.

Si didn't respond.

'If it's any consolation, eventually, the bad news becomes water off a duck's back. They always say no news is good news, but I've my own saying – lots of bad news is just *meh*.' The man started to cough. After it subsided, he said, 'Would you like a fag?'

In no mood for this, Si lifted his face from his hands and fixed the emaciated old man with a stare. 'Is that a good idea? It's not done you any favours, has it?'

The old man coughed again, smirked, and continued to smoke.

When it became clear that the man did not want to chat any more, Si felt a flicker of pity. 'Nothing personal. I've just run out of patience.'

'Meh to that as well! Who really has time for patience? I certainly don't. Just do what you feel.'

'That's kind of what brought me here,' Si said. 'Doing what I feel.'

The man winced as he rose to his feet. He held his back as he did so. 'Fifty cigarettes a day since I was fifteen. It started in my back though. Not my lungs. Smoking's not to blame.'

Si sighed. 'I shouldn't have said that, you know, before.'

'Forget about it. I have. Grudges were never my thing.'

'A good way to live.'

'Aye. I've had a good life. The only person I've ever truly hurt is myself. That's at least something to be thankful for. This place is full of people loaded with regret, but I don't really have any. It's a merciful place to be when it's your time.'

The old man waved and staggered away.

The only person I've ever hurt is myself.

Si thought of the horrified look on his daughter's face after he'd slapped her. He also thought of the desperate expression on Harvey's face all those years back while Miles Cook hovered over him.

Am I loaded with regret?

He buried his face in his hands. Several more patients came and went. No one else offered him a cigarette, or any words of wisdom. He never even bothered to raise his face to see who had taken up the seat beside him.

The night moved on. No one came to ask him to move. He assumed that it was too short-staffed and busy in the hospital for anyone to monitor the comings and goings of the nicotine club out front.

After a long time, he dropped his hands.

And gagged on the sudden impact of adrenaline.

Sitting in a wheelchair beside the adjacent bench, wearing a hospital nightgown was Harvey.

Si was reasonably near, but his old friend was yet to notice him. Maybe because his face had been in his hands for so long?

Despite joining the smokers as they drew shapes in the dark with their burning chemicals, Harvey wasn't smoking himself. He simply looked up into the sky, observing the stars.

Behind Harvey on the bench adjacent to Si was a much younger man fiddling on his phone. The police guard?

Si had never really had a plan, but he felt another sudden rush of adrenaline when he considered the opportunity offered by a neglectful guard.

He rose to his feet, keeping the wheel brace concealed beneath the jacket. His heart rate was flying now, but he forced himself to be slow and steady.

Preparing for the possibility of the target's and his guard's eyes swinging in his direction, he tightened his grip on the wheel brace in case he'd have to dive in, swinging.

No eyes moved. Harvey maintained his reverie with the stars, while the guard remained transfixed on his phone.

Si looked over his shoulder in the direction of A&E. There was an ambulance sliding up alongside it, but no one was currently walking this way. He looked back towards the entrance. No one was in the foyer.

He inched forward.

As he neared, he decided he wouldn't be averse to Harvey suddenly noticing him.

Look at me coming your way. See what you've brought upon yourself.

But Harvey still didn't look.

When he was near enough that the ambush would be a success, Si pulled his jacket away with his left hand, and raised the wheel brace with his right. 'Harvey!'

Harvey glanced up with jaundiced eyes; he looked pale and broken.

But not scared. *No.* The bastard did not look scared.

'Simon,' Harvey said. His tone of voice was filled with resignation.

Si was prepared to crush his skull.

'Drop that!'

The officer's outburst made Si jump. Lost in the eyes of the man he'd come to kill, he'd forgotten about the guard.

Si turned to the officer, who was already on his feet and launching himself forward.

He swung the wheel brace.

Clunk.

The officer hit the ground.

Si looked down at the officer, flat on his face, prepared to deliver another blow. When the officer didn't move, he switched his attention back to Harvey.

Harvey looked down at the injured officer, and then up at Si. He appeared sad now, but still not fearful.

'Aren't you scared?' Si asked.

'I've always been scared.'

'My heart bleeds.'

The officer on the floor moaned.

'I've never asked anyone for sympathy. Not yours. Not anyone's,' Harvey said.

'Why did you do this? Why did you take my daughter from me?'
'I didn't.'

'She was near your hut. The purse was there. Her purse.'

'Listen to me,' the officer said with a pained voice from the floor.

'Shut up!' Si hissed.

'I can help you—'

'*Shut up*, or I'll hit you again.'

'Okay... okay...' the officer moaned.

Harvey said, 'Don't make it worse, Si. Really. You've lost enough.'

'And why would you care? I should've killed you back then in the scout hut. Killed you and that pervert, Baloo, together.' Si felt tears well up in his eyes. 'She was innocent. My daughter was innocent. She'd nothing to do with *any* of that. Why, Harvey, why did you do it?'

'I didn't. I'd never have harmed a hair on her head.' He sighed. 'I loved her, Si.'

Si felt his insides melt. He waved the wheel brace at Harvey. 'Don't. Don't you dare. You twisted, diseased—'

'*Listen.* Not in that way, Si. Not in some perverse way. I loved her because she was the only person that showed me any kindness.'

Si screwed his face up. It made the tears break loose from his eyes and run down his face. 'Did you get her pregnant?' He touched Harvey's head with the wheel brace.

'I... I...' Harvey looked shocked now. 'She was pregnant?'

'Was it you?' Si said, pushing his head with the wheel brace.

'No, of course not. I didn't... I didn't even know.'

Someone started screaming from the foyer. Si looked up to see a middle-aged woman standing there in a state of panic. It gave the officer on the floor confidence. 'Call the police!'

'Shut up,' Si hissed at the officer. 'Shut up!' He pointed the wheel brace in the woman's direction. She put her hand to her mouth and ran back into the hospital.

Si threw his jacket down, freeing his hand so he could slap his forehead. 'Think. Think. *Think!*'

'Listen,' Harvey said. 'Listen to me.'

'Listen to you?' He shook his head. 'To you? You're insane!'

'Take me with you. *Now.* I won't struggle.' Harvey gestured down at his injured arms. 'I can't anyway. No energy.'

'Why?'

'So, we can talk. Work this out. You want the truth; killing me now won't get it for you.'

Si hit himself in the centre of his head again. 'Shit... shit...' He threw the wheel brace to the floor, seized the handles of the wheelchair and pushed his old friend quickly, away from the benches, and alongside A&E.

The wheelchair was old and lacked decent suspension, so it bounced the frail recluse from side to side.

Si stole a look over his shoulder.

Two hospital porters were helping the felled officer to his feet.

Si focused his attention back on his exit. He'd managed to pick up some speed now, and he flew past a parked ambulance with some velocity.

He took a sharp left onto a small zebra crossing and under the covered car park. The right wheel of the chair left the ground. Si gasped, expecting his captive to slide from the chair and crash into the ground. But the chair righted itself in time.

He glanced behind him and saw a sprinting man alongside A&E.

'Shit!' Si sighted the Lexus parked alongside several other vehicles, a couple of metres away from the long-arm barricade. The realisation that he hadn't validated the parking ticket hit him like a bullet. Was he trapped?

'Police. Stop!'

He looked back. The sprinting man was gaining on them.

Nothing for it. He threw everything into the final push, skimming alongside a parked Nissan, scratching it with his watch. When he burst onto the exit road that ran between the two sets of parked cars, there was a Corsa coming his way. He looked left at the driver's anxious eyes, wondering if the stopping distance was too short.

He heard the screech of the driver's brakes.

The Corsa halted barely a metre from them. The driver leaned out the window, shouting obscenities. Si completed the journey to the other side of the exit road, fumbling in his pocket as he neared the exit. He rustled around, feeling his house keys, but unable to get his fingers to the fob for the Lexus. Behind him, the driver of the Corsa revved the engine angrily before tearing off.

'Stop!' the police officer cried.

Si's fingers hit the fob. He pressed the button. The Lexus gave a welcoming flash and the doors unlocked with a clunk.

'There's nowhere to go!'

The officer sounded close, but Si didn't feel he had enough time to check exactly where he was. He stopped the wheelchair, circled around Harvey and opened the back door. 'In, now!'

Harvey rose from the seat. He looked frail and moved slowly. When Harvey leaned in through the back door, Si sighted the chasing officer out the corner of his eye. He was on the other side of the exit road alongside the Nissan he'd damaged with his watch.

Si pushed the leaning Harvey hard in the centre of his back. The recluse went into the rear of the vehicle across the back seats. 'Get in and pull in your legs.'

Harvey scurried all the way in and folded his legs so the soles of his feet pointed at the ceiling of the car.

Si slammed the door behind him and turned. The officer was partway over the exit road. He was a suited, tall man with slicked back dark hair. Si charged at the empty wheelchair, kicking it as hard as it could. It flew backwards.

The officer was going at such a speed, he had no choice but to hold out his hands to meet the obstacle. Blocking it did him no good. The wheelchair crashed into his legs, and he was turned over with the chair.

Si raced around the front of the car and jumped into the driver's seat. He didn't bother with the seat belt, but he did hit the internal lock.

He thrust the car into reverse and drove hard across the exit road, narrowly missing the officer and slamming into the Nissan's front bumper, making the watch scratch on the side of the vehicle the least of the owner's worries.

He looked left and saw the tall officer back on his feet, charging at the side of his car. 'Stop!'

Si turned his wheel to full right lock. At that moment, the officer got hold of the door handle on the passenger side. Si watched him yanking desperately at the locked door, his face screwed up. Si hit the accelerator and the car turned. The officer didn't give up the door and moved with the turning vehicle.

Si slammed his foot down on the accelerator and the car tore forwards, the insane officer still clutching the handle, running with all his might. Si pointed ahead at the car park barricade. The officer cast a look in that direction and then threw himself back from the car to avoid certain death.

Si smashed through the rising arm of the barricade, and pieces of debris rained down on the vehicle and the street around him. He took a sharp left and accelerated.

33

Having staggered away from his confrontation with Jack, Tommy used some of his last remaining energy to pound on Aiden's caravan door.

The door opened. He exchanged a quick look with the young man, who looked stunned, before putting his arm against the side of the caravan and leaning into it. 'We're buggered.'

'What's happened to you?'

Tommy spat blood on the ground and coughed. 'What always happens, I guess. The world outside. Found its way in.'

'Tommy, come in,' Aiden said. 'You need to sit. You look awful.'

Tommy found the strength to push himself away from the caravan and follow Aiden in. He muttered, 'Always the world outside.'

Once inside, Tommy sat on the front of Aiden's bed and then lay back. One eye was in the process of swelling shut, so he stared at the ceiling of the caravan with limited vision. 'I told you to leave her alone, didn't I? Last year. I told you.'

'You did.'

'But you didn't listen.'

Some dogs in the adjacent caravan started barking.

'What a way for it all to come crashing down,' Tommy said and coughed, making his face suddenly feel like it was on fire. 'Tell me you have painkillers.'

'Yes... What's happened Tommy?'

'You're going to have to hide me in here. They're going to come looking. Tonight.'

'Who is?'

'The pigs. Christ almighty, the day you started seeing that stupid bitch again, I should've taken us all away from this place.'

'Don't call her that. Please, Tommy, don't call her that.'

'Only myself to blame, I guess.' He swallowed blood.

'Just tell me for Christ's sake! Who did this to you?'

'Jack. Who else? My own fault. I went to see him to plead our case.'

Aiden didn't respond.

'Well, aren't you going to say anything? Aren't you going to ask how it went?' He grinned, and then winced over the pain. 'You've done this.'

'Your memory is messed up. I said I'd leave, remember? You forced me to stay. I wouldn't have carried on bringing her back here, and I'd have found a way for us to be together somewhere else. I didn't want to keep putting everyone in danger. None of this was my idea. You used the situation to your own advantage, Tommy.'

'*Our* advantage, you bastard! Jack came to Knaresborough. Who could have predicted that? Where were the options? Tell me. *Where were the options?*'

Aiden sighed and paced his caravan. 'We can still leave. Tomorrow, Tommy. Give the word. We just pack up and go. Let's cut our losses.'

'You want to run? They found your girlfriend dead by the lake!

You're a traveller. A scourge on their world. Pestilence! Where do you think this ends up?'

'It ends up where it belongs. With that old bastard in the hut!'

'Does it? Use your brain, Aiden. There's only one place this ends up.'

Aiden shook his head. 'You're being paranoid. You need rest; let me handle the police.'

'It's going to end up *here*. With us. No question. If they can get us, they'll get us.'

'They found Tia by his hut, Tommy! Not by my caravan!'

'It's too obvious, don't you see. It looks like a set up. Any lawyer worth his salt is going to be able to point that out. Not like there's any witnesses to the—' He paused and looked up at Aiden.

'What?' Aiden said.

'An idea. A way to put this shit show to bed.'

34

Rhys Hunt put the silver bracelet to his nose. He could still smell Tia.

He let the hand holding the gift from him to her on her twentieth birthday, fall to his lap. With the other hand, he put a glass to his lips and polished off the Scotch in one large, burning mouthful.

Turning the bracelet over in his hand, he thought of the moment he'd given it to her. The surprise in her eyes. Her attempts to reject the gift. Her claims that it was too generous.

He'd insisted. Told her that she was to take it. And, although it was too risky to engrave it in case her father should see it, that she should always wear it. So, when she looked at it, she would think of him.

But no, she'd resisted. Refused to take it from his house.

He ran the bracelet up and down his tear-stained cheek.

For a time, with his eyes closed, he saw her there. Her beauty demanding his attention as it always had done. He reached out to her, pressing his palm against her cheek.

Her cheek, like his, was damp with tears.

Then, he pulled her body tight against his. She quivered. He asked her to be still.

Yes, their union was a forbidden secret, but did that make it wrong?

He heard a cough.

When he opened his eyes, Lorraine was standing at the door to the spare room, watching him.

He didn't let his hand fall away. He kept the bracelet pinned to his cheek.

The couple stared at each other for a short time, before Lorraine turned and walked away.

35

Gardner ruminated on her sofa for hours.

Why the bloody hell had Tommy been at her home?

To talk to her about the investigation? Confess something regarding Tia, perhaps, or even point the finger at someone? Aiden?

And why had her brother taken offence at a traveller's presence? *Unless...*

A cold feeling spread over her chest. Did Tommy know Jack? Jack had been walking past the campsite today.

Had Jack been looking for Tommy, but then, after seeing her there, quickly decided to leave?

Not much of this was making any bloody sense.

She sat by her phone into the early hours of the morning, desperate to hear that Jack had been found, but no one called.

Shit! Had she made the right decision? Staying here with Rose. Should she have found someone to look after her? Joined the hunt for her psychopathic brother?

She refilled her glass with Merlot.

No. It was the right call.

Rose couldn't be with a stranger tonight. What if she woke screaming again? No. Her number one priority was that girl.

She didn't have anyone to talk to. Barry was useless these days. A few times she almost succumbed to the temptation to call Riddick but had held off. It'd be selfish. That man was in turmoil – let him get a good night's sleep.

The night wound on. Eventually, she received a phone call and answered it with a shaking hand. It wasn't about Jack. It was simply to inform her that Tommy Byrne was still missing. She'd already known that he hadn't returned to the travellers' site as the police had checked in there earlier, but she'd expected him to have turned up by now. Either in a hospital bed, or possibly, looking at the state of him earlier, dead in a ditch.

Disappointed, she finished the wine and passed out on the couch.

* * *

Marsh contacted her at six in the morning; there was a hint of fatigue in her boss' voice which was unusual. However, she suspected she herself sounded like shit.

She listened to the events involving Si and Harvey at the hospital late last night and sat bolt upright on the couch, her heart thrashing in her chest.

'Christ above! Why didn't you tell me as soon as it'd happened, ma'am?'

'After hearing about the situation with your brother and that traveller, I wanted to try and keep your plate a bit less messy for a few more hours. I was confident we'd pick Si and Harvey up without having to worry you. I was wrong.'

'What happened?'

'Well, we assumed he was in his own vehicle, so we lost some valuable minutes on him. By the time I received the licence plate from the officer that chased him from the entrance to the hospital, the bastard had a head start. Sorry, Emma, we never got eyes on him.'

'Whose vehicle?'

'He was borrowing an employee's vehicle. A one Larry Kempton. We've spoken to him, but he seemed none the wiser to where his boss had gone. I still held up hope the ANPR would tag him sooner or later, and let you rest. But I'm afraid that Si is no fool. We found the car abandoned, and both men gone.'

'Where?'

'Near Jacob Smith's Park off Boroughbridge Road.'

'Harvey wasn't in a good way. They must be moving slowly. Surely, they shouldn't be too hard to locate?'

'You'd think so... We're on CCTV now and it's very residential around those parts, so I'll get some of your team to start knocking. But, shit, Emma, we've messed up. If he's given us the slip! Heads are going to roll if we don't find them soon, and mine will be first.'

And they deserved it! Gardner gritted her teeth. The outlook was bleak for Harvey and, right now, she was convinced more than ever that he was innocent. How could they have let this happen to him? She relaxed her jaw and took a deep breath. 'How's the poor bloke that was minding him at the hospital?'

'Fractured skull, but alive, and should be okay, thank God. Could you imagine the shitstorm if we had two murderers on the run together?' Marsh said. 'And why not just kill him outside the hospital? Why bother taking the risk in getting him out of there?'

Gardner thought. 'Maybe he wants to make him suffer? Or... hopefully, he, like us, is uncertain over Harvey's guilt, and just wants to get the truth.'

'I hope so, Emma, because if he goes on some kind of rampage, you'll need a basket to catch my head in when they wheel out the guillotine.'

'I'm sure it won't come to that, boss.' But she wasn't convinced. She rubbed her temples. *Jesus. First, Jack and Tommy; now, Harvey and Si. All off the bloody radar.* 'I'll start contacting the team.'

'Changing the subject, Emma, have you any idea yet why this Tommy Byrne was in your garden with your brother?'

Gardner was surprised it'd taken Marsh this long to ask the question. 'Not yet.' She didn't want to take Marsh through the options she'd considered last night while drunk. 'But I will let you know as soon as I do.'

She hung up and rubbed her temples again. Her headache was worsening at speed.

Riddick answered Emma's call immediately. He sounded more drained than she did. So much for that good night's sleep she'd left him to. What did she expect? Never mind her having enough on her plate, Riddick had the monopoly on shit-covered plates. She updated him on the Si and Harvey situation, but spared him the chaotic situation involving her brother, still holding out some hope that it'd bear no relation to Operation Bright Day.

His response was predictably impetuous as always. 'I'm going to find him.'

'And where would you even start?'

'His home?'

'You don't think that's been tried?'

'So, what do you suggest, we sit on our hands?'

'Paul, listen to me. Deep breath. Okay?'

He sighed. 'Okay.'

'We've the right people looking. You...' *Potentially drunk*, she thought. 'Aimlessly driving over Knaresborough won't help. Trust our people. They'll come good. I need you at the briefing with me. Today, we've got to be sharper than ever, avert disaster. As soon as they're located, we'll move. Get yourself ready and I'll see you there.'

As soon as she hung up, she stood. *Painkillers first, then get ready for—*

Rose!

Shit! With Jack gone, who would take care of Rose if she went out?

She went upstairs and poked her head into the guest room. The poor little mite was sleeping with her little face pressed against the stuffed pug.

She thought, then sighed over the most obvious option. It made her want to cry. She'd have to contact social services, explain the situation, and then wait for her to be picked up.

First, her mother overdosing; then, her father almost killing someone on a lawn; and now bundled off into care.

This wasn't acceptable.

I'll help you Rose. You can be sure. Whatever it takes. I'll help.

Her mind quicky flirted with the idea of fostering, or even adoption, as it had done on many occasions since her vulnerable niece had shown up in her life. And, just like on all those other times, the idea veered towards that same brick wall. *My marriage is breaking. I barely see my own daughter...*

But still, Rose. I'll help you. And if this is what it takes, then, this is what it takes.

She left Rose, reasoning that Riddick would have to lead the briefing while she waited for them to collect the little girl. She turned to head back downstairs to the lounge where her phone was, when she noticed the door to the room Jack was staying in, ajar.

Had it been ajar last night?

Her head still pounding, she tried to think, but couldn't remember.

Was he back?

Holding her breath, she crept to the door, wincing when the floorboards creaked. She placed her hand on the door and listened, but all she could hear was her heart thrashing in her chest.

If he was here, was he a danger to her?

She thought of Malcolm's Maze of Mirrors. She thought of the x-ray of her fractured skull...

She peered around the door, her heart hammering.

Empty.

At first, she felt relief, but then there was disappointment over the fact that she still had no idea where he was. She opened the door fully and looked at his unmade bed, and then homed in on two sports bags on the floor.

She stared long and hard at them for a minute, her head still pounding. She chewed her bottom lip.

Who are you, Jack? Really? You say you've changed. That you're not the boy with the dead eyes who fractured my skull. Yet, I saw you last night. I saw that same hollow being out on the lawn almost beating a man to death...

Who are you, Jack?

She sat on the unmade bed and lifted the first sports bag onto her lap. She unzipped it and looked inside. She rustled through screwed-up clothing. She couldn't see anything of note. Still, she emptied the clothes onto the bed beside her and continued to sieve through it, wondering with a wrinkled nose, if he was doing his laundry. She'd given him complete access to her facilities but had no real idea if he was using them while she worked nearly every hour God sent. She checked a few pockets, found some loose change and a couple of scrunched up bus tickets but nothing of significance. She wedged the clothing back into the sports bag, zipped it, and then repeated the process with the second bag.

No clothes in here, just a heap of items: deodorant, shaving foam, an out-of-date passport, some packets of biscuits, a *Top Gear* magazine and other junk. After examining all the items, she felt the crushing weight of disappointment.

She'd learned he liked *Top Gear*. Great.

She pulled out the magazine and looked at three red Ferraris, accompanied by the heading 'Celebrating 75 years of speed, noise and red paint'. Then, she noticed the corner of something white poking out from between the pages.

She gripped the white corner and pulled out an envelope.

It was unmarked and carried some weight. It certainly wasn't a late birthday card for her.

She turned the envelope over; it wasn't sealed, so she opened it up and looked inside.

Her eyes widened.

Well, well. I thought you had nothing? I gave you food, shelter and money when you needed it. Yet, here I am, staring at a bundle of cash...

She pulled the money out and counted out five hundred and sixty pounds in ten- and twenty-pound notes. Almost six hundred pounds.

Six hundred pounds.

In her mind's eye, she watched Tia withdrawing two hundred pounds from the cashpoint at the Co-op service station on Boroughbridge Road. On three consecutive days.

Then, she recalled Tia's journey after every withdrawal.

Down Breary Flat Lane.

Towards Harvey by the lake.

But also towards the travellers on the rugby field.

Had she been right, after all? Had Tia been giving the money to Tommy so she and Aiden could continue their relationship? So, where the hell does Jack come into it?

Why did Tommy give the money to Jack? Did he owe him money? Why? How the hell did Tommy even know Jack in the first place? And why the fight? Was Jack still owed money? Was that why Tommy was here? To plead his case?

The rush of adrenaline brought rapid fire questions.

She didn't have the answers. But she knew one thing for certain.

Jack might run away from Rose, his flesh and blood, but he wouldn't run from almost six hundred quid.

She'd be seeing him again.

But he wasn't having this. She took the envelope and left the bags exactly how she'd found them.

As she left the room, she looked down at the envelope in her hand.

If this money was indeed the money that Tia withdrew then it was evidence for Operation Bright Day. If that was the case then, right now, Gardner should be on the phone and reporting this.

If.

She didn't want to weave herself personally into this case unless she really had to. The investigation was already burning hot with Harvey and Si in the wind without adding a large, potentially distracting and unrelated, angle.

She could rule it in or out by herself.

Still, Tommy was missing...

And how could she head to the rugby field now to demand answers from Aiden with Rose in her care?

Delaying the disclosure of finding this money for an hour or so was irresponsible, but taking Rose along in the back seat to a potentially dangerous place was obscene, and how would that help with her application to foster her?

She racked her brains. Who could she leave Rose with? Whose discretion could she count on? Riddick was the obvious choice, but she needed him to run the briefing...

She thought of Lucy O'Brien – the feminine heartbeat of her

male-dominated investigation room. Her gut told her she'd be a good call.

'Something's come up, Lucy. Something personal. I need a favour. An hour, if that.' Gardner explained the favour was to look after Rose.

'I'd be happy to, boss. I can be over in thirty minutes.'

She hadn't asked why. Gardner felt that she could count on her discretion. 'I'm so grateful, Lucy.'

She sighed.

After hanging up, she contacted Riddick to tell him he was leading the briefing. Of course, he probed her far more than O'Brien had done.

'It's about Jack,' Gardner said.

'I'm coming with you.'

'No, Paul, listen to me. I'm going to be telling Marsh I've suddenly got a bad gut, and that you will be running the briefing until I get myself right. If we're both absent, then tongues will start wagging. I need to get right with something first. It might be nothing. If it's something, you'll know soon enough.'

'Tongues are always wagging anyway. I don't like your plan.'

'I need this. Are you there for me?'

'Clever words, boss.' Riddick sighed. 'Guess I can't turn down someone who is always there for me.'

She phoned Marsh to report her sudden onset of diarrhoea. She wasn't best pleased, but Gardner assured her that once the Imodium started to kick in, she'd be available.

Rose woke up five minutes before O'Brien arrived at the house, and Gardner explained that a nice woman would be looking after her for the next hour. She didn't tell her she'd be contacting social services in the next couple of minutes to come and collect her later this morning. She felt numb inside.

At first, Rose looked worried, but after asking if the nice woman would watch television with her, and receiving an affirmative from Gardner, she soon settled.

Gardner left O'Brien and Rose in front of CBeebies, but only got as far as the front door before her phone rang. It was Barnett.

'Ray?'

'Boss. Have you checked your emails?'

'Not had a chance. Had a hell of a morning with my stomach.' She patted it, as if she was starting to buy into her own lies.

'We suddenly have two potential witnesses.'

'What?'

'Two young men out drinking by the lake the night of Tia's murder. They claim to have *seen* Harvey dragging the body from his hut into the patch of trees where she was discovered.'

'Bullshit!' Gardner said. 'Who witnesses someone dragging a body and then only comes forward several days after?' She shook her head. She didn't need to be distracted by a shit lead right this moment.

'Yeah, I know,' Barnett said. 'It's on your email – I just assumed you might want to take a quick look and dismiss it?'

'Yes, you're right, Ray, that would be prudent. It might help us in other ways. It seems someone is very desperate for the CPS to get a move on and build a case against Harvey... Go on, then, who are these two boys?'

'Two young travellers from the campsite on the rugby field.'

She sucked in a deep breath and steadied herself against the doorframe. 'Where are these travellers now?'

'Still on their site, I imagine. One of them contacted the emergency services and babbled it down the phone – it's only just worked its way to us. You want me to go down?'

'No, Ray, I'll speak to the two boys in question.' *As I'm on my way there, anyway.*

'But your stomach?'

'I'll get hydrated and deal with it. Paul is leading the briefing, anyway. Ping me the names of the two witnesses. Keep this emergency call recording under your hat for the moment, Ray, though. Our place has been like a sieve in the past. Last thing we need is more bullshit seeping out to the press. Remember the bloody Viaduct Killer.'

Silence.

'What's wrong, Ray?'

'Sorry, boss, the recording is uploaded on our system already, boss. About twenty minutes ago.'

'*What?* Who did that?'

'Marsh put it on the system, and then cc'ed the whole team the link.'

'Why would Marsh send it out to my team? I'm the SIO.'

'Efficiency? She probably thought you were feeling unwell and might not pick it up quickly. Anyway, I'll mention at the briefing that you're already following up on it. I'm sure everyone will be careful with the information,' Barnett said.

'I hope so.'

'As soon as you've spoken to the boys and confirmed it's bullshit, contact me, and I'll make sure everyone has put a line through it.'

Yes, I'll do that. And I'll find out whether this money in Jack's bag is Tia's while I'm there – if it's the last thing I do.

After climbing into her car, she contacted social services and put them on the hands-free as she made her way to the travellers' site.

And, after the call, her heart feeling like it was breaking into pieces, she made that same vow she'd made in Rose's bedroom before. Except, this time, she said it out loud, 'I'll help you Rose. You can be sure. Whatever it takes. I'll help.'

36

Down on his haunches, Si watched the early sunrays dance on the surface of the lake.

He was only metres from where he'd seen his daughter's body several days back, but he didn't feel the rage and despair that he'd felt then. For now, at least, he felt oddly calm.

From beside him, Harvey said, 'It's peaceful.'

Si didn't respond. Instead, he looked at the bleeding cut on the back of his hand. He'd done it on the fence helping Harvey over it. Of course, there'd been no option; out in the open, they'd have been spotted in no time. He wiped the blood on his shirt.

He surveyed the sides of the lake again to confirm there still weren't any fishermen.

Would anyone really come here after what had happened?

He thought of his daughter's body again.

Her shell. Not her. Not really.

'I call it Lonely Lake,' Harvey said. 'Everyone I see here looks alone. I think this is what this place is. A place to just hide away.'

Si looked down at his reflected face in the lake. 'Why'd you come to live here?' A breeze rippled the water and his face melted away.

'After my parents... it felt like the right thing to do.'

'Christ.' Si shook his head and then looked out over the lake again. 'All of this because of what that monster did to you?'

'All of what?'

'This retreat from everything.'

Harvey sighed. 'I really don't know. All I can tell you is that it feels right.'

'How something feels, and how something is, aren't always the same. This certainly doesn't seem right to me.'

'I'm happier alone. Was that because of Miles? Or is that just because of who I am? I can't really answer that. I mean, can you fully describe how your experience with Miles affected you?'

Si shrugged. 'I carried guilt. I should've helped you back then.'

'No, I don't mean the guilt,' Harvey said. 'I'm talking about what Miles actually *did* to you. It must have caused some—'

'What do you mean?' Si glared at the man sitting on the ground beside him. 'Did to me?'

Harvey looked away and didn't push it. Si was glad of this; the suggestion had briefly destabilised his composure.

'Anyway, I should've helped you,' Si said, turning his eyes back onto the lake. 'I'm sorry. I *should've* stopped him.'

Si waited for Harvey to respond. He didn't. All he heard was a breeze rustle the canopy above him. 'Are you bloody listening? I'm saying I should've helped. For God's sake! I've never stopped regretting that moment. Surely this is what you want to hear?'

More silence. Until some ducks on the other side of the river punctured it by loudly addressing one another.

'Whatever; don't speak then,' Si said. 'You may have convinced me that you didn't harm Tia, but you'll never convince me that you aren't insane. I should've helped you, but you can't blame your madness on me.'

'Blame?' Harvey said, shaking his head. 'I don't blame you. You were a child. As was I.' He turned his eyes back to Si. 'Which is why I couldn't help you, either.'

'Help me?' Si said, glaring again, but raising his voice. 'What're you talking about? Help me, how?'

'He abused us both, Si.'

'Shut your mouth. I was there barely a minute. You don't know what the hell you're talking about!'

'Are you sure?' Harvey was still looking at Si.

Si turned away from Harvey and spat on the floor. He could feel his hands starting to shake again. Control was fleeting. But what next? If it wasn't Harvey, because his old friend had put forward a compelling case for his innocence over the course of the night, then who was to suffer his wrath? And now this: suggestions he was abused? What a joke! 'He never touched me.'

'Do you have to be touched to be abused, Si?'

'He touched you,' Si said, rising to his feet. 'This is bullshit. I'm here for the truth about my daughter, not to be counselled by the local madman.'

'Do you think the truth about Tia, if I had it, would be enough?'

'Jesus Christ, Harvey, it'd be a start! I want to know who murdered my daughter. You've told me about your great friendship with her, but so far, I know nothing about who hurt her. And now you're talking about something that happened forty years ago. What does this have to do with my daughter's death? As I keep telling you, that monster never came anywhere near me! He certainly never touched me. So abuse? What abuse? I'd have castrated him if he'd even tried.'

Harvey sighed. 'I don't want to antagonise you, Si. I only want to help you.'

'Then help. We're here now because you offered a hand of friendship to my daughter for some peculiar reason. Why? To get back at me? To get close to me? Have you even made that clear to me yet?'

'I thought I had,' Harvey said. 'Tia simply came here.'

'And like I said, you should have turned her away. You said you liked being alone.' He waved his hand at the lake. 'And you moved here to be alone... So why the hell welcome my daughter in?'

'How many times, Si? I'm sorry, but she was lost, unhappy; she needed someone—'

'She *needed* you? Bullshit! She needed her father, that's what she needed.'

Harvey nodded. 'I agree.'

'She should have come to me. Not you.'

Harvey nodded again.

Si lowered himself back onto his haunches. He had tears running down his face. He wiped at them with the back of his hand.

'But she didn't,' Harvey continued. 'And, when she came... you have to believe this Si... it wasn't just the least I could do for her, but it was also the least I could do for you.'

Si picked up a stick and threw it into the lake. 'You've lost your mind. It was *me* who turned my back on you. You didn't owe me anything.'

'Maybe, we owe each other?'

'Because we were both abused?' Si said with a sardonic smile.

Harvey nodded.

'You're not going to let this go, are you? I *wasn't* abused.'

Harvey said, 'But you killed Miles?'

Si took a deep breath, his heart suddenly in a cold grip. 'What're you talking about?'

'You *know* what I'm talking about. You killed Miles, didn't you?'

'What could possibly make you think—'

'Where did he go then?'

'I don't know. To hell for all I care. Or *hope*, more like.'

'So, he just left Knaresborough and disappeared?'

'Yes. That's how I understand it.'

'Tell me the truth, Si. I've got your back. I cared for you then, I care for you now.'

Si looked over at the ducks. 'What does truth change anyway?'

'It changes everything.'

Si guffawed. 'How? She'd still be gone.'

'Yes, but at least it would free you. And I'm telling you the truth too, Si. I've always cared for you.'

Si eyed Harvey and almost said, *And I cared for you, too. That's one of the reasons I did what I did.* He bit the words back at the last second.

'What did you do, Si?'

Si sighed. 'What needed to be done. Something I should have done back then, back in 1982.'

He took Harvey back to that night twenty years ago, when he'd stumbled on the old, disused scout hut, drunk. The door had been locked forever by the council. Si had kicked it down and discovered old, crippled Miles, alone.

'You kept a key then, Baloo?'

The place smelled, and there was rotting food and rubbish everywhere. There was also a sleeping bag. Miles was looking through photo albums.

'What're you looking at, Baloo?'

Miles showed him. They were the photos of the many cubs he'd cared for over the years.

'How many, Baloo? How many lives have you polluted? How many have you destroyed?'

Miles had been losing his mind at that point. His answers hadn't made a great deal of sense. He was frail, and Si knew that one more

cold winter with only that sleeping bag to fend it off would probably be enough to end him.

'But he didn't deserve a natural death, did he?' Si said, looking
at Harvey.

Harvey didn't respond.

'You know he was sitting on that same chair that I saw you on
that night. That same white, plastic chair.'

'How did you...?' Harvey asked.

Si pulled out his Swiss Army Knife from the pocket of his jeans
and showed Harvey.

'SM?' Harvey said. 'Si Meadows.'

'Stuart Meadows, my father. God rest his drunken soul. He had
it when he was in the cub scouts. Everything always seems to have a
sick cyclical nature to it, don't you think?'

Si looked back at the lake and recalled the moment he'd killed
Miles. He'd died easily. Too quickly. He'd wanted him to suffer.

'I hope he heard my last words to him. I told him it was for all
those other boys he hurt.'

'And you, too?' Harvey said. 'Don't forget he hurt you too.'

Si shook his head. *Was I really abused? Was Harvey calling it
right? Have I blocked it out? Were they repressed memories? Had the old
monster actually...* He shook his head; it didn't bear thinking about.
'Miles is beneath the floorboards of that old scout hut. Decaying in
an unmarked grave.'

Just like all those innocent boys decayed... inside.

Si took a deep breath, suddenly feeling lighter. 'How did you
know anyway?'

'I just did. I don't know how, really. I just did.'

'Are we connected in some way, Harvey?' Si asked. He smiled
again. 'Do you believe in that kind of bullshit?'

Harvey shrugged. 'Maybe.'

'We fancied each other. So what? Nothing ever happened,

because of our circumstances. Again, so what? It's a tale that's been told a million times. Happening every day. That doesn't connect us.'

'It's not about the feelings we had for one another. Miles controlled you, Si. He used you. He used your sexuality against you and made you turn your back on me.'

Si flinched and looked away. He could feel himself welling up again.

'That was abuse,' Harvey continued. 'He may not have physically touched you like he touched me, but he destroyed some part of you, didn't he? We were both in this together. And that's why we'll always be connected.'

'Stop,' Si said, holding up the palm of his hand. He shook his head. 'Please.'

'I've finished,' Harvey said. 'That's all I have, anyway.'

Si wiped tears from his eyes. 'I hit her. Only once, but I hit her.'

'She never told me, Si.'

'The only thing that ever mattered to me. The only good thing to come out of my sorry excuse of a life, and I *hit* her. She must have hated me.'

'She loved you, Si. Trust me. You were her father, and you were everything to her.'

'If that's true, why come here? To you? Why?'

'It's just life, Si. She wasn't a child any more. She was a young woman. It was time for her to find her own way.'

'Did she really not tell you that she was pregnant?'

Harvey looked away. 'No, she didn't.'

'Did she tell you about a boyfriend? About who the father could be?'

Harvey shook his head but didn't meet his eyes.

'She's gone, Harvey. Now what? What next?'

Suddenly, in that moment, Si felt like he'd felt days ago when he'd first seen her body. He was down on his knees, his fists clenched, tears streaming down his face. 'There's nothing left. *There's nothing left.*'

He felt a hand on his shoulder. He jerked away. 'I don't want to be here any more. I just don't want to be any more!'

The hand settled on his shoulder again. He jerked again, but this time Harvey managed to keep his grip.

'Let it stop. Let me die.'

He kept trying to jerk away, but Harvey was persistent. In the end, he allowed it to stay as he cried. Then, he felt Harvey's entire arm move around his back.

Si sobbed with every part of his being.

Eventually, drained, he glanced at the recluse he'd been planning to kill earlier in the night, sitting alongside him.

Si let his head settle on Harvey's shoulder and watched the ducks cross from one side of the lake to the other. Soon, he felt settled, and regained some composure. He felt Harvey's fingers running through his hair.

'She's all I ever had, Harvey. I've always been worthless, and she was the one good thing.'

Harvey spoke quietly and gently. 'You're not worthless, Si. You've just spent your entire life hiding. Same as me.'

'I don't understand.'

Harvey continued to stroke his hair, consoling him. Si closed his eyes. It felt good. Tingles ran through his entire body.

'What's not to understand, Si? I hid from the world, while you hid from your true self. You say we're not connected, but we are. We've both spent most of our lives lost.'

Si focused on the hand running through his hair. Moments ago, it'd felt right. Perfect. Wonderful, even. But suddenly, now, it felt wrong. Agitation started to spread over his body.

'And because we've always been connected,' Harvey said, 'since that moment, it was only a matter of time before we found one another again—'

Feeling a rush of disgust, Si sat upright, yanking his head away from Harvey's fingers. 'Enough.' He stood. 'How dare you!' He pointed down at him. 'How dare you even suggest that my daughter's death has brought us together.' He realised he was suddenly furious. His eyes were wide, and his voice was raised. 'You old faggot.'

Harvey looked at him with sad eyes. He nodded and then turned his attention back to the river. 'There's only one way back for people like us, Si.'

'I don't want to hear it. Do you understand? I don't want to hear it.'

'We have to stop hiding.'

Si's mouth was full of tears. He spat on Harvey. 'You should have helped my daughter when she came to you. And you should never have tried to make this about us.'

Si started to walk away towards the fence.

Several metres later, he turned back to Harvey, who was still sitting on the ground, facing away from him and staring out over the lake.

He took a deep breath. He felt the pull. Even after all this, he still felt some desire to be close to him.

He shook his head.

It's just guilt. Guilt, pure and simple. You've no feelings for him.

The apology for leaving him had been made. Harvey was not relevant in his life any more. What was relevant was the father of his daughter's baby... and the person who did this to her. Nothing else mattered.

He continued walking. After he climbed over the fence onto Breary Flat Lane, he caught sight of someone jogging towards him. It was Colin Abbott, owner of Riffa Fabrications. It was one of the many businesses that fell under Si's own business umbrella. They also went back a fair way and were drinking buddies in another life, long back. The tall fifty-year-old, who seemed to be going at a relentless speed, stopped in front of him.

Colin plucked out his wireless earphone. 'Si... hey...' There was a look of concern on his face. Si suspected his kidnapping of Harvey had already made the national news.

'Hi Colin,' Si said. 'I'm in a rush—'

'Are you all right mate?' Colin asked, sweat running down his face.

'Yeah, fine... Just don't mention you've seen me, okay?'

Colin nodded. Si suspected Colin would keep quiet, but even if he didn't, it'd be irrelevant. They'd catch up with Si sooner rather than later anyway.

'I'm sorry about Tia,' Colin said.

Si nodded. 'Thanks.'

'Is Harvey with you?'

'Yes, but it's all settled now.'

Colin nodded over to the fence. 'Is he over there?'

'Yes, but as I said, don't worry. He's okay. I haven't hurt him.'

'Ah, good,' Colin said, wiping at his dripping brow. 'I'm glad. When I heard the news this morning about those two witnesses, I feared you'd—'

'What witnesses?' Si asked.

Colin wobbled. 'You haven't heard?'

'You think I'm walking around with my mobile phone while every plod in Yorkshire is onto me?'

'I see. No worries. I don't know for sure what's happened...'

'Colin, if you don't want to run the next mile with a broken leg, you need to tell me right now about these witnesses.'

'Shit. I'm sorry, Si, I really probably—'

'Now!'

'Harvey was seen, Si. He was seen with Tia's body.'

Si leaned back into the fence, his temples pulsing.

'Si?' Colin said. 'Are you okay?'

Si looked down; he felt like his head was going to explode. 'Keep running, Colin. Go now.'

'Si?'

'*Run!*'

Colin gulped and sprinted away.

Si turned. Back towards the lake.

37

When Gardner arrived at the camp site, she saw Aiden standing before the first caravan. It was almost as if he'd been expecting her.

She marched towards him, much to the dissatisfaction of the many dogs, who yanked at their leads, desperate to become closely acquainted with her.

Right now, she couldn't care less, such was the amount of adrenaline coursing through her system.

She didn't hold back on allowing Aiden insight into her emotional state. Enough was enough. She narrowed her eyes and glared at him. 'Did you love her?'

'Yes, I told—'

'Then be more bloody helpful.'

He flinched and looked away. For a moment, she wondered if he was going to burst into tears. Should she have come in so gung-ho?

Yes, she thought. *This feels like the right time.* The truth was close; sometimes you just had to reach a bit harder, and damn the consequences.

She wondered, briefly, if she was picking up habits from Riddick. And whether they were bad ones or not.

He looked back at her, fiddling with his moustache. 'I told you everything I know.'

'Six hundred pounds,' Gardner said.

'What?'

'The money Tia withdrew from the cashpoint. I mentioned it last time.'

He looked away again. 'I told you. I didn't know—'

Damn it. 'The truth, Aiden. Tommy was on *my* lawn last night with Jack Moss. Know him?'

Aiden shook his head. He didn't look at her.

'Where's Tommy?'

'I don't know. Why would I? He didn't come back last night. Your lot have already been here looking.'

'Aren't you worried about him?' Gardner asked.

Aiden nodded and looked at her for the first time in a while, but his eyes were twisting all over the shop.

'I saw the state of Tommy,' Gardner continued. 'Unless he gets treatment, he might not come home. If you know where he is, you're best telling me.'

'I don't,' he said and looked away again.

A dog close to her started barking again. 'Shut that bloody dog up!' She glared in its direction. There was no owner to heed her demand.

She stared back at Aiden.

'She may have been carrying your child.'

Aiden tightened his expression. He was forcing back tears but puffed up his chest to try and give a different impression. 'I don't know anything. I really don't.'

'I guess you're the leader in Tommy's absence?'

'I do what needs to be done. These're my people. Tia has gone anyway, and I'll protect what I have left.'

Aiden may have fooled others with this act, but he wasn't

fooling her. If she had time, she could break him, but what time did she have?

'Did Tia ever mention Rhys Hunt?'

Aiden shook his head. 'No.'

'Really? Did you know that there may have been another man in her life?'

'I don't believe it. You're just trying to wind me up. It won't work.'

'So, you've nothing to give me. Still. Even after what happened last night?'

He shook his head again. 'I wish I did.'

She sighed. 'Have it your own way.' She resolved to turn the money in at HQ. Let her brother be dragged into this sorry affair, and the forces descend on this camp. She'd probably be removed from the case but needs must. She sighed. 'You could have made this easier.' She recalled the other reason she was here.

'When I arrived before, you looked like you were expecting me.'

'Yes, I was expecting someone.' He played with his moustache as he considered his next words. 'Let me say, we're in as much shock as you about what Greg and Liam saw.'

'When did they tell you?'

'They told their parents after they made the call to you. I only just found—'

'You're aware that this is three days after the murder?'

'They're fifteen...'

'So, when you're fifteen, you don't have morals and just ignore a murder for three days?'

'No.' Aiden shook his head. 'They'd been underage drinking is all. They didn't want to get into trouble. Didn't want to bring the local council sniffing around again, checking on the camp children's wellbeing.'

'So, they saw someone dragging a body, and just, you know' – Gardner shrugged – 'blanked it out?'

'What difference does it make anyway? You know it's Harvey Henfrey. Everyone knows it's him. You should be grateful – those kids just made everything move a little faster for you.'

'And a little faster for you and Tommy, eh, Aiden? No more police sniffing around. Maybe, you can all slink away without any bother. After all, things have become a little troublesome for you and Tommy around here by the looks of it. Probably can't wait to be shot of Knaresborough... and Jack Moss.'

'As I said before, I don't know who you mean.' Aiden shook his head. 'And we'd nothing to do with Tia's death. Speak to Greg and Liam and you'll see that for yourself.'

'I intend to. So, let me ask you, when Harvey stands trial, are you going to drive Greg and Liam to the court, personally?'

He looked confused. 'Strange question. I... I don't know. Maybe. Me or someone else?'

'Do you think a jury will buy the fact that Greg and Liam kept schtum for three days? I mean, come on! What changed their minds anyway?'

'Guilt, I think. Aren't you best just speaking to them?'

'I will. One at a time.'

* * *

It didn't take long for Gardner to establish that the witness statements were bullshit.

The stories didn't match. The two fifteen-year-olds claimed to be fishing, while enjoying an illegal drink. Greg said they'd experienced great catch. Six flappers in total. Liam said they'd only managed two. She could tell from talking to these two boys that basic maths was always going to be a step too far for them; however, the difference between six and two would require a whole new level of idiocy.

Worse still was Greg's insistence that they'd not filmed Harvey dragging Tia's body on a phone camera due to fear, while Liam said it was because they never took their mobile phones fishing.

Not only did the inconsistency damn this evidence further, but what fifteen-year-old travelled anywhere without their mobile phone in this day and age anyway?

She marched out of the second interview, annoyed, and glared at Aiden. 'A waste of time. Whoever told them what to say should have done a better job of ironing out the details. I didn't even have to go that far out of the box to expose the inconsistencies.'

Aiden shook his head. 'He did it. Harvey did it.'

'I'm on the verge of arresting someone for wasting police time, Aiden. And you're looking like the best option.'

'I'm not wasting your bloody time!'

'I mean if it is Harvey, you're making it a damn sight harder to build a case! And, if it isn't him, you're giving the real killer time to get away. Last chance. Is there anything you want to tell me, Aiden?'

'Greg and Liam were the ones that phoned you! Stop blaming me.'

'They're fifteen. Look me in the eyes and tell me no one has put them up to it.'

Aiden shook his head and looked down.

Bloody hell!

'I need to make a call,' Gardner said. 'Don't go anywhere.'

She contacted Riddick and was sent straight through to voice-mail. *Typical.*

She then contacted Ray.

'Sorry, boss. Just let me step outside. We're in the briefing... Okay, I can talk now.'

'Could you go and get Paul please?'

'I'm afraid he didn't show. Marsh stepped in.'

Shit. She recalled his words. *I'm going to his house.* Surely, he hadn't meant it? *Paul, you're an absolute nightmare!*

'Listen, Ray, the witness statements are a complete fabrication. The worst concoction I've ever heard. Tell the team, and rule out that nonsense—'

'Boss?'

She gulped and was hit with dread. An interruption wasn't good. 'Yes.'

'I'm afraid the press did get hold of it.'

The dread quickly became a heavy, cold stone in her stomach. She looked at Aiden and hissed, 'Lies have consequences.'

'Sorry, boss?'

'Nothing. Is it out in the public domain, Ray?'

'Yes,' Barnett said. 'I'm afraid so. Marianne Perse, as per. We're too late—'

A loud explosion shook the air.

Gardner flinched and went to her knees. She heard gasping, screams and shouts from the caravans around her.

Up ahead, roughly where the lake was, countless birds rose above the treetops, squawking.

'What's that?' Barnett was shouting down the phone. 'Boss, are you all right?'

A cloud of smoke billowed above the treetops.

'Yes. You need to get the emergency services to the lake. There's been an explosion.'

All around her, people were piling out of their caravans to look towards the blast zone.

'Good lord! The lake. Is it Harvey's hut?' Ray asked.

'I suspect that whoever our leak is has just lit the match.' Gardner hung up and started to run in the direction of the lake.

38

Riddick *had* intended to run the briefing at HQ.

He *had* also resisted the urge to raid his kitchen cabinet despite withdrawal and the shaking in his hands.

Yes, there'd been a moment when he'd wavered under a stream of negative thoughts. *You're damned, Paul. One way or another. If Marianne's impending article doesn't burn you to the ground, then last night's drunken decision to make that phone call will do.*

Yet, despite these ruminations, he *had* still managed to get in his car and start the journey to HQ in Harrogate...

But then his phone had started ringing. The number unrecognisable.

He'd pulled over and answered, 'Who's this?'

'Paul...'

'Si?'

'Yes.'

'Whose phone is this?'

'A burner; I ditched my own. Listen—'

'No, you listen. You need to come in.'

'It's over, Paul.'

'What's over? Where's Harvey?'

'I'm going back to the moment when everything changed for me.'

'You need to be clearer...' Riddick paused, thinking over the words. *Of course! Where Tia was found. Where you saw her...* 'Stay at the lake, Si. I'm coming to you.'

'I'm not at the lake, Paul. I was. But no longer. The moment that everything changed was long before then. I'd lost her before she was even in my life. Doesn't that sound odd? Still, I'm through dwelling on it all. I know now. We're always destined to go back. People like me and you. Never forward. No matter how hard we try.'

'You're wrong, Si. We *can* go forward. I'll go forward, and so will you. Tell me where you are, and let me help—'

'The past never releases you, mate, but I think you know that too.'

'For the umpteenth bloody time, where the hell are you?'

'Just stay away. I'm armed, and I'll hurt you if you come. This is goodbye. I know you get it, when no one else ever did, or ever will.'

'Where. Are. You?'

No reply.

'You bloody idiot!' He'd banged the steering wheel, wondering if it was Si he was calling an idiot, or himself.

Both, more likely.

The moment that everything changed was long before the lake. I'd lost her before she was even in my life.

Of course. It was so bloody obvious.

And so, Riddick really *had* intended to go into HQ sober to run that briefing.

But plans have a habit of changing quickly, don't they?

39

Gardner arrived before the emergency services.

She knew she shouldn't be scaling that fence on Breary Flat Lane before the site of the explosion had been cleared, but she did so anyway.

The stone hut itself was in pieces. Wood, stones and books smouldered on the ground. She suspected a gas explosion. She recalled the tank of gas around the back. It wouldn't have taken much for someone to put that into the hut with its valve open, light a candle, close the front door, and then walk away before it went pop.

Or, worse still, sit *inside* the hut until it went pop.

She shuddered. Well, if that was the case, no one would've survived that.

However, she didn't go to investigate the remains of the hut just yet, because, en route, she saw Harvey sitting on the ground, looking out over the lake. Fortunately, he was some way from the blast zone. She paused.

'Harvey?'

She waited for him to turn. He didn't.

'Harvey?' She increased her volume.

There was still no response.

She glanced around the surrounding woodland. She couldn't see anyone else. 'Si?'

She paused to listen. 'Are you here, Si?'

Nothing.

In the distance, she could hear the wailing sirens of the emergency services. The phone in her pocket was buzzing. She considered answering it.

The sensible thing to do, Emma.

She turned and looked back and considered returning to the fence.

Also sensible.

But hadn't she already started the day off in a rather unsensible fashion? She might as well continue.

Taking a deep breath, she moved towards Harvey, slowly, surveying the trees around her for sudden movement.

Si could be here. And there was no doubt over how dangerous he was now.

She felt a familiar cold sensation in her chest. A timely reminder from her psyche that she'd suffered a life-threatening knife wound to the chest many years back, and she wasn't immune to it happening again.

Metres from him, she said his name again, despite knowing already he was dead. 'Harvey?' He was sitting upright, but his head was tilted forward. One hand lay in the mud beside him, palm up.

Shit.

She took a deep breath, steeled herself, and approached Harvey from the side, keeping some distance to preserve any evidence immediately around the body.

Harvey's face was pale. His eyes wide. His hospital scrubs were punctured and bloodstained. Stabbed. She felt that familiar sensation in her own chest again, and her breath was sucked from her body.

She leaned over, clutching her knees. *Not now, Emma. Get a grip.*

She looked up over the lake, and took long, deep breaths to steady herself.

Then, when in control again, she turned back to the body.

There wasn't much she could take from this tragic scene, but she was at least glad his face wasn't contorted in agony – something she'd seen before in other stab victims.

'Oh, Harvey,' she said, and sighed.

If anything, Harvey looked more at peace in death than he'd ever looked in life. Gardner looked out over the lake for a second time. The ducks were going about their business, none the wiser to the horrors occurring a stone's throw from their world.

Lucky them.

'Si... what have you done? What if it wasn't Harvey?'

Couldn't you just have been patient? Waited for the truth? Was this because of the news this morning? The false witness statements?

Was that it?

Were more lives ruined because of the leak in her department?

After the emergency services had arrived, she stood back on Breary Flat Lane, desperately trying to phone Riddick.

Each time she went through to voicemail.

Her messages began calmly enough as she informed him of the situation, but each time she contacted him, her messages became more and more hostile. The fifth one was laced with profanities.

After the SOCOs had arrived and gone to work, Marsh rang her to tell her that they still didn't have Si. Close to despair, she contacted O'Brien, apologising profusely, before asking if she could watch Rose a little longer while she oversaw another crime scene.

40

Riddick parked and approached the crumbling scout hut, shaking his head in disbelief. The front door was missing, and most of the roof had caved in. The council had surrounded it in 'No Entry' signs. Not only was it an eyesore, but it was dangerous too. The sooner it was demolished the better.

'Si? Are you here?' He called out. He suspected that his threat of being armed was a bluff, but he didn't intend to surprise him, just in case.

He stood at the opening to the hut, where the door used to be, and called Si's name again. He waited for a response. Nothing.

If Si was here, somewhere, he was doing a bloody good job of keeping quiet.

Riddick leaned into the hut. The air was cold and musty, and he could barely see anything in the gloom.

Si and Harvey weren't there. They couldn't be. The place was practically rubble.

He sighed. Had he got it wrong? He thought back to Si's words again. *The moment that everything changed was long before the lake. I'd lost her before she was even in my life.*

But this was where Si had witnessed the abuse and run. Wasn't it?

After ruling the interior of the hut out, Riddick circled to the back instead.

He saw a riverbank strewn with rubbish. It was probably a party spot for some of Knaresborough's wayward youth.

He approached the edge of the River Nidd. He kicked a bottle aside and sat.

Out of ideas, he took his phone out and stared at the screen.

Would Si phone again?

The screen lit up and he felt a burst of hope. But it was Gardner. No doubt desperate to admonish him for not being at head office already. He sent her through to voicemail and then sat gazing out over the River Nidd, wishing deep down he had his hip flask with him, but knowing it was a good job he didn't.

Gardner persisted.

He continued to ignore his phone. He threw some heavy stones into the water and began to wonder if today would be the day that Marianne's character assassination would hit the shelves outside petrol stations.

On full view for all to see.

Again, he sent Gardner through to voicemail, before casting another stone into the water. The ripples spread far and wide.

Maybe you're right, Si.

Maybe the past will never release me.

Maybe I can never go forward.

Maybe I should just climb into this river, lie face down, and float off downstream...

He felt a rush of adrenaline. *Is that what you did, Si?*

Rising to his feet, quickly, he surveyed the river, looking for signs of a body.

He heard loud, fast breathing.

He turned. Si Meadows was behind him, leaning over, clutching his thighs, catching his breath, staring straight ahead at Riddick.

Riddick moved towards the fugitive.

Si displayed the penknife in his hand. 'Sit back down, Paul.'

'Really?' Riddick said. 'Could that even break my skin?'

'It broke Harvey's...'

A cold wave passed over Riddick. He shook his head and felt nauseous.

Now you're damned, Riddick thought. *Just like me.*

'Don't pretend to be surprised, Paul. I warned you. Apples and pears. This is my justice.' He nodded his head at the scout hut. 'As Miles Cook found out, just before I buried him beneath those floorboards. Now, as I've told you, *sit*.'

Riddick sat.

'And turn back to face the river.'

'Why?'

'Do it.'

Riddick turned. 'It won't matter if you kill me now. They'll find Miles' body when they demolish the hut anyway.'

'Good. It'll be a warning to all those other monsters out there.'

Riddick felt another cold wave. Si knew his time was up. And he really didn't sound like he cared all that much.

'I knew you'd come,' Si said.

'Why's it so important I did?' Riddick asked, staring at the water. 'What's your endgame?'

Riddick's phone rang.

'Answer it,' Si said.

Riddick heard him moving closer behind him.

'It's my boss. For you, it's probably not a good idea.'

'This *is* the idea,' Si said. He was much nearer to him now. 'So answer it.'

'And if I don't?'

Riddick felt something prodding into the back of his neck; his chest tightened. The knife.

'I'm not bluffing,' Si said.

No, Riddick thought. *I don't suppose you are.*

'Answer it.'

Riddick answered the phone. 'Hello.'

'Where the hell are you?' Gardner asked.

'I came to try and find Si and Harvey.'

'Harvey's dead.'

I know, Riddick thought. 'Shit.'

'Where *are* you?'

'Home, I'm...' The knife point dug into the back of his neck; he winced.

'Are you okay, Paul?' Gardner asked.

'Yes, I'm—'

'Just tell her the truth, Paul,' Si said.

'Who's that?' Gardner asked.

'It's...' Riddick broke off.

'Tell her,' Si insisted.

'Is that Si?' Gardner asked. 'Paul, are you in danger?'

Riddick sighed. 'Good question. I'm not actually sure. I'll ask.' He held his phone out. 'My boss wants to know if I'm in danger?'

'What do you think, Paul?' Si said. 'Talk to her.'

Riddick pulled the phone back to his ear. 'Looks that way. He's got the knife he killed Harvey with.'

'Paul, where are you?'

'Listen. I'll handle it.'

'No! *Where are you?*'

'Middle of nowhere.'

'Tell her where you are, right now, Paul.' His head was pushed forward by the sudden pressure of the knife point on the back of his neck.

'Paul, you damn well do as he says, and tell me!'

It was spiralling out of control, but what could he do? 'I'm behind the old scout hut.'

'Hold on, keep him talking. Help's coming.'

Gardner rang off.

'I guess we're going to have fireworks now,' Riddick said.

'I guess so.'

'It's what you wanted, isn't it?'

'Keep looking at the river. I don't want you to get up, and I don't want you to look at me, but we can talk. Until... the end.'

The knife left the back of Riddick's neck. He reached around and rubbed it. Damp. He looked at the blood on his fingers. His? Or Harvey's? He dropped his hand and stared at the houses over the river. Would this be the last thing he ever saw? Those houses... this river?

And then what? His legacy – what was left of it – completely tarnished by Marianne's article? Would he become a benchmark of failure in the force? A warning to others of what not to become?

Jesus, was he really going to die?

Well, behind him stood a man on the edge. And a man on the edge was capable of anything.

I should know, after all.

'Two unhappy men together at the end of the world, eh?' Si said.

'I'm not happy,' Riddick said. 'Not happy at all, but that doesn't mean I want to die today.'

'Can I ask: did you call that number I gave you?'

'Yes.'

'And how did it make you feel?'

'I don't really know to be honest. And, with a knife to the back of the neck, my feelings are all over the place right now.'

'Did it give you any relief?'

'Nothing will ever give me relief,' Riddick said, before flinching at the thought of what his words could imply. 'But that still doesn't mean I want to die. How about you? How does what you've done to Harvey make you feel?'

'Nothing.' He paused. 'I feel nothing.'

'So, stop then, Si. None of this is worth it.'

Si grunted. 'Since my daughter died, it's hard to measure anything in terms of worth.'

'I hear you, Si. I hear you loud and clear. But I think our pain must be a call to us. That we should not tear everything down around us. That we should, I don't know, maybe try and build that worth elsewhere.'

'Enough, Paul. Let's be quiet for a time now. I just want to think about Tia for a few moments longer, you know... *before*.'

* * *

Riddick tried to strike up several conversations with Si over the next few minutes, but he was asked to be silent on each occasion. Si didn't get angry or prod him with the knife point again; he simply demanded more time to think about Tia.

Eventually, Riddick gave up and looked down at the ground he was sitting on, hoping to formulate a way out of this predicament. There was a large piece of glass from a smashed bottle lodged in the dirt. He moved his legs, slowly and gradually, until his bent knees were above the glass. Then, he slipped his hand cautiously beneath his legs, so he could work the glass free. Riddick hated the thought of hurting Si. Their lives had been fractured in similar ways. He felt no anger towards him, only sympathy, because he knew first-hand the turmoil that drove a person to insanity.

However, Riddick had been telling the truth before when he'd said he didn't want to die today, and anything could happen when those *fireworks* arrived.

'We used to smash bottles here,' Si said. 'Way back when. Stones on bottles. Me and Harvey.'

Riddick felt his heart beating faster. *Why did he bring up smashed bottles? Has he seen me work the glass free, and is looking on smugly, knowing I won't have the chance to use it?*

'Si. Have you thought about a different ending? A better one?'

Si grunted. 'Such as?'

Good question, Riddick thought, realising he didn't quite have an answer just yet. He thought about what the therapist had said to him once when he'd told him he felt suicidal. *There're always new beginnings, Paul. You must know that, and you must hold onto that.*

'We can all start again. You could use some of what you've experienced to help others...'

'From a jail cell?'

There was a screech of brakes behind him. Followed by another. The vehicles were piling in.

Armed response.

'I'm asking you, Paul, not to turn around. Not once. If you don't, then it might not be too late for you. But if you turn, then you'll leave me no choice.'

Riddick felt the glass digging into his palm as he gripped it tightly. He listened to vehicle doors being flung open, the sound of boots on the ground, a couple of shouts between team members.

Time was running out.

Everything quietened down quickly.

Behind him, Si breathing. Ahead of him, some ducks ambling past.

A loud, female voice broke the quiet. 'Si Meadows. Put the weapon onto the ground and step away from it.'

'No,' Si said.

'Si,' Riddick said. 'They'll put holes in you.'

'Shut up, Paul!'

Should he turn, thrust the glass into Si's leg, bring him down, disarm him? Sudden movement could stimulate gunfire. It could end them both...

'This is my *second* clear warning, Si Meadows,' the female officer tried again. 'Put the weapon in your hand onto the ground—'

'And you heard my response the first time. *No.*'

'Si, *please* listen to me; I've an idea,' Riddick said, chancing a slight turn of his head.

'Don't you turn around. Do you hear me? Look at the river.'

'Si, listen.' He poked the sharp edge of the glass out between his fingers. Should he take the chance? Thrust it into his leg? Scurry up on top of him after he'd hit the floor? Scream at armed response to hold fire?

'Look at the river!' Si shouted.

'Put the weapon down!' The volume of the officer's warnings was increasing.

'Okay, okay,' Riddick said, turning his head back. *Shit.* This was suicide!

'Si?' It was Gardner.

Not now. 'Boss, please!' Riddick's heart thrashed in his chest. 'Get away—'

'Shut up!' Si demanded.

Riddick felt the knifepoint on his neck again. *Christ. Emma. Do you know what you're doing?*

'DCI Gardner, I need you to stay back,' the officer said.

'Si, I need to talk to you,' Gardner said.

Riddick could hear her edging closer. She was ignoring the request.

You really don't know what you're doing, do you?

'I must *insist* now, DCI,' the officer continued.

'Okay,' Gardner said. 'I'll stop... here... Listen, Si, I can only imagine the pain you're going through.'

'Imagine?' Si laughed. 'How could you have the foggiest idea? Paul might do, but you? How?'

'Okay, if that's the case, Si, then listen to Paul. I'm sure he's spoken to you. Nobody wants what's about to happen.'

'Nobody?' Si laughed. 'You sure about that? Those officers behind you look very enthusiastic. And as you can see, I'm not averse to the idea.'

It's the wrong approach, Emma, Riddick thought. 'Si, listen to me.' He winced as the pain from the knife intensified on his neck, but he didn't scream out. If he did, they'd fire.

'Enough!' Gardner called.

'DCI, do not take any more steps,' the officer said. 'One more step and we'll take down the assailant. We cannot risk any more escalation, do you understand?'

'Okay, okay, I've stopped. I promise. Easy with those fingers.' She sighed. 'Okay, listen, Si, you need to know that you killed the wrong man. Harvey didn't do this.'

A moment of silence.

'Are you listening?' Gardner continued.

'No!' Si shouted. 'Liar. The witnesses? There were two of them!'

'I'm sorry, Si,' Gardner continued. 'It was a lie. The travellers on the old rugby field made up the story.'

'I don't believe...'

The knife came off Riddick's neck.

'They did,' Gardner continued. 'Nobody saw Harvey with your daughter. That never happened.'

'But why'd they lie?' Si asked.

'To protect themselves from investigation. I spoke to the witnesses; there were too many inconsistencies.'

'Then why did you let it out in the bloody news?'

'It was a mistake. I'm sorry; it shouldn't have happened.'

'No, shut the hell up! No... no... You're tricking me!'

Riddick could tell that Si was moving away from him now. *Towards* Gardner. He readied the glass.

'Stand back,' the leader of armed response shouted. 'Another step, and we *will* shoot.'

'You're lying,' Si continued. 'He killed my daughter. That bastard—'

'He didn't.' Gardner's voice was loud. It drowned out everyone.

Everything fell silent.

It's working, Riddick thought. *True or not, whatever you're saying, Emma, it's working.* 'This changes everything,' Riddick said. 'The person who did this, they're still out there. We still need to find them.'

No response.

Process it, Si, Riddick thought. *You need to fight another day...*

'Put the weapon down, Si,' Gardner said. 'I promise you that this is the right way.'

Still no response.

'Now, Si,' Gardner said.

'I... I...' Si said. 'No.'

Riddick shook his head. *You stubborn old prick.*

'It changes nothing,' Si said. 'What can I do from a prison cell?'

'Nothing,' Gardner said. 'Because we'll handle it. We're close and you'll get justice. I promise.'

Shit, no! Riddick thought. *Wrong word. Si has a different definition of justice.*

'Justice?' Si said.

Riddick tried to intervene. 'What she means is—'

'Justice, DCI?' Si interrupted. 'Like the justice you got for that man behind me, Paul Riddick?'

It was spiralling. Riddick looked at the shard of glass in his hand again.

'His entire family dead, and the killer enjoying three hot meals a day?'

'Put the weapon on the ground,' the officer continued to demand.

'Nah,' Si said. 'It just ain't good enough. None of this is good enough. Paul? You understand what must happen here. Listen to me. If it wasn't Harvey, you find whoever did this to Tia.'

'Yes, of course. Put the weapon down, and I'll do whatever you need me to,' Riddick said.

'I can't do that. But I trust you to find them and do what's right. You owe me now, remember? I gave you justice, so you can give me mine—'

Riddick swung, dived forward and jabbed the glass into Si's leg. He yelled in pain. The DI reached out for his leg to pull him down, but the large man yanked it away at the last second.

Shit!

Si darted towards Gardner with his leg trailing behind him, and Riddick knew it was over, even before the gunshot and the sound of the body hitting the floor.

41

Gardner marched after Riddick.

'Paul, stop!'

Riddick halted at his car door, opened it, but before climbing in, turned and faced Gardner. She saw tears in his eyes.

'I could've stopped him,' Riddick said.

'How?'

'If you hadn't have shown up. There wouldn't have been so much distance between us. I'd have been able to stop him. Bring him to the floor.'

'Ifs and maybes, Paul.'

'I'd take ifs and maybes right now. Better than dead.'

Gardner shook her head. 'You're emotionally drained, Paul. Si brought this on himself. Even if you'd wrestled him to the ground, you think he'd have lain there, knife in hand, happy for your help? No. He'd have fought back and' – she threw a thumb in the direction of armed response – 'they'd have still ended it. Just with the added risk of hitting you in the process.'

Riddick turned and pounded his fist on the roof of the car. 'When did everything turn into such a shit show?'

Gardner put her hand on his shoulder. 'You're not the same as him. He experienced something terrible, but that's where your similarities end. He chose a different path to you, and we both know that those paths always end in failure. You're going to beat this, Paul. We're going to beat this.'

Riddick took a deep breath. He looked up at the sky, then shook his head. 'It's too late.'

'It's never too late. Marianne Perse won't win.'

'Not that. Not the article. Something else...'

She recalled Si's words in those final moments. *You owe me now, remember? I gave you justice, so you can give me mine.*

Owe him what? What justice? She opened her mouth to ask him but quickly closed it again. Now was not the time. She needed to calm him down, not wind him up further.

'Just do yourself a favour, boss, and get as far away from me as possible,' Riddick continued. 'I'm more like Si than you realise.'

Her phone rang. It was O'Brien.

'Lucy?'

'Sorry, boss. I'm so sorry. I let you down. I can't—'

'Woah, Lucy, slow down. What happened?'

'Rose is gone.'

'What?'

'I'm sorry. Her father took her.'

Gardner steadied herself against the roof of Riddick's car. She felt like someone had punched her in the stomach, knocking all the wind out of her.

42

Gardner was too shaken up to drive. Riddick shook off his own demons to take her home.

En route, he probed her for answers. She gave him them, telling him all about Jack and her suspicions that the money she'd found was Tia's, as well as her maverick approach in the travellers' camp-site earlier. 'I need to be hung out for it.'

Riddick looked at her. 'No one's being hung out. We don't even know if the money was Tia's. And if it was, you followed your instincts. Tried to shut this lead down before it escalated and poten-tially wasted time and resources.'

'What a great bloody job I've done!'

'Shit happens. You tried. Over my dead body is anyone going after you for this. You're the best thing that's ever happened to this place. Trust me, if you recall, I know your predecessor well. You just chuck that money back under his bed and let me dig it out now.'

She stared at him. *Reckless, as always.* 'We're not having this conversation. Bloody hell, Paul, if anything has happened to Rose...'

'She'll be fine. Jack's her father. He loves her, I'm sure.'

'You don't know him like I do, Paul. He doesn't understand the meaning of the word *love*.'

When she saw the ambulance outside her house, she darted from the car before Riddick had even brought the car to a complete standstill.

She located O'Brien beside the ambulance, holding a bloody rag to the back of her head, arguing with a paramedic.

'Lucy?' Gardner said. 'Oh Lord, this is on me, I'm sorry.'

'I'm fine, boss, *seriously*.'

Gardner put her hands on the young officer's shoulders. 'It's my fault. I never—'

'Boss, seriously—'

'I'm *so* sorry.'

'Why? I let *you* down. Your niece is gone.'

'Nonsense. Tell me what happened Lucy.'

'Your brother got in without me noticing.'

Because he has a key, Gardner thought. *How could I be so sodding stupid?* She shook her head, forcing back tears of shame.

'He surprised me in the kitchen and clocked me with a pan. When I came to, Rose was gone. He's her dad. She'll be okay, won't she?'

'Yes,' Gardner said, not sure whether she believed this. 'He loves her.' Or at least feels for her in whatever way his limited capacities allow.

'Excuse me?' the paramedic said. 'I really need you to talk some sense into your colleague. She needs to get to the hospital for a check over.'

'I'm fine; how many times?' O'Brien narrowed her eyes at the pestering paramedic.

'No,' Gardner said. 'You go into the hospital. I'll call you as soon as we've found them.'

She looked up and saw Riddick talking to some officers outside her house. She went into her home, up the stairs and into Jack's room to confirm what she already knew. The bags were gone.

She went into her own room and retrieved the hidden envelope stuffed full of cash, looked down at it with tears in her eyes, and then contacted Barnett.

'Boss!' Barnett said. 'I've just heard. You all right? Shit, is Paul all right? The shooting! I don't know which way to look.'

'All eyes out for my brother and my niece. We *must* find them Ray. They won't have got far.'

'Already in process, boss. Marsh has thrown the kitchen sink.'

Gardner sighed. 'I've also got to come clean about something. You got a pen and paper ready?'

'Yes, boss.'

Gardner told him about the money she found this morning, and her visit to the travellers' site, which was cut short by the hut exploding. 'That was the reason Lucy was here at my house, Ray. I told her to look after Rose while I went to ask Aiden about this money.'

Barnett didn't speak for a moment. She wondered if he was too stunned by her confession, or just making notes.

'I wasn't able to link it to Aiden or Tommy, but I *think* it's linked, I really do.'

'Okay... so you were just trying to find out...'

Don't you start! 'No, Ray, you're not hearing this. I shouldn't have sat on it. I should've reported it straight away, instead of going off on my own.'

Barnett was quiet again for a moment.

'Are you listening, Ray?'

'Yes, boss, but I'm not actually sure what you want me to say?'

'Go and speak to Marsh, tell her your concerns.'

'I don't have concerns.'

'Ray!'

'Okay, boss, *shit*; whatever you want.'

'Then, could you send someone to come and collect the money. We should submit it for forensics. Although, we know it'll have my DNA on it now.'

She chatted about several other leads Barnett was following before quickly ending the call to run to the toilet.

43

After vomiting twice and drinking two glasses of water to replace the lost fluids, she sat on her sofa, trembling, while Riddick went to boil the kettle.

She saw Rose's pug on the table and her heart sank. She reached over, picked it up and clutched it to her chest.

She cried for a moment, pausing occasionally to shake her head over her reckless behaviour.

Riddick came into the room, holding two cups of tea. 'Look at the pair of us.' He placed them down on the table. His phone rang; he looked at the screen and then answered. 'Yes, ma'am... she's here...'

Riddick handed her the phone, mouthing, 'Marsh.'

Here it was. The bollocking to end all bollockings. Suspension? The least she deserved.

'Ma'am.'

'Breathe easy, Emma, we have them,' Marsh said. 'Rose is safe and Jack is in custody for assaulting Lucy.'

Gardner felt an indescribable rush of relief, the likes of which she'd never experienced. 'Where is Rose?'

'With social services.'

Out of my hands now, then. But safe, at least she's safe.

'I want you to take five, Emma, and then come back to HQ.'

'Of course. I take it Ray spoke with you, ma'am?'

'He has.'

'And?'

'And Rose is safe, Lucy will be fine, but we still don't have Tia's killer. So, I've no other priorities right now. Hear that? No other priorities right now.'

She hung up and told Riddick the news, who'd already picked it up from the conversation. She drank her tea in silence, with Riddick looking over her.

Not right now.

So, she lived to fight another day.

But this hadn't been the last she'd heard of it. Not a chance. And rightly so. She'd been negligent. But as she reflected on it now, she realised that it wasn't her career she was worried about. It was the potential blow to her chances of fostering Rose that terrified her most.

Riddick's phone rang. He answered. 'Yes, Phil... I'm with her, yes. She's just taking a few minutes...' He stood. 'You can speak to me if you want—'

Gardner thrust her hand out so hard that Riddick jolted back to avoid a thick lip. 'Give me the phone.'

Riddick handed it to her.

'Phil?'

'Boss, you need to hear this.'

Gardner stood. 'I'm all ears.'

'Poking around Tia's finances, something struck me as odd. There's been a lot of money going into her account from the White Bull. And I mean *a lot*. I gave the landlord, Bertie Thomas, a call to query it. He assured me it was overtime, but you know, unless she was working twenty-four hours a day, seven days a week, I'm not buying it. Especially as she's another job with Tesco, which takes up a fair chunk of her working hours. So, I told Bertie to send over his copies of her payslips to correlate with her bank account.'

Gardner, who'd been lost to despair merely minutes before, suddenly felt an awakening inside. 'And?'

'The money on the payslips which Bertie possesses does not match the money that was going into Tia's account from the White Bull. Either he slung *me* some false payslips, or whoever handles payment has slung *him* some false payslips.'

She began to pace, anticipation burning in her stomach.

'So, after finding out that Tia wasn't on quadruple time, I asked Bertie who's responsible for organising payments,' Rice continued. 'Well, it's not a brewery. The White Bull is privately owned by Bertie. It seems Bertie employs Benjamin Murphy of Murphy Ltd to organise his finances. And get this, boss, Benjamin Murphy is also Rhys Hunt's financial manager.'

Gardner's entire body started to tingle. 'And?'

'That's it up to now.'

Riddick was staring at Gardner, wide eyed. He mouthed, 'What?'

'Phenomenal work, Phil,' Gardner said.

'So, can I go and see Benjamin Murphy and query the false payslips, and the excessive pay? I doubt he'll give us anything until he has a solicitor, but we can try nonetheless?'

Barnett would normally be her go-to for a job like this, because although Rice was stellar behind a desk, away from it, he was a risk. But how could she say no after he just tore this gold nugget from the mine?

'Okay. Could you ask Ray to follow up on Bertie, then, please?'

'I don't think he's involved.'

'Probably not, but double check anyway. In fact, treble check.'

'Yes, boss. Thank you for freeing me from the desk... I think I'm now in love with you.'

'If you ever say that again, I'll take the freedom back off you. *Permanently.*' She looked up at Riddick. 'Myself and Paul will go and see Rhys again. Find out if it's his money that has found its way into Tia's bank account...'

And potentially into my brother's deceitful hands.

44

The conversation between Gardner and Riddick on the journey to Rhys Hunt's home went at breakneck speed, flitting between the investigation and the source of the leak. Riddick suspected Rice. Why wouldn't he? He despised him.

During her previous investigation, Gardner had suspected Rice of leaking information to the press herself. But now she wasn't so sure. He just seemed too eager to please. He chased praise, and despite those horrendous attitudes from a bygone era, he was bloody effective at times. Would he really jeopardise his growing reputation?

'There's no one else in your team that would go that low, boss. No one. You need to listen,' Riddick said.

Gardner sighed. 'I am! Well, whoever it is, they've cost two men their lives today. As soon as we put Operation Bright Day to bed, we're going to have to plug the leak, no matter how hard it is.'

After parking, they approached Rhys Hunt's impressive home on foot down the driveway. En route, Riddick stopped Gardner with a hand on her shoulder. 'Are you okay, Emma?'

He didn't usually use her first name. She stopped and smiled at him. 'I'm fine, Paul. Stop worrying about me.'

He nodded. 'You spend enough time worrying about me; figured I owed you.'

'Thanks... and you, Paul, are you fine?'

He looked away. 'Yes.'

Liar. Si's needless death... the impending article... you're a bloody mess, aren't you? And here you are, directing your energies into me.

She felt her heart warming. She hadn't experienced friendship like this since Michael Yorke, her DCI back in Salisbury.

'What a pair we are,' Gardner said.

They continued to the door. This time, Riddick didn't make a song and dance over the hand-carved naked women depicted on the door knocker and rapped it against the wood insistently.

Lorraine Hunt answered the door. Her eyes were glassy and her hair unkempt. She was also red-faced and sweating. Gardner and Riddick exchanged a look.

'Can I help you?' Lorraine asked.

Gardner smiled. 'Sorry to disturb you again, Mrs Hunt—'

'Again?' Lorraine looked confused. 'I don't recall... Sorry, who are you? I'm not too well, you know.'

Bloody hell, Gardner thought. *How strong is that medication the doctor has you on?*

'DCI Emma Gardner and DI Paul Riddick,' Gardner said, trying to assist her memory.

'Okay, yes, I recall...'

Gardner could see in her eyes that she still didn't have a clue.

'Are you exercising, Mrs Hunt?' Riddick asked.

'Exercising? What makes you say that?'

'You look flustered,' Riddick continued.

Lorraine touched her damp forehead and looked at the perspiration on her fingers. 'Oh... just tidying. My husband is a pig, you know.'

Gardner and Riddick exchanged another look.

'Is your husband, Rhys, home?' Gardner asked.

'No. He's out.'

'Do you know where exactly?' Riddick asked.

'Work, I guess... That's usually the case.'

'Are you okay, Mrs Hunt?' Gardner asked.

'Yes. Like I said... just, you know, tired, and running about the place. I don't sleep so well these days.'

Gardner nodded. She leaned closer so she could speak more quietly. 'Are you in any danger, Lorraine?'

Lorraine shook her head slowly. 'No, of course, not. Why would I be?' Her face brightened momentarily. 'I do remember yesterday now. I'm sorry. I showed you those pictures.'

'Yes, you did,' Gardner said and smiled.

'I'm sorry. I take medication, you see. It's strong. It keeps me... calm. But sometimes everything goes a little fuzzy.'

'I understand,' Gardner said. 'We tried your husband's number, but we can't get through to him. We assumed he'd be here with it being the weekend...'

'Doesn't matter to Rhys,' Lorraine said. 'He spends most of the weekend in his office.'

'Okay, thanks, we shall catch him there then.'

And if he's not there, we'll just have to locate him by his phone.

'Is there anything else I can help you with?' Lorraine asked.

Plenty, Gardner thought, *but I'd like to talk to Rhys first.*

Riddick handed her a card. 'If he calls and gives you his location, can you contact us?'

'What's it concerning?'

'Same as yesterday,' Gardner answered.

Lorraine narrowed her eyes. 'Yes. Now, I come to think of it, I remember. You got my husband into a right state.' She took a step back. Gardner noticed the large tattoo of the eagle on her ankle she'd seen the day before.

'I feel rather sick,' Lorraine said. She reached up to her neck and took a pendant of a bird between her thumb and forefinger. The bird had long, outstretched wings, and Gardner wondered briefly if this too was an eagle. 'I think I need to lie down.'

'Of course,' Gardner said. 'We'll try his office and go from there.'

On the way back to the car, Riddick said, 'Is it appropriate these days to say someone is peculiar?'

Gardner didn't respond. She had birds and eagles on her mind.

Something was bothering her.

Back in the car, her phone rang. It was Rice.

'Phil?'

'I've spoken to our suspicious financial accountant, Benjamin Murphy.'

'And?'

'He went pale when I showed him a copy of the dodgy payslips, but that's as far as we got. He wants a solicitor. Only positive is that he's agreed to come to the station without a fuss.'

'I'll leave it in your capable hands, Phil. We're heading to Rhys' office.'

After ringing off, she fed back to Riddick, and then said, 'You see the tattoo on Lorraine's ankle?'

'The eagle... yes. Bold, huh?'

'Why do you think she chose an eagle?'

Riddick shrugged and started the car engine. 'She likes birds of prey? She wants to present herself as a powerful person? Although that isn't working out so well. Seems like her husband has really done a number on her... ground her right down.'

'And she had a pendant. She was fiddling with it. That looked like an eagle, too.'

Riddick checked his mirrors and moved the car out onto the road. 'I didn't notice... sorry.'

'So, do these eagles remind you of anything over the last couple of days?'

'No, but they do you by the looks of it. It'll come to you when you least expect it. You know how it works. Take your mind off it for the moment. Tell me whether or not you fancy Rhys for the murder?'

'I think the DNA results will show that he got her pregnant. He's obviously paying for her silence. Paying for a good life for Tia and a future illegitimate child.'

Riddick shrugged again. 'Makes sense. Drip feeding Tia a lot of cash to support her is far safer than a large lump sum which may be noticed.'

'Also, by using this system, he avoids contact with her. Protecting himself from Si Meadows, and the wrath of his wife.'

'Yep. Completely washing his hands of the whole thing. So why kill her? By killing her, he risks exposing the payslips, which would almost certainly have gone unnoticed otherwise. Not like he couldn't afford to maintain the status quo?' Riddick asked.

'Unless Tia changed her mind and threatened to expose him. Maybe Aiden and Tommy put more pressure on her to up her demands?'

Riddick nodded as he indicated right. 'Clear motive.'

Gardner's phone rang. It was Barnett this time.

'Ray?'

'I'm no mind-reader but I'm fairly convinced Bertie was none the wiser. You might want to take another run at it, boss, but I reckon he'll be twiddling that bow tie and serving shit beer for years to come.'

'Thanks.'

After the call, Gardner looked out of the window and watched a flock of birds draw patterns in the sky...

And a memory exploded in her mind.

Another bird pendant in between a thumb and a forefinger.

Aiden Poole's thumb and forefinger.

'Pull over, Paul,' Gardner said.

'Why?'

'Do it!'

As he did so, she fumbled around in her pocket for her notepad.

'Talk to me,' Riddick said from the driver's seat.

'Maybe... yes...' She flicked through the book until she had Aiden's phone number. 'I need to make a call, but I need you to make a call too. I'll leave the car – you use your hands-free.'

'What is it? You've got me tingling all over!'

She told him.

'Shit, if you're right—'

'Now!'

She jumped out of the car onto the pavement and phoned Aiden.

'Yes?'

'Aiden, it's me, DCI Gardner.'

Aiden sighed. 'It's over. I heard.'

Over! 'I need to ask you a question.'

'Why? We're leaving. You folk got your way, as you always do. Shifted us on. And as I've told you, that story those kids told you has nothing to do with me—'

'Just listen. It's nothing to do with that. It's about that pendant around your neck.'

A moment of silence followed by a snort. 'What? The eagle?'

'Yes! That one! I saw you playing with it the other day when I first spoke to you. Where did you get it?'

Aiden paused. 'Wait... am I being fitted up for something here?'

'Did you love her, Aiden? Do you want the truth? Because the truth is that Harvey Henfrey did not take Tia from you. If you want to know, tell me where you got the goddamned pendant.'

A pause.

'Now!'

'From Tia, okay? She gave it to me.'

'Okay... okay... Why?'

'It was a gift. Well, I guess it was kind of a gift. It was hers, but she didn't want it any more. I started wearing it to wind her up. Then, you know, when it happened, I didn't really want to take it off.'

Gardner suddenly felt as if thousands of volts of electricity were shooting through her. She turned and realised she'd paced a fair distance from the car. 'Who gave it to her, Aiden?' *Please say you know... please tell me who.*

'She never said.'

Shit. Stay with it, Emma. That's not the end of it. 'Okay... okay, she just gave it to you, and said she didn't want it any more. There must be something else? Did she at least tell you why she didn't want it?'

'Yes, it was odd what she said.'

Gardner took a deep breath. *Please... Please...*

'She said the person who gave it to her had said: an eagle waits... watches... and swoops only when it is ready. I thought it sounded quite cool, but she didn't. In fact, it seemed to unnerve her. She wouldn't tell me who it was, but she said it was someone she was very close to, someone she did wrong by.'

Gardner breathed out. Her instinct had been right. She saw it all now. Clear as day.

'Someone she did wrong by? And you didn't think to tell me?' Gardner said.

'I... I... honestly didn't think. She didn't make that much of a big deal out of it.'

She stopped short of telling Aiden that he was one of the reasons that an innocent man had just died. She opted to hang up instead.

She ran to the car, opened the door. She'd had Riddick on a long shot, and didn't expect much here, but when she saw his wide eyes, she knew her second hunch had also struck gold.

'Yes, Lorraine Hunt does have her own business, online, in fact. She makes stainless steel pendants.'

'Turn the car around, Paul. *Now*.'

45

Riddick was in no mind to waste any time calling in backup.

Gardner wasn't that stupid. She contacted HQ and then joined Riddick on his march to the front door. She was out of breath when she caught up to him.

She could see from his wide eyes that he was pumped. Riddick thrived on moments like this.

He used the door knocker, but there was no answer.

'We have about five minutes until the cavalry arrive,' Gardner said.

Riddick didn't reply. He knocked again.

Still no answer. 'I'm not waiting,' Riddick said.

She looked down at his clenched fists. 'If I wasn't here, you'd already be in there, wouldn't you?'

'With two valid reasons. First, Lorraine Hunt looked sick. She's now not answering the door even though we know she's in. Is her life in danger?'

'Valid. And the other reason?'

'Well, if you're right – we know the other reason.'

'I'm right. It's valid too,' Gardner said.

He took a step back to kick the door down.

'At least try the handle first,' Gardner said.

Riddick shrugged and did. The door glided open. 'She was obviously keen to get back to whatever she was doing,' he whispered.

'Unless she did it on purpose. Go steady.' Gardner slipped in first. 'Mrs Hunt?' Gardner called out. 'We came back to ask you a few questions.'

Gardner paused, waited for a response. Nothing came.

'We have entered your house to check on your safety. You looked unwell when we saw you before.'

No response.

Gardner looked back at Riddick in the doorway.

He shrugged and mouthed, 'Fair game. Let's go.'

They made their way into the lounge. Gardner glanced over at the photograph of a muscular Lorraine holding first prize in a bodybuilding competition. She looked at the sofa and remembered the photographs of the festivals. Lorraine's fondest memories. Gardner looked over at the bar where Rhys had poured himself drinks. It'd been neat and tidy yesterday; today, there were bottles strewn all over it.

She heard Lorraine's words in her head. Her claim that she was tidying. *My husband is a pig, you know.*

She looked at Riddick; she wondered if her deputy had been drinking again. She suspected he had.

'Mrs Hunt?' Gardner called out.

They paused. Still no response.

'It's a big house,' Riddick said. 'But she'd have heard us by now. She's either passed out, or ready to swoop like that bloody eagle on her ankle.'

'You're right,' Gardner said. She looked at her watch. 'I think we should wait for backup.'

'It's your call.'

Gardner paused to listen but could hear nothing in the house.

She led Riddick through into a corridor off the lounge that ran adjacent to an impressive staircase.

She tried calling again. Predictably, nothing.

Riddick pointed at a door in the wall beneath the stairs. 'Maybe she's down in a bunker?'

'Maybe,' Gardner said. 'We've only three minutes to wait and we can find out.'

Riddick stepped forward and opened the door. 'Open.'

'What happened to "it's your call"?' Gardner asked.

Riddick looked back at her and shrugged. 'I'll take a quick look. You keep the stairs covered and wait for the cavalry.'

'While you march off into the dark?'

He switched on the light. 'Happy?'

'No,' she said, following him down.

The stairs were modern and didn't creak on their descent, but this was only a small mercy. The silence was suffocating and she felt her dread intensifying. The coldness in her chest where the knife had entered her all those years ago, flared up. She paused near the bottom. 'This is a mistake, Paul.'

Riddick reached the final step and turned into the cellar.

She clutched her chest and took deep breaths to try and steady the rising panic.

She listened for Riddick's movements, but all she got was the overwhelming silence. 'Paul?' she called out.

He didn't reply.

She turned and looked up the stairs at the open door, hoping to see assistance, but seeing only that they remained alone, and vulnerable.

She turned back, breathing quickly. 'Paul! Where the bloody hell are you?'

Nothing.

'Paul!'

Riddick poked his head around and looked up at her. 'All clear. No one here, but you have to see this, boss.'

She breathed a sigh of relief and headed down the stairs, the sensation that had flared up in her old wound subsiding.

Gardner looked around the well-organised cellar. It was certainly a far cry from her cellar back in her house in Salisbury which was piled high with half-empty paint tins and junk.

This was an efficient working space. She looked around at the equipment carefully laid out on the tables. She walked over to an Apple Mac sitting in the corner and looked at the shelves above it. There were labelled glass boxes full of pendants. She read a couple of labels: honeybees; crucifixes; leopards; seagulls. She followed the boxes along until she reached hawks and eagles. She then looked back around at the equipment. She went over to Riddick. She pointed at the walls. 'Soundproofing.'

Riddick nodded. 'Not that it matters, she isn't in here—'

'Wait,' Gardner said. 'Look.'

She strode to the end of the long room to the final shelf which was covered in labelled jars and boxes. The shelf was several feet away from the back wall, but she could see through a gap between two boxes.

She pointed and turned to look at Riddick. 'There's a door there. You can see its handle poking through the proofing.'

Riddick came alongside her. 'Well, we've come this far—'

Gardner heard something and put her hand on his arm. 'Listen; do you hear that?'

Riddick listened.

Gardner heard it again. It sounded like a whipping sound. Far in the distance. She squeezed Riddick's arm.

'I hear it,' he said, pulling away and slipping past the shelf.

'Wait, Paul!'

He yanked opened the door.

With the soundproofing breached, the next whipping sounded close and vicious.

Then came a muffled moan.

Her heart racing, Gardner slid around the shelf and sprinted into the adjacent room after Riddick. As she did so, there came another dreadful whipping sound, followed by another pained moan.

This soundproofed room was much smaller than the one they had come from, and it was almost completely bare. Naked, on his knees, and hugging a long pipe at the end of the room, was Rhys Hunt. His back was a bloody mess.

Lorraine, still dressed in the nightie that she'd opened the door in earlier, was standing with her back to the two officers.

'Lorraine,' Riddick said, closing in on her. 'Put the belt down.'

She was unperturbed. She drew the belt back and struck her husband again.

Rhys' sobbing and moaning remained muffled; he must have been gagged. Gardner shuddered when she thought of Lorraine's sweaty face at the front door. This torture had been going on for a long time.

Knowing that Lorraine's history of bodybuilding would make her a strong adversary, Gardner was relieved when she offered little resistance to Riddick. Riddick wrapped his arms around her, and she hung loosely in his grip.

Gardner, meanwhile, darted over to Rhys. She looked down at his back. A mess of welts and frayed flesh. He was, as she'd suspected, handcuffed around the bar. She yanked the tape off Rhys mouth, so he could let his moans and sobs out properly.

She looked up and saw Riddick reading Lorraine her rights as he led her out of the small room.

Gardner surveyed the empty room. Her eyes fell to the loose pile of bricks in the corner. She thought of Tia's head wound.

Rhys managed to speak. 'I didn't know... I *really* didn't know.'

'How could you not have known, Mr Hunt? This is your home!'

'I never...' He winced and gasped for air. 'I never come down...' He sobbed in agony. 'I can't hear anything down here.'

'Tia was pregnant with your baby, wasn't she?'

Rhys nodded; his face scrunched up. Tears ran down his face.

'You were giving her money?'

He continued to nod.

'I loved her.' He clenched his teeth, clearly fighting the agony. 'I loved her.'

'So everyone keeps telling me,' Gardner said. 'Yet, no one helped her. No one *saved* her.'

Rhys looked up at Gardner, tears and snot streaming down his pain-contorted face. 'How could I know? I never told Lorraine! I never told her!'

Gardner could hear feet pounding on the steps leading down into the adjacent cellar; backup had arrived.

'I thought it was the freak by the lake, like everyone else.' He put his head against the bar and looked as if he was going to pass out.

Several officers and a paramedic suddenly flanked her.

She stood back to allow him to retrieve treatment.

* * *

After Lorraine Hunt was taken away, Riddick and Gardner waited by the ambulance until Rhys had been freed.

He was led towards the ambulance on a trolley. He lay on his side with an oxygen mask on. As he drew alongside Gardner, his eyes were open.

She looked at the paramedic. 'I need another word.'

'I don't think—'

'It's important. Two minutes. Is he comfortable?'

'As much as he can be. He's had a fair jolt of painkillers. He might not make too much sense.'

Gardner knelt so she was looking directly at Rhys' face.

'You said you didn't know that Lorraine knew?'

Rhys pulled off his mask. 'I didn't.' His eyes rolled. He looked relieved to be freed from agony but remaining conscious was still proving a burden for him. It wouldn't be long. 'Last night, she brought me a drink and told me that Tia had confessed to her. Over a week ago, in fact. Can you believe it? Silly girl! Oh, that poor, sweet, silly girl! The guilt was too much for her, so she'd asked for Lorraine's forgiveness.'

'She didn't get it,' Riddick said. 'She got a pendant and a warning.'

Rhys closed his eyes and Gardner wondered if that was all he was giving up. She was about to sigh when he opened them.

'Did Lorraine then tell you what she'd done to Tia?' Gardner asked.

'Not exactly. She told me that Tia came here later on the night I'd seen her at the White Bull – the night she died. Apparently, she'd wanted to speak to me, but I'd already passed out on the sofa, pissed. Tia told Lorraine that she was here to tell me that she never wanted to see me again... that she didn't want the money any more. That she was leaving Knaresborough with some traveller boy she'd hooked up with.' His eyes filled with tears. 'Jesus. Why couldn't that have been enough for Lorraine? Why did she then have to go and do this?'

'So, she admitted to it?'

'She said she'd show me what had really happened to her. It was then I realised the drink she gave me was drugged. When I woke up I was in the cellar... well, you know the rest.' He closed his eyes.

Gardner stood and looked at Riddick. She gave him a nod, indicating that this would do for now, and said thank you to the paramedic.

The paramedic wheeled Rhys to the back of the ambulance.

Rhys' eyes opened and he called out, 'Lorraine!'

Riddick and Gardner exchanged a glance. He was clearly out of it now. They started to turn.

'Lorraine!' Rhys said again. 'She's not herself... she never used to be like this. She used to be sweet, fun-loving, good humoured... and so fit. We have a gym out back and the bench pressing... I used to love how strong she was.'

Gardner looked at Riddick and then back at Rhys again. He was pitiful.

'Do you think she fully understands what she's done... what she was doing? Is there any hope for her? I couldn't live with myself if I caused this...'

Gardner opened her mouth to reply but closed it just in time.

The man was a mess at the moment. Let her words sit and wait for a while until she was sure he would fully acknowledge them. So, as the ambulance rolled away, she thought over those words.

'The decision over what happens with Lorraine will be for someone else. All I know, right now, is that poor choices have been made. Too many poor choices. And three people have now died as a result. A young girl with her life ahead of her. A father who loved his girl more than anyone can claim to in my opinion. And a man who has been tortured his entire life by the society around him... so I think it is better that you try and find someone else who can give you the peace of mind you believe that you're entitled to.'

46

In the interview room, Lorraine Hunt was still in her chair while her eyes stared vacantly at some part of the wall high above where Gardner and Riddick sat.

When yet another question failed to illicit a response, Gardner wondered if Lorraine was in the process of closing herself off from the world.

Lorraine had been provided with some clothing so she could change out of her nightie. The long-sleeved T-shirt she'd been given was tight on her, and Gardener regarded those muscles bulging through. Lorraine's days of bodybuilding may have been long behind her, but she still retained an impressive build.

Enough body strength to not only deliver a fatal blow to Tia's head, but enough to put her victim in a fireman's lift as she scaled that fence at Breary Flat Lane...

'Why Harvey?' Gardner asked. 'Why choose him?'

The wall she stared at remained far more interesting to Lorraine. If, in fact, she was *seeing* the wall and had not already retreated into the dark recesses of her mind.

Gardner and Riddick exchanged a glance. No doubt he'd be

thinking the same thing. Would they ever get the truth from Lorraine as to why she planned it this way?

Unless the truth was just plain obvious?

Wasn't Harvey the easiest, available target?

I mean, initially, apart from Gardner, no one had batted an eyelid over his guilt.

It was a solid plan, really, wasn't it, Lorraine? Just blame the local madman. Easy to throw him away. No one was going to spare resources raising hell over something so obvious.

In another life, with another SIO, Lorraine, you might just have got away with it.

She raised an eyebrow at Lorraine. *Maybe you're not really out of it? Is this just a bluff?*

When the solicitor, organised by her husband, arrived, he pounded his fists on the table and demand a psychological assessment for his client.

Here we go. I've seen this one before. Diminished responsibility.

'We won't need a confession, Lorraine,' Gardner said. 'One of those bricks in the corner of that room we found you in had blood on it. If that turns out to be Tia's, as I suspect it will do, we have the murder weapon.'

Look at me, Lorraine. Just look at me once. Let me see that your madness is a bluff.

'You whipped her, Lorraine. You struck a young, pregnant woman again and again on the back. I can only imagine the pain she felt before you took her life.'

Lorraine's eyes didn't move.

'An innocent young girl.'

Was that a flicker in her eyes? Had she responded to the word 'innocent'?

She felt a hand on her shoulder. She looked at Riddick. His nod said it all.

That was it. Time to go.

They'd done their bit. Supplied the perp and the physical evidence. It was now up to the judge and jury to determine her guilt and her destiny.

As she left the interview room, she took one last look back at Lorraine Hunt.

'I just don't understand the brutality, Lorraine. Your anger over her pregnancy, yes. The bitterness over the end of your marriage, yes. But to kill someone with such fury... such aggression... Did you really believe Tia deserved such pain? Such cruelty?'

Nothing.

Gardner sighed, shook her head and started to turn.

She stopped. Had she just seen the ghost of a smile flicker across Lorraine's face?

Gardner waited, and when it seemed unlikely that Lorraine was going to break her silence, she finally turned for the exit.

'Would you ask a bird of prey why it needs to be so brutal?' Lorraine asked.

Gardner quickly turned back. Lorraine was still staring off into the nothingness.

Gardner approached the table again, determined for more answers. She fired off more questions as she prodded the table. Five minutes later, and it was quickly apparent that Lorraine had again retreated into her shell. That one comment was all she was allowing them.

Would you ask a bird of prey why it needs to be so brutal?

'No,' Gardner said. 'Because who am I to question nature? But don't be deluded, Lorraine, into thinking that anything you did was natural. What you did was as far from natural as you can get!'

Gardner studied her just a moment longer, until Riddick, who already knew this was a lost cause, pulled her away from the interview room and the investigation.

47

Gardner received an awkward, congratulatory phone call from Marsh.

At the end of the praise, Gardner asked, 'So the other matter is going to be under consideration now?'

'The leak?'

'No... well, yes, *obviously* the leak. But I was referring to my negligence.'

'Negligence? You just wrapped up Operation Bright Day, Emma.'

'You know what I mean. The money. Ray told you. It was the wrong call. It wasn't professional.'

And to make matters worse, I'm still no closer to working out how Jack is connected.

There was silence on the phone.

'Ma'am?'

'You're an interesting person, Emma.'

'I don't follow.'

'Asking to be held to account. I've spent most of my career with people desperate to avoid accountability.'

'If we don't hold ourselves to account, how can we expect to do the same to others?'

More silence.

'Ma'am?'

'Okay, Emma, I'll hold you to account if that's what you really want.'

'It is.'

Marsh sighed. 'Congratulations again on the case.'

And then she was gone.

Gardner asked Riddick to hold a final briefing with the team to delegate and ensure all loose ends of Operation Bright Day were tied up. She also asked him to keep a close eye for any suspicious behaviour. The leak had cost lives. Someone may be jumpy.

'I will,' Riddick said.

'And not just on Phil, either.'

'Well, he won't be jumpy anyway. The man is spineless.'

She sighed. 'And apologise to everyone for my absence.'

'You sure you don't want to come into HQ before you speak to him? He's not going anywhere.'

'No. I have to do this now. I *need* to know.'

48

Jack looked up at Gardner from the other side of the desk. She didn't speak right away. Instead, she tried to read his expression, but, as had always been the case with her younger brother, she failed.

It'd been the same that day he'd hit her with a rock in Malcolm's Maze of Mirrors.

Now, like then, Gardner saw *nothing*.

Not the same kind of nothingness she'd seen in Lorraine Hunt's face. No. Jack was very much *here*. He was still connected, in some way, to the world around him. This was a completely different kind of nothingness. More of an absence of the things that make most humans, well, human.

She sat down opposite him and, like him, she tried to keep her own expression blank. She wondered briefly if she was succeeding, before quickly deciding she wasn't. No one who'd been on the emotional rollercoaster she'd been on the past twenty-four hours was keeping a straight face. Not unless you were sociopathic of course.

Not unless you were Jack Moss.

'I've disappointed you... again,' Jack said.

Gardner gave a brief nod.

'I'm sorry.'

She raised an eyebrow. 'Are you?'

Jack tilted his head, considering his response. 'Yes.'

'Just be honest with me, Jack. For once. You're not sorry, are you? Not really.'

Again, he considered. 'No, Emma, I think I am. And, in a way, I've always been sorry.'

In a way.

Nice.

'There're things I need to know,' Gardner said.

'I understand Sis—'

'Don't call me that.' Gardner pointed at him. 'Don't *you* ever call me that again.'

'But it's what our parents would've wanted.'

She stared at him for a moment, trying to work out if he really meant that, if he really *believed* that. But it was just the same old nothingness in his face. 'Our parents would understand.'

Jack nodded. 'Okay... whatever you wish.'

She stared at him for a time. He was clearly following her lead, but right now, she was struggling for words. The best she could manage was, 'Why?'

'Why what?'

'Why did you do what you did?'

'I thought it was obvious?'

'When has anything ever been obvious with you?'

'Think about it, Sis... *Emma*... It's about Rose. It's *always* been about Rose.'

'Bullshit! If you cared about Rose, you wouldn't have put her through what you did! You traumatised her!'

For a moment, he appeared genuinely sad. He lowered his eyes.

The reaction stunned Gardner, momentarily, but then she shook it off. He was just playing her, like he always played her, and everyone else.

He lifted his eyes. 'No. I'd never hurt Rose. *Never.*'

'Okay... so what about the rest of us? Are we just fair game?'

'I'd never hurt you either, Emma.'

She guffawed and pointed to the scar on her head. 'Have you forgotten about this?'

Jack sighed. 'No, but in a way, yes.'

Gardner shook her head. 'What're you on about?'

'That memory is peculiar. Strange to reflect on. Faded. Fragmented. When I look back, it seems different... *I* seem different. Even now, I see mist, confusion—'

'Can I stop you there, Jack?' Gardner said with her palm out. 'I'm not here to journey into your psyche. That accursed place is your own playground.'

'I understand, but listen, Emma. Everything is clearer these days – unusually so – and I'd never hurt you or Rose. Ever.'

'Instead, you risked killing one of my officers which, indirectly, would've completely ruined my life, but still.'

'She took me by surprise. I didn't mean to hurt her as badly as I did.'

Gardner held up the palm of her hand again. 'Anyway, let's park that for the moment. I want to start with Tommy Byrne. What's the connection between you two?'

He didn't speak for a time. This concerned Gardner. He was clearly uncertain of how much to divulge. 'This isn't being recorded, Jack.'

Jack thought for a moment longer and said, 'Fine. Because it's you, Emma, I'll tell you. For anyone else, the question would be redundant. I know those travellers, and they know me. They were in Wiltshire several years back, running with some other people I knew. I know of some things they were responsible for. So, when I realised they were up here, in Knaresborough, I saw an opportunity. And I took it.'

'You asked for money for your silence?'

Jack nodded.

'The money I found.'

Jack nodded again.

Gardner leaned forward. 'What did you have over them? What were they responsible for actually?'

'I can't tell you that... if I do, then this opportunity may never present itself again.'

'The opportunity to extort money? Come on, Jack. Could you really do that in jail anyway?'

Jack shrugged. 'I don't know, but I don't intend to burn that bridge. It's irrelevant to you, Emma. You were right about our connection – that will suffice.'

'How much money did you ask him for?'

'A lot. More than I got. I knew Tommy had access to money.'

'From where?'

'I watched the travellers for a while at the rugby club. I saw that girl, Tia, going into that boy's caravan many times. I found out who her father was. A very rich man, and according to some, a dangerous man.'

'Was. He died.'

Jack's expression didn't change.

'So, it was you? *You* got Tommy to extort the money from Tia?'

'It wasn't really extortion in the end. She gave the money willingly. Aiden just made up some rubbish about some gambling debts that he had to clear before someone sank him in the river. It worked well too. They could have kept it going until I had the three grand I expected from Tommy.'

'Except the poor girl died.'

'Yes.'

'Were you disappointed?' She forced back a sneer as she asked this question.

He shrugged. 'I never really get disappointed, but if I'm accurate in my interpretation of what happened, I wasn't at fault for her death.'

'You didn't help matters when it came to the investigation though, did you?'

'I guess not. I'm sorry.'

'Why did you beat Tommy half to death on my lawn?'

'He came around to ask me to reduce my demands. I decided against it. Told him he could have two weeks to find the rest of the money. That he'd have to get some of his people working if that's what it took. He got a bit nasty then. Started to threaten me. Told me he'd tell you that I'd got my hands on Tia's money.'

'So, you almost killed him instead? What was your thinking? Replace a lesser crime for one that was far more serious?'

'No. I didn't hurt him because of his threat. I hurt him because of his manner with my daughter.'

Gardner creased her brow. 'I don't follow.'

'Rose came to the door. He was angry and frustrated. He chose to tell Rose that her father was a dead-behind-the-eyes psychopath. He also told her to run for her life, which is also irresponsible.'

'So you did that to him in front of a child?'

'Of course not. I sent her up to her room first. There's a line, Emma. He crossed it. Do you appreciate that?'

She shook her head. 'She was hiding beneath her bloody bed. She was terrified!'

He shrugged. 'I couldn't allow him to upset Rose like that.'

'No matter the consequences?'

Jack didn't respond. Why would he? When had he ever cared about consequences?

'And now what? Is this how you envisage it all turning out?'

He tilted his head slightly but didn't respond.

'You in jail, Rose desperate for a new home.' She froze. And it hit her like a cannonball. She turned her head slowly from side to side. Her eyes widened.

A new home...

It made perfect sense.

The police had found Jack and Rose ambling into Knaresborough train station. He'd hardly gone to ground.

'You did envisage this, didn't you?'

Jack straightened his head. She thought she caught the ghost of a smile on his face.

'You bastard! You wanted to be caught. You've used me.'

Jack took a deep breath. 'I may not think and feel as you do, Emma, but I still understand the world. And I understand inevitability. More than most, perhaps. A man like me doesn't stay free for long. It simply isn't allowed. And, even if I did evade inevitability, then what? My daughter follows in my footsteps. Another dead-behind-the-eyes psycho! No. You see, you underestimate me, Emma. I do have the capacity to care. If I didn't have a heart, then how has that darling little girl managed to melt it?'

Jack smiled.

It wasn't his usual smile.

This one *was* genuine.

'So, I'm now out of the picture,' he said.

'And you've left me burning that same torch for that little girl as you have.'

That smile again.

'You've manipulated the situation,' she said.

'I've done the right thing. Her mother isn't long for this world anyway, and even if she does survive, Rose will end up in care. I couldn't just ask you all those months ago to be a mother to my daughter, Emma. But now, I can. And now, you'll say yes.'

'It's not that simple.'

'You're a DCI. You're respectable. You're married. It'll happen.'

'Married! Barely!'

'You'll make it work, Emma, because me and you are more alike than you realise. We both make things happen. Give her a good life.'

He knocked on the table. The door opened and the guard leaned in. 'I want to go now.'

The guard looked at Gardner, who nodded and sighed.

Jack stood and approached the guard. Just before he reached the door, he turned back.

'And one more thing. That money I took from Tommy. Tia's money. It was never for me.'

Gardner took a deep breath. 'It was for Rose, wasn't it?'

'Everything has always been for Rose.'

And then Gardner saw something she never thought she'd see.

A tear running down Jack Moss's face.

49

Now Riddick could no longer see his dead wife, he was left with only the photographs. He swiped through the pictures on his phone.

Rachel had been beautiful. And smiling. Always smiling. How could any person have been so consistently happy in *his* presence? He'd been so bloody lucky!

He swiped and swiped. So many duplicates.

When Rachel was alive, she'd spent many evenings selecting the best images and deleting the duplicates. Riddick, on the other hand, had always been too busy for that. It'd been an excuse. Until now, he'd never seen the point of looking over photographs, content to live in the here and now, twenty-four seven.

Of course, things had changed. There was no contentment in the here and now.

A few times his finger hovered over the bin icon on his phone as he toyed with the idea of deleting a duplicate just like his conscientious wife would've done, but each time he decided against it, and swiped on.

Eventually, he gave up trying to force his finger down onto the bin icon. It was never going to happen, was it? Why delete a single image of Rachel, or his children, despite the poorer quality of some?

He looked around his kitchen. Would anyone ever smile in this house again?

Paula. Yes, she'd smiled. He curled his lip. False smiles. Weaponised smiles. Smiles that would lead to his eventual destruction.

He grunted.

Maybe, Si Meadows made the right decision, after all? Which mug is sitting here, miserable? Not him...

He shook his head and sighed, searching his conscious for some positivity.

He'd resisted a drink all day. And his reward for doing so? The closure of Operation Bright Day. He may have still been miserable, but that was something, wasn't it?

He looked up at his kitchen cabinet. There wasn't anything in there. He'd emptied all the bottles as soon as he'd arrived back. He wanted to be sober when he faced the potential destruction of his career and life. Who knows? Being sober might just give him the clarity he needed to save himself.

He stood and stretched out. He turned from the table, preparing to head to bed.

His mobile phone, still on the table, buzzed.

Emma?

He turned quickly, almost excitedly, over a potential message from his friend. He couldn't say why exactly, but she just had this way of making him feel, you know, a little bit brighter.

But it wasn't Gardner, and his eyes widened when he saw who it was from.

He opened the message.

I'm sorry, Paul, for the pain I caused you. You've been through so much, and I added to that. I did it for money, to help someone close to me, but that's no excuse for my selfish behaviour, and I'll never expect you to forgive me. You were a good father, a good husband, and you're a good man. I've told Marianne that I want to be removed from the article. She tells me that without my consent the article will die. I hope you will one day find it in your heart to forgive me. You've fought your way out of despair, and I won't be the one to cause you to go back into it. Paula x

Riddick took a deep breath.

'Corruption: Back from the Dead' was no more.

And I've just put myself through a living hell.

'And the worst thing is, Rachel,' he said. 'I could have saved Si.' He looked towards her seat, but it remained empty. 'And I don't mean by the River Nidd. I mean *before*. I could have saved him *before*. I could have told him things that have helped me over time. Things that kept me going. But I didn't. I was being too self-indulgent. Wallowing in my own misery. And by taking that number off him...' His blood froze.

The number.

What have I done? What've I set in motion?

He felt a crushing pain in his chest. He doubled over and clutched the edge of the table.

By taking the number from Si, I condoned what he then did to Harvey.

Everything's my fault.

And it's going to get worse...

He flew to the kitchen drawer, pulled out a charged unregistered phone and rooted through a pile of letters by the breadbin.

'Shit. Where're you? Where the bloody hell are you?'

Unable to locate the number, he angrily pushed all the letters on the floor. *Bollocks!*

He threw the phone down on the kitchen table and put his hands to the sides of his head. 'Think... think... *think*.'

He ran to his kitchen bin and emptied it out onto the floor.

He dropped to his knees and dug through almost a week's worth of rotting food until his hand fell on the beer mat that Si had scribbled the number onto.

After rising to his feet, he charged back to the table, almost tripping over some single-use plastic containers. He laid the beermat out and punched the phone number into the burner phone.

'Hello?'

'It's me... It's Paul Riddick. We spoke before... I paid you...' He kept pumping the words out. A stream of consciousness. He must have sounded like a maniac. Crazy. When he'd finished, he was out of breath.

The man on the other end of the phone was silent.

God, let him be there. Please don't hang up on me. I'm not a madman.

The man was still there, and eventually he spoke. 'It's too late.'

And then the phone went dead.

Riddick smashed the phone onto the table again and again until it was in pieces. He went over to his glass bin and thrust his hand inside it. He pulled out the tequila bottle. He opened it and tipped it over his mouth. A couple of drops came loose and stung the back of his throat. He tried again with the vodka bottle. He was luckier this time. He was treated to a small, fiery trickle.

He threw the vodka bottle against the wall. It shattered. Glass rained down.

He fell to his knees in a week's worth of rotting food.

50

When Ronnie Haller opened his shower door, he received his final warning that he was about to die.

The first warning that he was facing an imminent demise had come much earlier. A screw had come to his cell to tell him that he was taking his shower with Group D instead of Group C this evening, because one of the five shower heads was broken, and, due to Group D being reduced to three men after two releases this week, Ronnie had been selected to switch for the time being.

However, it hadn't been until the second warning that Ronnie had taken notice. Two of the three prisoners accompanying Ronnie and the screw to the shower blocks had started to fight. The brawl had been quickly broken up with the assistance of two other screws. The two prisoners had been escorted away to solitary confinement, leaving Ronnie, one screw, and the prisoner, Lewis Caulfield, to continue to the shower block.

Lewis was a murdering lifer with no hope of parole and an elderly mother he loved dearly with care costs which were going through the roof. So, here had been the third warning that Ronnie was set for the great unknown. At this point, Ronnie *should* have run. Where to was anyone's guess – as there was nowhere to run *to*. Yet, despite this, he still should have tried. Creating a drama might have attracted attention. Given him a fighting chance. Still, Ronnie, an old man in poor health, had dawdled, and his options had narrowed to practically none.

Feeling like a condemned man, Ronnie had taken his shower, which was cut off, precise as always, at three minutes. After towelling himself dry, he opened the shower door.

And there was his final warning.

The screw was gone.

These days, screws weren't incompetent. There was simply too much training, scrutiny and accountability for that to happen.

But that didn't make them all honest.

So, if a screw abandoned you, as this one clearly had, they did so because they were having their palms greased. The money they made to leave you vulnerable was clearly worth the risk to their profession.

With no weapon, Ronnie held the corner of his towel, planning to use it as a whip, and strode out naked.

To his right stood Lewis, leaning against his own shower door. He was still fully clothed. He had some rudimentary, handcrafted knife in his hand.

Ronnie tightened his grip on the corner of his towel. In his earlier years, he may already have rushed Lewis, but poor health had been catching up with him and his chances of overpowering this tall, strong prisoner with little to lose were slim to none.

'You like to look at naked old men, Lewis?' Ronnie asked.

Lewis smiled. 'Only to see what I've got to look forward to when gravity takes hold.'

Ronnie smiled. 'Not much, son. Not much at all. I thought we had an understanding?'

Lewis shrugged. 'Understandings change, I guess. Look, you've always been good to me Ronnie, but... well, you know how it is. We may have free accommodation, but we all have bills to pay.'

'Still, if you kill me, you won't be long for the world yourself.'

'Well, see, I've had a good think about that. My first thought was that I was never getting out and my mother's health takes priority, but then I had a second thought. You're not as popular as you once were... you certainly don't have as many *friends*. You know how it is; the longer you're locked away, the weaker your hold on the outside world. I don't think anyone will come for me.'

'You're taking quite a gamble there, Lewis.'

'Been taking those gambles my whole life.'

Ronnie raised an eyebrow. 'And look where you are.'

'True, but I don't look at it that way. I look at it like this. One day my luck is going to come in.'

'A fool's errand.'

Lewis nodded. 'Probably. Anyway, shall we get to it? You going to whip me? See where that takes you?'

Ronnie sighed and dropped the towel. 'There's no point is there?'

Lewis shook his head. 'You've been around longer than me. You know how this plays out.'

'At least tell me who paid for this. The king's head can't have been cheap.'

'You'd be surprised, Ronnie. You'd be surprised at how our value drops.' He paused to think. 'It's probably best if I don't tell you... you know?'

'Why not? What difference does it make? I can't tell anyone.'

'Well, just wouldn't be professional, would it?'

'I've made plenty of enemies, but I'm not convinced any of them would be stupid enough to do this, unless...' He paused and thought about it. 'No... could it be? Really?'

Lewis had already edged nearer, the blade ready in his hand but yet to strike. Maybe he was curious over whether Ronnie would get it right.

'Was it Paul Riddick?'

Lewis smiled.

'The policeman, Paul Riddick! The man who put me here, is also getting me out of here – just not in the way I'd have preferred.'

'You did kill his entire family,' Lewis said.

Ronnie nodded. 'Aye. I did. Some would think I've got it coming.'

'We've all got it coming, Ronnie.'

'Ain't that the truth, son. Paul Riddick. I'll be damned.'

Lewis came in quickly, his hand darting in and out. Ronnie felt like he was being repeatedly punched. The wind was being knocked out of him. After Lewis backed away and Ronnie looked down at his punctured, bloody chest, he realised that being winded was the least of his concerns.

He went down to his knees and rather than look up at his murderer, because he was simply the weapon and not that relevant, he turned his mind to Paul Riddick, and smiled. 'Atta boy.'

He fell forward onto the floor and down into the darkness.

51

The caravans were towed from the old rugby pitch as the sun started to rise.

Watching the vehicles pass, Aiden sat on one of the boulders that he and his people had dragged aside weeks earlier to gain access to the old rugby pitch. He waited until his caravan was standing alone, hooked up to his battered old Ford. Then, he surveyed the field that was to be joyously reclaimed by the many dog walkers in Knaresborough. For Aiden, however, it would always be home to his fondest memories.

He felt a hand on his shoulder. He looked up to see the bruised face of Tommy looking down at him. 'Let's get a move on, lad. If we go now, we won't only miss the traffic, but we'll miss the locals lining the street, clapping our departure.'

Aiden nodded. He looked down at his clenched hand. He thought about what he was holding. He'd still not completely made up his mind what he wanted to do with it. 'Just one more minute, Tommy.'

'Okay... okay...' Tommy said, but Aiden could hear the frustration in his voice. He turned to walk away.

Aiden continued to stare, recalling the first time Tia had *finally* agreed to come into his caravan and spend a few hours with him—

'I don't want to sound cold,' Tommy said. He'd obviously turned back to get something off his chest. 'But you *do* know the truth now, lad.'

Aiden creased his brow and looked up at him. 'And what's the truth, Tommy?'

Tommy shrugged. 'Don't shoot the messenger. I'm just trying to make you feel better. You were wrong about what you had with her, that's all. It wasn't as special as she made you believe. No one thinks any less of you. But you need this to help you move on. Use it. Turn it into a positive.'

Aiden shook his head and looked down.

'Take this minute you wanted, lad, and then let's get shot of this place. It's for the best.' Again, Tommy turned to walk away.

Aiden rose to his feet. Yes, he knew it was 'for the best' to just ignore the irritating bastard, and head for his caravan. However, he was rather sick of doing what was 'for the best'.

In fact, some of what had happened could have been avoided if he'd only done something that wasn't for the best. Like follow Tia to the prick who'd got her pregnant and put him down before he could do her any more harm.

He turned back towards the camp leader. 'Oi Tommy!'

Tommy kept walking.

'Listen, I'm sick of doing what's for the best.'

Tommy shook his head and continued walking.

'I wasn't wrong about Tia.'

Tommy raised the back of his hand in the air to gesture a farewell.

'Turn around and talk to me, you bastard, or I'll tell the pigs why Jack Moss found it so easy to—'

Tommy stopped. 'Careful, lad.' He turned. 'Careful.'

But Aiden was riding a wave of adrenaline now. He marched forward. 'Or? You don't look in any shape to do anything. Give me an excuse to finish what Jack started.'

Now this really wasn't for the best.

But did he care any more?

Not one bit.

Tommy fixed him in a stare. He took a few steps towards Aiden, and then stopped with his fists clenched at his side. He looked as if he was preparing to launch.

Come on then. I'm ready.

Tommy eased backwards. 'I see you're in pain, Aiden, so I'll let this slide.'

Aiden guffawed.

'Just hurry your arse up—'

'We *were* in love. Completely and utterly. You're wrong.'

Tommy snorted and shook his head. He looked left and right as if there was an audience who could acknowledge how ridiculous Aiden's comments were, but they were alone. 'It wasn't your baby. It belonged to that old suit with money.' He rubbed his thumb and forefinger together. 'That's why you stick with your own, lad. Because we're *nothing* to these people. You were *nothing* to Tia. She had her sugar daddy. You were a bit of rough.'

Aiden shook his head, his cheeks flushed. 'She told me. She told me about this man... this *Rhys... before.*'

'What did she tell you?'

'That someone close to her, someone she thought of like another father, was using her. Threatening to tell her real father what was happening between me and her. He *forced* her.'

'She told you this... and what did you do about it?'

'Nothing. She wouldn't give me his name, damn it!'

'You could've found out—'

'Yes, I could, but she asked me not to. She was just trying to keep me safe. She was adamant her father would kill me. She said if I loved her, I'd leave her to handle it herself.'

'That wasn't sensible.'

'I know. Do you think a single second passes when I don't think of that?' Aiden had tears in his eyes. 'That man, that Rhys Hunt, he took advantage of her, used her.' He thumbed his chest. 'It was me she loved. *Me*. It should've been my baby. Not that bastard's.'

Tommy sighed, shook his head and looked down. 'Listen, lad. This is leading nowhere good. Nowhere good at all. It's over now. You need to move on... stay with your people. There's nobody in our group who wouldn't put themselves on the line to see you right. This is where you belong.'

'But why didn't I tell the pigs what she told me?'

'You know why. You didn't want to invite suspicion on yourself. Am I right?'

Aiden nodded. 'I'm spineless. She never told me she was pregnant because it wasn't mine. If I'd have told that DCI that I knew the baby wasn't mine, she'd have been all over me like a rash, accusing me of jealousy, fitting me up for the murder. So, I'll tell them the truth now, shall I? Make sure that Rhys bastard gets what's coming to him.'

'Ha!' Tommy said. 'You think they'll take your word over one of their own? Don't waste your time. You'll give them purpose though. A reason to turn you to sodding sausage meat. They always do.' Tommy put a hand on his shoulder and sighed. 'Okay, lad, you've convinced me. I believe you. She loved you, and you loved her. Take that with you. But its time now, Aiden. In fact, there's never been a better—'

Aiden pulled away from Tommy and started to run in the direction of the lake.

'Aiden lad, you bloody fool!'

* * *

Clutching his knees, sweat pouring down his face, Aiden stood at the edge of the lake.

When he'd first started running here, he'd not been sure as to the reason why, but in the last few minutes, the reason had presented itself clearly.

Although he wasn't physically standing where she'd died, this was roughly where she'd been abandoned, as if she was nothing but a piece of meat, cast aside and left to rot.

It was here that he'd make his promise. His vow.

He reached into his pocket and clutched the eagle pendant. He looked at it once, with disgust, not quite believing he'd had a gift from Tia's killer around his neck for these last days. Then, he cast it far into the water.

'I promise I'll never forget you, Tia.' He wiped a tear away and sighed. 'And I promise to come back one day and pay a visit to Rhys Hunt in both your name and the name of your child.'

52

TWELVE DAYS LATER

Gardner looked at her freshly made-up face in the dressing table mirror.

It'd been so long, she barely recognised herself.

Shaking her head, she tipped some make-up remover from the bottle onto a cotton pad, and then lifted it close to her face, catching her eyes again in her reflection as she did so.

So, so long.

She inched the pad closer to her face.

No. You can be this person... you can be whoever you want to be...

She dropped the pad onto the table and then said the words she'd said out loud to her daughter, Anabelle, on so many occasions. 'You can be whoever you want to be. *Whenever.* Never forget that.'

She smiled, admiring her painted lips, and then her doorbell went.

She looked at her watch.

Bloody hell, Hugo. There's fashionably late, but is fashionably early a thing?

She rose, looking at her low-cut red outfit in the mirror as she did so.

Too much?

She sprayed some perfume on.

Hell, no!

* * *

She opened the front door, expecting to see a freshly scrubbed Dr Hugo Sands standing on her doorstep with immaculate hair, wearing an ironed shirt, tailored trousers with shoes reeking of polish, holding some flowers, or maybe even a bottle of wine.

Instead, there was Paul Riddick, with out-of-control hair, especially at the sides, a dishevelled suit that longed for the dry cleaners, and a pair of scuffed old trainers. He was, at least, holding a bottle of wine.

Although, it did look almost empty.

Riddick was currently on his second week of medical leave following his nasty experience behind the scout hut at the River Nidd. Gardner had checked in on him by phone but had not actually seen him in over a week. This visit was unexpected. 'What the hell, Paul?'

He smiled.

It confirmed her worst fears. 'You're pissed, aren't you?'

He looked her up and down. This made her uncomfortable. 'Shit...' he said. 'You look good.'

'When did you start drinking again?'

'What's that got to do with how good you look?'

She felt like bursting into tears. This was her fault. She should have been keeping a closer eye on him.

Gardner looked left and right to see if any neighbours were poking inquiring noses in this direction. Of course, no one was.

Still... paranoia was an intense motivator; she ushered him in quickly.

As he passed, he said, 'You smell good too.'

'Well, you don't. And stop.' She shut the front door and turned to him. 'You sound like you're flirting. It's making me cringe.'

'Bloody hell, thanks. Is me flirting with you really such a horrible prospect?'

'Looking at the state of you – *yes!*'

Riddick put his bottle down on a table in the hallway, held his arms up and looked down at himself. 'State of me? My flies are done up! But yes, I guess I've had better days. But you... sorry... *you*...' He grinned. 'Sorry... I won't say another word.' He mimed zipping his mouth close.

She sighed. 'You should've spoken to me. Come to see me... *before* this happened again.'

'You had bigger things to worry about. Fostering that niece of yours.'

His comment hurt her. She flinched. 'I'd have been there for you, Paul. In fact, *I'm* here for you.'

'How is that niece of yours?'

'Fine... it's in process, moving slowly.'

'And what's with the get-up?' He nodded at her dress.

'Ed Sheeran.'

'Ah yes.' He smiled, but she sensed anything but happiness behind it. 'With the formidable Dr Hugo Sands?'

Gardner rolled her eyes and checked her watch. 'Yes... and the formidable Dr Hugo Sands is due here in about twenty minutes.'

'After he finishes stitching someone back up?'

'Nice.'

Riddick reached for the bottle. He held it up. 'Well, twenty minutes is time to share a glass then?'

'Two problems with that, Paul.'

'Go on, boss, I'm listening.' He put on an overly serious expression.

'Firstly, we would definitely be *sharing* that glass as there's only about one left in that bottle.'

He nodded. 'Right you are. The second problem?'

'You're an alcoholic.'

'Shit... you're a good detective. What gave it away?'

'If you want my company, Paul, you need to hand that bottle over to me to tip away and I'll make you a cup of tea.'

He made a pantomime of looking between the bottle and Gardner several times.

Keeping his eyes on Gardner, he slammed the bottle back down on the table. 'Tea it is then, boss. Did I ever tell you that red is my favourite colour?'

Knowing that he was referring to her dress, she blushed. 'Go and sit down, dickhead.'

He disappeared into the living room singing 'Lady in Red' by Chris de Burgh.

She grabbed the bottle, went into the kitchen, put it on the table, and shook her head.

Now what?

She was supposed to be going on a date with Hugo in twenty minutes, and now one of her close friends was in the other room.

Laughing, joking, smiling...

As his life went up in flames.

* * *

When she went back into the lounge, Riddick was unconscious on her sofa.

She put the two cups of tea on the table, sat down and looked over at him. His mouth was hanging open, and he was drooling onto the collar of his shirt.

You ridiculous man. I thought we'd got this behind you... set you free...

She sighed and rubbed her temples.

Who are you kidding, Emma?

Free? How could anybody be free after that experience?

She sat back on the sofa and looked up at the ceiling. She'd been stupid to think that she could save him. That their friendship would sustain his sobriety. That his job, as he argued, helped him with the healing process.

How could that job help anyone heal from anything?

She sighed. He couldn't go back to work now, could he?

He needed help, *serious* help, and she wasn't the person to give it to him, no matter how much she cared for him—

The doorbell went.

* * *

Hugo Sands did scrub up well.

He also came armed with flowers.

The compliments he passed were also measured – just like his forensic analysis – and far less coarse than Riddick's had been.

However, she still sent the disappointed doctor away with his two Ed Sheeran tickets.

Her excuse was that a good friend needed her.

It wasn't a lie.

He looked irritated and asked who it was. She declined to tell him.

As soon as she closed the door, she ran to the kitchen and finished Riddick's wine straight from the bottle.

Then, she opened her own bottle.

* * *

When Gardner woke in the early hours of the morning, she realised she was not alone on the sofa.

It took a couple of seconds to recall the earlier events of the evening.

She looked to her side where Riddick was sitting upright, staring off into space.

'I hope I didn't wake you,' he said.

'No... but you did ruin my evening.'

'I'm sorry.'

'Don't be. I don't like Ed Sheeran, anyway.'

'How about Hugo Sands?'

Gardner grinned. 'He's a good pathologist. Thorough.'

Riddick nodded. 'He is.'

'Okay, I'm going to head to bed. You can sleep down here, and we will come up with a plan of action in the morning. You'll beat this, Paul, like last time.' She rose from the sofa. 'And next time, we'll make sure you—'

She felt Riddick take her hand, stopping her from walking away. She looked down at him. Despite it being dark, she could see the tears in his eyes.

'Can you stay?' he asked.

'Isn't it best we get some sleep?'

'Please?' He still had hold of her hand.

She sat down beside him.

'Emma. I need to tell you something.'

She felt a rush of blood to her head.

What was it?

Did he have feelings for her?

A large part of her enjoyed the idea; another large part of her realised the mess it could make.

'Listen, Paul, we're tired. I'll stay if you promise to sleep.'

'Can't I just get this off my chest. It's too much... too much of a burden.'

The grip on her hand tightened. She felt an urge to slip her arm around his shoulders and pull him in close.

She resisted. *It'd be a mess...*

'In the morning,' she said, patting his hand. 'I promise.'

She slipped her hand from his and closed her eyes.

'I don't know if I'll have the courage to tell you about this in the morning.'

That's probably a good thing, she thought. Although her sinking heart would no doubt disagree.

ACKNOWLEDGMENTS

Bringing the tumultuous relationship between Gardner and Riddick to life against the scenic backdrop of North Yorkshire is not, by any means, a straightforward task.

However, with Boldwood on my side, and a wonderful team of editors in Emily Ruston, Candida Bradford and Susan Sugden, I am able to give it my best shot!

A special thank you this time for my children who always know how to bring a smile to my face. It gives me great pleasure to dedicate this book to you, although it will be many years before I allow you to read it!

Not forgetting the rest of my family, Jo included, who are forever supportive, and tolerate the daydreamer in the corner of the room.

Again, I extend my gratitude to all bloggers and ARC readers, including Donna and Sharon, who even made it up to a recent launch party of *The Viaduct Killings*.

I look forward to seeing you again soon when Gardner and Riddick are drawn into an investigation involving the caves in Knaresborough...

ACKNOWLEDGMENTS

MORE FROM WES MARKIN

We hope you enjoyed reading *The Lonely Lake Killings*. If you did, please leave a review.

If you'd like to gift a copy, this book is also available as an ebook, large print, hardback, digital audio download and audiobook CD.

Sign up to Wes Markin's mailing list for news, competitions and updates on future books.

https://bit.ly/WesMarkinNews

The Viaduct Killings, the exciting first instalment in Wes Markin's Yorkshire Murders series, is available to buy now...

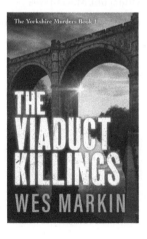

ABOUT THE AUTHOR

Wes Markin is the bestselling author of the DCI Yorke crime novels, set in Salisbury. His new series for Boldwood stars the pragmatic detective DCI Emma Gardner who will be tackling the criminals of North Yorkshire. Wes lives in Harrogate and the first book in the series The Yorkshire Murders was published in November 2022.

Visit Wes Markin's website: wesmarkinauthor.com

Follow Wes on social media:

 twitter.com/MarkinWes
 facebook.com/WesMarkinAuthor